"KISS ME, KATYA. WE CAN'T HAVE YOU
APPEARING TOO INNOCENT, NOW, CAN WE?"

"I thought you said that my appearance of innocence was
my greatest strength."

"True. But there is such a thing as carrying it too far. A
chaste and virtuous mistress—how very appalling. Think of
my poor reputation."

A shaky smile curved her lips. "You have a remarkable
way of rationalizing whatever you want, don't you?"

"Is it always this difficult to coax a kiss from you?" he
asked.

Although she was clearly waiting for him to make the next
move, he found himself strangely unwilling to let her simply
succumb to his caress.

"Touch me," he commanded softly.

Nicholas felt a slight shudder run through him as she
brushed her hand lightly over his chest. Unable to hold back
any longer, he wrapped his arm around the small of her back
and pulled her tightly to him.

The seducer was quickly becoming the seduced.

Dell Books by Victoria Lynne

Chasing Rainbows
What Wild Moonlight

What Wild Moonlight

Victoria Lynne

A DELL BOOK

Published by
Dell Publishing
a division of
Bantam Doubleday Dell Publishing Group, Inc.
1540 Broadway
New York, New York 10036

ISBN: 0-440-22331-8

Printed in the United States of America

Published simultaneously in Canada

October 1998

10 9 8 7 6 5 4 3 2 1

OPM

For Bob Sr.,
for the Taming of the Tarasque.
And for Bob,
for everything else.

Prologue

"*T*ell me the story, Mama."

Katya Zofia Rosskaya Alexander didn't specify which story, for there was only one: her story. She knew it word for word, yet she never tired of hearing it. She snuggled beneath the thick blankets that covered her bed and released a contented sigh. Moonlight streamed in through the window of their small, private compartment as the train's wheels rolled rhythmically beneath her, nearly lulling her to sleep. With all the stubborn determination a six-year-old could summon, she fought the drowsiness. Not yet. Not until she heard her story.

"Tell me, Mama," she repeated. "Please."

Her mother gave her a soft, indulgent smile and sat on the edge of her bed. After extracting a promise that Katya would go to sleep as soon as the story was finished, she began.

"Once, a long, long time ago, a beautiful young girl lived in a castle overlooking the sea. The young girl's name was Sacha Rosskaya and her father was a rich and powerful count, one of the richest and most powerful men in the land. There was great joy in the castle one day, for on that day Sacha's father betrothed her to Marco DuValenti, the son of another great family.

"All the preparations were readied for the wedding feast. The banns had been published weeks before. The walls were decorated with tapestries, fresh rushes covered the floor, and sweet spices burned in the cauldrons above the fire. Wine flowed freely and the tables were laden with rich and exotic fare. Scores of guests filled the cavernous hall. Troubadours strolled about, entertaining the assembly with singing, dancing, and tumbling. It was a time of great merriment and festivity, but there was one person who was not smiling that day."

"Sacha's grandmother," Katya burst out.

"Yes. Sacha's grandmother. For she was a gypsy—"

"Just like us."

"Just like us," her mother agreed. Then she patiently continued in her soft, bedtime voice, "But Sacha's grandmother had special powers, for the old woman was the castle seer. She could read the future by the shape of a cloud, tell how many children a woman would bear by studying her palm, and predict whether a crop would thrive or fail by examining the stones in the ground.

"Many in the castle thought the ancient gypsy called on evil and brought it to descend on those who displeased her. But in truth, she simply read the omens that drifted through the sky, looking for signs of dark foreboding or coming joy. Those very signs were telling her that there would be a score of deaths that day, and many more to follow. A portent of evil hung in the air, as thick and menacing as the castle walls themselves."

"But it was too late to call off the wedding, wasn't it?"

"It was," her mother sadly acknowledged. "With a blare of trumpets Count Rosskaya entered the great hall with his daughter Sacha. The young bride wore her best clothing: a pale linen chemise; a silk tunic trimmed with dark fur; a velvet surcoat; and a deep blue mantle shot through with purple thread, meant to bring out the wondrous lavender color of her eyes. On her tiny feet were shoes of fine leather that had been embellished with gold."

"Her eyes were the same color as mine, weren't they, Mama?"

"Yes, Katya. The same color."

Her mother hesitated for a moment with a troubled frown. Slowly she continued, "Marco DuValenti was a tall, darkly handsome man, but he had a sinister heart. As he stood to greet his bride the ancient gypsy grandmother glared at the man and his warrior knights. She had never approved of the union, despite the fact that it had been decreed by the king himself. The DuValentis were an ambitious, hot-blooded, unscrupulous family, swift to revenge and furious in battle. They were no match for the Rosskayas, regardless of the wealth to be gained when their lands were joined.

"The two families met in the center of the hall as an emissary of the king moved to join them. The count and his daughter made their marks on the king's official ledger and passed the book to the groom. Marco DuValenti signed his name with a flourish, then pressed his signet ring into the hot wax beneath it. A stark, forbidding image of a Maltese falcon rose to life within the wax.

"The last of the formalities completed, the king's emissary called forth a second man. The scribe stepped forward carrying a pewter tray draped in rich gold velvet. The emissary lifted his arm for silence, then announced to the gathered assembly, 'A token of esteem from His Majesty, given on the joyous occasion of this marriage. May the union be long and fruitful.' He turned to the pewter tray and removed the velvet cloth with a flourish. A gasp of muffled awe echoed through the crowd as the contents of the tray were displayed to one and all. Resting before them was a glistening, pale blue diamond the size of a man's fist."

Knowing what was coming next, Katya felt a shudder run down her spine. "The Stone of Destiny," she whispered.

Her mother nodded gravely. "The Stone of Destiny. Sacha's grandmother had finally found the source of the premonition that had haunted her all morning. But she was too late to stop it now.

"The DuValenti warriors surged forward for a closer look at the glistening jewel. They were met by the Rosskaya knights, who gathered protectively around the Stone. The wary trust that had existed between the clans promptly shattered. Thick tension filled the air as muffled shouts of anger led to bouts of fervent shoving. From within the huddled, seething mass of bodies there came the quicksilver flash of a sword raised in anger. The sword sliced through the air and lashed down with swift, deadly menace as a woman's piercing cry echoed through the hall.

"The knights staggered back, their mouths agape with horror. As the crush of bodies slowly parted, the tragedy concealed within their midst was revealed. Marco DuValenti knelt on a thick bed of rushes, his young bride gathered tightly in his arms. His hands moved frantically over Sacha's side, attempting to stem the flow of blood that poured from her wound, but his effort was in vain. The radiant spark that once filled the young girl's magnificent eyes had dimmed forever. She was dead.

"The stunned silence that swept over the assembly was broken by Count Rosskaya's roar of anguished rage. Violence exploded in the great hall as cries of vengeance filled the air. The wrath of the Rosskayas was unleashed on the DuValentis. Soon the blood of both clans stained the rushes. The DuValentis, badly outnumbered but stronger warriors, fought their way down to the harbor and retreated onto the ships that awaited them.

"The ancient gypsy watched as the DuValenti ships slid out to sea. Then she scanned the keep, assessing the disaster that had descended upon them. Her beloved granddaughter was dead and the Stone of Destiny had been stolen during the melee. She had been powerless to stop any of it. Her heart heavy and her bones aching with age, she abandoned the vaulted hall and slowly made her way up the dark, winding steps to the Saint's Tower.

"She stood alone as morning faded to afternoon, and then to twilight. Hungry for portents of what was to come, the old woman focused intently on the wind, reading the signs. The omens were not good. The battle between the Rosskayas and the DuValentis had just begun. There would be more deaths for generations to come. As the breeze blew stronger, the prophecies it carried grew clearer. In the distant future another lavender-eyed Rosskaya bride would stand beside a DuValenti groom. Once again the Stone of Destiny would lurk between them, casting an evil shadow over their union."

In the silence that ensued, Katya asked in a small voice, "And then what?"

The troubled frown returned to her mother's face. She studied Katya for a long moment in silence, then she gently brushed a wayward ebony curl from her face. "I can tell you no more, Katya Zofia. We shall have to trust in fate to decide the rest."

The answer was always the same, and as always it left Katya deeply dissatisfied. Her mother kissed her goodnight, then stood and left the compartment, softly pulling the door closed behind her. As the moonlight shadows danced over the walls and the train's wheel's clicked rhythmically beneath her, the question repeated itself over and over in Katya's mind.

And then what?

One

"Pink."

"Blue."

"Yellow."

"Green."

The wager was set: one thousand pounds to the man who correctly divined the color of the ribbons on the serving girl's garters.

Nicholas Duvall, the Earl of Barrington, listened to the guesses of the other men gathered at the table of the busy roadside tavern in southern France. Then he studied the serving girl in question. She was of medium height and endowed with a lush little body that she clearly delighted in showing off to maximum advantage. Her scoop-necked top was cut low, allowing daring glimpses of her full, generous breasts. Her narrow waist was tightly nipped in by her apron, and her clingy wool skirt revealed the smooth, softly rounded lines of her hips.

Her eyes glistened with excitement as Nicholas's gaze moved up and down her body. Her rich brown hair had been artfully arranged to cascade about her face in loose, wispy tendrils that suggested both underlying sensuality and girlish innocence. Despite her obvious enjoyment of the attention she was receiving, there was a demure coyness in her expression that gave Nicholas the answer he sought. Standing before him was a young woman of vast experience and knowledge—a woman who clearly enjoyed playing the part of the perfect virgin.

"White," he said.

"It's done then," Lord Rigby announced, assuming a jo-
vial yet businesslike air. He clasped his chubby hands together and rubbed them briskly. "And now, my girl, if you
would be so kind as to lift your skirts for us. . . ."

A look of irritation flicked through the barmaid's dark
eyes. She quickly recovered herself, however, once her gaze
returned to the fifty-franc note waiting on the table.

"Oui, monsieur," she murmured demurely. Relaxing
back into the posture of an innocent seductress, she shot a
glance around the busy tavern. Apparently satisfied that her
actions would go unnoticed in the smoky, overcrowded
room, she bent down and grasped the hem of her skirt.
Moving with seductive deliberation she raised the fabric to
reveal a pair of trim, feminine ankles encased in sheer white
cotton stockings. She lifted the garment further, allowing an
enticing view of her shapely calves, rounded knees, and the
soft swell of her lower thighs.

Abruptly she hesitated. Her skirts hovering above her
knees, she chewed her bottom lip and lowered her gaze to
the floor, as though racked with maidenly doubt and uncertainty.

It was a pretty act, Nicholas conceded, but it rang as false
as a church sermon delivered by the town sinner. Rather
than the ill-timed surge of chastity and repentance she had
tried to project blatant greed had glistened in her eyes before
she coyly lowered her lashes. Stifling a sigh, he removed a
second fifty-franc note from his wallet and placed it on top
of the first. "Pray, don't keep us in suspense, mademoiselle."

"You are too kind, monsieur," the barmaid cooed. Her
voice was honey-sweet, yet edged with the brittle insincerity
of a practiced courtesan.

She lifted her skirts once again, this time displaying no
virginal hesitation. The fabric traveled up her pretty legs,
moving swiftly past her calves and knees. She exposed not

only her lacy garters and the finely knit mesh of her stocking tops, but a generous portion of the smooth, creamy skin of her thighs as well. Nicholas took all that in with a glance, and one thing more.

The ribbons on her garters were white.

"Damn it all," blustered Rigby, thumping the table in drunken good humor. "You win again, Duvall."

Nicholas inclined his head with a graceful nod as he collected his winnings. "So it would appear."

"Let me know if I can be of any further assistance, messieurs," the barmaid said, her voice rich with invitation as she smoothed down her skirts. She deftly collected her francs, picked up her tray, and moved to go. But before she left, her gaze traveled one last time over the men seated before her. As she briefly surveyed her customers, a look of haughty disdain filled her eyes and a triumphant smile curved her lips. Then she turned and sauntered away, her hips provocatively swaying as she moved through the crowded room.

Nicholas caught her parting look but was neither angered nor insulted by it. If anything, he thought, the woman's judgment of character was remarkably astute. He understood all too well what she had seen as she scanned their table. It was hardly an inspiring sight. Seated beside him were five of England's most noble sons, all of them men of wealth and stature. But other than their titles and their lineage, there was little to recommend them. Beneath their elegantly cut suits, their intricately tied cravats, their sleek and highly polished boots, and their fancy gloves protecting their effeminate hands from the cold, they were little more than overstuffed fops and fools.

The group was part of the annual pilgrimage made to the dazzling new mecca that beckoned from abroad: Monte Carlo, where the fashionable went to play after the Season was over for the year. Society came in droves, exchanging the thick fog of London for the Mediterranean sunshine.

Nicholas Duvall had taken his place among his peers, playing the part of an indolent, arrogant lord, because it temporarily suited his purposes. His patience with the charade, however, was quickly wearing thin.

"We need another wager," declared Henry Bickford, his voice somewhat slurred from the hearty Bordeaux they had all been drinking since midmorning. "How about this . . . we'll wager on the age of the next person to walk through the door."

"God, man, are you really that dull?" countered Samuel Parr.

Bickford frowned and reared back in drunken indignity. "Dull, am I? Then what do you suggest?"

"Something a little more interesting," answered Philip Montrove. His steel-gray gaze moved slowly around the tavern as though seeking inspiration. "Perhaps a way for the five of us to win our money back from Duvall."

Instantly alert, Nicholas's dark gaze shot across the table and locked on Philip Montrove. Their dislike was mutual and intense, despite the surface cordiality.

"I have it," declared Edward Fletcher, his florid cheeks flushed even redder from drink. "A seduction. Either Duvall has to seduce the next woman to enter the tavern or he forfeits the money he's won from us this morning."

"Not bad," said Philip Montrove. He hesitated a moment, as though considering the idea carefully. "But in the past hour, I've seen nothing but barmaids and servant girls from the local inns enter this establishment. That's hardly a wager worthy of the Lord of Scandal, is it? Rather like wagering on a wolf's ability to devour a lamb."

Nervous, uneasy laughter sounded among the men. Nicholas had, of course, heard himself referred to as the Lord of Scandal—particularly after Allyson's untimely death—but never had a man been so bold as to call him that to his face. He waited a beat, letting the silence stretch between them, then replied in a silky-smooth voice, "Hardly sporting, indeed."

Montrove arched one pale brow in response as a small smirk played about his lips. "I thought you might agree."

"Then what's the wager?" demanded Bickford.

Montrove tapped his empty wineglass with a fingernail, his lips pursed in thought. "Perhaps—" he began.

His words were cut short as the tavern door suddenly flew open and a group of wind-blown travelers staggered in. The small party consisted of three women and four men. Two of the men supported a third, who appeared able to walk only with their assistance. He was doubled over and groaning loudly, clutching his belly as he lurched forward. A bed in a back room was secured for the ailing man, followed by calls for a physician, soothing wine, and blankets.

The plight of the travelers quickly became apparent. The driver of their coach had taken ill on the route between Esterel and Cannes and was unable to continue. Because the tavern owner also served as the local agent for the coach company, the group besieged the man to supply them with another driver. But their pleas were met with little more than vague sympathy and an ultimate shrug of indifference. When the driver was well again, they would continue. Whether that took days or weeks was out of the tavern owner's hands.

"Such a shame," murmured Philip Montrove, shaking his head at the misfortune of the small band of travelers. Yet as he spoke, a distinct glimmer of satisfaction entered his eyes. "Although," he continued slowly, "we might be able to remedy their situation."

"Are you proposing we give them our rail tickets?" asked Lord Rigby, releasing a deep boom of laughter at the absurdity of the suggestion.

"Not precisely." Montrove steepled his fingers, glancing from man to man around the table. Abruptly his steel-gray gaze locked on Nicholas. "I'm suggesting that we give them a driver."

"I don't follow you," said Bickford.

Philip Montrove lifted his shoulders in a casual shrug. "You wanted another wager and here it is. If Duvall agrees to assume the post of driver and to guide the coach and passengers into Monaco, he doubles his winnings. If, however, he fails to complete the journey, he forfeits his winnings and returns them to us. It's that simple, gentlemen."

The other men at the table shifted uncomfortably in the ensuing silence. "Rather brash, isn't it, Montrove?" muttered Lord Rigby.

"I would say so," concurred Samuel Parr, nervously clearing his throat.

Nicholas fought back a smile at their obvious discomfort. For a member of the peerage to seduce an innocent young servant girl was well within the bounds of acceptable behavior. But for a lord of the realm to lower himself enough to accept a task as menial and degrading as driving a coach? That was simply not done.

Putting that hypocrisy aside for the moment, Nicholas considered the wager. The money was of little consequence, but there were other elements to consider. First and foremost, Montrove was apparently as anxious to be rid of him as Nicholas was to be rid of the lot of them. Interesting, but ultimately inconsequential, he decided. He knew better than to let his innate dislike of the man color his judgment.

Second, accepting the wager would mean parting from the group until they were reunited in Monaco. As the journey would take less than a day, and his traveling companions appeared intent on acquainting themselves with as many taverns as they could along the way, he doubted that this would do any harm. Separating now was infinitely preferable to

spending an afternoon neck high in drunken wagers, maudlin reminiscences, and soggy toasts to health and good fortune.

Last, Nicholas briefly considered what accepting the bet
would mean to his reputation. He had done worse in his life,
far worse indeed, but his prior exploits were hardly a matter
of public record. Accepting this meaningless wager would
undoubtedly be viewed as reckless in the extreme by the
soft-bellied lords and elegant ladies who awaited his arrival in
Monaco. And that, after all, was exactly the type of reputation he needed to cultivate in order to shield his activities.

He paused, surveying one last time the men with whom
he traveled. Was the killer he sought among this group of
elegant sycophants? Perhaps yes, perhaps no—it was simply
too soon to tell.

With that in mind, Nicholas pushed back his chair and
rose to his feet. "Gentlemen," he said, "you have a wager."

Katya Alexander shifted from foot to foot, her heart racing
as she stood inside the crowded tavern. She clutched her
faded carpetbag tightly against her chest, struggling to rein in
her mounting sense of alarm. She had to reach Monaco by
tonight, she simply had to. If she didn't . . . well, she
wouldn't think about that yet. She hadn't traveled all the way
from London only to give up now.

But despite her mental reassurances, the conversation between the tavern owner and her fellow passengers sounded
bleak indeed. No, there was no other driver available. No,
the owner couldn't leave the tavern and drive the coach
himself. No, he couldn't think of a local tradesman who
might want to finish the route. Perhaps in a few days, he
suggested, the driver would be well again. In the meantime
they could all stay and enjoy the beauty of Cannes.

On another occasion the offer might tempt her, but not
right now. Not when she had to reach Monaco by nightfall

or she would lose everything. Everything. Think, Katya, think! she commanded herself. No matter how desperate the situation, blind panic and utter hysteria were rarely productive emotions—nor were they particularly attractive. Taking a deep, calming breath, she considered her options.

There was the train, of course, but since she hadn't been able to afford the steep price of a rail ticket when she had left the port of Toulon, she could afford it even less now that she had already paid the regular coach fare. She could always try to rent a small buggy, although the thought of negotiating the rugged Cornice on her own left her feeling distinctly queasy. Her mind raced. A fishing boat perhaps? Or a farmer driving a wagonload of produce north to market?

"Pardon me, but do I understand that you're in need of a driver?"

Katya spun around at the sound of the smooth male voice behind her. Her gaze flew to a tall man of perhaps thirty. He spoke in fluid French but his accent, subtle though it was, sounded decidedly British. His clothing marked him an Englishman as well, suggesting a recent visit to an exclusive London haberdasher. He wore his dark brown hair a bit longer than was currently considered fashionable; it cascaded in thick waves just past the collar of his shirt. But it was his eyes that truly captured her attention. They were black, luminous, piercing—the most compelling aspect of the man.

All things considered, he did not seem the type who would charitably come to the aid of a group of stranded travelers. Nevertheless, at least he seemed interested in their plight, which was more than she could say about the tavern owner.

"How much?" she inquired in English, boldly addressing the stranger directly.

As though aware of her presence for the first time, the man turned to face her. The moment his eyes met hers, Katya felt a tremor run down her spine and a rush of heat flood through her limbs. His gaze was neither lewd nor intimidating, yet something about the way he looked at her sent a blistering shock through her system.

The kiss of fate, her mother would have called it. That brief, infinitesimal moment when fate allows us a glimpse into the future, showing us what will be. But the thought of her fate being somehow entwined with this mysterious Englishman's struck Katya as patently absurd.

Dismissing the notion entirely, she returned her attention to the subject at hand. "How much will you charge to take us to Monaco?" she repeated.

"Twenty-five francs a person," he replied.

"I'll pay twenty."

The Englishman arched one dark brow in a look of mild surprise, then with a careless shrug of his broad shoulders said simply, "Agreed."

He must need the money more desperately than she had imagined to consent so readily to the lower fare. Katya felt a momentary twinge of guilt for depriving him of his income, but she quickly brushed the feeling aside. After all, she reasoned, she was certainly in no position to be generous.

The negotiations complete, she dug into her carpetbag and removed the money. She held the notes out to him, then abruptly pulled her hand back as a thought occurred to her. "I don't suppose you have any references as to your good character?" she demanded, eyeing him distrustfully.

"My what?"

"Your good character, sir. Something to assure us that you are a man of honor and integrity."

A sardonic smile touched his lips, as though he found the very idea mildly entertaining. "Even if I had such references—and I can assure you they don't exist—I doubt very much I would carry them around in my pocket, waiting to show them off to every stranger I met in a roadside tavern."

"Then how are we to know you truly intend to see us to

Monaco, rather than just rob us of our possessions and abandon us on a seaside cliff?"

"Do I look the part of a notorious highwayman?" he challenged.

Katya's eyes once again swept over his rich, meticulously tailored attire. Aware that he was waiting for her reply, she tilted her chin, forcing herself to meet his cool, mocking gaze. "The quality of a man's clothing is hardly an accurate measure of the quality of his character."

"How aptly put. I suppose that means you'll just have to trust me, won't you?" He studied her for a moment longer, then lifted his shoulders in a bored shrug, as though their discussion had suddenly grown tedious. "Or you can wait here for the next coach. The choice is yours."

Unfortunately, she was in no position to wait. Her appointment with Monsieur Remy was scheduled for eight o'clock that evening, and she couldn't afford to miss it. Yet still she hesitated. There was something about the mysterious Englishman that reminded her of midnight—a quality that was dark, elusive, and vaguely dangerous. But despite whatever grave doubts she might harbor as to the true nature of his character, she had little choice at the moment but to hand over her money and hope for the best.

"You'll take the coach all the way to Monaco?" she pressed, holding out two ten-franc notes.

He inclined his head with a graceful nod. "All the way to Monaco."

"Fine." Remembering one more thing, she snatched the money back once again as he reached for it. "By tonight?"

The hint of a smile she had seen earlier now blossomed into a full-blown, cocky grin. The sudden splash of pearly white teeth, contrasted against the bronzed glow of his skin and the ebony fire in his eyes gave him a startling, almost luminous air of sensuality. He crossed his arms over his broad chest, studying her for a long moment in amused, rather patronizing silence.

"Is this some sort of a game you're playing, Miss . . . ?"

"Alexander," she supplied briskly. She knew she looked the part of an untraveled fool, but she infinitely preferred a teaspoon of caution to a cupful of reckless remorse. "I do not mean to play games, sir. I merely wish to assure that we will arrive safely in Monaco by this evening, that is all. I have rather urgent business to attend."

"I see."

His dark eyes swept over her once again, this time moving in a slow, open appraisal. His gaze traveled from the unadorned straw hat on her head to the reading spectacles perched on the end of her nose, then on to the few wayward ebony curls that had sprung free from the tight bun in which she had captured them that morning. His undisguised assessment coolly continued as he took in the dark gray, high-collared and loose-fitting traveling ensemble and low-heeled, practical boots, and it finished with the scuffed and well-worn carpetbag she clutched in her hand.

He seemed to come to some conclusion, for the light that had filled his eyes only moments earlier abruptly dimmed. "In that case," he suggested flatly, "I suggest we delay no further."

He took her money and tucked it into the pocket of his jacket. Then he turned away without another word, seeing to the needs of the other passengers.

Rather than being offended by his curtness, Katya found herself wishing she had selected a more becoming gown when she had dressed that morning. Or that she had at least bothered to remove her spectacles. Puzzled by her ridiculous reaction, she abruptly dismissed the matter of her appearance. What she wore was entirely sensible, given the dirt and debris she encountered while traveling the dry, dusty roads that lined the Côte d'Azur. Beyond that, she was still in mourning for her parents. The fact that her attire apparently didn't meet the lofty standards of their newly acquired coachman was hardly a matter of concern.

Fortunately the tavern owner had no objection to the Englishman serving in their driver's stead. Not knowing what else to do with herself, Katya listened as the stranger extracted his fee from the other passengers and then took direction as to the proper handling of the stage: the route he should follow, the stops he was required to make, and where he should deposit the horses and coach once they reached Monte Carlo. The business was finalized in short order and the group was ushered out of the dimly lit tavern and back into the stuffy confines of their coach.

The vehicle rocked and swayed as the Englishman climbed to his open-air perch above their cabin; then it jerked forward as the horses established a steady rhythm. Relieved that the stranger could apparently handle the team, Katya turned her attention to the other occupants of the coach. Her seatmates included a rather portly businessman from Marseilles who stank of fish and began snoring almost as soon as the vehicle was in motion, a pair of young lovers who sat scandalously close to one another and whispered back and forth in fervent Italian, and an elderly couple from England, Lord and Lady Stanton, with whom Katya had recently made an acquaintance.

"Heavens, Miss Alexander, you needn't balance that heavy bag on your lap all the way to Monaco," Lady Stanton protested as Katya settled her carpetbag on her knees. "We may be a bit crowded in here, but surely we can make a bit more room."

"That's quite all right, I don't mind."

"Nonsense." Lady Stanton tapped her husband authoritatively on the arm. "Do help her with her bag, my dear."

Katya hesitated briefly, then released her bag to the smiling, elderly lord, who placed it on the floor beside his wife's.

"There now, isn't that better?" Lady Stanton inquired pleasantly.

"Yes," she admitted. "Thank you."

"I should think so." Lady Stanton sniffed approvingly. "Now that we're all comfortable, my dear, do allow me the liberty of making a few suggestions for your trip." The older woman abruptly launched into a long-winded but well-meaning lecture, directing Katya to all the glorious sights awaiting her within the tiny principality of Monaco.

Katya listened politely, nodding from time to time as she feigned interest in what the other woman said. The information offered, however, was of little use to her. She was twenty-three years old, alone, and nearly penniless. She could ill afford to waste either time or money on idle pleasure-seeking.

As Lady Stanton rambled on, Katya's thoughts turned inward. For what seemed like the hundredth time since she had left London, she questioned the wisdom of this trip, particularly now that her meeting with Monsieur Remy was so close at hand. What if he should deny her request? She had foolishly refused to even consider the possibility months ago, but now she could think of almost nothing else. What would become of her if Monsieur Remy said no? The question echoed through her mind with the haunting finality of a funeral bell.

At last the coach rumbled to a stop, jarring her out of her depressing reverie. She heard the springs creak and groan above her as their newly acquired driver climbed down from his seat. He opened the door with a flourish and let down the passenger stair. "Ladies and gentlemen," he announced, "Nice."

Katya stepped out of the stuffy dimness of the stage. Brilliant Mediterranean sunshine flooded the courtyard, providing a welcome relief from her dismal thoughts. Once her eyes had adjusted to the light, she couldn't help but gaze around in open admiration, instantly charmed at what she saw.

Directly to her west was the Baie des Anges, the Bay of Angels, a sparkling azure port filled with an assortment of pleasure boats and fishing vessels. On the rocky beach below them fishermen barked out their prices, selling that morning's catch. Their calls competed with the bustling shouts coming from the marketplace, which consisted of a thriving series of stalls and intricate alleyways. A fountain bubbled in the center of the square, providing the music of softly gurgling water to the scene around her. To her east was an area that looked primarily residential. Tall pink buildings with red tile roofs were stacked tightly together and connected by a maze of laundry lines. A soft breeze carried a myriad of rich scents: fresh soap, rich coffee, sizzling meat, the salty tang of the sea, and the sweet fragrance of lemon blossom.

As her fellow passengers disembarked and headed toward a café, Katya hesitated, loathe to be again confined inside on such a beautiful day.

"Are you coming, Miss Alexander?"

She turned to find the Englishman waiting for her. Shaking her head, she replied instead, "I believe I prefer to stretch my legs a bit first."

"Don't get lost. We'll be ready to depart again in thirty minutes."

Irritated by his autocratic tone, she turned without a word and strode purposefully toward the marketplace. Her appetite was stimulated by the open air and the tantalizing aromas wafting around her, and she stopped at a *boulangerie* to choose one of the shop's luscious offerings. Finally she selected a crusty slice of thick, freshly baked bread that had been liberally sprinkled with olive oil, basil, and oregano, then piled high with chunks of ruby ripe tomato, shiny black olives, grilled eggplant, and rich cubes of pungent goat cheese.

She ate as she strolled through the marketplace, eyeing the vast selection of merchandise. She walked past shops displaying bolts of traditional Provencal fabrics, rough clay pottery, spectacular beaded jewelry, silky lace shawls, candied fruit, purple cabbages, plump little sausages, lush stalks of gladioli, and fragrant bunches of mimosa. Although she would have loved to while away the afternoon exploring the town, she was too mindful of time passing to fully enjoy herself. Reluctantly she turned and made her way back to the coach.

She found the square with no trouble, but their coach remained empty. Apparently the other passengers were still inside the café. Her spirits buoyed by the fresh air and a full stomach, Katya set down her carpetbag and took a seat on the edge of the courtyard fountain.

Her gaze was drawn almost at once to the old Nice castle. Built centuries ago to protect its residents against Saracen invaders, its thick rock walls jutted up almost mystically against the harbor, as if it had risen from the sea itself. Its crenelated walls, ancient turrets, and crumbling battlements seemed to teem with life and cast an odd medieval spell over the city. Katya closed her eyes and imagined herself under the castle's protection, watched over through the centuries. It was a purely whimsical thought, but one which pleased her nonetheless.

Suddenly the warmth of the sun disappeared and a chill ran through her, as though the castle's protection had abruptly vanished. She opened her eyes to discover the driver standing beside her, his long shadow looming over her. Her first thought was that he was standing too close to her. On closer reflection, however, she realized that he stood no closer to her than anyone else. Yet his presence seemed somehow magnified, almost as though he were touching her.

He had removed his jacket and cravat, she noted immediately. Unable to stop herself, her gaze moved briefly over the Englishman's body. His crisp white shirt was slightly open at the neck, revealing a glimpse of his broad chest and a light smattering of coarse, dark hair. He had also rolled up the sleeves, drawing her attention to his powerful forearms and fine brown leather riding gloves. His dark hair was swept back and tousled by the breeze; his skin was bronzed from the sun. In the bright light of day his ebony eyes appeared even more dark and mysterious.

Katya considered the man silently. While there was nothing distinctly offensive or improper about him, he seemed to exude a rugged, almost aggressive air of sensuality that she found faintly disturbing. He reminded her of a pack animal that had been cast out and was forced to hunt alone. A beautiful animal perhaps, but one that was ultimately dangerous. Bearing that in mind, she sent him a curt nod, then gathered her belongings and stood to leave.

As she took a step away from him she was confronted by the sight of the young Italian lovers with whom she had shared the coach. They were standing against a thick clay wall and presumably believed that no one could see them. Locked in a scandalous embrace, they shared a deep, intimate kiss. As the young man's hand moved caressingly up his inamorata's thigh, Katya turned abruptly away, blushing furiously.

Unfortunately she turned directly into the Englishman's arms. As he brought up his hands to steady her, she was immediately engulfed by the heady, warm scent of his skin. Not knowing where else to look, she bravely tipped back her chin to meet his eyes. Judging from the knowing smile on his face, it was all too evident that he had also witnessed the scene.

She stiffened her spine and stepped back. "Are we departing soon?" she inquired coolly.

"In a minute." His gaze skimmed over her once again. His eyes were so dark they seemed to absorb the sunlight; yet they offered back none of the sun's warmth. A slight frown touched his brow as he looked at her, as though she were a puzzle to be solved and the pieces didn't quite fit. "American?" he asked.

"Pardon?"

"Your accent. I've been trying to place it."

Rather than explain her entire history, Katya found herself giving the same answer her mother had always given. "Gypsy."

"Of course. I should have guessed."

Determined to ignore his subtle condescension, Katya turned pointedly away. "If you'll excuse me . . ."

"One moment, Miss Alexander," he said, stopping her. "There was a reason I came out here to speak with you. Have you checked your belongings recently?"

She turned, frowning back at him. "I don't know what you're talking about."

"I'm talking about that carpetbag you were clutching to your chest in the tavern back in Cannes. Surely you weren't so foolish as to entrust its safety with Lord and Lady Stanton."

"How did you—"

"Your voices carried through the top of the coach."

"I see." Katya drew herself up. "Thank you for the warning," she replied stiffly. "That being the case, I shall take care to monitor our conversations more carefully."

A tight, mocking smile touched his lips. "The warning was not meant to ensure the privacy of your conversations."

"Then what—"

"Lord and Lady Stanton have indicated that they've changed their minds about continuing on to Monaco. It occurred to me that their abrupt change of heart might stem from a desire to escape undetected with whatever valuables they were able to sneak from your bag, rather than from a sudden desire to tour the town of Nice."

Her eyes widened as she stared at him for a moment in

stunned, speechless shock. "You can't be serious," she finally managed.

"You didn't wonder why a lord and lady of the realm were taking a third-rate coach into Monaco, rather than the train? Or where their servants might be? Or why Lady Stanton was so insistent that you give up control of your bag?"

Now it was Katya's turn to smile. "You seem to take great delight in making rather absurd and offensive assumptions about people, don't you?"

"I suggest you check your bag, Miss Alexander."

"Very well," she replied, matching his patronizing tone. "After I do, I shall be happy to accept your apology on behalf of Lord and Lady Stanton."

That said, she bent down, flipped open the leather straps of her carpetbag, and reached inside. Secure in the knowledge that she was entirely correct, she unfastened the tiny buttons that lined the inside front pocket, opened it, and peered inside.

Nothing.

The black silk pouch in which she stored her jewelry and cash was missing.

Katya smothered a shocked cry as her heart slammed against the walls of her chest. Swallowing hard, she resisted the urge to immediately dump her bag upside down and rifle through its contents in search of the missing item. The truth was inescapable. She had checked the tiny pouch before she boarded the coach and had found everything in good order. Now her jewels and money were gone. The only time the bag had been out of her hands all day was when Lady Stanton had insisted Katya put it on the floor between her and her husband.

The Englishman's deep voice rang out from above her. "I'm sorry, Miss Alexander. In this particular instance, I had hoped that I was wrong."

Katya squeezed her eyes shut, unable to bear his sympathy.

She was furious with herself for her carelessness, furious with the Stantons for their deception, and furious with him for pointing out her witless naïveté and clumsy ineptitude. "Surely you weren't so foolish as to entrust its safety with Lord and Lady Stanton." It was bad enough that her belongings were missing, but she needn't compound the beating her pride was taking by admitting that to the arrogant Englishman. She was quite capable of getting her possessions back without any help from him, thank you very much.

Forcing an expression of smug righteousness onto her face, she straightened and coolly met his gaze. "It appears that everything is perfectly in order," she lied. "Or perhaps you would like to check for yourself." She extended the open carpetbag toward him.

A look of mild surprise touched his features, although he didn't look the least bit embarrassed at his mistake. "I believe I can take your word for it," he replied, then gave a slight bow. "Do convey my apologies to Lord and Lady Stanton."

"I shall do nothing of the sort. I wouldn't dream of insulting them." She bent once again to fasten her bag, then straightened. "I suggest that in the future you refrain from leaping to such absurd conclusions about people. Especially people of quality. It is painfully evident that this is a subject with which you are horribly ill acquainted."

A tight, mocking smile once again appeared on his lips. "It might surprise you to know that I was once a gentleman myself."

She tilted her chin. "Frankly, sir, I find that rather difficult to believe."

Rather than taking offense at her words, his grin only widened. "Frankly, Miss Alexander, so do I."

Two

The smile stayed on Nicholas Duvall's lips as he watched the prim little Miss Alexander move toward the café where the other passengers had gathered for a late afternoon meal. Clearly his warning about Lord and Lady Stanton had offended her, though he couldn't imagine why. It had been meant as a simple word of caution, nothing more.

Now that he thought of it, Nicholas didn't know why he had bothered to issue the warning at all. Surely it wasn't his protective instincts toward the fairer sex that had impelled him to do so, for those instincts had run dry years ago. Then again, never had he seen a woman more in need of a firm guiding hand than Miss Alexander. Everything about her, from the way she had vested her total trust in the Stantons, to the crimson blush that had stained her cheeks at the sight of the young lovers exchanging passionate kisses, to the stiff-collared, droopy state of her attire, spoke of her complete naïveté.

Nicholas shrugged the idle thoughts away. How the prim and proper Miss Alexander chose to conduct herself was none of his business. Not only that, he had more important things to do than waste time pondering buttoned-up innocents. With that resolution firmly in mind, he moved to collect his passengers.

He strode to the café and opened the door, then stepped inside and briefly scanned the crowd. His gaze fell immediately on his small group, who were in the process of collecting their belongings and departing. While he watched, Miss Alexander leaned forward and accepted Lady Stanton's farewell embrace. Nicholas took a step toward them and then abruptly stopped, frozen in disbelief.

Bloody hell, he thought, as a shocked smile slowly stretched across his face. I'll be damned.

It appeared he had been entirely wrong as to who was the thief.

As the two women concluded their embrace, Miss Alexander dipped ever so gracefully into Lady Stanton's bag and artfully transferred a black silk pouch from the elderly woman's bag into her own. The switch was performed with such infallible timing and grace that he would have missed it entirely had his gaze not been focused on them.

Nicholas's shock at witnessing the petty crime quickly turned into an absurd sense of admiration. He shook his head, unaccountably pleased by the discovery. Rarely was he fooled in life, yet Miss Alexander had deceived him completely. So she wasn't the prude little innocent she pretended to be, he thought, eyeing her with renewed interest.

He hesitated a moment, debating what action he should take. The honorable thing, of course, would be to immediately denounce Miss Alexander and demand that she return the pouch to its rightful owner.

Then again, the hell with that. Nicholas was rarely burdened by what was honorable . . . particularly when his own needs were so much more compelling. It came to him with startling clarity that the corrupt little Miss Alexander might well offer a solution to one of his most pressing problems.

Somewhere ahead of him in Monaco—or perhaps in the group he had left behind—lurked a cold-blooded killer. Miss Alexander might be the perfect tool for helping him find the man. She was obviously resourceful, talented at sleight of hand, and gifted with a set of wonderfully ambiguous moral standards. If she was smart, she might even make a tidy little profit by helping him. He quickly formulated a plan, amazed at the ease with which it came to him. It had never before occurred to him to seek out an accomplice in his search. Now that he considered it, he wondered why he hadn't thought of it before.

Abruptly deciding that Lady Stanton could well afford the loss of whatever petty baubles she had carried in her bag, he stepped forward, announcing that it was time to depart. He ushered his remaining passengers into the coach without further ceremony and then climbed aboard and gathered the reins. He edged the team out of the café's open courtyard and onto the busy Quai Rauba Capeau, heading northeast toward Monaco. Once they left the bustling town of Nice the traffic diminished considerably, allowing him an opportunity to relax a bit and enjoy the spectacular scenery.

The road widened as they entered the charming fishing harbor of Villefranche. Nicholas stopped briefly for the fisherman from Marseilles to disembark. He made a second stop less than an hour later in the ancient hilltop village of Eze, where the young Italian lovers took their leave. As Lord and Lady Stanton had elected to remain in Nice, that left him with just one passenger for the remainder of the journey into Monaco: the charmingly corrupt, intriguing Miss Alexander.

While Nicholas guided the team, he pondered the best way to approach her with his proposition. Should he appeal to her sense of greed by baiting her with a monetary reward, cajole her with flattery for her talent as a thief, or directly threaten her with exposure if she didn't agree to help him?

As he silently considered the merits of each tactic, a stiff breeze abruptly kicked up. Nicholas glanced around, noticing for the first time the commotion in the underbrush around him. Thrushes, hares, and marmots scurried to find cover, reminding him of the sudden burst of activity on shipboard as sailors hurry to prepare for a storm. And there would be a storm, no doubt about it. Looking over his shoulder he saw a bank of thick, dark clouds sweeping in from the west and bearing down on the coastline.

He let out a sharp curse and rapidly calculated the odds of beating the storm to Monaco. Slim to none, he guessed, as the azure sky quickly darkened to indigo and the sharp spring breezes became violent gusts strong enough to rattle the coach. They were probably only six to seven miles away from their destination, but it might as well have been sixty to seventy. He was barely able to control the horses now and knew it would be even more difficult once the skies really opened up. Nor was there room on the rugged Corniche to turn the coach around and return to Eze. It would be suicide to even attempt the maneuver. The road was little more than a narrow ledge carved into the mountainside; alongside it was a sheer drop to the sea below.

Unfortunately they had no choice but to seek shelter within the coach and ride out the storm where they were. No sooner had Nicholas come to this reluctant conclusion than a burst of deep, booming thunder rumbled above them. A resounding crack of lightning blistered the sky as the clouds split open and rain poured down in torrents. The horses tossed their heads and pranced nervously back and forth, ready to rear. One wrong move could send them plummeting over the side of the cliff.

"Easy," Nicholas crooned, keeping his voice low and soothing as he leaped from his seat and stepped gingerly behind the horses. Feeling his way in the driving rain, he blindly searched among the tangle of leather straps and metal harnesses, working until he had unhitched the badly spooked team.

Once the horses were free from the burden of the coach, he breathed a sigh of relief and stepped back onto the path where he nearly tripped over his remaining passenger. Miss Alexander was soaked to the skin, fighting the driving gusts of wind and rain just to remain upright.

"What the hell are you doing out here?" he shouted, barely making himself heard over the fury of the storm.

Her gaze flashed to the frightened team of horses, then back to him. "What are *you* doing?"

"Get back inside the coach," he ordered, unwilling to waste time explaining the direness of their predicament. Nicholas took her arm to guide her back inside, but she immediately shook off his grip.

"You gave me your word," she said.

His brows shot skyward in astonishment. "You're blaming me for the storm?"

"You're the driver. You promised we would make it to Monaco by tonight."

"I try to drive that team in this weather and I'll kill us both."

"That is not your decision to make," she informed him heatedly. "You've been paid your fee and are honor bound to meet the terms on which we agreed. I have to make it to Monaco by tonight. I have to."

A rolling boom of thunder shook the ground around them as Nicholas let out a series of scathing oaths. "And I don't care if the bloody prince himself is waiting to see you," he shot back. "Neither of us is going anywhere in this storm."

She studied him in furious silence. "Very well," she said, then turned abruptly away and stalked toward the coach.

Nicholas watched her march away, her skirts dragging in the mud as she moved. She might be angry, he thought, but at least she was listening to reason. He let out a weary sigh and moved to join her, intending to wait out the storm from within the relative warmth and safety of the coach. But rather than reboard as he had instructed her, Miss Alexander merely reached inside and removed her carpetbag. Once that item was securely in her grasp, she spun around and began to march defiantly down the rugged Corniche.

He caught her arm as she tried to pass him. "What the hell do you think you're doing?"

"I'm walking. And I would appreciate it if you would cease swearing at me."

Ignoring her prim little reprimand, he stared at her in stunned disbelief. "*You're walking*? All the way to Monaco? In *this*?" A sharp gust of wind whipped the rain around him, punctuating his words.

"Apparently I have no choice."

"I don't think you quite understand our situation."

"On the contrary," she shot back, "I understand completely. You gave me your word and now you are reneging on your promise. Clearly my instincts were right about you from the very beginning. I should never have trusted you. You are no gentleman, sir." Tilting her chin as she peered down her rain-streaked spectacles, she finished with cool disdain, "I hope you'll earn your twenty francs by seeing to it that at least my trunk arrives safely."

Nicholas studied her in silent disbelief, doubting both her sanity and her will to live. The woman was soaking wet, her clothing was drenched, her hair was completely undone and running down her back in a tangled mass of thick ebony curls, and she was standing up to her ankles in a current of swift-flowing mud. Given her present state, one would think she would realize that the only option they had was to wait out the storm. Instead, she had the audacity to chastise him for the unpardonable sin of wanting to protect both their lives.

Allowing his anger to take precedence over common sense, he released her arm. With an elegant gesture more appropriate in a crowded ballroom than on a rain-soaked cliff, he motioned her forward. "By all means, madame, do proceed."

With a haughty toss of her head, she lifted her sodden gown and swept past him. She hadn't made it more than ten feet in the blinding rain, however, when her gown caught and twisted in a tangled mass of thorny shrubbery. Glancing back over her shoulder she gave the fabric one impatient jerk, then another. When both attempts to free her gown failed, she planted her feet in the muddy ground, gathered the fabric between her hands, and tugged with all her might.

Nicholas's silent amusement at her self-created predicament abruptly faded. With a surge of horror, he realized how perilously close she was to the edge of the cliff. If she did manage to wrest her gown free . . .

"*No!*" he shouted, lunging toward her.

His warning went unheard in the raging storm. Just as he had feared, after several angry tugs the fabric jerked free so suddenly that she stumbled backward, loosing her footing in the mud. Her arms flailing, she scrambled on the slippery slope to regain her balance. As she did, a bolt of lightning illuminated the sky. In that single, fleeting moment—a moment that seemed to stretch into infinity—she appeared poised in midair, as helpless and fragile as a china doll that had been tossed from a balcony window. The lightning abruptly faded and the sky went black once again.

Miss Alexander gave a scream of terror and tumbled over backward.

Nicholas dove for her, hurling himself with all his might toward the spot where he had last seen her.

As his last hope of reaching her in time plummeted, his fingers brushed against a sodden, kicking appendage. Recognizing it at once as her ankle, he immediately tightened his grip, holding on to her with both hands. But his relief at catching her quickly vanished. Propelled by the slushy mud beneath him, the momentum of his lunge, and the sheer force of Miss Alexander's fall, he was about to be carried over the edge along with her. For instead of bringing them both to a stop, his body continued to skid toward the edge of the precipice.

Nicholas frantically glanced around for a foothold in the torrent of mud and rain, searching desperately for some sort of anchor to stop their fall. Nothing.

His arms slid over the cliff wall.

He stuck out his legs, hoping to hit a root or a rock—anything to stop their deadly plunge.

His head slid over the cliff wall.

Refusing to let her go just to save himself, he dug his heels into the ground. But there was nothing to hold him. Nothing but mud and slush and tangled shrubs.

His chest slid over the cliff wall.

Muttering a vivid oath that fell somewhere between a swear and a prayer, he kicked out his legs one last time . . . and finally felt something connect with his boot. He immediately hooked both ankles around the unknown object as he and Miss Alexander jerked to an abrupt stop. Although he couldn't see what had blocked their fall, it felt as though he had hooked his boots over a thorny shrub.

Letting out his breath in a gush of relief, he took a second to reassess their position. Despite the direness of the predicament, the absurdity of their situation didn't fail to impress him. He could well imagine the collective and comic shock of his peers were they to see Nicholas Duvall, the Earl of Barrington, hanging upside down over the face of a cliff. Both his hands were firmly gripped around one of Miss Alexander's ankles, while her opposite leg flailed about, coming back every four seconds or so to strike him somewhere about his shoulder, back, or head.

While this was undoubtedly a nuisance, his attention was nonetheless diverted by the fascinating effect gravity had had on her skirts.

Hanging upside down as she was, Miss Alexander's skirt and petticoat had taken flight and were gathered inside out and upside down over her head. His position, hanging over the ledge with his head between her ankles, offered him an uninterrupted look at her legs—encased in serviceable black stockings—as well as her hips and belly—chastely covered by white cotton drawers edged with delicate pink ribbon.

A decidedly interesting view, but one he was not at liberty to enjoy.

That point was driven home most effectively when the shrub around which he had wrapped his ankles bent abruptly, sending him slipping another inch or so over the abyss. His heart slammed against his ribs and he heard Miss Alexander's muffled cry of shock and distress as it echoed through her skirt and petticoat. Immediately returning his thoughts to the task at hand, he moved one hand up her leg, attempting to pull her toward him. He shifted one gloved hand to her calf, then placed his other hand on her lower thigh.

Miss Alexander released an immediate squeal of maidenly protest, followed by a storm of even stronger outrage. Nicholas heard something that sounded vaguely like *villain! scoundrel!* and a third, more shocking word he would have wagered good money was not even in her vocabulary. She squirmed wildly, fighting him with all the verve and gusto one might properly reserve for a lowly mugger in Piccadilly Square.

Nicholas squeezed his eyes shut and clamped his hands even more tightly around her leg, imagining for a moment the sheer bliss of granting her will and letting his ungrateful captive slip free from his clutches.

Deciding against that course of action, however tempting it might appear, he ignored her protests and slowly inched his way up her leg, pulling her closer to him. To his dismay, she was much heavier than she had appeared. Finally he realized why. As he was desperately struggling to keep his foothold on the tangled shrub—which might give way at any second—she was using both her hands to clutch her bulky carpetbag above her head.

Amazement, fury, and disbelief gripped him in turn. "Let go of that damned bag!" he shouted.

"What?!" came back her muffled reply, her voice buried beneath the layers of her skirt and petticoat.

"Drop your bag!"

Another reply from her, this one too indistinct to be understood.

The shrub gave again, sending them both sliding another inch forward.

Nicholas's back was breaking, his arms ached, and his shoulders burned as though they were about to be wrenched from their sockets. He raised his voice, shouting himself nearly hoarse. *"Drop the bloody bag! Now, dammit!"*

His words appeared to have finally sunk in, for she released one hand while swinging the bag with her other, as though to fling it away from herself. But rather than allowing it to drop, she hurled the bag upward with all her might.

The carpetbag flew full force directly into his face.

Nicholas released a startled roar of both pain and anger as the rough canvas bounced off his nose and cheek, then catapulted from his shoulder to land with a heavy thud on the path above them. After delivering yet another curse in a long stream of heated profanity, he jerked her to him and worked his way up her leg, finally managing to catch her around the waist.

Holding her thus with one arm, he extended his free hand and shouted in a furious tone that was not to be ignored, "Take my hand!"

Fortunately she obeyed almost instantly, blindly reaching upside down through the tangle of her skirts to grope for his hand. Nicholas caught her palm in his. No sooner had she bent forward, straining to a half-sitting position, when his glove, slick from the rain and mud, slipped from his hand. Her body hurled backward once again. If not for the grip he had maintained on her waist, she would have tumbled to her death.

Miss Alexander gave a startled, panicked cry and reached for his hand again almost instantly, this time without any prompting from him. As her bare hand struck his, Nicholas tugged her forward. Using his body as a human bridge, she scrambled clumsily over him, reached the narrow path, and pulled herself up. He followed immediately, digging his fingers into the rock and mud as he scaled the cliff after her. She tugged at his shirt and trousers as he climbed, doing her best to assist him. Finally, with all the grace and dignity of two drunken monkeys falling out of a tree, they reached the ledge.

Too exhausted to move, breathing hard, they lay sprawled out side by side in a current of mud. Neither one spoke as the rain pelted their bodies. They didn't have to. The silence between them carried a mutual, unspoken emotion: astonishment that they were still alive.

Nicholas had no idea how long they stayed like that, but gradually he became aware of a change in the weather. Like most storms in the region, this one had swooped down with a sudden, violent intensity out of a clear blue sky, only to vanish almost as quickly as it had come. The rain, which had poured down in torrents only minutes earlier, now began to soften. A light, misty drizzle blurred the horizon. The ground seemed to steam, almost purr, with luxuriant relief at the passing of the storm. The chirping of birds and the sounds of animals thrashing about in the bushes filled the air once again.

Nicholas rolled over onto his side, looking at the prostrate form of Miss Alexander. "I trust you're unharmed?" he asked.

She waited a beat, then shifted experimentally. Looking thoroughly dazed, she slowly sat up and opened her eyes. "I believe I lost my hat," she replied. "Other than that, I'm quite all right. And you?"

Nicholas inclined his head and matched her polite, drawing-room tone. "Aside from the bruises you gave me with your kicking and ungodly struggles, I expect I'll live."

"You were accosting me, sir."

"I was trying to save your wretched, ungrateful life."

"You were doing so in a most unchivalrous manner."

"In the future, Miss Alexander, should you ever again decide to plunge headfirst over the face of a cliff, I shall endeavor to grasp your ankle in a more genteel fashion."

His sarcasm was lost on her. "I would appreciate it," she replied, primly victorious.

That said, she bent her head, removed her spectacles—which had somehow miraculously managed not to tumble over the cliff—and turned her attention to the task of cleaning them. Apparently satisfied that she had removed as much of the dirt and grime as she could using her sodden gown, she propped the glass lenses once again onto the bridge of her nose.

Nicholas watched her, absurdly wishing she had left them off. Her eyes, when not obstructed by those thick, clumsy spectacles, were truly amazing. The most unusual shade of lavender he had ever seen.

"Well," she said crisply, "now that our little adventure is over, I trust we may proceed on our journey."

"Indeed," Nicholas replied, drawing his thoughts back to their journey. He glanced over at the horses and coach. Although still skittish, the team appeared to have settled down enough to be manageable. He rose to his feet and offered her a hand up.

She gently placed her delicate hand in his larger one. Although he hadn't noticed it earlier, it occurred to him now how small her hand was within his, how light and absurdly fragile.

The realization stirred an unexpected surge of protectiveness within him. Fixing her with a reproving glare, he intoned sternly, "Had you listened to me in the first place, Miss Alexander, that entire incident might have been avoided. We would both be safely ensconced in the coach right now, waiting out the last of the storm in relative comfort and—"

A sharp, deafening crack cut off his words. Nicholas swung his gaze sharply to the left, narrowing in on the source of the sound. What he saw made his blood run cold. A mud slide, a not uncommon by-product of the region's sudden torrential rains, churned down the mountain, carrying with it a mass of rocks and debris. As it gained in size and speed, the force of the avalanche snapped a tree in half.

Now the slide was hurtling straight toward them.

Three

With no time to do anything but dive out of the path of the torrential avalanche, Nicholas lunged once again for his passenger. He knocked her down in a rough tackle and rolled sideways, desperately attempting to propel them both to safety.

The ground shook as the slide rolled past them, missing their bodies by scant inches. It slammed into their coach with a thunderous crash, hitting the conveyance broadside and knocking it flat. As the coach tumbled past them, Nicholas instinctively shielded Miss Alexander beneath him, covering her body with his own. He heard a sharp crack within the tumult of the avalanche—the coach being ripped in half, perhaps? A second later the sound of splintering wood and steel filled the air. Nicholas clenched his jaw, his muscles tensing as he felt a sharp, agonizing sting lash his back.

For one heart-stopping moment he thought the entire coach was about to come crashing down upon them. But in the next second the conveyance was gone, careening over the cliff edge as it exploded against the rocky shore below. After a minute or two the deafening roar of the slide slowly faded to a dull rumble. As the muffled protests and squirming motions of Miss Alexander slowly penetrated his consciousness, he rolled over and let her slip out from beneath him.

She sat up and gazed in stunned disbelief at the deep river of mud that flooded the path where they had stood just moments earlier. Biting back a groan, Nicholas struggled to a sitting position and glanced around as well. Aside from the steady current of mud streaming slowly down the mountainside, the landscape was once again peaceful and serene. At least he had had the foresight to unhitch the team at the onset of the storm, he thought. At the start of the mud slide the skittish animals had taken off in a terrified gallop. The horses were safe—albeit halfway to Monaco by now.

After a minute or two of contemplative silence, Miss Alexander let out a doleful sigh. "My trunk was atop that coach."

Ignoring the plaintive remark, he pointed to a small scrap of lace showing beneath her skirt hem. "Your petticoat . . ."

With an indignant frown, she immediately swept her skirts over the offending bit of lace. "A gentleman would not have noticed."

"The gentleman is bleeding to death."

Her brows snapped together. "What?" she said. As her gaze flew to his back, an expression of shocked horror filled her face. "How did that happen?"

"I believe it was the coach's harness straps."

"Does it hurt?"

Holding back the sharp retort that sprung to his lips, Nicholas bit out between clenched teeth, "If you would be so kind as to allow me the use of your petticoat . . ."

Finally understanding that he meant to use it to bandage his back, she hesitated. "Oh, dear, it's one of my best . . ."

Nicholas reached for her petticoat without another word and ripped off a generous length of the rain-soaked cotton.

"Really!"

He slipped off his shirt and fumbled with the bandage. As he did so, her startled gaze flew across his naked chest. A soft, ruby glow infused her cheeks, visible despite the layers of mud and grime that coated her skin. Determined to ignore her puritanical sensibilities—sensibilities that were likely as false and hollow as the rest of her prim facade—

Nicholas continued his task without a word. After a few minutes of fumbling on his part, she finally intervened.

"Here, let me do that."

He released the makeshift bandage without a word, hoping she would make a better job of it. Her touch was surprisingly soothing, light yet firm. Forgetting his pain, Nicholas found himself wondering what it would be like to feel her hands on other parts of his body. What a shame that his back had been injured, he thought absently, rather than his upper thigh. Now that would have been interesting.

"It would appear that the two of us are cursed, Miss Alexander," he said after a moment. He wasn't particularly eager for conversation, but it seemed the best way to divert his attention from the sensual, fluid feel of her hands as they moved across his skin.

"I don't believe in curses," she replied absently. "My mother did, naturally, but I don't suffer from the same old-fashioned thinking."

"Why is it natural that your mother would have believed in curses?" he asked, his curiosity aroused.

"She was a gypsy."

"I thought you said you were as well."

"True, but I don't enjoy it."

Certain she was joking, a small smile touched his lips. "You don't?"

"It's in the blood," she conceded with a small sigh, "but I'm not like my mother at all. I'm more of a modern gypsy, I suppose. I don't particularly like to travel, nor do I sing and dance, nor do I search the skies for signs of evil."

"I see." He studied her for a moment in amused silence. "Then what do you do?"

"Do?" she repeated.

"What brings you to Monaco?"

"Oh." A look of anxious distress clouded her features. "I had an appointment with a certain gentleman at eight o'clock this evening. A rather critical appointment." She lifted her sodden gown with one hand, then let it fall with a dejected sigh. "Now everything's ruined. Even if we were to reach Monaco in time, I couldn't go looking like this."

"Surely he'll understand."

"Not Monsieur Remy," she said, letting out another sigh. "He's very particular about punctuality and appearances. Besides, everything was arranged over a month ago. Now I don't know what I'll do."

"You'll find another Monsieur Remy."

Her brows drew together in a confused frown. "I don't know what you mean."

"I trust the purpose of your meeting was to determine whether the two of you might be suitable for matrimony."

She stiffened her spine in righteous indignation. "What an insulting assumption."

"Young, unmarried girls rarely travel halfway across the globe without the benefit of a chaperon merely to enjoy the sights," he stated flatly, lifting his broad shoulders in an indifferent shrug. As she opened her mouth to object, he continued smoothly, "There's no shame in it, Miss Alexander. In Monaco, where the wild game consists of wealthy dukes, earls, viscounts—all blessedly free of the encumbrances of both spouses and common sense—hunting is practiced without permit and throughout the year."

"How very reassuring," she replied.

Her tone was as icy as the north wind, but there was no denial in her words. So his instinct had been right, Nicholas concluded silently, she had come to Monaco to find herself a rich man to marry. That and to rob as many people blind as she could. It was an uninspired plan on her part, but one which fit nicely with his own needs.

"Which do you have your sights on," he continued blithely, "a title or money? Poor, unchaperoned women rarely command both, even those with the distinct, rather creative allure of modern-day gypsies."

She met his gaze with a look of cool disdain. "I'm beginning to understand why our coach wrecked. Obviously you were too busy jumping to ridiculous conclusions about me to properly focus on handling the team."

Nicholas let out a low laugh—albeit one that was cut short as, with an abrupt motion, she pulled the bandage tight and knotted the strip of cotton. At his involuntary jerk away from her, she released a satisfied sigh. "There," she said briskly, "that should hold. How does it feel?"

His back was stiff and bruised, the binding was uncomfortable, and the lacerations stung like hell. "Fine."

"Good." She rose to her feet. "Now what do we do?"

Nicholas stood as well. "Now, Miss Alexander, we walk."

"All the way to Monaco?"

"All the way to Monaco. Unless you have a better plan."

She thought for a moment, studying the horizon as though a solution might be offered there. "I see your point," she conceded.

They hadn't moved but a few steps when he reached for her carpetbag and wordlessly took it from her hand. She studied him with a surprised frown, as though the small courtesy were completely unlike him. "Thank you," she said.

Nicholas merely nodded and continued walking. As they strode along the Corniche the final details of his plan took shape in his mind. The prim little Miss Alexander was a thief and a fraud—but she was good at both, and that was what mattered. When Lady Stanton discovered that her jewelry was missing, Miss Alexander would be the last person anyone would suspect.

Not only was she a good thief, he thought, but she apparently had nerves of steel. They could easily have been washed over the cliff and smashed to bits on the rocks below, yet she had just picked herself up and started walking. Remarkable, really, when compared to most of the women he knew. Anyone else would have fallen to pieces.

Miss Alexander would suit his purposes very nicely, he thought. The only question that loomed unanswered was whether she would be able to blend in with his peers. He sent her a sideways glance, silently assessing the woman. At the moment her drab gown was covered in mud, her hair was caked with debris, and her spectacles gave her an unflattering, decidedly spinsterish quality. But if she were cleaned up, dressed in an exquisite gown, and decorated with a few jewels? Perhaps then his plan would work.

As Nicholas considered the question, he was struck by the memory of what her rain-slick thighs had felt like against his hands. Although he hadn't been at liberty to fully enjoy the sensation at the time, the memory aroused within him a carnal curiosity to finish what they had inadvertently begun. She would do just fine, he decided. Just fine, indeed.

They arrived in the principality of Monaco just as twilight was descending. Gaslights lit the beautifully manicured parks, regal coaches rolled down the wide avenues, and a general atmosphere of indolent merriment seemed to fill the air. Richly dressed pedestrians crowded the sidewalks, and the cafés bustled with activity. Although they drew several openly appalled glances, given the ragged state of their attire, Miss Alexander didn't slow her purposeful stride or appear the least bit embarrassed. Instead, she met the rude stares of passersby with a cool, composed gaze—another point in the woman's favor, Nicholas decided.

As they turned a corner on Rue Grimaldi, she drew to an abrupt stop. "This is where I'm staying," she announced.

He looked at the modest structure she indicated. The villa was respectable enough, though far from first class. It consisted of three narrow floors, all freshly whitewashed. The windows were framed by intricate wrought-iron balconies,

and a neat bed of shrubbery filled the garden. A ROOMS TO
LET sign hung above the front door.

He shifted her carpetbag from his grasp and set it on the
ground beside her. "Your bag, Miss Alexander."

"Thank you, Mr.—" A startled expression flitted across
her face. "I don't know your name."

"Duvall. Nicholas Duvall."

She nodded. "Mr. Duvall." She took a deep breath, then
primly offered him her hand. "Farewell. I trust this is the last
we shall see of each other."

A smile touched his lips at her haughty words of parting.
From the corner of his eye, Nicholas caught sight of a young
girl selling flowers. With a nod he called her over and examined her wares. He selected a long-stemmed white rose
and handed the girl a coin.

Once the flower girl had departed, he bent over the mud-
stained hand Miss Alexander had offered. But rather than
shake it, as she had obviously intended, he brought it to his
lips and graced it with a kiss.

"Not farewell, Miss Alexander. Merely au revoir." He
straightened and passed her the rose. Then his eyes locked
onto hers. "Until we meet again, little gypsy."

Katya swallowed hard, her cheeks burning beneath the
sensual heat of his dark gaze. *Little gypsy*. The endearment,
whispered in a deep voice that was low and honey-smooth,
caused a distinctly uneasy churning sensation to fill her belly.
Fortunately the moment didn't last long. Nicholas Duvall
eased his grip on her hand and allowed her to pull free. She
stepped away immediately, driven by the same instinct that
would impel her to lift her hand from a burning stove: pure
self-preservation.

For an instant, as he had given her the rose, she had felt
sure he was going to kiss her. Properly kiss her, that is—on
the lips, rather than on the back of her hand. She shook her
head, mentally chastising herself. The mere idea was idiotic,

not to mention highly indecent. Undoubtedly the strain of their journey was beginning to cloud both her thinking and her judgment. Anxious to put a little distance between them, she took another step backward, stumbling as she did so over a small potted plant.

"Yes, well . . . goodbye."

With those awkward words of parting, she turned and strode toward the villa. The landlady answered the door at the second knock. After a long and horrified appraisal of Katya's filthy attire, the woman reluctantly accepted the fact that she was indeed the lodger who had written over a month ago to secure a room. With a beleaguered sigh, she ushered her new guest inside.

As Katya followed the landlady across the threshold and into the villa, she took one final glance over her shoulder. Nicholas Duvall had vanished completely and his disappearance caused a pang of dismay to sweep through her. Ridiculous, really, when she didn't even like the man. Resolving to push all thoughts of the enigmatic Englishman aside, she followed the landlady through the modest house and to her room.

She set down her carpetbag and glanced around the small chamber. Although distinctly unglamorous, it was entirely adequate. It contained a narrow bed, a chest of drawers, and a table with two chairs. She also noted a privacy screen, behind which rested a small tub for bathing, a stand with a pitcher and water basin and—an unexpectedly gracious touch—a stack of jasmine-scented soaps.

As she crossed the room, Katya caught a glimpse of herself in an oval looking glass and gave a gasp of horror. Her hair was completely undone and thoroughly matted with mud and leaves. Her face and hands were coated with a thin film of grime, as were her spectacles, and her gown was caked with mud and various bits of debris. No wonder her landlady had looked so horrified.

A wry, self-deprecating grin touched her lips. No wonder the Englishman had vanished so quickly. Who could blame him? Deciding to immediately avail herself of every bucket and pail of hot water she could carry from the kitchen to her room, she set about the task of bathing. By the time she had finished and changed into the crisp white linen nightshirt she carried in her carpetbag, her bathwater ran black.

She dumped the stale water in the vegetable garden outside her window and quietly padded back for more hot water for her clothing. That accomplished, she knelt down in front of the tub and placed her garments inside. As she rinsed out the clothing she felt a thick lump in the pocket of her skirt. She reached inside, expecting to find a fistful of rocks or perhaps an undissolved clump of mud.

Instead she discovered a man's leather riding glove. Katya stared at it in perplexed silence. Then with a sudden rush of understanding she realized how it had come to be in her possession. The Englishman's glove had slipped off in her hand as he had tried to pull her up the cliff. Although she didn't recall doing so in her panicked state, she must have tucked it into her pocket.

Abandoning her wash for the moment, she squeezed the glove free of excess moisture and brought it with her to the table. She sat down and turned the glove this way and that, unaccountably fascinated by the item and—though she was loathe to admit it—the man to whom it belonged. Without stopping to examine her motives she lifted the glove close to her face. It carried a compelling mixture of aromas: leather, horses, the sweet jasmine of the soap, and the heady, unmistakably masculine scent of the Englishman's skin.

She rubbed the smooth leather between her fingers, then slipped her hand into the glove. As she did so she felt a small, round object strike her third finger. Frowning, she removed her hand and gave the glove a hard shake. A ring tumbled out onto her palm. She must have been gripping Nicholas

Duvall's hand so tightly that she had pulled off his ring along with the glove.

As Katya studied the ring a chill ran up her spine, making her shiver despite the warmth of the room. There was something oddly ominous about the thick band of gold, something she couldn't define. It was a portent of some sort, that much she knew. But a portent of what?

Confused by the strong emotions the ring evoked within her, Katya examined it more closely. The band was heavy and doubtless very valuable, for it appeared to be made of solid gold. It looked like a signet ring of some sort, one that had likely been passed down from generation to generation. Ancient, intricate carvings decorated the sides of the band, giving it a feeling of timelessness. The stone that crowned the center of the band was solid onyx, as black and as fathomless as the Englishman's eyes. The onyx had been carved as well, but she couldn't quite make out the design.

Her curiosity whetted, she found a candle and dripped a bit of hot wax onto a sheet of paper; then she pressed the onyx into the wax. As the wax cooled, she recognized the figure of a bird of prey. A hawk, or perhaps an eagle or a falcon. There was something profoundly unsettling about the figure of the bird, but she couldn't quite articulate it. She peered inside the band for an engraved name, date, or set of initials, anything that might tell her more about the ring. What she found instead was a squat cross with an inverted V at each of the four ends.

Katya dropped the ring with a gasp of horror.

The cross on the inside of the ring was the Maltese Cross.

The bird of prey carved into the onyx was a Maltese falcon.

Duvall . . . DuValenti. Clearly this was a modern version of the ancient family name.

Katya stared at the ring that sat on the table before her. With a shock of apprehension and disbelief, she realized that she had just accomplished what centuries of her ancestors had been unable to.

She, Katya Zofia Rosskaya Alexander, had found the Maltese, her family's mortal enemy.

Four

"*R*egrettably, Miss Alexander, your request is impossible."

Katya sat in a rickety wooden chair in the cluttered office of Monsieur Remy, theater manager for Monte Carlo's stunning new entertainment hall. She had enjoyed very little sleep the night before. Her thoughts had swung between the grim state of her financial affairs, the momentous encounter she had had with Nicholas Duvall, and her nagging worry that Monsieur Remy would refuse to see her at all, since she had missed their appointment the previous night.

But the man had consented to see her—albeit after keeping her waiting outside his office for a good hour. Unfortunately the meeting wasn't going well. She shifted in her chair, struggling to maintain an air of poised composure. Displaying any sign of the naked desperation she felt inside would hardly endear her to Monsieur Remy, nor would it help her secure the post she sought.

She leveled her tone to one of cool professionalism and persisted, "But certainly, monsieur, you can see my position."

"I see nothing," he replied flatly. He pulled a timepiece from his breast pocket, frowned at it, then snapped the case shut. "I expected you last night, not this morning. Punctuality and reliability are of the essence in this business, Miss Alexander. You have done nothing to demonstrate why I should possess any confidence in you in either regard. If a performer cannot meet a simple appointment, I have little faith he or she can meet a schedule as rigorously demanding as one imposed by life in the theater. Our discussion is finished."

Katya regarded him without moving. The man was short in stature and given to pudginess, a trait he tried to disguise with his immaculate dress. He wore his hair slicked back with perfumed oil; his body reeked of heavily scented cologne. While she certainly hadn't expected sympathy from him, neither had she anticipated such callous disregard. For the first time since she had stepped into his office, anger replaced the fear and trepidation that had overwhelmed her.

Her father, after all, had been the Great Professor Alexander, Wizard of the North, King of the Conjurers, Magician Extraordinaire. Her mother? None other than the legendary Anastasia, dark-eyed assistant to the great professor. Her parents' final performance had taken place on Monsieur Remy's stage, a mere fifty feet from where they sat. Given that fact, surely it was not asking too much that he treat her with a modicum of professional courtesy.

Resolved to terminate the interview with her dignity intact, she stood and slowly pulled on her gloves. "Would you be so kind as to inform me to whom I should speak regarding the shipment of my parents' costumes and props to London's Egyptian Hall? Mr. Townsend, the manager there, has already indicated a great interest in being the first in the world to introduce a female magician who can perform the Gun Trick."

This was pure fiction. In truth, her correspondence with Mr. Townsend had been returned unopened, as had her letters to every other theater manager. She mentioned the competing hall only as a way of saving her pride. But to her considerable surprise, Monsieur Remy's head snapped up, his eyes alert with interest. "You didn't mention the Gun Trick."

"On the contrary, monsieur. I said that I was fully able to perform every illusion in my parents' repertoire." She moved to the door and paused. "Now then, to whom shall I speak regarding those shipping arrangements?"

Monsieur Remy stood. With a tight smile that revealed a row of tiny yellow teeth, he gestured toward a chair. "Perhaps we've both been a bit hasty, Miss Alexander. Do sit down."

Katya studied the chair in silence, as though debating whether to accept his offer. Inside, however, she was quaking with both relief and apprehension. The Gun Trick had frightened her since she was a little girl. It was among the most deadly feats a conjuror could perform and was practiced only by the most skilled magicians.

On the surface, the act was simple. A gun along with three bullets were given to a random member of the audience. He was instructed to inspect the weapon for any signs of trickery, and if he found the piece sound, to load the bullets into the chamber. The gun was then passed to another member of the audience, who was invited to join the magician onstage. The first two bullets were fired at a piece of lumber, proving the weapon's deadliness. The last bullet was fired directly at the magician, who—God willing—caught it in his hand. It required precise timing, nerves of steel, and an inordinate amount of luck. The trick had become infamous not only for its sheer dramatic power, but for the number of magicians who had been killed onstage while attempting to perform it.

Pushing any thoughts of her own peril aside, Katya sank smoothly into the chair offered by Monsieur Remy. "Was there something else you wanted to discuss?" she asked, affecting an air of complete indifference.

Remy strode back and forth behind his desk, absently running a hand over his well-oiled head. "As it happens, I do have an opening for a performer on Saturday evenings."

She flicked an imaginary piece of lint from her sleeve. "Really."

"Given that your props and costumes are already here in Monte Carlo, it would seem logical to feature your act here first, rather than bearing the expense of shipping it all off to England."

Katya made a noncommittal sound.

"I can promise you top billing."

Thick silence hung between them. After a long minute, she inquired coolly, "At what rate of compensation, monsieur?"

Monsieur Remy named his price.

"Very amusing. Double that figure and we shall have a bargain. Otherwise . . ." Allowing the threat to speak for itself, she lifted her shoulders in an indifferent shrug.

Remy's jaw worked in clenched silence; he was clearly irritated at having lost the upper hand in the bargaining. Finally he spit out, "Agreed."

Katya favored him with a gracious nod. "How lovely that we were able to come to terms."

As she moved to pass him, he studied her with a look of acute discomfort. "You realize, mademoiselle, that you'll be performing on the very stage where your parents . . ."

"Died," she finished for him. She swallowed tightly, once again checking her emotions. "I am well aware of that fact, monsieur."

She had little choice in all of this. Her parents had spent money as extravagantly as they had lived, leaving Katya nothing but mounds of unending debt. Rather than making that shameful fact public, she said simply, "It was always my parents' wish that I continue the act in their stead."

"I see." He nodded, clearly relieved at having dispensed with the awkward topic. "I shall inform the local press that you will be performing the Gun Trick as the finale to your show on Saturday evening." Anxious to broadcast word of his latest theatrical coup, he moved to the door and held it open for her, thus indicating that their interview was at an end. "I trust that settles everything, Miss Alexander."

She picked up the tightly rolled stack of playbills beside her chair and passed them to him on her way out. "Will you see to it that these are posted around the casino grounds? I'll expect the orchestra for rehearsal on Friday morning, and I'll need two men capable of heavy lifting to meet me at the theater this afternoon. I would also like a word with your head usher sometime tomorrow. Should I have any other requirements, I'll let you know. Good day, monsieur."

He stopped her with one final thought as she turned to leave. "Will you be in touch with your parents' manager?"

She frowned. "I beg your pardon?"

"The man who came to claim your parents' props and possessions. I would have turned the lot over to him had I not received your letter first." At Katya's blank look, he lifted his shoulders in an indifferent shrug. "If he comes again, I will have him speak to you."

"Please do."

Determined not to waste any time getting underway, Katya left Monsieur Remy's office and walked backstage. There she met the two stagehands who would be assisting her with her act. With a bright smile pasted on her face she greeted the men with what she hoped would pass for eager excitement rather than acute anxiety.

Maintaining that pose proved far more difficult than she could have imagined. First she battled an overwhelming surge of nostalgia and melancholy while going through her parents' trunks of props and costumes. It was one thing to think about reviving her parents' act in the abstract; but actually working onstage without them made their sudden absence from her life all the more painfully tangible. Then she discovered that her fingers, after an absence from the world of magic, weren't quite as nimble as they used to be. Nor was her memory of the flow of routines as tight as she had presumed. Fortunately her new assistants worked patiently with her, performing a trick over and over again until she had perfected the timing and the rhythm.

Saturday night arrived all too quickly. At eight o'clock precisely she stood backstage in costume, dressed to perform. Ignoring the nervous flutters that filled her belly, she reviewed the stage set one last time. The effect she had tried to achieve was that of stepping into Aladdin's den. Lush Turkish carpets and overstuffed pillows covered the floor. Gauzy curtains were opulently draped across the stage. The seductive whine of the Indian sitar, the steady beat of the Turkish kanun, and the soft jangle of Arabian bells added to the mood of Eastern exoticism and mystery.

Katya had decided to open the show with the Birth of the Butterfly. As the curtain parted the audience found her two assistants center stage. They were dressed entirely in black and gold, complete with turbans, satin slippers with turned-up toes, and huge, deadly scimitars strapped to their hips.

The music gradually changed from an ancient rhythm into a flowing, gentle melody reminiscent of the soft sounds of springtime. On cue, her assistants lifted a sheet of opaque parchment and spun the paper around a dense wire hanging from center stage, like two moths spinning a cocoon. Once the cocoon was complete they sent it spinning, whirling in midair. The music tempo rose until it became almost frenzied. Abruptly the cocoon and the music came to a synchronized stop.

The audience heard a faint scratching from within the cocoon, one that grew steadily louder until the cocoon was split in two. A single, elegant hand emerged from within the parchment, wriggling as though it had just been given life. Finally the cocoon burst open to reveal Katya, attired in the guise of a sophisticated butterfly woman. Keeping her motions slow and provocative, she stretched to her full height, lifting her arms to reveal huge monarch wings.

A crackling murmur of tension and disbelief rippled through the theater as Monsieur Remy stepped forward and greeted the audience. "Ladies and gentlemen," he bellowed to the astonished assembly. "I give you Katya, the Goddess of Mystery!"

Her assistants marched across the stage and stopped beneath the cocoon. Each man took one of Katya's outstretched hands as she settled herself on their shoulders like a princess settling herself on a royal throne. Slowly they lowered her to the stage floor.

From that point forward, Katya moved from one illusion to the next with an ease and fluidity that was the result of years of practice, despite the time her skills had lain dormant. She worked her father's magic and spoke in the Magyar of her youth, her mother's language, the language of her gypsy ancestors. She flirted with the audience like an accomplished courtesan, drawing them ever closer; then she pushed them away as she performed an illusion too impossible to comprehend. By the time she reached her finale and performed the Gun Trick, her audience gasped in stunned awe, then burst into thunderous applause.

At last the curtain fell and she took her final bow. She walked through the backstage maze of props and stage sets to her dressing room, feeling both exhausted and exhilarated. The show had been a success. With that contented thought in mind, she opened the door to her dressing room and stepped inside.

She stopped abruptly, her gaze riveted on her dressing table and the two items that rested there.

The first was a long-stemmed white rose.

The second was an engraved ivory card.

A shiver of apprehension coursed through her as she moved to the card and lifted it. There were no words, no note of any kind. Just a name.

Nicholas Duvall, Earl of Barrington.

So the Maltese wanted to see her.

Although Katya had been too busy with rehearsals to actively seek him out, Nicholas Duvall had never strayed far from her thoughts. His presence haunted her, lingering in her consciousness like an ominous shadow. Never in her life had she imagined that she would be drawn into the ancient blood feud that existed between their families, yet now that reality seemed inescapable.

She had been given the kiss of fate. Rosskaya and DuValenti together again. The time for a resolution to a centuries-old feud had finally come. She could no more walk away now than she could sell off her parents' props and stage sets—to do so would be to deny her heritage.

Her thoughts whirling, she stepped behind the tall screen in the corner of her dressing room and removed her stage attire. She slipped into a loose silk robe of pale lavender and belted it tightly around her waist. Next she unpinned her hair, allowing it to tumble free around her shoulders. Although she had lost her trunk when the coach crashed, her parents had stored nearly every piece of her extensive traveling wardrobe. While some of the rich and exotic garments had been designed for the stage, most of the clothing was meant for everyday wear.

As she scanned the assortment of gowns, she heard the door to her dressing room open. Assuming it was the cleaning woman, Katya called out, "I'll be out of your way in a minute, Marie."

Silence greeted her words, then the door clicked softly shut. From the other side of the screened partition, she heard the echo of heavy footsteps followed by the distinct and unmistakable sound of a cork being popped from a bottle of champagne.

Katya stepped out from behind the screen with a frown. "Marie?" she began. She stopped in midsentence.

Nicholas Duvall sat before her, looking supremely relaxed

and perfectly at ease. A bottle of champagne and two tall crystal goblets rested on the table near his elbow.

"There's no hurry, Miss Alexander," he intoned politely.

Her hand flew instinctively to the immodest neckline of her dressing robe. Gathering the fabric protectively to her throat, she demanded, "What are you doing here?"

"I came to help you celebrate your opening night."

"You were not invited."

"Champagne?"

"I'd like you to leave."

He let out a weary sigh. "It may reassure you to know that I am not in the habit of intruding on the privacy of a woman's dressing chamber."

"I know nothing of your habits. But I certainly hope they aren't as bad as your manners."

"Worse, I'm afraid." He lifted his glass and took a deep swallow of champagne, studying her with a look of mild amusement. "Come now, Miss Alexander, surely you're aware that I mean you no harm. I did, after all, save your life."

She lifted her chin. "A true gentleman would never remind me of that fact."

"But we've already established that I'm no gentleman, have we not?"

Katya had no reply to that statement; certainly none was expected. She remained where she stood, regarding him in wary silence. Now that the shock of seeing him had worn off, she felt the same astonishing jolt of intimacy that she had experienced at their first meeting. As his dark gaze moved unswervingly over her body, a familiar tingling sensation filled her belly and a slow heat spread through her limbs. She wondered idly if it was fear she felt, or a primitive recognition of her family's ancient enemy, or perhaps just the rush of nervous energy a soldier felt before stepping into battle.

But in truth, the feelings that coursed through her were

like none of these things. What she experienced instead was an indefinable sense of eager curiosity and dark foreboding, a startling awareness of the man who stood before her. It was as though some invisible bond had been forged between her and Nicholas Duvall centuries ago. She felt powerless to ignore it—nor was she entirely sure that she wanted to.

DuValenti. Duvall. They were one and the same. No wonder her reaction to the man was so very peculiar. Danger and sensuality were entwined within him. She could not separate one from the other.

In the week that had passed since she had last seen him, Katya had convinced herself that he couldn't possibly be as handsome as she remembered. But in truth, his appearance was even more striking and self-assured. Katya paused, studying him with a frown. If she had considered the DuValentis at all—something she rarely did—she had always imagined them as monsters. Ugly, horned beasts with scaly tails and hairy palms. But that was obviously far from the case with Nicholas Duvall.

While she assessed him, his dark gaze moved appraisingly over her.

"So my little caterpillar has turned herself into a beautiful butterfly," he remarked.

Katya wasn't certain whether he was referring to the opening act of her performance, or to her transformation from the mud-soaked girl he had left a few days earlier into the immodestly clad woman who stood before him now. In either case, it didn't sound like much of a compliment. She told him so.

He lifted his shoulders in an indifferent shrug. "There wasn't a man in that audience who wouldn't desire you in his bed."

"I'm not sure that's a compliment, either."

A knowing smile curved his lips. "Given tonight's crowd, you may be right."

It was an odd remark to make, especially since the audience that night had been comprised mainly of what was considered the better class: lords and ladies of the realm, the gentry, the wealthy, and the titled. Essentially, Katya thought, Nicholas Duvall's peers.

Remembering his card, she asked, "You are an earl, are you not?"

"I am."

She studied him in a new light, wondering why she hadn't seen it earlier. Of course the man was wealthy and titled. That explained his haughty arrogance and air of complete self-assurance, his immaculately tailored clothing and his entrée into Monaco's most exclusive gatherings. So the DuValentis had prospered all these years, while the Rosskayas had for centuries barely managed to scrape by. The DuValentis had acquired wealth and status, while the Rosskayas had fled from country to country, forever hunted and persecuted by their ancient blood enemy.

"Do I detect a frown?" he inquired. "I disappointed you. Perhaps you were expecting a duke or a marquis."

She coolly raised her gaze to meet his. "I expected an Englishman who was down on his luck and looking to earn a few extra francs. Money you would have doubtless thrown away in the casino upon arrival in Monte Carlo."

He lifted one dark brow as a tight, mocking smile curved his lips. "Apparently I didn't impress you as the type of man who would be able to withstand the lure of the gaming tables. Or any other temptation, for that matter."

"Frankly, you did not."

His gaze moved slowly over her form. "How very perceptive of you, Miss Alexander."

She ignored the blatant suggestion in his words and stood her ground, refusing to be diverted. "If you weren't desperate for money, why did you agree to drive our coach?"

"It was a foolish wager, nothing more," he replied, impatiently dismissing both the question and the topic. His eyes locked once again onto hers. "Katya, the Goddess of Mystery. Is that truly your name? Katya?"

"Yes."

"Katya." He said her name slowly, as though experimenting with the feel of it on his tongue. "It suits you. Exotic, yet not unapproachable."

"What are you doing here?"

He took a long swallow of champagne, studying her for a moment in thoughtful silence. Finally he replied, "I attended your performance tonight. Very impressive. Do you know which part of your act I enjoyed the most?"

"Do tell."

"I believe you called it Flying Purses. Wasn't that the part where various possessions belonging to different members of the audience magically flew into your hands onstage? Watches, pipes, brooches, rings, even one woman's tiara. It was quite impressive—especially when those audience members swore you hadn't been anywhere near them."

"I'm glad you enjoyed it. Now if you'll excuse me—"

"In fact, I was so impressed, I couldn't help but try to fathom how you accomplished it. It occurred to me that you must have gotten physically close to them at some point in order to snatch their belongings. Suddenly I remembered an elderly, bumbling usher who seated a few of the guests for tonight's performance—the very guests whose possessions found their way into your hands. That usher was you, was it not, Miss Alexander?"

Katya hid her surprise and dismay. Had she been that obvious? It was on the tip of her tongue to deny it, but she could tell by the smug expression on his face that that would be fruitless. "Congratulations, Lord Barrington, you win a prize."

"Don't look so disheartened. I sincerely doubt that anyone else saw through your disguise."

"How very comforting."

"I did have an edge, after all," he continued blithely. "I witnessed you employ your considerable talents on the road to Monte Carlo."

She studied him with a puzzled frown. "I'm afraid you're quite mistaken. I didn't perform any magic on the way here."

"Really?" An odd light filled his eyes as his enigmatic smile returned. "I believe you have something of mine, Miss Alexander."

Katya's first thought was that he was referring to the Stone. Then she noticed that he had held up his right hand, subtly indicating his third finger. *His glove and ring,* she realized with a start, reaching into her reticule for the items. She passed them to him with a murmur of apology.

"They came off in my hand when you tried to pull me up the cliff," she reminded him.

"Did they?" There was a note of condescending disbelief in his tone, as though he were humoring a small, corrupt child.

Her brows snapped together. "Are you suggesting that I deliberately stole your possessions?"

"Didn't you?"

"Certainly not."

He studied her with a look of total bewilderment, as though astonished that she might take offense at the suggestion that she was a thief. "You needn't defend yourself, Miss Alexander. The fact is, I thoroughly enjoyed your performance." He paused for a moment, then continued smoothly, "Though I do wonder if Lady Stanton was equally entertained."

"I'm sure I don't know what you mean."

"I saw you take that silk pouch from Lady Stanton's bag," he replied. "Granted, you were far smoother onstage this evening, but it was an impressive display nonetheless."

Katya's thoughts spun in a tangled disarray. He thought she was a thief? She had assumed that Nicholas Duvall had sought her out in order to find some resolution to the ancient feud that existed between their families. Instead, he was under the misguided notion that she was a common pickpocket.

"You needn't look so stunned, Miss Alexander," he said smoothly. "Even the best thieves are eventually caught."

"I hate to disappoint you, but you are entirely mistaken, Lord Barrington. What you saw, that is, what you *think* you saw, was merely—"

"I have a proposition for you. One that will benefit both of us."

"I'm not interested."

"There is an object I need recovered," he continued, as though she hadn't spoken at all. "I have reason to believe the person who stole it is here in Monte Carlo. Someone of your particular talents could make the task of finding the object considerably easier for me. In turn, I could make your stay in Monaco considerably more profitable for you."

She stared at him in amazement. "You're asking me to steal for you?"

"Not at all. I'm merely asking you to recover an object that rightfully belongs to me—and I need to know from whom you recover it. I'll take care of everything after that."

He paused, a look of somber reflection on his face. "I have a few ideas as to who might have stolen it, but I'm not certain. The item is small enough that whoever has it might very well be carrying it on his person. Then again, he may have secreted it in his residence. I'd like you to discreetly search both the men themselves and their rooms. Of course, you're welcome to keep any stray baubles or petty cash you come across during the course of your search."

His voice sounded vaguely distracted as he spoke, as

though he were discussing ledgers and accounts, rather than the astonishing suggestion that he employ her as a thief.

"And if I say no?" she asked.

"Will I attempt to blackmail you into accepting? Alert the management that they have a thief in their employ?" He hesitated for a moment, as though contemplating the idea; then a tight, mocking smile curved his lips. "No, I think not. I need a willing accomplice in this venture or none at all. I had hoped that the elevated status of the men from whom you'd be stealing would be incentive enough for you to agree. After all, why waste your skills pilfering paltry jewels from the Lady Stantons of the world, when I can give you access to the valuables of England's richest men?"

"Why indeed."

He shifted impatiently in his seat. "What do you say, Miss Alexander? The path to riches begins with one single step."

"So does the road to ruin," she murmured absently. Although she knew she should turn him down and walk away, she found herself caught in the mysterious web he had spun around her. Her curiosity aroused, she inquired, "What am I to look for?"

"A parchment scroll. It has little actual worth, but great sentimental value to my family."

Katya's breath caught in her throat. A parchment scroll, she repeated in her mind, as the stories and ancient legends that had filled her childhood rushed through her mind.

She needn't ask what the scroll looked like, for she had held one nearly identical to his in her own hands. It had been passed down through the generations within her family. The DuValentis held one third of the scroll, the Rosskayas held a third, and a third resided at an isolated abbey. According to ancient lore, when the feuding clans came together and the three scrolls were joined the Stone of Destiny would be returned.

Putting the legends aside for the moment, the absurdity of

the situation hit Katya with a sudden, shocking impact. He was asking her, a Rosskaya, to retrieve the DuValenti parchment. Nicholas Duvall had absolutely no idea who she was.

Then again, she thought, why should he recognize her? The parchment was passed down through the women in her line—women whose names changed when they married, women who moved from country to country, women who had a tendency to die young and leave their legends and their legacies to their daughters. Perhaps over the centuries the DuValentis had simply lost track of the wandering Rosskaya women.

Katya's mind raced as she considered the ramifications of what he was proposing. Not only would her immediate financial problems be solved, but the wrong that had been done to her family centuries ago would finally be avenged. She sank into the chair beside him, her thoughts careening in clumsy turmoil. Spying the glass of champagne sitting on the table before her, she reached for it and took a long, comforting swallow.

Aware that he was awaiting a response from her, she forced her mind back to the question at hand. "How do you suggest I get close enough to these men to search their persons?" she inquired.

He shrugged. "However you normally do it. I won't question your methods, Katya, so long as they bring results."

Ready to object to the familiarity, her eyes flashed toward him at the sound of her Christian name on his tongue.

Guessing her intention, he immediately forestalled her objection. "What else should I call my new mistress, if not her given name? And you, of course, shall call me Nicholas."

Her eyes widened and her champagne glass nearly slipped from her grasp. "Your mistress?"

"What better way to explain your sudden appearance by my side? I saw you perform this evening and instantly fell under your spell." An odd, burning light filled his eyes as his gaze traveled slowly over her body. "And your charms are considerable, indeed. Katya, the Goddess of Mystery. That suits you far better than the prim little spinster you feigned earlier."

Katya bit back a nervous bubble of laughter. That hadn't been a farce at all. If she had appeared a prim little spinster, it was because that was exactly what she was. Yet now she was actually contemplating playing the part of his mistress. Could she do it? Could she match wits against him and come out ahead? The virgin playing the part of the sophisticate. The mere idea was ludicrous, not to mention dangerous. If he should discover her real identity . . . A cold shiver ran down her spine despite the warmth of the room.

The DuValentis are a merciless clan, not to be trusted at any cost. They are fierce in battle and swift to revenge. They will do anything to get their hands on the Stone. The words echoed through her mind as she struggled to piece together her memories of the ancient legends. *Follow the Maltese and he will lead you to the Stone.*

"I presume you mean mistress in name only," she stalled.

A sardonic smile touched his lips. "Evidently I vastly overestimate my appeal to the fairer sex."

"That's not an answer."

"No, it's not." His eyes locked on hers. "Very well. In name only. Consider it our little masquerade." He raised his glass to hers. "What do you say, Katya Alexander? Do we have a bargain?"

Their little masquerade.

The idea was preposterous . . . horrifying . . . and yet strangely intoxicating.

For the first time in her life, Katya felt the fire of her gypsy ancestors spark within her. She touched her glass to his and tilted her chin, her eyes bravely meeting his.

"Yes, Nicholas Duvall. We have a bargain."

Five

Katya awoke shortly after dawn to the sound of her landlady arguing with the local butcher as to the quality of the pork that was being delivered to her door. She let out a low groan and rolled over, stuffing her head beneath the pillow. As she tried to lull herself back to sleep, memories of the night before suddenly flooded her thoughts. A jolt of nervous energy coursed through her veins, leaving her wide awake.

Had she truly agreed to pose as Nicholas Duvall's mistress?

She sat up in bed and rested her chin on her knees, drawing her rumpled nightclothes tightly to her. At the memory of her unprecedented act of daring, a shaky smile touched her lips. Never in her life had she acted with such wanton disregard for propriety and convention. Granted, it was all a charade—but one that had dire consequences.

What if Nicholas Duvall should discover who she was? While he had not asked her if she was a member of the Rosskaya clan, she was nonetheless guilty of committing a lie of omission. Katya had never been one to lie or dissemble. But as far as she could tell, she had little choice in the matter. If the DuValentis were as fierce and unscrupulous as legend indicated, revealing her identity would not only be foolhardy, it might even put her in danger.

That unsettling thought led directly to another. She would be in constant contact with Nicholas Duvall. As she remembered the way his burning ebony gaze traveled over her body last night, a feeling of vague queasiness spread through her limbs. Yet she was also possessed of a strange eagerness to see him again. Despite her grave doubts as to the virtue of his character, something about the man was undeniably compelling. Would she be able to hold him at bay should he renege on his promise that their little masquerade was in name only? What would happen if she didn't?

Realizing that her thoughts were only serving to fuel her anxieties, she brushed away the possible repercussions of her actions and began to dress. What was done was done. Undoubtedly she was worrying for nothing. The Earl of Barrington saw her as nothing but a petty thief and a means to an end. If she stood to profit from his insulting and misguided assumptions, so much the better.

It was too early to leave for the theater and begin her day's rehearsals, so Katya decided to take a brisk stroll through the principality instead. She returned to the inn an hour later, feeling awake and refreshed. But the sight that greeted her brought her to a dead stop and defeated all the feelings of cautious optimism she had cultivated while on her walk.

A regal, plushly appointed coach stood in the street before the inn. Given that such expensive vehicles were a rare occurrence in this section of town, her first thought was that Nicholas Duvall had come to pay an unexpected call. There was no sign of the man, however. Upon closer inspection she noted that two groomsmen were busily tracking back and forth between the inn and the coach, their arms loaded with an assortment of clothing and miscellaneous personal belongings.

Her clothing and personal belongings.

Katya sucked in her breath as a rush of furious indignation flooded through her body. She stalked toward the coach and demanded of the tall, elegantly attired man who stood supervising the groomsmen, "Just what do you think you're doing?"

The man turned toward her. He was probably in his mid-thirties, but had the authoritative air of someone much older. His pale blue eyes surveyed her from head to toe, revealing nothing but polite disinterest. "Might I presume that you are Miss Alexander?"

Katya drew herself up and nodded tightly. "And you are?"

He gave a small bow. "Allow me to present myself. Edward Litell, Lord Barrington's personal secretary."

"Just what do you think you're doing with my belongings, Mr. Litell?"

"Lord Barrington instructed me to see to their transfer to his villa."

"By whose authority?"

Litell arched a dark blond brow. "His own, I presume."

The reply was uttered with such cool indifference that Katya was momentarily taken aback. Then her ire rose.

"I believe that I locked my room before I left," she stated tightly.

"Indeed." He cast a significant glance toward the inn's front landing. "I can assure you that the proprietor of this household was amply compensated for the trouble of letting us inside."

Katya saw her landlady standing beside the stoop, a contented smile on her face as she counted the thick stack of francs in her hand. Obviously, Nicholas Duvall thought he could buy whatever he wanted—including her. Her fury mounting by the minute, she watched as the groomsmen loaded the last of her meager belongings into the coach.

Litell pulled open the coach door with a flourish. "If you're ready, Miss Alexander, I believe Lord Barrington is waiting to see you."

Katya took a deep breath and resisted the urge to vent her anger on the punctilious head of Edward Litell. After all, she reasoned, the man was just doing as he had been directed. With that in mind, she gave him a curt nod and stepped wordlessly into the luxurious confines of the coach. She would save the heat of her wrath for Nicholas Duvall, the man who deserved it most.

The coach rolled to a smooth start as the driver eased the vehicle into the midmorning traffic peppering the Rue Grimaldi. They moved quickly through the bustling markets, past the fortresslike Palais du Prince, then past the magnificent Grand Casino, which rose like a glistening, confectioner's castle from the rocky promontory that overlooked the sea.

From there they turned west, climbing slowly up a seemingly endless series of narrow roads that gave access to the district of Moneghetti, where the exotic landscape and lushly tended gardens were interspersed with a series of exclusive villas.

Once they reached the summit the coach driver made a sharp turn, directing the team of matched chestnut geldings into a broad, stone-paved courtyard. He reigned the team to a stop as one of the groomsmen leaped down from his post and opened the coach door. Katya stepped out and gazed at the site before her in appreciative wonder, temporarily putting aside her anger.

The courtyard was awash in color. Fragrant bunches of mimosa, chamomile, oleander, bougainvillea, and wild roses blossomed in rich abandon within the stone planting beds and enormous clay pots that lined the walk. Tall eucalyptus, generous palms, and wizened olive trees swayed in the soft breeze like gently dozing sentries. The villa itself had been constructed of the same native stone that paved the courtyard. The deep beige-and-brown stone was offset by a roof of terra-cotta tile and flanked by deep green shutters. A brilliant sapphire sky hung above the scene, framing the villa with its rich hue.

Before Katya was able to fully absorb the beauty of the sight, Edward Litell materialized at her elbow, politely directing her forward. "If I may show you inside, Miss Alexander . . ."

She nodded and stepped toward a pair of ornately carved front doors. As she moved through the interior of the villa, Katya briefly surveyed the furnishings. Gobelins tapestries, Aubusson carpets, Sevres vases, Biedermier desks, Dutch and Flemish paintings, crystal chandeliers, velvet draperies, and silk-covered settees were placed about the rooms with meticulous perfection, giving the estate an air of rich, if somewhat overstated, opulence. Nevertheless, an air of frigid pomposity echoed through the villa.

Litell stopped before a closed door and knocked briskly. At the sound of the murmured assent from within, he pulled open the door and ushered Katya in.

She stepped into a large, bright room that obviously served as the main parlor. In stark contrast to the stuffy interiors she had just seen, the room was decidedly more welcoming, with an attractive blend of masculine mahogany tables, feminine settees, gold-leaf mirrors, and free-standing bookcases. A series of tall, glass-paned doors opened at the rear of the room to a sun-washed terrace, filling the parlor with the fragrant scent of the nearby gardens and the salty breezes from the Mediterranean. Katya took all of this in, then immediately transferred her attention to Nicholas Duvall.

Judging by his attire, he had been out riding. He wore a simple white linen shirt that was open at the collar, revealing a generous expanse of the bronzed skin of his chest. His dun-colored trousers were perfectly fitted and tucked into a pair of rich leather riding boots. His deep brown hair was windswept, and a hint of color flushed his ruggedly sculpted cheeks. He held a sleek riding crop in his hands and absently toyed with it as he silently regarded her.

Everytime she saw him Katya felt a jolt of raw recognition

rush through her. She experienced it even now, as though she were seeing him after an absence of years, not just hours.

Nicholas broke the silence that hung between them. "Here she is at last, my magic gypsy," he announced. A hint of a smile played about his lips as he strode across the room. He lowered his voice to a seductive, conspiratorial tone as he neared her. "Or should I say, my partner in crime?"

She lifted her gaze to meet his. "Frankly, I find both descriptions offensive."

He arched one dark brow as he studied her face. "You're angry because I took the liberty of sending my men to fetch you and your belongings."

"Of course I am. That was a liberty you had no right to take without consulting me first."

He gave a light, indifferent shrug. "When you agreed to play the part of my mistress, you agreed perforce to reside under my roof. Obviously it wouldn't do for you to stay in a dreary boardinghouse on the outskirts of town."

"That boardinghouse suited me just fine."

"It didn't suit me."

"Are you always this overbearing?"

"Yes." He crossed the room and leaned against a sturdy mahogany desk. Tapping his riding crop absently against his thigh, he asked, "Are you always this difficult?"

She regarded him for a moment in cool silence. Finally she said, "When I agreed last night to take part in your little scheme, I was not under the impression that you would play the organ grinder and I the obedient monkey leaping to satisfy your every whim and command. If that is what you had in mind, this arrangement will not work after all."

His languid smile returned. "An obedient monkey. No, that was not what I wanted from you."

"Then what—"

"How very honorable and virtuous you sound, Katya. Almost as though you don't stand to profit at all from our arrangement."

She tilted her chin. "I merely mean to ascertain your intentions."

"I think you know my intentions."

His hot, liquid gaze seemed to burn right through her. She swallowed hard and reminded him primly, "Our agreement was for this charade to be in name only."

"So I recall. What exactly are you objecting to?"

"I object to the high-handed manner in which your servants bribed their way into my room and helped themselves to my belongings without so much as a by-your-leave."

"And?"

"And I object to the way you arrogantly assumed I would blithely agree to live under your roof."

"Is that all?"

Rather than deluge him with a list of trivial grievances, she replied tersely, "For the moment, yes."

"What remarkable principles you have. I should have thought profit would be your primary concern—that and a consuming desire to not get caught with your hand in somebody else's pocket." He shrugged, as though bored with the topic. "To this end, I will supply you not only with a facade that will put you above suspicion, but with entrée into the richest and most exclusive society in all of Monaco. You'll have your pick of any number of baubles or trinkets. In return," he finished coolly, "you shall from time to time be required to satisfy a few of my 'high-handed whims.'"

Her brows snapped together. "What sort of whims?"

A knowing smile curved his lips. "Let us get to the heart of the matter, shall we? I have no intention of disturbing the privacy of your bedchamber." He paused, then continued smoothly, "Unless, of course, you invite me to."

Katya stiffened her spine. "I can assure you that will not happen."

A low, smoldering heat filled his ebony eyes. He stepped away from his desk and slowly crossed the room, stopping only inches in front of her. He reached out and lightly stroked her hair, capturing one stray ebony curl in his palm. Then his gaze locked on hers. In a deep voice that was no more than a whisper he inquired, "Won't it?"

Katya trembled inside and a tingling warmth began to radiate through her limbs. Before she could summon a dignified reply, the sound of a cane thumping on the parlor's thick carpet echoed from the doorway.

"For Heaven's sake," an imperious voice interrupted shrilly, "stop toying with the girl, Nicholas. And move out of the way so I can see her property."

With one last languid look, Nicholas accommodated the curt request. As he stepped back and shifted his body slightly to the left, Katya's gaze moved to an elderly woman who was looking with undisguised curiosity at her and Nicholas. As she recalled the disgraceful content of their conversation, her cheeks flushed crimson.

Nicholas, however, remained entirely unaffected by their indecorous circumstance. He grasped Katya lightly by the elbow and ushered her forward, stopping before the other woman.

"Aunt Eleanor, may I present Miss Katya Alexander," he said, smoothly performing the tardy introductions. "Miss Alexander, my aunt, the Comtesse de Fiorini."

Katya managed an awkward curtsy and pushed aside her embarrassment enough to murmur a few customary words of greeting. As she did so, she briefly surveyed the other woman. The Comtesse de Fiorini had the same piercing coal-black eyes as Nicholas, the same aristocratic bearing and chiseled features. Her body appeared thin and frail beneath her gown of gray silk chiffon, yet inner strength and an indomitable spirit emanated from her unwavering gaze. Her elegant silver hair was coiffed into a neat chignon at the nape of her neck; three long ropes of glistening black pearls hung about her throat. One elegant hand, slightly weathered with age, rested on a polished walnut walking cane with an intricately sculpted ivory handle. Katya had the distinct impression that the cane was used more to summon others than for any weakness in the Comtesse.

The older woman moved into the room and seated herself on a chintz-covered sofa. Then she returned her attention to Katya, studying her in cool, contemplative silence. Finally she remarked, "My nephew tells me that you are a thief, Miss Alexander."

Before Katya had a chance to respond to that astounding statement, the Comtesse turned to Nicholas and said, "She certainly doesn't look like one, does she? A wayward schoolgirl, perhaps, but not a thief. How very intriguing."

"Yes, it is remarkable, isn't it?" Nicholas replied. A hint of amused admiration filled his voice.

The Comtesse nodded thoughtfully. "I daresay one would hardly suspect."

"My thoughts exactly."

"She could use a bit more polish though, couldn't she?"

Katya shifted, growing increasingly impatient with their none-too-subtle examination. "Shall I open my mouth so you might check my teeth and gums," she put in, "or have you both seen enough?"

Nicholas turned toward her with a wry smile. "Do I detect a note of dissatisfaction?"

"I am not accustomed to being discussed as though I weren't in the room."

"Indeed?" The Comtesse raised one brow in haughty disdain, as though she had just been corrected by an impudent servant. "Very well. I shall address you directly. That odious shade of yellow does not flatter you at all, Miss Alexander. You're old enough to know that by now."

Katya stiffened her spine, coolly meeting the challenge in

the Comtesse's dark gaze. "Had I known that I was to be summoned before so august an audience, I would have been better attired. Unfortunately, your nephew neglected to inform me of his plans—as you no doubt heard."

"There is no need for you to take that tone with me. I am merely offering a constructive criticism. With your coloring, you should wear nothing but blues, lavenders, and purples, to bring out the extraordinary shade of your eyes. At least, from what I can see of them behind those ghastly spectacles. Are the glasses truly necessary?"

"They are if I wish to read."

"Well, you're not reading now, are you?" She gestured impatiently at the settee across from her. "Do sit down. Gazing up at you like this is most uncomfortable."

Katya settled herself on the settee across from the Comtesse, refusing to let herself be rattled by the elderly woman's tactics. Nicholas took a seat in a sturdy armchair that sat at right angles to the two women. A heavy silence filled the room as their conversation came to an abrupt halt.

After a moment, the Comtesse lifted her lorgnette and examined the modest strand of opalescent pearls that hung about Katya's neck. "If you must wear paste, my dear, do so only at night, when it is not so easily discerned."

"The pearls belonged to my mother, and they are quite genuine."

"Really? How remarkable."

In the series of thrusts and parries that had comprised their conversation, that was little more than a small jab. Katya therefore decided to ignore it, focusing instead on divining the purpose behind the gathering.

. A discreet rap sounded at the door. Edward Litell entered, balancing a heavily laden sterling-silver tray. He set the tea service on the plush ottoman between the settees.

"Thank you, Edward, I shall pour," the Comtesse said,

dismissing him. Once the tray was settled, she turned to Katya and inquired briskly, "Do you prefer India or China?"

It took Katya a moment to realize the Comtesse was referring to the tea. "India," she replied, accepting the fragile cup and saucer the older woman passed to her.

Nicholas accepted the steaming cup of tea his aunt gave him with a nod of thanks. He relaxed back into his chair and stretched out his legs, appearing perfectly at ease.

"Edward," he called as his secretary reached the door, "you may instruct Melinda to settle Miss Alexander's personal belongings in the peach room. Once she has properly sorted the clothing, I'd like a few of Miss Alexander's better gowns sent down. You may also see to it that the family jewelry is brought down from the vault." He thought for a moment, then added, "The lesser jewels, I think. No need to make a show of it on our first night out."

At Edward's nod of assent, Nicholas turned toward Katya. The subtle smile that curved his lips was just short of patronizing. "That is, if the arrangement meets with Miss Alexander's approval."

Katya lifted her cup and took a sip of tea, regarding him in thoughtful silence. He was obviously giving her an opportunity to decline the arrangement and have her possessions transferred back to her room at the inn. Now that the heat of her anger had faded somewhat, she considered that option. In truth, while she still didn't care for the arrogant manner in which he had taken control earlier that morning, she realized that she had little to gain by running back to the shelter of the boardinghouse. If her intent in uniting with Nicholas Duvall was to search for the scroll, she would be in a much better position to do so if she were well established within his household.

"I believe that arrangement will be satisfactory," she replied.

A hint of triumph showed in Nicholas's eyes. Keeping his

gaze fastened on Katya, he said, "You may see to it, Edward."

As the door closed behind the man, silence once again filled the room. Nicholas was the first to raise the conversational gauntlet, offering a rather banal comment on the weather. Katya murmured a polite response in return, as did the Comtesse. The discussion lurched awkwardly forward, rambling on in a loose, faltering fashion. They touched on opera, politics, travel, music, and religion, moving from one topic to the next in a seemingly random order.

As the talk wound down and a lull fell over the three of them, Katya inquired politely, "Do I pass the test?"

A look of almost startled surprise showed in the expressions of both aunt and nephew.

Katya lifted her shoulders and continued smoothly, "I presume your purpose in arranging this little gathering is to judge whether I am fit to play the part of the Lord of Barrington's mistress." She set aside her cup and plate and met their gazes directly. "Did you find my manners adequate, my discourse satisfactory, my knowledge of the arts and current events tolerable? Did I slurp my tea? Commit the gross offense of scratching my elbow? Or have you decided that I might be somewhat presentable after all?"

Nicholas set aside his own teacup and studied her with a long, lingering look—challenging almost. "You'll do just fine, Katya."

"You have a rather brash demeanor and a sharp tongue, Miss Alexander," the Comtesse countered. "It would serve you well to keep your opinions and insights to yourself. At least until you become accustomed to the rudimentary protocol under which polite society operates."

Katya eyed the older woman coolly. "I believe I'm quite familiar with the laws of etiquette and propriety."

The Comtesse arched one brow, a look of haughty disdain on her face. "As I understand it, your parents were in the theater, and you employ your own peculiar talents as a magician to rob unsuspecting admirers of their belongings. That's hardly a reassuring background. Nor is it one that would reflect a natural grace and ease while moving about in society."

Katya smiled sympathetically. "Yes, it is rather difficult to find a properly bred thief these days, isn't it?"

"There is no need for your sarcasm, Miss Alexander," the Comtesse bristled. "I am merely stating a simple fact. No matter how much one polishes brass, it cannot be expected to shine like gold."

A soft rap on the parlor door spared Katya the chore of replying. A pretty young maid entered carrying a few of Katya's better gowns. Behind her was a stern-faced footman who held two broad wooden cases in his arms. He set the cases down on a table beside Nicholas, then quietly retreated.

"Very well, Melinda," said the Comtesse, imperially thumping her cane on the carpet, "let us see what you have found."

The maid had brought in four gowns, each of which had been custom ordered for Katya while she and her parents performed in Paris. A rustle of silk filled the room as Melinda held out one gown after another, displaying each rich, shimmering creation to its best advantage. Katya had considered selling her few remaining gowns and possessions to pay off a portion of her parents' debt, but a combination of pride and vanity made her suddenly glad that she hadn't.

Once the presentation was complete, the Comtesse nodded decisively. "You may leave the indigo gown, Melinda. Take the others upstairs." Although there were no words spoken to acknowledge the quality and style of the gowns, neither did the Comtesse offer any criticism. That in itself, Katya had already learned, was high praise indeed.

The Comtesse turned to her nephew. "And now, Nicholas," she intoned regally, "let us see to the jewels."

Nicholas opened the cases and carelessly upturned them over the polished table. Clearly the DuValentis had done well for themselves. The lesser pieces, as he had called them, covered nearly the entire surface of the table and must have been worth tens of thousands. Katya watched in mild horror as Nicholas and the Comtesse shuffled idly through the jewelry, considering and discarding the assorted pieces like unsavory bits of candy. Could a person ever become like that, she wondered? She doubted it. What they said about the nobility was true—one had to be born to it.

After much debate, they decided on a discreet pair of diamond drop earrings, a necklace that alternated intricate clusters of brilliant sapphires and diamonds, and a glistening diamond comb for her hair.

Once the matter was settled, the Comtesse rose regally to her feet. She eyed Katya sternly as she rested her hands on her walking cane. "I do hope you won't disappoint us, Miss Alexander."

Uncertain how to reply, Katya responded simply, "I shall do my best."

"See that you do." With those imperious words of parting, the Comtesse swept out of the room.

In the silence that followed, Katya asked, "Your aunt, does she live here with you?"

He shook his head. "The Comtesse does tend to come and go as she pleases, but she has her own lodgings—a guest villa she has furnished as her own." He gestured vaguely to an unseen point beyond the gardens.

"I see."

That topic exhausted, Katya turned her attention to the rows of books that filled the mahogany cases. She skimmed the titles, making a mental note of those she would like to borrow. When she returned her gaze to Nicholas she found him watching her, his languid smile back in place.

"You did very well, Katya."

She tilted her chin. "The fact that you sound so surprised somewhat lessens the value of the compliment, does it not?"

His smile widened. "I suppose it does," he conceded. He set aside his teacup and strode across the room. Stopping before a tall armoire, he removed a crystal decanter filled with amber liquid and splashed a generous portion into a glass. He lifted it to his mouth then paused, silently offering the glass to Katya.

She tightened her lips and primly shook her head.

A look of mild amusement softened his normally harsh features. "No, of course not," he said, speaking almost to himself. He took a deep swallow then absently toyed with the drink, watching the liquid as it swirled in a tight, wet pool within the confines of the glass. After a moment he asked softly, "Who taught you to steal? Did you learn that under your parents' tutelage?"

Katya's head snapped up as her gaze locked on his. "Certainly not," she answered automatically. "At least, not in the way that you mean. They simply taught me the art of borrowing an item from a member of the audience during the course of a performance. But it was only an act—honest thievery, if you will. Whatever was taken was always returned. My parents never stole from anyone, ever."

"And yet, that's the path you chose. Why?"

She froze, startled by the question. Until that moment, it had never occurred to her that he might question her motivation. She quickly searched her mind, looking for a plausible reason for taking up a life of petty crime. Short of telling him that she was only after the scroll, what could she say?

Deciding to stick as close to the truth as possible, she replied, "Unfortunately, my parents were not as financially astute as they were artistically gifted. Upon their deaths, certain debts were left to me which became my responsibility to resolve." She hesitated for a moment, then added as an afterthought, "In my defense, I never stole from anyone who could not afford to lose what I took."

"How very commendable." He thought for a moment, then shrugged. "You needn't apologize to me. Virtue has never been a trait I particularly admire. It appeals to the weak, the hesitant, the penny-ante players. Such people do not exist in Monaco. If they do, they have the courtesy to remain hidden."

"I see," she murmured uneasily. Eager to change the subject, she glanced significantly toward her indigo gown and the jewelry he and the Comtesse had selected for her. "It appears as though we have an engagement."

"Yes, we do."

His expression sobered, then he turned away from her and moved to stand beside the tall, paned-glass doors that overlooked the terrace. Her presence temporarily ignored, he stared unseeingly at the glittering azure sea. A soft breeze whipped around him, ruffling his shirt and gently mussing his deep brown hair. Despite the brilliant sunshine that flooded in around him, there was something dark and vaguely brooding about his stance. After a long moment he turned toward her, his ebony gaze unreadable.

"Tonight, little gypsy, the masquerade begins."

Six

At precisely ten o'clock that evening, the seventeenth-century Louis XIV mantelpiece clock began to toll. Nicholas absently counted the chimes as he paced back and forth in his study. A gust of wind blew in from the sea, scattering the papers that littered his desk. He ignored the mess, just as he had ignored the papers themselves. While it had been his intention to use the afternoon to catch up on his correspondence from London, he had accomplished nothing. The interview he had had earlier with Katya seemed to muddle his thoughts, turning them dark and pensive. Or perhaps it was the house itself that had set his nerves on edge. Coming back stirred too many memories—memories that were better left dead and buried.

Nicholas glanced impatiently around the ornate room, vaguely displeased. He had never felt at home in his father's house. It was too plush, too ornate, too excessive. He hadn't set foot in it for over three years, not since he had returned for his father's funeral. As his gaze moved over the stunning collections of books, paintings, and fine furnishings, memories of his father crowded in around him. Even those who knew and liked him readily admitted that William Harrison Duvall had been profligate, amoral, quick-tempered, given to petty grudges and gross overindulgences. In his blacker moments, Nicholas was certain he was becoming a mirror image of the man who had sired him.

A restless eagerness to get out of the house and escape his gloomy thoughts suddenly seized him. Impatient to leave, he turned to call one of the servants to summon Katya. She had been instructed to present herself downstairs at ten o'clock precisely, not five minutes past. As he turned, however, a slight movement at the door to his study caught his eye. He heard a soft rustle of silk, then Katya stepped inside.

Nicholas stopped short, gazing at the woman in appreciative wonder. He had known Katya would look attractive in the indigo silk gown, diamonds, and sapphires that had been selected for her. Any woman would. But he had not expected her to look so magnificent.

By simply changing her clothing and forgoing the wire-rimmed spectacles she normally wore, she managed to look both worldly and seductive, yet fetchingly innocent as well. Her flowing ebony hair had been pulled up and secured at the crown, leaving just a few loose curls to cascade along the nape of her neck. The deep indigo of her gown imbued her pale skin with a gentle, rosy glow. Lavender satin roses and long streamers of midnight-blue velvet ribbon decorated the bodice and brought out the intense color of her eyes. The décolletage was cut low and trimmed with creamy lace, offering a tantalizing glimpse of her breasts. The intricate bustle softly swayed with her every movement, drawing attention to her hips and derriere. Despite the striking, sensual appeal of her attire, the gown itself was well within the bounds of fashion—modest, in fact, compared to some he had seen.

Belatedly realizing that she was waiting for some sort of comment from him, he said, "You look lovely."

"Thank you."

"I trust you found your room satisfactory."

"Quite."

"If there's anything else you need, just let one of the servants know."

"Very well."

The stilted conversation came to a swift and dull close. The ire Katya had displayed earlier that morning seemed to have evaporated. A shame, he decided, as he had enjoyed her fire and spirit. Now only a polite emptiness rang between them. They stood regarding one another like two strangers on a train brought together only because they were traveling to the same destination.

"If you're ready," he said, "the groomsmen are waiting with the coach."

She nodded her assent. They moved silently through the villa and stepped outside into the balmy night air. A full moon glowed softly overhead, illuminating the inky black sky. Nicholas assisted her into the coach then took a seat opposite her. The driver eased the team to a gentle start, rolling smoothly down the hillside toward Monte Carlo. As the coach gently rocked and swayed, Katya pushed aside the heavy curtains that blocked the window and studied the passing countryside.

Although she seemed pointedly disinclined to conversation, he reasoned that some discussion would be necessary if they were to believably play the part of enraptured lovers. Therefore he broke the silence that hung between them by instructing, "Say my name."

She turned toward him and arched one dark brow in cool surprise. "I beg your pardon?"

"My name. Say it."

She gave a light shrug. "Lord Barrington."

"Nicholas," he corrected.

"Nicholas."

"Say it again."

"Why?"

"I don't want it to sound awkward on your tongue. If you are to play the part of my mistress, you should seem perfectly comfortable saying my name—rather than looking as though you had just bitten into something you couldn't wait to spit out."

"Nicholas. Nicholas. Nicholas."

He held back a smile. "Very good. Now tell me about

yourself. Your age, your home, your likes and dislikes, anything that comes to mind."

"Is this really necessary?"

"Yes."

"Very well." She let out a long-suffering sigh and recited in a flat monotone, "I'm twenty-three. My home is wherever I happen to be at the moment. I enjoy long walks, good books, and rich chocolate desserts. I dislike being in debt. There—is that enough?"

This time he didn't bother to hide his smile. "Any unusual birthmarks I should know about?"

She stiffened her spine in clear affront. "Certainly no one would ask so vulgar a question."

"Perhaps, perhaps not."

She studied him with a look of scandalized disbelief. Then she took a moment to compose herself, idly adjusting the buttons on her long silk gloves. "You needn't worry about me, I'll manage," she finally said. "I assume there are dozens of petty thieves available for hire in Monaco. If you are confident enough in my abilities to select me over anyone else, I suppose that should signify for something."

"It wasn't merely your abilities as a thief that impressed me. In order for this little ruse to work, I also needed someone who could pose as my mistress." His gaze traveled briefly over her form. "You suit that role far more than I could have hoped."

She brought up her chin. "Am I to be flattered by that?"

Nicholas gave a light shrug. "Either excessively flattered or excessively insulted, depending on whom you ask."

"How very reassuring."

"At least I'm being honest with you."

"Are you?" she challenged.

He folded his arms across his chest and settled back against the plush leather seat. With a polite nod of his head, he indicated for her to continue. "Obviously you have something on your mind."

"What exactly am I to expect tonight?"

"The party is being hosted by the Duke of Westerly and his new bride," he answered directly. "I suspect we shall find a stuffy, crowded ballroom and an odd assortment of over-dressed and underfed guests who have had far more to drink than good taste and common sense would allow. The conversation, if you can call it that, will center exclusively on gossip and the latest *on dits,* and will last far too long into the night. Ultimately, someone will insult someone else, either directly or indirectly. At least two couples will embark on shocking extramarital affairs. By four o'clock in the morning, the party should have waned enough for the hosts to gather the assembly and serve a ten-course, late-night supper consisting of nauseatingly rich sauces and fatted meats. Then the guests shall be sent home in a bleary, drunken stupor. As a final affront, we shall suffer an interminable wait of at least an hour in the early morning fog while the coachmen jostle each other for position in their frenzied rush to retrieve their charges. By tomorrow afternoon, the party shall be deemed a brilliant success."

"You're not serious."

"I'm afraid I am. The only thing that will set this evening apart from any other is the fact that a few of the guests will leave with their pockets a little emptier—the result of their seemingly innocent contact with the Earl of Barrington's new mistress."

"I see." Katya made a face that clearly expressed her disapproval. She gazed out the window at the moonlit landscape in thoughtful silence, then said tightly, "I'm sorry that you choose your friends so ill."

"My friends," he echoed. A harsh laugh escaped his lips. "That limited circle of acquaintances, the men and women whom I truly trust and admire, remain back in London.

What you are about to meet tonight is a gathering of elegant sycophants whose tolerance for me exists only because they covet my money, my possessions, and my title."

"I suppose their opinion of you is as poor as yours of them?"

"Worse." He thought for a moment, then continued, "Perhaps you should be forewarned that you are keeping company with the Lord of Scandal. At least, that's the name that is whispered behind my back."

If he had been trying to shock her, he had failed. Her expression remained carefully blank as she turned from the window to face him. "The Lord of Scandal? I imagine the name suits you quite admirably."

He lifted one dark brow as a small smile played about his lips. "Do I detect a note of satisfaction in your voice to hear that I am thus libeled?"

"No more than I heard in yours. Something tells me that the name pleases you as well. Why do I suspect that it's a title you went to great pains to earn?"

Not only was Miss Katya Alexander captivatingly beautiful, Nicholas thought, she was extraordinarily perceptive as well. For in truth, he had secretly taken a quiet satisfaction in the fact that he was viewed as a roguish outcast by the very society that he loathed. But no longer. Regret and remorse took hold where pride and arrogance had once flourished. He couldn't help but wonder how things might have changed if he had acted differently.

"This scroll you expect me to find," she continued slowly, "it must be rather important to you if you're willing to go to such extreme lengths to get it back."

Something in her tone caught his attention. Her voice sounded slightly disingenuous, a combination of both vague opportunism and bad acting. Almost as though she were testing him out, or knew more than she was letting on. It suddenly occurred to him that the enterprising Miss Alexander might be considering recovering the scroll—and then marketing it to the highest bidder.

With that in mind, he replied harshly, "The scroll itself is of no importance. As I explained at the beginning of this venture, the value to me is in knowing who stole it. Therefore, should you be entertaining any thoughts in that pretty little head of retrieving the scroll and selling it off to the highest bidder, you had best rid yourself of that notion now. I can assure you that whatever profit you might make would not be worth the weight of my wrath were I to discover your deceit."

Katya eyed him coolly. "Charming. If you are attempting to warm my affections for the tender ruse we are about to undertake, I suggest you try another tact."

"I merely mean to impress upon you the consequences of your actions should you be considering such a course."

"In that case, you may consider your goal accomplished. You have done so with all the grace and civility an English landlord might display toward his Irish tenant. How very commendable."

Nicholas smiled despite himself. "Have you always had such a sharp tongue, Katya, or do you unleash it solely as a weapon to use against me?"

"Frankly, you do inspire a certain amount of hostility within me," she admitted breezily. "I suppose I should just ignore your character defects for the sake of this . . . venture, as you call it, but I find that I'm curiously unable to do so."

He nodded in solemn commiseration. "How very trying that must be for you."

If she was at all aware of the sarcasm in his voice, she ignored it completely. "Be that as it may, if we are to successfully work together, there are a few questions I would like answered."

"Very well, do proceed."

"Thank you." She nodded primly and shifted in her seat, as though adopting a more businesslike pose. The brush of the thick satin against the plush leather had a dramatic effect on her gown, however. Rather than move with her, the fabric adhered to the seat, pulling the line of her bodice significantly downward. The fact that the move was almost certainly unintended did nothing to lessen its effect on Nicholas—in fact, just the opposite was true. His eyes fastened on the soft skin of her breasts with a fascination bordering on total absorption. Within the silver glow of the moonlight pouring in through the coach windows, he could just make out the rich, rosy curve of her nipples.

"Were you listening to me?"

Embarrassed, Nicholas quickly averted his gaze. He was not normally given to peering down women's gowns like some lecherous drunkard on a crowded trolley car. "I'm sorry, I didn't hear . . ."

Katya let out a sigh and shifted impatiently. The bodice of her gown slid back into place. Whether Nicholas was relieved or disappointed at the loss of erotic distraction was hard to judge. At least now he was able to properly focus on her words.

"What makes you think that the man who stole the scroll will be in attendance tonight?" she asked.

Although the question was simple and straightforward, the answer was far more complicated. "The scroll was taken from my home in London by someone who knew not only of its existence, but also of its exact location. That information was limited to a very few members of the peerage."

"Or to an ordinary thief," she suggested, "who was in league with a servant?"

He shook his head. "There were objects of far greater value nearby that might have been taken as well, but nothing else was touched. The only item the thief was after was the scroll."

"But that still doesn't answer my question," she persisted. "If the scroll was taken from your home in London, why are you so certain that whoever has it is here in Monaco?"

Nicholas hesitated, unwilling to give her more information than necessary. "That requires a rather laborious answer," he finally replied, adopting his most soothing, persuasive tone. "And you look far too lovely for me to bore you with all the petty details."

A mocking smile curved her lips. "How very kind. Fortunately, however, the fact that I have attired myself in an elaborate evening gown and put up my hair will not impair my ability to comprehend your reply."

He shook his head, studying her in growing admiration. The woman was definitely not one to be patronized—or to be glibly brushed aside. Realizing he would be far better served to give her at least a little background on the theft, he said, "You've told me before that you don't believe in curses. What about legends? Are you equally as skeptical as to the power of legend?"

"I suppose that depends on the legend in question."

"In that case, I shall let you judge for yourself." He thought for a moment, then settled comfortably back into his seat and began, "Over six hundred years ago the ownership of this entire region—what is now the south of France—was fiercely contested. In an attempt to breed loyalty to the crown, the king decreed that two of the region's most prominent families be joined. The eldest daughter of the lord of one clan was promised in marriage to the eldest son of the lord of another clan. In return for this act of loyalty to the crown, the king offered to double the size of their lands, and he promised that an even more formidable gift would be delivered on the morning of their betrothal."

"And what was that gift?"

"A stone," he replied. "More precisely, a glittering blue diamond rumored to be as large as a man's fist, known as the Stone of Destiny."

"I see." Across the coach, Nicholas heard Katya draw in a shallow, fluttery breath, as though she were striving to maintain an air of calm indifference. That didn't surprise him. Mention of the Stone made even cautious men wild with greed and had done so for generations. "Did the king make good his promise?" she asked.

"Unfortunately he did."

"Unfortunately?"

"The Stone is cursed. That's why the king was able to demonstrate such largesse in giving it away."

Her brows snapped together. "Cursed? I never heard anything—" She stopped short, as though abruptly recalling herself. "I never heard anything so preposterous."

Nicholas lifted his shoulders in a light shrug. "Legend has it that the young bride and groom fell deeply in love during their courtship, despite the wariness that existed between their clans. The marriage was never consummated, however. On the morning of the wedding feast, the bride was cruelly slain and the Stone was stolen. That set in motion a bitter feud that raged on between the families for centuries."

She thought for a moment, as though she were carefully weighing his words. "Am I wrong to assume that this Stone is somehow connected to the scroll stolen from your home?"

"Actually, I would say that you're remarkably astute."

"So what has the scroll to do with this Stone of Destiny?"

"As I mentioned, a bitter and bloody feud erupted between the clans. The feud lasted for generations, with each side launching violent raids against the other in their fierce quest to regain possession of the Stone. By this time, the lands in the area had passed into the possession of Louis IX.

Determined to put an end to the warring once and for all, the king dispatched a small army of knights to the region with instructions to capture the Stone and bring it, along with the leaders of both families, to a local abbey. After laying siege to both keeps, the knights succeeded in doing so. The monks who resided at the abbey took the Stone into their own possession and secreted it away, preparing a scroll that detailed its location. Each family received one third of that scroll; the remaining third was held at the abbey. As decreed by the king, once the families overcame their bitterness and presented themselves at the abbey united and in peace, the monks would turn over the third portion of the scroll and the Stone would be recovered."

"Did that ever happen?"

He shook his head. "After centuries of feuding, the families were too proud to reconcile. Time passed and a variety of events, ranging from famine and plague, to warfare and political upheaval, tore the region apart. The lure of the Stone waned with the passing of the years, and the clans drifted away in search of better lives. My ancestors eventually settled in England. As to the fate of the other clan," he paused, lifting his shoulders in an eloquent shrug, "I believe they settled somewhere near Prussia—but that's merely a guess."

"I see."

A thoughtful silence fell between them as she considered his words. Nicholas watched her, somewhat surprised at her acumen and intelligence. Then again, nothing about Katya was ever predictable. There were so many different facets to her, he couldn't help but wonder which was the real woman. The prim, prudish spinster; the confident Goddess of Mystery who captivated an entire audience; the sophisticated seductress who sat before him now; or the opportunistic thief he had lured into stealing for him. In the end it didn't matter, he supposed—as long as she succeeded in re-trieving the scroll.

"I trust that brings us to the present day," she concluded briskly. "Until the scroll was stolen from your home, was there any indication that someone was after the Stone?"

Very good, he thought, once again congratulating her on her mental agility. If he was learning nothing else from the conversation, at least he would not make the mistake of un-derestimating her intelligence.

"Six months ago," he replied, "certain events transpired in Monaco that led me to hire a private investigator to ex-plore their cause. In one of his reports, the man mentioned that an abbey not far from here had been broken into. It was none other than the abbey in which the third portion of the scroll has rested for centuries."

"The abbey was broken into?" she echoed, visibly un-nerved. "Was the scroll taken?"

"Fortunately not. The scroll, along with several other an-cient documents and artifacts, had been moved to another portion of the abbey before the theft occurred. At the time, I attributed the crime to the work of local thieves. But the abbey was broken into again two months ago. Clearly the thief is determined to get his hands on some object in partic-ular. Now that the scroll has been stolen from my own home, it would appear obvious that he's after the Stone."

"Indeed. I would have drawn the same conclusion," she murmured, almost as though speaking to herself.

The coach slowed to a leisurely, rumbling stop. Nicholas heard the creak of harness leather accompanied by the sound of other horses and carriages. Glancing outside the window, he saw that they had joined the long line of carriages queu-ing up before the Duke of Westerly's villa.

"I trust that I have given you ample information from which to proceed," he said.

"Almost," she returned. "You mentioned earlier that

something occurred here in Monaco that led you to hire a private investigator. What was it?"

"That needn't concern you." Regrettably, his tone was harsher than he had intended, but that couldn't be helped. His brother's death was not a matter for discussion.

"I've given you this background, Katya, so that you might understand the gravity of the situation. Whoever stole the scroll is serious—one might even say deadly. Therefore . . ."

"Therefore," she finished for him, "should I suddenly find myself intimidated by the task, this is my opportunity to bow out."

"Quite."

"I take it that this is your way of allowing me to renege on my word."

He inclined his head. "I would not think less of you were you to decide not to pursue this further."

"How very reassuring."

The coach pulled to a smooth stop. One of the groomsmen climbed down from his perch, opened the door, and offered Katya his hand in disembarking. She gathered her black lace fan and satin reticule, then stepped out onto the neatly manicured lawn, mingling with the other guests who were disembarking for that evening's fete. As Nicholas joined her she took a few steps away from the gathered assembly, moving discreetly out of earshot. That accomplished, she met his gaze and said firmly, "Fortunately for both of us, I believe I'm quite up to the chase." She hesitated for a moment, then added smugly, "Furthermore, I am not in the habit of breaking my promises."

Her expression was so primly self-righteous it was all he could do not to smile. While the incongruity of a self-confessed thief proudly proclaiming herself a woman of her word had obviously escaped her, the irony was not lost on him. Deciding that this was not the time to remark upon it, however, he replied solemnly, "I'm delighted to hear it." He placed his hand on her elbow and gently ushered her forward. "Now let us go inside. It's time for the lords and ladies of Monaco to meet my new mistress."

Seven

Katya took a deep, steadying breath as Nicholas took her elbow and ushered her inside. She tried to sort out her heightened emotions but they were too jumbled for her to properly think straight. Had the scroll that had been in her family for generations already been stolen? It had not occurred to her to check that it was still hidden among her mother's possessions. But now a dark suspicion loomed before her: if the person after the scroll knew enough to find the secluded abbey and the DuValenti scroll, wouldn't he also know the whereabouts of the Rosskaya scroll?

On the heels of that thought came another, even more horrifying. Had her parents' deaths been connected to the search for the scroll? A feeling of newfound dread spread through her limbs as she considered the possibility.

"Nervous?"

Lost as she had been in her own thoughts, Katya nearly jumped at the sound of Nicholas's low voice in her ear. "Pardon?" she said.

"You needn't look so terrified. I expect the worst we shall have to endure tonight is a rather tasteless display of unending boredom and priggish snobbery."

She forced a tight smile, trying her best to appear both sophisticated and at ease. "I believe I'll be able to bear it."

He nodded and placed his hand on the small of her back, gently propelling her forward. Although she tried to channel her thoughts to the task ahead of her, her attention was ridiculously diverted by the feeling of Nicholas's palm against her gown. Her mother had often told her that the key to a man's soul was visible in his hands. While Katya did not possess the same degree of skill that her mother had in the art of palmistry, certain things were clear even to her.

An unusual combination of mastery and gentleness was revealed in Nicholas's touch. She felt strength in his hands, an innate sense of confidence and subtle finesse in the way his long fingers lightly caressed her back. Katya hadn't given it much thought at the time, but she suddenly remembered the ease with which he had assumed the position of driver and directed their coach into Monaco. Nicholas Duvall was obviously a man accustomed to handling horses. She could easily imagine him riding a restless stallion across a wind-swept field.

He would soon find out, however, that he could not control her as easily.

With that thought in mind, Katya smoothly withdrew from his grasp as the Duke of Westerly's footmen opened the villa doors and bowed for them to enter. Although the gesture had been merely symbolic, Nicholas had not missed its significance. Rather than react to her subtle provocation, he merely arched one dark brow and gallantly gestured for her to proceed him, as though amused by her presumption that she could exert her will over his.

A steward showed them through a long, vaulted hall that led to a set of ornate double doors. They stepped through the entranceway and entered a magnificent formal ballroom. Katya drew in a deep breath as she watched the guests meander about the crowded room. She had forgotten the glamour and elegance that great wealth could radiate, the confidence and condescension possessed by the very rich.

The vaulted room resonated with the hush of polite conversation, the rustle of silks and satins, and the soft strains of a seated orchestra. Crystal chandeliers hung from the ceiling, giving the huge chamber a soft, almost ethereal glow. The mirrored walls reflected the dazzling sparkle of the brilliant jewels worn by the guests and created a sense of vivid movement. Servants circulated discreetly through the assembly offering tall glasses filled with bubbly wine.

Katya suddenly experienced a surge of doubt and misgiving regarding the task she was about to undertake. Before she could turn back, however, she felt Nicholas's hand return to her elbow, subtly urging her forward. Hiding her nervousness she tilted her chin and stepped regally into the room, moving with the same grace and confidence she would have exhibited onstage.

As they strolled through the crowded room her self-consciousness slowly faded. Much to her relief, she received nothing but an occasional curious glance. Her escort, however, did not enjoy the same level of indifference. In fact, just the opposite was true. Judging from the open disdain visible on the guests' faces, it was quickly impressed upon her that Nicholas Duvall, the Earl of Barrington, was viewed as a pariah of sorts.

While he never received what was formally known as a cut direct, the reaction to his presence by those attending the gala was nothing short of shocked disapproval. The crowd parted before them like the sea before Moses, leaving an excited murmur of conversation in their wake. Throughout it all Nicholas remained coolly composed. On second glance, however, Katya realized that he wasn't as impassive as she had first thought.

A quiet, simmering tension radiated through his frame. It wasn't anger, but something else . . . something akin to the indefinable aura of danger she had perceived in him on the day they first met. A murky combination of vengeance and honor seemed to emanate from deep within him. His dark, hawkish eyes scanned the room as though seeking out his prey, while his proud carriage asserted his irrevocable right to move among his peers.

Although he had warned her that he was known as the Lord of Scandal, she had assumed that the title was nothing but a bit of self-mockery, or at worst, manly conceit at his various carnal exploits. But the fissure that existed between Nicholas and society obviously ran deeper than a bit of minor debauchery.

She watched as his gaze fastened on an elderly gentleman whose squat frame had been stuffed into a black, double-breasted formal suit with coattails that reached nearly to the backs of his knees. His attire was both the height of fashion and, given the man's short, portly frame, the height of unsuitability. He looked like a proud, waddling penguin.

"Come," Nicholas said. "I'll introduce you to our host."

They made it halfway across the crowded room when the opening strains of a waltz began and their elderly host stepped onto the dance floor with a tall, graceful young woman attired in ruby red silk.

Nicholas turned back to Katya, as though giving a mental shrug. "Shall we join them?"

She studied him in shocked surprise. "You mean dance?"

He studied her with a quizzical frown. "Of course."

"But I thought—" she began, then stopped abruptly as she realized the absurdity of what she was about to say. Until that moment, Katya's focus had been on finding the Stone, rather than on what it would mean to play the part of Nicholas's mistress. She had vaguely considered that since their agreement was for the farce to be in name only, it was merely a matter of making introductions and letting others assume what they may. But as Nicholas took her arm and ushered her toward the dance floor, that ill-conceived theory took on a whole new reality.

He pulled her into his arms and grasped her hand in his, holding it lightly but securely. The fingers of his opposite hand spread open across the small of her back, nearly spanning her waist. A nervous thrill shot down her spine as they moved across the floor, as though they were embarking on a journey of momentous proportions, rather than a few steps across a ballroom floor. A skilled dance partner, Katya did not have to pay close attention to the steps or the rhythm of the dance. Nicholas guided her through the waltz with an easy, athletic grace, leaving her mind free to wander. Which was fortunate, she supposed, because at that moment she could focus on nothing but the enigmatic man with whom she danced.

Although they stood the requisite distance apart, he felt much too close. Unlike most men of his station, he wore no cologne. His skin had a clean, fresh scent and the heady, masculine aroma seemed to drift around her, leaving her warm, giddy, and intoxicated. She found herself fascinated by the way his dark hair curled slightly as it touched the top of his collar. She shifted her hand onto his shoulder, noting as she did so that his jacket lacked the customary padding found in most men's coats. Nicholas Duvall was lean, solid muscle through and through.

To her shock and embarrassment, her iron-willed resolve to remain unaffected by his touch faded completely. Although Katya tended to look upon herself as proper, decorous, and strong-willed, she had not spent her life in a nunnery. Her parents—sometimes much to her dismay—had been rather shocking freethinkers and had given her tremendous freedoms. In her travels she had been exposed to a variety of different cultures and mores. Given her rather unorthodox and unsheltered background, she considered herself fairly sophisticated when it came to understanding men.

But she had vastly underestimated the impact Nicholas Duvall would have on her. Much to her dismay, the smug confidence she had had in her ability to resist the lure of his potent attractiveness vanished like household silver at a thieves' convention.

As they swirled to the music of the waltz, Katya experienced a curious sensation of both raw awakening and comforting familiarity. Almost as though she had known Nicholas Duvall her entire life, yet had only now dared to touch him. The air between them seemed to crackle with primal tension. Like a wave pounding rocks into sand, her blood pounded through her veins, disabling all the defenses she had erected against him.

She was suddenly overwhelmed by an astonishingly wicked and unprecedented urge to let her body "accidentally" brush against his. Just once. Just one forbidden touch to satisfy the insatiable curiosity that threatened to overwhelm her. The mere idea of doing so sent a warm quiver spiraling through her limbs and made her knees go weak.

Fighting her reaction, she straightened primly and held herself deliberately erect, striving to put as much distance between herself and Nicholas as the dance allowed. She reminded herself that the Lord of Barrington was a direct descendant of her family's ancient enemy. The man was autocratic and arrogant. He had attempted to bribe and blackmail her into her present position. All of that was undeniably true, yet its importance seemed to melt away with each fluid step they took.

"My congratulations, Katya."

Startled at the intrusion of his voice, she gathered her errant thoughts and repeated, "Congratulations?"

"Indeed. You have brought bad acting to the height of perfection."

A deep flush stained her cheeks as she realized he had somehow managed to read her mind. Somehow he had discerned that she was battling a thoroughly embarrassing urge to abandon all sense of propriety and press her body against his.

"I don't understand what you mean," she murmured awkwardly, unable to meet his eyes.

"It may be an unbearable chore for you to dance with me,

but I would appreciate it if you would make that fact a little less obvious."

Katya's head snapped up. So much for his being able to read her mind.

"You have two choices," he continued, speaking in a pleasant but iron-willed tone that only she could hear. "One: you may gaze into my eyes as though you are so overcome by lust for me that you have been temporarily rendered senseless."

She swallowed hard. As that was far too close to the emotions that had been running through her only seconds earlier, it was definitely not the most attractive of options. "And the second choice?" she asked.

"You may engage me in conversation. To do neither would indicate that a profound dislike exists between us. Need I remind you that this is exactly opposite the relationship we are trying to convince everyone in this room that we share?"

She quickly searched her mind for something to say, but was unable to find a suitable topic. Mistakenly interpreting her silence for consent to act the part of lovers, Nicholas shifted his fingers until he was gently cradling her wrist in his hand. As his ebony eyes locked on hers, he slid apart the buttons of her glove. Moving his thumb with deliberate care, he stroked the tender skin of her inner wrist in a slow, provocative caress. The gesture was profoundly sensual, yet intimate enough that only those truly close to them could see it. Before Katya could react, he lowered his head and placed a gentle kiss against her wrist, brushing his lips against the exact spot he had warmed with his thumb. Her breath caught in her throat and her pulse skyrocketed.

"What would you like to discuss?" she blurted out, her voice high and shaky.

A small, knowing smile touched his lips. "It doesn't matter. Anything. What are you thinking about right now?"

"Very well." Latching quickly, almost desperately, onto a topic, she said, "I'm wondering what sort of crime you could have committed to receive such an outlandish reception from your peers."

"Crime?" he echoed. "What an interesting turn of phrase."

Although his tone remained pleasantly mild, Katya sensed she had stumbled onto some fundamental truth. Unfortunately she had neither the knowledge nor the background to unearth it completely. Before she could pursue the subject further, he lifted his shoulders in a light, unconcerned shrug.

"My family name is tarnished," he said flatly. "My personal reputation is abominable. My money, however, remains as potent an enticement as ever, gaining me unlimited access to events such as this. Remarkable what one can buy for the right price."

Assuming he was referring to her, she stiffened at his words and drew back.

Nicholas instantly recognized his gaffe. "My apologies, Katya," he said, moving his hand reassuringly along the small of her back. "I was not referring to you. Just to the exalted group that surrounds us." With a slight nod of his head, he indicated the elderly man he had sought earlier. "Our host, for example. The esteemed Duke of Westerly. A disillusioned, dishonored, disappointed man. Nothing but an aging Narcissus desperately trying to avoid the reflection in the pool."

She followed his gaze, frowning as she studied the short, balding man and the voluptuous, crimson-clad young beauty with whom he danced. "There must be a few admirable traits to his character," she protested. "Just look at the way his granddaughter dotes on him."

"The lady you're referring to happens to be his wife."

Her brows shot skyward. "His wife?"

"I believe the occasion of this gala is their one-month wedding anniversary."

She studied him for a moment in silent disapproval. "Why does shocking me seem to be a particular goal of yours?"

"Are you shocked?" he asked, sounding genuinely surprised. "Personally, I find it rather sad. A bitter old man vainly trying to cheat death by acquiring a youthful wife. I suppose the spectacle would be humorous were it not so trite."

"That's easy for us to judge now, when old age is nothing but a distant glimmer on the horizon. I suspect the lines will not be so easily drawn once our bones are brittle, our hearts are weak, and death is knocking at our door."

"I sincerely doubt that fate has anything so kind in store for me," he returned. "I expect that I shall be cut down in my prime, perishing from the bite of a rabid French poodle, or something equally embarrassing."

Despite her attempts to restrain it, a burst of laughter bubbled from her lips at the image conveyed by his disgruntled words. As the last strains of the waltz faded to a close, he drew her tightly to him.

"You should laugh more often, little gypsy."

Her startled gaze flew to his. His eyes were dark and fathomless; yet within his expression lurked a suggestion of the same stark, earthy desire she herself had felt only moments earlier. Katya's heart slammed against her ribs and her mouth suddenly went dry.

Wordlessly taking her hand in his, Nicholas led her off the dance floor to a semisecluded corner that had been partitioned off from the rest of the room by a group of potted palm trees. Once there, he slipped his arm around her waist and drew her tightly to him. Katya's breasts pressed against the solid expanse of his chest; her thighs entwined with his. His dark, slumberous gaze brimmed with both sensual conquest and bold confidence. Without granting her time for consent or refusal, he lowered his head and moved his lips over hers.

His kiss was feather light, a mere brush of his mouth against hers. Barely had she adjusted to the shock of that intimate contact when the kiss abruptly changed. Nicholas increased the pressure of his jaw, gently coaxing apart her lips. Boldly he thrust his tongue into her mouth. Katya stiffened instinctively at the unexpected intimacy. She tried to jerk free from his grasp, but he had guessed her intention and tightened his hold, drawing her body even more fiercely against his own. His hips pressed against hers, rocking with a slow, languid motion that mimicked the rhythm of their kiss.

The steady movement was both deeply comforting and unbelievably exciting. Within seconds her shock and dismay turned to a pure, liquid pleasure that coursed through her veins and warmed her very bones. She tightened her arms around his neck as a jolt of fiery passion shot down her spine. For a moment she felt as though her body would surely melt into his. But she was not yet ready for total surrender. From somewhere deep within her, a small spark of self-preservation remained lit. She turned her head and pulled back, slipping free from his embrace.

The spell was abruptly broken. Like a sleepwalker jolted awake to find herself in strange and unfamiliar territory, Katya gazed up at Nicholas in anxious wonder. She took a deep, shuddering breath and protested softly, "I think you go too far."

"But you're not sure, are you?" His eyes locked on hers as he lifted his hand and traced one finger gently from her temple to her cheek. "I can't decide whether your innocence pleases me or not. I only know that it never fails to astound me."

"Indeed?" The question meant nothing, but Katya could think of no other way to respond. She felt as though she were floundering, completely lost and out of her element.

"The Goddess of Mystery," he said softly. "How apt a title. Nothing about you is as it appears, is it? Beneath your prim little facade there is a fire waiting to be unleashed. I envy the man who can do so."

"But it won't be you." The words tumbled softly from her lips before she could stop them.

"No, it won't." A look of both regret and decisiveness crossed his darkly chiseled features. "Perhaps, had we met under different circumstances, it might have been. But not now."

Before she could summon a response, his gaze shifted almost imperceptibly, focusing on something just beyond her left shoulder.

"One of the men I am about to introduce you to is Lord Thurston Teecham," he murmured against her ear. "I suggest we begin with him. If he is carrying the scroll, I presume it will be somewhere on his person, rather than secreted away."

The abrupt shift in topics left her momentarily speechless. Foolishly she had imagined that Nicholas had succumbed to the same magnetic pull she had felt between them. But as he stepped slightly aside, Katya noted a group of three men who were studying them with looks of undisguised interest. With a jolt of mortifying recognition, she realized that the searing look of desire he had given her—and the kiss that followed—had merely been for the benefit of this audience.

Shame and embarrassment poured through her. The kiss had meant nothing to him. Nothing. She had allowed the line between illusion and reality to blur—but she would not make that humiliating mistake again.

That firmly resolved, she turned her focus to the three men who were approaching. They appeared to be in their early fifties and emanated a kindred air of stodgy pomposity. As Nicholas performed the introductions, she felt their curious gazes move over her body from head to toe, heedless of all decorum and propriety. Had she been anywhere else, she would have wasted no time in removing herself from their offensive presence. Nicholas must have sensed as much, for he kept one hand pressed firmly against the small of her back, as if to remind her to bite her tongue.

As the orchestra began a new set, he suggested smoothly, "Perhaps Lord Teecham would care to lead you through this next dance, Katya." He turned to the small circle of men with whom they stood, and continued, "Normally I would reserve that pleasure exclusively, but Miss Alexander has made it clear that she wishes to spend the evening dancing. While I would like nothing better than to indulge her every whim, I twisted my ankle while riding this afternoon and so I find myself shamefully unable to do so."

A look of surprise crossed Lord Teecham's face, then he puffed out his chest and gravely offered her his arm. "The honor would be mine."

Katya hesitated. Although she had known that this moment would come, she was nevertheless profoundly unprepared for it. She suddenly felt like a reckless spendthrift forced to reconcile her debts. Her heart beat wildly within her chest, her breath felt shallow, and her smile was tight and strained. Never in her life had she stolen anything. Granted, she had retrieved her own money and jewels from Lady Stanton; and in a portion of her act she did demonstrate her ability to "magically borrow" the personal possessions of various members of her audience, but these were entirely different things.

But she had no time to reconsider the bargain she had made. Nicholas increased the pressure of his hand against her back, gently propelling her forward.

Katya shot him a dark look, then turned to Lord Teecham. "You are too kind, my lord," she murmured, taking his arm.

Fortunately the dance was a reel, not a waltz, and therefore she would not be subjected to the same intimacy she had shared with Nicholas. Realizing that she would have no better time to search for the scroll, she took a deep breath and steeled her nerves for the task. She lifted her right hand and brushed it lightly against Teecham's chest. She felt the pleats of his stiffly starched shirt, a watch fob in his breast pocket, and a thick bulge of flesh around his torso, telling her that he wore a corset of some sort to give himself the appearance of a slim waistline.

She felt nothing, however, that resembled a parchment scroll. Emboldened by the fact that he had not noticed her touch, she tried again, checking the pockets of his coat. Again, nothing. As the rhythm of the dance changed, Lord Teecham pulled her stiffly back into his arms. Should she dare to check his pants? The notion that he might conceal the scroll somewhere within his britches seemed preposterous, yet shouldn't she at least confirm that it wasn't there? With that thought in mind, she shifted her hand and brushed it experimentally against his thigh . . .

"Looking for something, my dear?"

Katya gave a horrified gasp and snapped back her hand. Her heart slammed against her chest and her breath lodged in her throat. Aghast at being discovered, she bravely forced herself to meet Teecham's eyes. "I beg your pardon?" she managed hoarsely.

"I said, what brought you to Monaco? Was it the climate, the gaming, the company, or were you looking for something else?"

Raw relief flooded through her. He hadn't perceived her touch after all. "I have an engagement with the theater," she replied, hoping her voice didn't sound as thin and tremulous to him as it did to her.

"Of course, of course. Our own Goddess of Mystery. I hadn't made the connection. And what of Lord Barrington? Have you two been long acquainted?"

"Less than a week, actually."

Teecham arched both brows in a look of feigned surprise. "And yet he's managed to capture your affections in so limited a space of time." He paused, favoring her with a knowing smile that fell just short of an outright leer. "How charmingly impetuous."

Katya ignored the blatant insult that her body could be had for the price of the highest bidder. "You flatter me, Lord Teecham," she replied coolly, pulling away the moment the music stopped.

As the evening wore on Katya rotated through a variety of partners. She quickly discovered that Lord Teecham was neither the most ill bred nor the most well mannered among the men with whom Nicholas urged her to dance. She endured a long series of clumsy partners, mindless small talk, and vague insinuations. Her feet ached from having been constantly twirled around the dance floor, her nerves were raw from the constant stress of having to search the men with whom she danced, and her head was spinning from too many glasses of champagne.

Finally she could take no more. The music drew to a close and her current partner took her arm and led her back to Nicholas. He stood to greet her, another eager gentleman at his side ready to be foisted off on her. But before he had the opportunity, she announced, "If you gentlemen will pardon me, I should like a moment to tend to my gown." That said, she turned and walked away. It was perhaps rude, but she was in no mood to be polite and refined.

She strode briskly across the vaulted hall and entered the small retiring room set aside for the ladies in attendance. It was without doubt the most inviting room she had seen in the villa. The walls were papered a delicate shade of rose, the gas lamps were turned down low, and the soft murmur of female conversation filled the air. Perhaps a dozen women were in the room, not including the handful of snoring dowagers who lay sprawled out on sofas, their maids sitting by their sides. The younger ladies were occupied freshening their gowns, chatting among themselves, or just generally recovering from the pace of the party.

Katya sank onto a red velvet settee, grateful for the temporary respite from the hot, frenzied pace of the ballroom. She parted the filmy curtains that covered the windows to look outside. A faint lavender light glowed in the eastern horizon, telling her that dawn was finally approaching. A weary smile touched her lips, as relief that the night would soon be over flooded through her. She was not normally given to bouts of nerves, but tonight was clearly an exception.

After a few minutes a bell rang, summoning the guests to a late-night supper. Aware that she could hide no longer, Katya sighed and stood. As she made her way from the ladies' retiring chamber and back into the hall, a petite blond woman in a gown of vivid emerald silk stepped before her, blocking her way. The woman was strikingly beautiful, graced with porcelain skin, wide hazel eyes, and smooth golden-blond hair that had been swept up into an elegant chignon. Her presence made Katya feel large and ungainly.

"You certainly don't hesitate to take what you see, do you?" the woman said.

Katya once again experienced a rush of irrational horror that her sleight of hand had been discovered. But something about the woman's expression made her hesitate. "I'm afraid I don't understand," she replied coolly.

"Why, Lord Barrington, of course. You're the first woman he's been seen with publicly since . . . how shall I put it delicately . . . since that unfortunate incident with Allyson Whitney."

Although Katya didn't have the slightest idea what she was talking about, she was instinctively loathe to admit it. "Is that so?"

"Indeed. It does one good to see him out and about in

society again." She gave a soft sigh and blithely continued, "Well, at least he appears to have learned from the experience. He doesn't appear at all as possessive of you as he was of Allyson."

"Really? How kind of you to remark upon it."

The blonde studied her for a moment in silence, then smiled with satisfaction. "You don't know, do you?" she said, nearly purring with delight. "How very naughty of him to keep such secrets from you."

Before Katya could manage a reply, the woman's gaze shifted. "Good evening, Nicholas. I was just chatting with . . ." She hesitated for a moment, then continued in a shocked tone that rang patently false, "Oh dear, we haven't even been introduced, have we?"

Despite the blonde's stunning beauty, Nicholas regarded her with a curiously flat gaze. With a slight bow, he performed the introductions. "Miss Katya Alexander, allow me to present Miss Corrina Jeffreys." He hesitated a moment, then continued, "Miss Alexander and I were just going in to dine. Would you care to join us?"

"Perhaps another time," Corrina Jeffreys replied, smiling sweetly. "I fear that I've neglected my escort for too long as it is. Do excuse me." With these parting words, she lifted her emerald skirts and gracefully made her way back into the crowd.

An awkward silence hung between them as they watched her go. Searching for an opening for the questions that had suddenly blossomed in her mind, Katya remarked, "She's quite beautiful, isn't she?"

"Indeed," he agreed. "Evidence, no doubt, that unremitting selfishness truly is wonderful for the skin."

She turned toward him in surprise. "What a cruel thing to say."

He gave an indifferent shrug. "An ice sculpture is lovely to admire as well, but I wouldn't want to find it in my bed."

Abruptly closing the subject of Corrina Jeffreys, he asked, "Are you hungry?"

"Not at all."

"In that case, may I suggest that you spend the next five minutes working up a ravenous appetite."

He took her arm and led her through the villa and downstairs to the formal dining area. The meal began as soon as the guests were seated. Course after course was brought to the table, accompanied by free-flowing wine, champagne, and elaborately confected sweets and pastries. It was, she thought, a fitting finale to a night of gross overindulgence. At last the supper ended and they were able to take their leave.

Once inside the coach, Katya sank against the plush leather, exhausted to the point of feeling numb. Relieved that the evening was finally over, she leaned her head against the back of the seat and stared blankly out the window as the coach climbed the steep terrain toward Nicholas's home.

"I trust you did not find the scroll," he said after a minute, breaking the silence that hung between them.

"No," she answered. "I didn't."

"I didn't think you would. But at least it gave us a start. By noon the word will have spread throughout Monaco that I have a new mistress, and your presence will be sought after by all the curiosity seekers and morbid spectators in the principality."

"Fortunately I am not vain enough to believe that there exists enough interest in either you or me to stimulate that kind of widespread speculation."

"Then you vastly underestimate the pettiness and gossipmongering of the men and women in whose company we just passed the last seven hours."

Katya lifted her shoulders in a bored shrug, not caring enough to debate the subject.

"I hope you managed to extract a little profit from the evening," he continued.

She had anticipated that Nicholas would want to confirm her abilities and had prepared for it. She pulled open the strings of her reticule and dumped the contents out onto the seat beside him with what she hoped was the cool aplomb of a professional thief. From within the satin confines of her bag tumbled Lord Teecham's watch fob, Sir Garvey's sterling silver fountain pen, the Duke of Pallister's diamond stickpin, and Lord Rutherford-Green's gold-plated snuff box.

His dark gaze skimmed briefly over her plunder. "It appears you've had quite a profitable evening."

"Yes, I suppose I have."

"You must be pleased."

"Of course," she agreed woodenly.

Oddly enough, pleased was the last thing Katya felt. Although she should have been thrilled that everything had gone according to plan, she felt strangely dissatisfied. In truth, Nicholas's cavalier treatment of her had bothered her more than she wanted to admit. The raw force of his personality was almost overwhelming, yet she had felt unexpectedly vulnerable when she wasn't near him.

Confused by her emotions, she turned to face him. He had removed his cravat; it sat crumpled on the seat beside him. His shirt was open at the collar. Other than that, he looked as immaculately groomed and fresh as he had at the beginning of the evening. He was, she thought dispassionately, a strikingly handsome man. Unlike the other men who had attended that evening's gala, there was a rugged virility to him, coupled with a sense of quiet determination and absolute power. While he had foisted her off from one man to the next, he had kept himself slightly apart from the gathered assembly, as if he were somehow above the very crowd that scorned him.

The carriage slowed, then jutted forward as they moved

around a bend in the road. As Nicholas turned to glance out the window his expression abruptly darkened, almost as though a shadow had fallen between them.

Katya followed his gaze, and saw nothing but a dense out-cropping of sharp, white-capped rocks, their craggy surface devoid of vegetation. Nothing existed beyond them but a sheer, vertical drop to the sea.

"What is this place?" she asked.

Nicholas studied her for a moment in silence, as though carefully choosing his words. Finally he replied, "Rocks, Katya. Nothing but a pile of dull, lifeless rocks."

Realizing she would get no further information, she nodded without speaking and turned away, looking out the window. The sun was rising, filling the eastern horizon with brilliant bands of crimson, orange, gold, and rose. A dense fog rose up from the ocean; liquid silver drops clung to the mist, glistening like diamonds in the rays of the morning sun. The scene had an unearthly, almost spectral beauty.

Her mother had often told her that the winds carry warnings, if only she would pay attention. Katya had never tested the theory. She had scoffed at the archaic gypsy superstitions, preferring science to speculation. But that the blood of her ancestors ran through her veins could not be denied. As she surveyed the site an icy chill ran down her back, as though a hand had reached out from the grave and touched her.

The message the wind carried was clear, even to her.

Death was in the air.

Eight

*N*icholas urged Avignon into a full gallop, recklessly racing the black gelding down the steep, hairpin curves that led away from his villa and toward the bustling center of Monaco. The black responded to the command with unrestrained power as his long legs tore up the dirt path beneath him. Throwing caution aside, Nicholas leaned low over the gelding's neck, striving for more speed. The wind whipped sharply against his face, stirring up bits of sand and dirt to sting his skin. His breakneck pace was risky in the extreme, but he had no intention of slowing—not yet.

He rounded a bend, only to come face-to-face with a team of docile grays ploddingly guiding a farmer's dray up the steep slope. The team reared in wild-eyed fright, frantically lashing their hooves in the air. Avignon reacted in kind. The gelding reared upright, pitching Nicholas from his saddle and flinging him headlong through the air to land in a bone-jarring stop in a dense, thorny patch of holm oak.

He lay motionless for a moment, flat on his back and blinking up at the sky in stunned silence. Then he shifted experimentally, assessing the damage to his body. No bones were broken. He was stiff, sore, scraped, bruised, and thoroughly embarrassed, but nothing more serious than that. He had been lucky. Had he been thrown to the left, he could easily have been pitched down the steep, rocky bank to the sea below.

He slowly raised himself to a sitting position and looked around. The farmer with whom he had nearly collided was struggling to calm his team. At last he soothed the grays and brought them under control. Seeing that Nicholas was alive, he waved his fist in a universal gesture that conveyed his disdain and contempt.

Before Nicholas could offer either apology or restitution, the farmer urged his team back into their plodding pace up the hill. He watched them go, then turned his gaze to his mount. Avignon stomped his forelegs nervously as he paced; sweating and breathing hard, a slight shudder ran through his powerful frame. Biting back a groan, Nicholas rose to his feet and moved toward the black. He shook his head in disgust as he ran a soothing hand over his mount's flanks. He had been reckless in the extreme to risk injuring the animal.

Rarely did he let his emotions run away like that. Racing down the slope in guilt and self-loathing, he had desperately tried to outdistance the past. He glanced around at the sight where he had unceremoniously landed. It came as no surprise that fate had brought him down in the exact spot he had been trying so desperately to avoid—the thick outcropping of white-capped rocks that flanked the steep path. Resigned to face what he had been recklessly trying to avoid, Nicholas gathered Avignon's reins and led him to a patch of early spring grass where the gelding could graze as he cooled down.

Then he moved resolutely toward the base of the jagged rocks. He hesitated a moment, then climbed slowly to the summit. The wind blew back his hair and plastered his shirt against his chest; gusts of tangy sea air sprayed his face. Looking down, he saw nothing but a sheer, vertical drop to the sea. Waves pounded against the sharp, spiky rocks below, churning and crashing in a tumultuous struggle between land and sea.

As he stood at the top of the cliff, Nicholas wondered what it would be like to pitch oneself over the crest and plummet onto that deadly arsenal of jagged rocks below, to be swallowed up by the sea. During the second or two it took to reach the dagger-sharp rocks, what thoughts would run through one's mind? Terror? Acceptance? Anger? Resolve? Try as he might, Nicholas could not imagine it. He also could not comprehend that ultimate state of sadness and despair, of feelings so hopeless that they would cause one to take one's life.

Never would he have believed that such a state would overcome his own brother.

He stared blindly at the shimmering azure sea, lost in regret and reminiscence. Nicholas was only two years older than Tyler, yet the gap that separated them had been broader than either of them could span. Perhaps because they were so fundamentally different. Perhaps because they were both too stubborn to see the other's point of view. Whatever the cause, arguments and bitterness had separated them for years.

Looking back, a sense of waste and regret coiled over him. If they had tried to overcome their differences perhaps none of this would have happened. But it was too late for that now. Nicholas was not one to canonize the dead; his brother had had his faults, perhaps as many as Nicholas. But Tyler's most obvious flaw was self-centeredness; he would not have willingly given up his own life. Therefore it followed logically that someone else had killed him. Whether Nicholas reached this conclusion because he was looking for release from his battle with guilt, or because there was some shred of truth to it, he did not know.

Only one thing was clear: there was too much death around him. First, Tyler's death here in Monaco, then months later, Allyson's death in London. The only thing connecting the two events was him. The Lord of Scandal.

And possibly, just possibly, the scroll.

It was a tenuous link, but the only one left for him to explore. With that thought in mind, he turned away from the rocks and moved to collect Avignon. He mounted the black and sat with the reins in his hands, contemplating his next move. He had planned to spend the afternoon riding, but the aching soreness in his back and legs considerably lessened the appeal of that activity.

As he scanned the empty path that lay before him, his thoughts turned to Katya. She had performed admirably the night before, better than he had expected. Nicholas took a moment to review the evening. As far as he could tell, no one guessed that the beautiful conjuror was anything other than what he presented her to be: his newest mistress.

A small smile curved his lips as he considered her. Everything about Miss Katya Alexander had been unpredictable. She pleased him in an odd, undefinable way. Granted, she was a thief, but she was more honest and direct than most people he had met. Moreover, she had an uncanny ability to alternately shock, challenge, and amuse him. He enjoyed her company, her prim manners and sharp tongue, her quick wit and natural grace.

Deciding that she was the perfect antidote to an afternoon spent mired in his own dismal thoughts, he tapped his heels against Avignon's flanks, urging the black—at a more cautious and prudent pace—toward the the Grand Casino of the principality. Time for a visit with his little gypsy.

Katya moved alone backstage, relieved to see that there were no other performers about. Normally Monsieur Remy was present, or various stagehands and ushers, but today she found the theater absolutely quiet. She sent up a silent prayer of thanks. Ever since her discussion with Nicholas the night before, one question had been ringing incessantly through her mind: had the scroll that had belonged to her mother been stolen?

Determined to immediately resolve the matter, she opened a musty trunk and began riffling through her parents' belongings. Rather than wasting time looking for a chair, she sat on the floor, her skirts bunched up around her knees and ankles. Her parents had been chronically averse to throwing things away; the trunk was nearly brimming with outdated materials. Katya, preferring to be neat and orderly, had always scolded them for their sloppy sentimentality. But now she saw that what she had perceived as junk was nearly priceless treasure. Various old playbills, reviews of past performances, rough sketches of their elaborate costumes and stage sets, childhood drawings she had done, and train tickets from their travels spilled out into her hands.

Battling her emotions, she reverently emptied the contents of the trunk, spreading the mementos around her. Once that was accomplished she carefully pulled back the worn lining and felt along the base for the tiny spring that opened the trunk's false bottom. She found it and touched the lever; the hidden compartment instantly sprang open. Her father had designed the space as a place to store his secrets of the trade. A lifetime of collected works of magic and tricks that had been refined over centuries were contained within.

Katya sorted through the various books and pamphlets until she found what she had been seeking—a small bundle of letters and papers that had belonged to her mother. Even now the pages had about them the same mystical quality they had had when Katya was young.

As she touched the frayed, brittle parchment, she remembered the words her mother had spoken the first time she had shown them to her. *You have been given the kiss of fate, little Katya. Someday the blood of your gypsy ancestors will fire your veins.* As though it were both a blessing and a curse. Katya set the bundle in her lap and pulled free the purple ribbon that bound the pages.

Her hands went first to a tightly rolled, ancient document that was attached at both ends by narrow reeds, like a scribe's proclamation from a powerful medieval king. Her family's scroll. So it had not been stolen. Breathing a sigh of relief, she slowly unrolled it and studied the intricate document. Hand-lettered in the flamboyant style of thirteenth-century monks and bordered by ornate drawings on all sides, the scroll was doubtless valuable by itself. When joined with the two scrolls that led to the Stone of Destiny, it was priceless. Katya spent a few moments studying the document, then set it aside, burying it beneath the papers in her lap.

Next she lifted one of the yellowed, brittle pages that had been bound together with the scroll. The collection of letters and notes had been passed down through her family for centuries. The pages were mixed and out of order; many sheets were too badly smeared or worn to be legible. Her curiosity piqued, Katya removed her spectacles from her reticule and propped them on her nose. Then she lifted a page at random and held it up to the light.

It took a few minutes to decipher the ancient Latin. Once she did, she saw that she was holding an inventory of the preparations for a wedding. The page listed the various foods and wines to be served and which tapestries should be hung; it indicated that cloth weaving, rush weaving, candlemaking, and other household chores must be completed before the grand event. Interesting, perhaps, but not particularly relevant.

She set the sheet aside and lifted a second page. It took a good bit of scrutiny before she made sense of the tightly scrawled writing. Suddenly she did, and her heart felt as though it had leaped into her throat.

I met my betrothed today. Marco DuValenti arrived at the keep with his clan and warrior knights. He possesses a handsome figure and face, is well spoken, and does not seem at all as ruthless or as cold as I had been warned he'd be. He brought me a gift of fine blue silk and presented it quite prettily. He is not the barbarous heathen of whom I had been warned. Mother and father remain wary of the man. Secretly, I am both pleased and surprised. I wonder what impression I made upon him?

Katya stared at the ancient journal entry, feeling a pang of grief for the innocent young bride murdered on her wedding day. Then a puzzled frown touched her brow. She had always heard that Sacha had done her duty, marrying against her will for the sake of her clan. But now, after reading the journal entry, she wondered if there was some truth in Nicholas's version. Had she truly come to care for her family's ancient enemy?

"I thought I might find you here."

Katya gasped and dropped the parchment at the sound of the deep male voice behind her. She whirled around to find Nicholas Duvall standing behind her, one broad shoulder propped against the wall. How long had he been standing there watching her? What had he seen? She stifled an almost overpowering urge to frantically dump all of the papers back into the trunk and slam it shut. Fortunately, years of training in dealing with calamities onstage helped her maintain her poise. She schooled her expression into one she hoped gave an impression of relative serenity. Then she folded her hands in her lap and sent him a reserved smile.

"I didn't expect to see you here," she said simply.

"I apologize if I startled you." His gaze moved pointedly to the messy stack of documents in her lap. "It appears as though you're busy."

"Not really. Just sorting through a few odds and ends."

"No rehearsal today?"

Was there something in his voice? A tone that suggested he knew exactly who she was and what she had been doing? Or was it her own mind, her own guilt and fear, that combined to play tricks on her? Unable to resolve the question, she answered simply, "Not today. I've found that too much rehearsing can be as bad as too little. It turns a performance stale."

"Very wise." He moved toward her, crossing the space between them with three long, confident strides.

"Your jaw is bleeding," she observed.

"Is it?" He lifted his hand to his face, absently brushing it along the side of his jaw. Frowning at the blood he saw smeared across his fingertips, he removed a white linen handkerchief from his jacket pocket and pressed it against the gash.

As she watched him, Katya noted the light coating of dust and dirt that clung to his normally immaculate clothing. "Have you been in some sort of brawl?"

"Not exactly." Having stopped the blood, he folded his handkerchief and returned it to his pocket. "I spent the morning riding."

"I see." She gave his rumpled, disheveled attire a pointed look. "I believe it's customary to sit atop one's mount, rather than allow oneself to be dragged along behind it."

A small, self-mocking smile touched his lips. "Thank you for that advice. I shall bear it in mind next time."

"I thought you were good with horses."

"I am. But I am extremely poor at managing my own moods."

Sensing that the remark was not meant for her to understand, she let it pass.

Nicholas raised one skeptical brow at her position on the floor, a slightly amused expression on his face. To her astonishment, rather than looking for a chair, the Earl of Barrington lowered himself onto the floor beside her. He stretched out his long legs and propped up one elbow, resting his cheek against his fist. Looking perfectly comfortable and at ease, he regarded her with a look of quiet expectation.

Before she could react, he plucked a piece of ancient parchment from her lap.

"I'd rather you didn't—" she began, but it was too late. He already had the page in his grasp.

Katya clamped her jaw and pulled her fists to her side, forcing herself not to snatch the page from his grasp. She watched as he studied it in silence, a slight frown on his face. Her pulse pounded in her veins as her mouth went dry. What did he have? What did it say? Had he selected a piece that had the DuValenti name on it? Short of craning her neck around to see what he was holding, there was nothing she could do but wait.

After a moment, he passed it back to her. Then his eyes locked on hers. "I don't recognize the language."

Her gaze flew to the document he had held. *Beware the Maltese.* These three simple words were all that filled the page. She let out her breath in a rush as hysterical laughter threatened to rise up and choke her. Absurdity mixed with horror—of all the papers for him to pick.

"It's Magyar," she managed. "My mother's tongue."

"Ah. Gypsy talk. What does it say?"

She frantically wracked her brain for a suitable reply. "It says, 'Sacha's diary,'" she improvised.

"Sacha?"

"My grandmother."

"Grandmother?" he repeated with a frown. "These documents appear far more ancient than that."

Katya lifted her shoulders in a mild shrug. She casually gathered up the scattered papers and secured them with the purple ribbon in which they had been bound, intent on keeping them firmly out of his grasp. "Well, I suppose technically she wasn't my grandmother, more like my ancestor. In Magyar, we refer to all our ancestors as grandmother or grandfather, no matter how far reaching. It's a rather lovely custom, really, if you stop to consider—"

"Am I making you nervous?"

Her head snapped up. "What makes you think I'm nervous?"

"The way you're fiddling with your spectacles. I've noticed that you have a habit of doing so whenever you're nervous."

Finding that her hand was indeed on her reading glasses, she lowered it immediately to her side with an embarrassed smile.

After a moment Nicholas continued, "And if you're not wearing your spectacles, you fiddle with your hair." Before she could guess his intention, he reached forward and twisted a stray ebony curl gently around his finger. "Like this," he said.

Katya's stomach flipped at the unexpected gentleness and intimacy of his gesture. His dark gaze burned into hers, sending a nervous thrill coursing through her body. It suddenly occurred to her that they were completely alone in the theater. The air seemed to quiver with possibility. Her limbs suddenly felt hot and trembling; she was consumed by a strange combination of heat, curiosity, desire, and recklessness.

The moment seemed to stretch forever between them. Finally Katya pulled back. Slowly, but distinctly. Perhaps it was cowardly on her part, but she couldn't help it. Things were already far too complicated between them without tangling the matter further by responding to his silent sexual invitation.

"If you are trying to seduce me," she said boldly, "you are wasting your time. We have no audience here, therefore the chore of pretending to be intimate is rather unnecessary, is it not?"

"What gives you the impression it's either a chore or a pretense?"

She primly straightened her spine. "Because that was our agreement. If nothing else, at the very least I expect you to be a man of your word."

He nodded solemnly. "Far be it from me to fail to meet the least of your expectations."

"Why did you come here?"

A shadow seemed to cross his face as the ebony curl he

had been holding slipped away and out of his grasp. Was it disappointment she read in his eyes, regret, or merely somber acceptance? Whatever it was, the emotion was quickly replaced by his customary expression of aloof, mocking superiority.

"Curiosity, I suppose." He gave a light shrug. "I wanted to see what you do when you are away from me. You don't pass the hours pining away for my company, I gather?"

"Hardly." She gestured to the scattered papers that surrounded her. "I am far too busy with my work. Now that you see how I spend my time, I would think you'd find me perfectly boring."

"You would be wrong."

He held her gaze for a long moment, then shifted his attention to the papers she had indicated. "Do you mind?" he asked, gesturing to the stack of old playbills, ticket stubs, and various debris her parents had collected over the years.

As Katya had already sorted through the pile and knew it held nothing incriminating, she shook her head. "Not at all," she replied, giving him leave to satisfy his curiosity. While his attention was thus absorbed, she deftly tapped the scroll into her reticule, then placed the diary inside as well. This accomplished, she watched him as he sorted through the stack of flyers commenting on her mother's beauty, her father's renown, and the reputations of the famous people for whom her family had performed.

Nicholas surprised her by asking, "Do you enjoy your work?"

"My work?"

"This." He nodded toward the props and costumes that filled the backstage. "Donning the guise of the Goddess of Mystery and performing for a new audience night after night."

She shrugged. "I take pride in my work and try to put on the best show I'm capable of. I suppose there's a great deal of satisfaction in that." She thought for a moment and continued, "I suppose I never thought about it in those terms before. It's simply something I've always done. I've performed onstage with my parents since I was a child performing simple feats of prestidigitation."

"Pre . . . ?"

"Sleight of hand," she replied, demonstrating as she spoke by deftly plucking the flyer from his hand, closing it tightly in her fist as though to wad it up into a tight ball, then opening her palm with a dramatic flourish to show that the flyer had disappeared completely.

"Very nice," he acknowledged.

To Katya's surprise, Nicholas was a relaxed, amusing conversationalist. Their discussion drifted this way and that as she shared her childhood memories of life onstage. She found herself revealing how blessed she had been by her parents' love and affection, but how she had resented their busy schedules and having to constantly share them with the public. His questions were insightful rather than judgmental and showed a remarkable amount of both understanding and genuine interest.

"We performed before heads of state, queens and kings, children in foundling homes, and the sickly in hospitals," she finished. "The audience didn't matter, as long as there was an audience. My parents thrived on it; it was in their blood."

"Where are they now?"

Katya's gaze moved automatically to a dark corner where a tall glass-and-wood booth stood by itself. A shudder ran through her as she looked at the ominous underwater contraption. "They died while performing onstage here in Monaco," she replied. "They had added a new escape routine to their act but the trick somehow went awry."

Nicholas looked aghast. "What happened?"

"I'm not sure. It was a relatively simple trick, but apparently the escape latch refused to give."

"You weren't here at the time?"

"No. As I grew older I functioned as a manager for my parents, rather than appearing with them onstage. I was in London when it happened, making arrangements for their next tour."

A look of quiet sympathy showed in his eyes. "That must have been awful for you."

"It was." Katya hesitated for a moment, then continued, "I suppose the hardest thing to accept is the permanence of it all—that and the regret. The words that went unspoken, the letters unsent . . ."

"I know."

Emboldened by the genuine understanding she read in his face, she admitted softly, "In truth though, I found a strange sense of comfort in the way they died. I think they would have preferred to die like that. Onstage, performing, locked in each other's arms." She let out a small, wistful sigh. "My parents were so gloriously happy together," she said, "so in love. That was the real magic they shared. I doubt I'll ever find anything like that."

"Why?"

"I'm not certain I have what it takes."

"And what does it take?"

"Fearlessness," she replied succinctly. "It takes a strength I don't possess to abandon one's fears and doubts and to love that completely. To trust another person with your very soul."

An odd, intent look marked his features as he studied her. "We all have fears, Katya."

"I can't imagine you being afraid of anything," she said. At his silence, she looked away, embarrassed by the sentiments she was expressing so freely. "I sound foolish, don't I?"

"You sound inexperienced," he corrected gently. "Naive. But there's no shame in that."

Although she understood rationally that he had not meant his words as either a challenge or a slur, she couldn't help but take them that way. "Once I've gained the vast experience that you possess," she said, "what will I have learned?"

"Not to expect so much—from yourself or anyone else."

"What inspired advice. Is that what made your relationship with Allyson Whitney so extraordinary?"

He looked surprised—and distinctly displeased. "Who told you about Allyson?"

"Corrina Jeffreys."

"I see."

Nicholas's expression abruptly sobered. Katya had meant to encourage him to speak about himself. Instead, she had spoiled the moment completely. The intimacy they had shared was over.

"Speaking of the informative Miss Jeffreys," he said, "she is hostessing a shooting party this afternoon. I thought it might be wise if we make an appearance."

"Should I return to the villa and change my gown?"

He gave her attire a cursory glance. "You look lovely."

Katya knew a perfunctory compliment when she heard one, but she let it go, considering the question herself. She wore a simple white linen blouse with a square neckline that had been minimally adorned with lace. Her full skirt was tailored in rich navy cotton. It was a simple ensemble, but not unattractive. Fortunately she had thought to complete the outfit with her most fetching hat. The straw bonnet had a broad brim that turned up in front to frame her face. It was trimmed with white ostrich feathers and pink satin roses; a length of pink satin secured it beneath her chin. It gave her otherwise plain attire a festive look.

"When do you want to leave?" she asked.

He stood and offered her a hand in rising. "Now, if you're ready."

"Very well."

She led the way through the cluttered backstage area, leaving via the performers' exit. They stepped outside and were immediately bathed in the light and warmth of the brilliant Mediterranean sun. Nicholas took her arm and guided her to the side of the building. He stopped before a magnificent black gelding that stood tethered in the shade.

Understanding immediately that he meant for the two of them to ride together to Corrina Jeffrey's afternoon gathering, she regarded the animal dubiously. "I assumed you had a carriage waiting."

"Consider it romantic."

"I consider it unseemly."

He smiled. "My prim, proper little gypsy." Without giving her time for further protest, he closed his hands around her waist, and lifting her as easily as he might a child, settled her in a sidesaddle position on the gelding's back. Then he mounted behind her with one fluid movement and gathered the reins in his hands.

As he tapped his heel against the gelding's flank, Katya's heart gave a funny little leap and her pulse seemed to race through her veins. Although she was literally wrapped within her enemy's arms, she felt ludicrously safe and secure. In the silence that surrounded them, she was acutely aware of every last detail: the steady drumming of the horse's hooves against the dirt road; the riot of purple and indigo flowers blooming on the hillside; the heat of the sun on her skin and the gentle breeze against her cheeks; the taste of salty sea air on her lips.

The way Nicholas's warm, silky breath fanned her neck.

The feel of his thighs pressed against hers.

The spicy, masculine scent of his skin.

Her reticule tapped against her leg as they rode, causing her thoughts to turn to the scroll and journal contained within. As she considered the documents, the words of Sacha, her ancient ancestor, drifted through her mind.

He is not the barbarous heathen of whom I had been warned.

Nine

$\mathcal{T}$he isolated village of Roquebrune sat perched on a craggy slope overlooking the sparkling vista of Cap Martin. The dwellings and stores that comprised the medieval town were built on top of rocks or dug into the sides of them. The castle that crowned the site had also been constructed of stone. Connecting everything was an intricate labyrinth of narrow streets and alleys that burrowed their way about in all manner of tunnels, arches, and covered passageways.

"The castle is one of the oldest in France," Nicholas said to Katya as he guided Avignon up the steep path that led around the perimeter of the village. "Some say it dates back to the tenth century." His thighs brushed against hers as he shifted to allow her a better view of the ancient fortress. "This is one of my favorite places in all of Monaco. In all of France, for that matter."

She silently absorbed the information, wondering what it told her about the man. The castle was ruggedly beautiful, yet profoundly isolated from the surrounding villages and towns. Viewed from a distance, it might even seem unreachable.

"Do we have time for a tour?" she asked.

"Perhaps on our return. The keep is best viewed at twilight in any case."

She watched with regret as they rounded a bend and the fanciful, storybook-like castle disappeared from view. Determined to get a better look, she made a silent vow to hold Nicholas to his word and return later that afternoon for a proper tour.

They rode away from the village, moving in a smooth,

rolling canter toward a rocky promontory that was flanked by a grove of cypress, olive, and pine. An assortment of fashionable carriages and elegant mounts was stationed beneath the trees. But other than a collection of well-dressed groomsmen who attended the horses and buggies, there appeared to be no one about.

Nicholas reigned Avignon to a halt beside the other mounts. He dismounted, then turned to help Katya. Before she could ask where the other members of the party had assembled, a burst of gunfire exploded in the air around them, shattering the idyllic silence of the site. Katya jumped and gave an involuntary gasp.

Not the slightest bit disturbed by the sudden explosion of gunfire, Nicholas continued his task of tying the reins to the branch of a cypress tree. That accomplished, he turned and took her elbow. "It appears they've started the shoot without us," he said once the volley had stopped.

Following the noise of the gunfire, he led her to a steep, rocky path that appeared to plummet off the edge of a cliff. The sharp rise led to a grassy plateau that jutted out over the rocky cliffs. There the shooting party had gathered. Katya scanned the assembled group of thirty or so, recognizing most of the faces from last evening's gala at the Duke of Westerly's.

"As you can see, ours is a rather haughty, incestuous group," Nicholas said. "Rarely do we allow anything as invigorating as a new member into our midst."

"You must have been reading my mind."

"That's one of the reasons your presence caused such a stir last night."

"Really? And what were the other reasons?"

Although she had meant the question as nothing more than a bit of conversational rhetoric, an odd expression crossed Nicholas's face, telling her that the answer might have more significance than she suspected. Before she could pursue the topic further, however, Corrina Jeffreys detached herself from the men with whom she had been speaking and made her way toward them.

Katya watched her approach. The woman looked almost absurdly feminine in a frothy gown of pink satin that was trimmed with a profusion of delicate cream lace. She wore a matching broad-brimmed hat and pink satin shoes, and she carried a parasol made from the same delicate lace as that which adorned her gown. Her golden hair framed her face in a profusion of neat, shiny curls. Katya realized how disheveled her own hair must look in comparison, how simple and plain her clothing. But she restrained the urge to lift her hand to her hair and fuss. It would be useless to try to attain the air of smoothly coiffed perfection that seemed to come so naturally to the other woman.

"Why, Nicholas," Corrina cooed, "I'm so delighted you could make it."

"Corrina," he replied. Taking her offered hand, he pressed it briefly to his lips, then let it drop. "You remember Miss Alexander," he prompted, drawing Katya closer to his side.

"Of course. How good of you to attend my little gathering, Miss Alexander," she said, somehow managing to make her words sound both hollow and gracious at the same time. A call to gather for the next shooting match saved Katya from the pretense of summoning a polite response.

Corrina clasped her hands together like an excited child and turned with an animated smile toward a series of shallow caves carved within the face of the cliff wall. "Do watch closely," she urged, wrapping her delicate hand tightly around Nicholas's arm. "I think you'll find this most exciting. Lord Tenley has the most kills for the day—fifty something, I believe—but Viscount Geffert is not far behind. Rumor has it that they wagered over ten thousand pounds on the match."

Katya followed the direction of the other woman's gaze. She saw a dozen men standing with their backs to the cliff, their rifles hanging loosely at their sides.

"Take aim," shouted a portly, middle-aged man whose black-and-red uniform distinguished him as some sort of gaming official.

The shooters obediently cocked their weapons and hefted them to their shoulders.

"Ready . . ." called the official.

A murmur of eager expectation ran through the crowd. Five young men with matching black-and-red jackets crouched down near the face of the cliff. Behind them, half-hidden within the dim recesses of the caves, were a series of huge bamboo cages.

"Release!"

The young men sprang to life. They slapped open the bars of the cages, then leaped backward against the cliff face. From within the bamboo cages flew hundreds of doves, squawking in confusion as they flew blindly from the dim recesses of the caves into the bright, dazzling sunlight. They were greeted by blasts of gunshot as the shooters immediately commenced firing. The birds flew in chaotic circles with frantic urgency, disoriented by the smoke and barrage of loud, echoing shots. As the shooting progressed they dropped one by one, plummeting from the sky in a rain of blood and feathers. The doves that hadn't been killed instantly flopped about like fish on dry land.

Once the shooting died away, Corrina turned back to them with a satisfied glow on her face. "Remarkable, was it not? Such an exciting sport."

Rather than voice her disgust, Katya remained conspicuously silent.

"How does one determine who earns victory for each shot?" Nicholas asked. His tone was entirely impassive, giving no clue as to his true reaction to the spectacle they had just witnessed.

"The officials mark the rifle powder of each contestant with a colored dye. They'll check the birds now for traces of the dye, tabulate the results, and add these to the men's previous scores." As she spoke, the senior official and his five young assistants were already circulating among the dead and wounded birds.

Corrina let out a dramatic sigh. "It's the only way to tell, but it is rather tedious," she lamented, forming her lips into a pretty pout. She tucked her arm through Nicholas's and tugged him forward, neatly usurping Katya's place by his side. "Come," she said. "I suppose I ought to behave like a proper hostess and share you both with my other guests."

Nicholas took a step, then turned back with a frown when Katya remained where she was, unmoving. "Are you coming, Katya?"

"I'll be along shortly. I'd like to enjoy the view for a moment first."

Corrina sent her a cool smile. "Don't be long, Miss Alexander. You don't want to miss the next round of shooting."

Katya managed a polite nod and turned away without a word, moving down a rocky path that led to the cliffs. Oddly enough, she was thankful for the way Corrina had interposed herself between her and Nicholas, for she needed the distance to collect her thoughts. It felt as though the more time she spent with Nicholas, the less she behaved like herself. Normally her actions were prudent and sensible, perhaps even dull. But not now. For the first time in her life she was behaving wholly irrationally—and actually enjoying it. Even as she recognized the folly of her actions, she couldn't bring herself to change her course.

Beware the Maltese.

The warning was doing as much good as admonishing

Pandora not to open the box. She reminded herself that the Lord of Barrington was a direct descendant of her family's ancient enemy. That he was quite possibly dangerous. That he viewed her as nothing but a mildly amusing thief. None of it mattered. She seemed intent on flinging herself headlong into disaster, just as Sacha had done so many centuries ago.

As she reached the path's end, she found more than just a stunning view of the Mediterranean. Looming before her was an ancient, semicircular structure comprised of massive stone columns, each connected to the other by means of an ornately carved pediment. It appeared as though a chunk of the Parthenon had been transported to the shores of southern France and deposited on a cliff overlooking the sea.

Although such a find would normally have absorbed her complete attention, she discovered that her thoughts were curiously unfocused. She stared vacantly at the massive stone structure, circling aimlessly around it, but she couldn't come up with a single coherent resolution for her predicament. It seemed that all she was capable of was a jumble of simmering, misdirected emotions.

"Do watch your step, Miss."

Katya started and spun around as a tall, dark-haired man stepped out from behind the ancient structure. Her first thought was that Nicholas had followed her down the steep, rocky path. Once the man stepped out of the shadows, however, she realized that the resemblance was only superficial. Although the stranger shared Nicholas's height and coloring, his features were far less defined. He wore a pair of wire-rimmed spectacles not unlike her own and held a tattered book in his hand.

Sending her a rather bashful, apologetic smile, he said, "Forgive me if I startled you. I didn't intend to disturb your privacy, but you seemed rather preoccupied, and you continued to move closer and closer to the edge. . . ." He lifted one hand and gestured vaguely at her feet.

Katya glanced down to see that she had indeed moved precariously close to the edge of the cliff. "Oh," she said. "So I did. Thank you." She stepped back toward safer ground.

The stranger shifted awkwardly from foot to foot. After a long pause, he nervously blurted out, "This monument was erected to honor Emperor Augustus."

"Yes. I saw." She nodded toward the carvings that ran along the bottom of the structure.

"You read Latin?"

"Yes."

"How extraordinary."

She arched one brow in mild reproof. "You're surprised that a woman is capable of reading Latin?"

A look of stark dismay crossed his features. "Not at all," he stammered. "I didn't mean to suggest . . . I'm simply surprised that a guest of Corrina's would entertain an interest in the classics. I suppose I've become rather accustomed to being the odd man out. Do forgive my tactlessness."

His distress was so genuine and his apology so sincere that Katya immediately regretted putting him so ill at ease. Softening her tone, she said, "I don't believe we've met. My name is Katya Alexander."

He gave a polite bow. "Jeremy Cooke. It's an honor, Miss Alexander." He hesitated a moment, then said, "I believe I saw you arrive with Lord Barrington."

"Yes, I did. Is he a friend of yours?"

"A friend?" Jeremy Cooke echoed, looking both flustered and astounded at the suggestion. "No. Merely a passing acquaintance."

"I see."

An awkward silence fell between them. "Our fathers were well acquainted, however," he volunteered after a moment.

"Oh?"

Although her reply was meant as nothing more than a polite rejoinder, he immediately interpreted it as a request for more information.

"You see, my father believed he had uncovered scholastic evidence proving that King Arthur and his knights truly existed. His treatise on the subject was quite brilliant, really. He was a formidable talent in the arena of historical research. All he lacked was the funding necessary to prove his theories. Fortunately the senior Lord Barrington was generous enough to provide that funding."

"He acted as your father's benefactor," she surmised.

"In a manner of speaking, I suppose he did." He paused, fumbling for a moment with his spectacles. "But if you'll forgive me, my pride is such that I must protest the term *benefactor*. It has too much of a charitable ring to it. I prefer *investor*. For had my father succeeded in finding the remains of King Arthur's court, it would have been lucrative for them both."

"Did he find any evidence to support his theories?"

"Nothing conclusive. We were on the brink of some rather amazing discoveries when the senior Lord Barrington passed away. Unfortunately the current Lord Barrington canceled his family's financial support shortly thereafter."

She frowned. "Did Nicholas explain why?"

Jeremy Cooke gave a light shrug. "I suppose he thought the search was pure folly." He took a deep breath and sent her a reassuring smile. "Fortunately all is not lost. I've received quite a bit of interest from the historical society at Oxford College. They have indicated that they may be willing to undertake partial funding of my father's research."

Katya gave him a smile that she hoped conveyed both sympathy and encouragement. His plight was not unique among scholars, for there seemed to be a universal shortage of funds and support.

Searching for a way to continue their faltering conversation, she glanced toward the book he held. "I see you're reading Euripides."

"I am," he replied, shifting his attention to the thin volume. "Though in truth, I don't know why I bother. I've read him so many times I believe I could recite the lines verbatim without the benefit of the text before me."

She matched his soft smile with one of her own. "Which of his works is your favorite?"

Apparently this was all the encouragement Jeremy Cooke needed. He eagerly seized the question and embarked on a long-winded discourse detailing the relative merits of the ancient scholar's writings. Katya listened politely, nodding occasionally. Her gaze moved briefly over the man's attire as he spoke. It was well made, but showed signs of wear, suggesting a family that had once been affluent but had lately fallen on hard times. He reminded her of the countless young men she had met while traveling. Awkward, earnest, and enthusiastic. Scholarly, brilliant, and socially inept.

"My, how you do prattle on, Cooke," called a disdainful voice from their left.

Katya turned to see a tall, immaculately dressed man watching them. He stood with one shoulder propped against a tall stone column; his arms were crossed casually over his chest. His sandy-blond hair showed no sign of thinning, nor were there wrinkles around his steel-gray eyes. Katya guessed his age to be thirty years. Were it not for the expression of haughty amusement that marked his features he might have been handsome.

"It appears as though I'm interrupting," he said.

"Not at all," replied Jeremy Cooke. He took an automatic step away from Katya, as though they had been discovered standing too close.

The stranger pushed off from the column and moved

toward them. He sized Katya up with a ruler's glance, cool and thoughtful. "Aren't you forgetting your manners, Cooke?" he said after a moment, his gaze resting on Katya.

Jeremy Cooke fumbled uneasily with his book, like a student caught with his lesson incomplete. "I beg your pardon?"

"I believe an introduction is in order."

"Of course. Do forgive me." He nervously cleared his throat. "Miss Alexander, may I present Lord Philip Montrove. Lord Montrove, Miss Katya Alexander."

Montrove gave a low, gracious bow. "It's a pleasure, Miss Alexander."

Katya managed to summon a similarly polite reply, though in truth, she felt distinctly uneasy meeting the man.

"I believe I saw you last evening with Lord Barrington, did I not?" Montrove inquired.

"You did."

"How remiss of him to leave your side."

"Not at all," she replied coolly. "As you can see, I've found admirable companionship in Mr. Cooke. We were just enjoying a discussion on the works of Euripides, when you arrived."

"Were you? How very fascinating." He turned toward Jeremy Cooke. "Pray don't let me interrupt, Cooke. Do go on."

For an instant, Katya thought she caught a flash of quiet fury in Jeremy Cooke's dark eyes. But it must have been a reflection of the sun against his spectacles, for when he spoke his voice held nothing but the mild tone of a bashful scholar. "Perhaps another time."

Montrove smiled. "Yes. Perhaps another time."

A sharp volley of gunfire filled the air, drawing their attention back to the party that was proceeding without them.

"I see you're not participating in the contest, Cooke," Montrove remarked once the blast had died down.

A look of distaste crossed Jeremy Cooke's face. He shook his head. "I'm afraid that firearms are not my forte."

"Nor are they mine. Particularly when Lord Barrington is expected to attend and draw arms. The man does have a rather fearsome reputation, does he not?"

"I suppose he does."

"Deadly, one might say."

Thick silence hung between the two men as Cooke shifted uncomfortably. "Surely we can find a more suitable topic of discussion," he suggested, pointedly nodding his head in Katya's direction.

Montrove lifted his shoulders in an indifferent shrug. "It's only fair that the lady be warned."

"Warned? Deadly?" Katya interjected, irritated at having the conversation carry on in circles around her. "What dire words to use in conjunction with Lord Barrington."

"And yet curiously appropriate. He is a dangerous man." Montrove looked to Cooke for confirmation.

Jeremy Cooke studied the ground, looking as though he wanted to be anywhere else. "Those rumors are all unfounded, are they not?" he finally remarked. "Nothing was ever proven in a court of law."

Icy satisfaction glistened in Montrove's eyes. "How very true," he concurred with a sigh. "Nothing was ever proven in a court of law."

Katya had the impression that Philip Montrove had just neatly accomplished his goal—to plant seeds of doubt in her mind as to Nicholas's character and reputation. And, loath as she was to admit it, he had succeeded. But other than indulging his taste for malicious gossip, she wondered what he stood to gain by doing so.

"What a fascinating man the Lord of Barrington must be," she replied lightly, "to be surrounded by so much ru-

mor and innuendo. Particularly when he is not here to defend himself."

"Perhaps he will defend himself." Montrove said. His gaze
moved to a point just beyond her left shoulder, then returned to her. "Here comes Lord Barrington now."

Ten

*N*icholas strode across the rocky terrain to join the small group gathered at the base of the ancient monument. Deciding to forgo the customary rite of polite conversation, he exchanged cursory greetings with Montrove and Cooke and took Katya's elbow.

"If you gentlemen will excuse us," he said, "I promised Miss Alexander a tour of the castle before night falls."

He led her away from the monument and toward the ancient castle. After a brief walk they passed through a broad opening in the fortresslike walls and gained entrance to the keep itself. The narrow, cobbled streets were bustling with activity. Vendors stood in the arched doorways with carts of merchandise, calling out to the tourists who flocked around them. Painters attired in white smocks splashed oil across their canvasses at an almost furious pace, striving to capture the rich twilight hues before the colors faded into night.

They moved through the lively pedestrian traffic and up a series of steep stone steps. Finally they reached a tall rampart that overlooked the entire keep. From there the view stretched out across the rugged cliffs and gently sloping hills, continuing until the rich lavender and indigo of the horizon melted into the deep azure of the sea.

Katya let out a contented sigh and rested her elbows on the thick stone wall. "This is lovely," she sighed.

"Yes, isn't it?" he agreed, but he wasn't studying the horizon. Instead, his gaze was fixed on her. In the gently fading light, her complexion took on the warm glow of ivory satin. Her body was as slim and lithe as a young girl's, yet graced with the seductive curves of a grown woman. But of all

Katya's natural attributes, her eyes captivated him the most. Not just the rare lavender color or lush black lashes—although these were quite striking—but what he saw within her gaze. Her attempts to appear sophisticated notwithstanding, her eyes shone with wide-eyed wonder and childlike innocence. It gave her an air of artless vulnerability, despite the plucky confidence she tried to project.

As he studied her, a sharp gust of wind blew over the parapet, lifting her hat from her head and sending it skittering across the rough stone floor. Nicholas bent to retrieve the satin and straw creation.

"Thank you," she said with a flustered smile.

Her hand moved to her hair in what he assumed was an automatic attempt to smooth her wayward curls. Judging from the abundance of pins that secured it in place, she was constantly striving to control it. As he watched her, it occurred to him that he would love to see her hair fly free, to see it cascade unrestrained down her back in a riot of wanton, luxurious curls.

"Do you ever wear your hair down?" he asked.

"My hair? No, never—"

"You should."

He moved closer to her, so close that he could almost feel the heat of her skin. One rich, ebony spiral brushed his cheek, moving across the line of his jaw like a sweet, silken caress. "You should," he repeated. "It's a waste to hide something so lovely."

"That would hardly be proper."

Although he knew she meant her words as a prim rebuttal, her expression conveyed the opposite meaning. She tilted her head back and met his gaze with a look of burgeoning curiosity and breathless expectation, as open and trusting as a young child's. Unfortunately her expression of utter innocence awoke not only his latent desire, but something even more remarkable—and heretofore unknown—within him: his conscience.

He studied her for a long moment, then stepped abruptly back. "This was a mistake," he said curtly.

"You mean coming here?"

"No. I mean you."

She studied him blankly. "I don't understand."

He let out a sigh and raked his fingers through his hair, searching for the right words. "Perhaps I should have explained something to you at the very beginning. The society here in Monaco is worldly. My acquaintances, both men and women, tend to be profligate, informal, and sexually broadminded. They drink, cheat, lie, flaunt their wealth, and abuse their servants. Husbands ignore their wives and live with their mistresses, wives bear their lovers' children, and everyone involved behaves with sophisticated civility. You don't fit in."

"I see." An expression of startled embarrassment flashed through her expressive eyes, then she brought up her chin. "I'm sorry I disappoint you."

"You misunderstand me. I meant that as a compliment of the highest order."

"Did you?" she asked tightly.

"I did. There's an innocence about you that separates you from everyone else here. At first I thought that that was a tremendous advantage, for who would suspect you for a thief? Now I fear that that very quality will make you vulnerable to men like Montrove."

"Vulnerable in what way?"

A vision of Allyson's battered, lifeless body flashed through Nicholas's mind. But this was hardly the time to unburden himself by sharing that grim bit of background with Katya. He pushed the stark image away, saying simply, "He's a dangerous man—perhaps even deadly."

"How remarkable. He said the same thing about you."

A small, humorless smile curved his lips. "And what about Jeremy Cooke? Did he try to warn you away from me as well?"

"Actually, he tried to defend you."

"Really? How very gallant of him."

"You would do well to model yourself after Jeremy Cooke," she retorted. "I found him to be a perfect gentleman."

Nicholas gave a sharp laugh. "God, I can't imagine anyone more dull to emulate."

"Why did you cut off the funding for his research?"

"Because it was a waste of time and funds for everyone concerned."

"Your father didn't think so."

"My father is dead. The money he left is to be used at my discretion, and at my discretion only."

"You don't believe in science?"

"Yes, but not charity. If Cooke spent as much time working on his estate, rather than letting it fall down around his head, as he does begging for funds—"

"A scholar seeking patrons is hardly begging for funds."

Nicholas took a deep breath. "Can you tell me why we're having this idiotic debate?"

She studied him for a moment in surprise. "No, I can't," she said; then her lips curved in a slow, wavering smile. "That's not entirely true. I don't suppose there's a woman in the world who reacts well to being told she is completely unsuitable as a mistress—even when it is nothing but a ruse. If I reacted poorly, it was because my pride was wounded. It was foolish on my part."

Amazed at her candor, he replied gently, "Then you misunderstood me. You suit me too well, little gypsy. That's the problem."

"I don't understand."

"I can't protect you. Seeing you alone with Philip Montrove only underscored that fact."

"But I wasn't alone. Jeremy Cooke was with us the entire time."

"That doesn't signify," he said, dismissing her objection immediately. He thought for a moment, then asked, "Were you able to get close enough to Montrove to check to see if he held the scroll somewhere on his person?"

She sent him a look of amused disdain. "This was hardly the occasion for me to do so. I couldn't ask him to dance right there atop a windswept cliff, could I?"

"No, I suppose not," he concurred. He raked his fingers through his hair and turned away from her, staring blankly out over the sea.

"What is it?" she asked.

He shook his head, unable to define the restless impatience that suddenly consumed him. He couldn't shake the feeling that he was acting like a pawn in someone else's game. That the person who had the scroll was watching every move he made, and laughing. He felt as impotent as a caged animal pacing back and forth on display before the crowds in London's zoo.

When he had accompanied Katya to the Duke of Westerly's, he had positioned himself so that he could watch her every move. Today he had not been able to do so, and it had bothered him far more than he would have suspected. If they continued on the course they had set, there would be more moments when she would be alone with Montrove and others like him. More moments in which she would be entirely vulnerable. Perhaps no harm would come to her. Perhaps she would find the scroll and he would be able to clear his name. Perhaps everything would be all right.

But perhaps the person who had killed Allyson would make Katya his next victim.

On the heels of that sobering thought came the stark realization of what the proper course of action should be: send her away and search for the scroll alone. It was an honorable solution, but one that was highly impractical. Given Katya's talents at sleight of hand, she was far better suited to the task than he. And now that he had presented her to society at large as his mistress, it served both their interests to continue their pretense. But beneath this rationale lurked a purely selfish motive as well—a desire to keep her entirely to himself. His whimsical little thief pleased him far more than he ever would have guessed.

"You may consider me duly warned," she said, interrupting his thoughts. "If you can't protect me, I suppose I shall simply have to protect myself. Fortunately I'm twenty-three years old, so the task is not entirely unknown to me."

Pushing away his bleak worries, he turned back to her, forcing himself to match her breezy tone. "Twenty-three?" he echoed. "I had no idea you were so ancient."

"Indeed. Practically decrepit."

"On the shelf."

A thoughtful silence fell between them as they studied each other in wary hesitation, as though taking new measure. Her smile faded slightly and a somber light entered her eyes. "We seem to be forever at odds, don't we?"

He studied her in surprise. "Does it feel that way to you?"

"Generally, yes." She thought for a moment, then suggested, "Perhaps it's because we're trying to appear intimate when we really know so little about each other. I imagine that this would put a strain on anyone."

"I imagine so," he agreed, although he hadn't considered it at all. In truth, the thought that a man and a woman might need to know anything about each other in order to be intimate was rather astounding to him. He considered his relationship with Allyson Whitney. He had enjoyed her beauty, her style, and her expertise in bed. She, in turn, had enjoyed his company and his wealth. Allyson had spent her nights in bed with him and her days making the rounds of various milliners, couturiers, jewelers, and seamstresses, selecting a wide assortment of items she "simply could not live without" and sending the bills to him.

Although their relationship had seemed perfectly acceptable at the time, he could not imagine Katya falling into a similar role.

"What do you suggest we do to alleviate this strain?" he inquired.

"There's an old gypsy custom that says if you want to make an enemy your friend for life, you must trade secrets. That way you'll always have something to hold over the other."

A sardonic smile curved his lips. "How touching. A friendship based on fear, mistrust, and the ever-present threat of extortion."

"Are you saying you won't give it a try?" she retorted, a distinct glimmer of challenge in her eyes.

"Not at all. I have no doubt that this is the basis for some of mankind's most enduring relationships." He crossed his arms over his chest and leaned back against the parapet wall, giving her a polite nod. "Ladies first."

She thought for a moment, then an impish smile curved her lips. "I stole a lion when I was five years old."

Nicholas smiled. "Very impressive. I presume, however, that you mean a specimen from a taxidermist."

"No. A real lion," she insisted. At his dubious look, she admitted reluctantly, "Well, a three-day-old lion cub. My family was traveling with a circus troupe when the cub was born, and I decided he'd make the perfect pet. Unfortunately my parents didn't see things the same way—nor did the mother of the cub. I was forced to give him back."

"Is that how you began your life of crime?"

"My life of crime?" she echoed blankly. Suddenly, startled understanding dawned. "Oh—of course. My life of crime. Yes, that's where it began."

There was something artificial in her tone, but before he could consider it further, she sent him an overly bright smile and announced, "Now it's your turn. I want to hear a secret of yours."

He mentally reviewed the dark skeletons of his past, searching for something to share. He had secrets; far too many of them. But none that were suitable for her to hear. Finally he said, "I dislike goat cheese."

Her lips pulled down in a disappointed frown. "Surely you can do better than that."

He lifted his shoulders in a resolute shrug. "It appears that my life is far less extraordinary than your own."

"I highly doubt that."

"It's true."

She arched one dark brow, the expression of a stern schoolmistress on her face. "Very well. You leave me no choice but to discover a secret or two by myself." She stretched one thin, delicate arm in his direction. With the cool demeanor of a royal princess, she demanded imperiously, "Your palm, Lord Barrington."

"I thought you didn't believe in that sort of nonsense."

"I am not above resorting to desperate measures when the situation calls for it. As it happens, my mother was highly skilled in the art of palmistry. I may not have inherited her consummate talent, but I should be able to discern a thing or two."

The whole idea struck Nicholas as utter nonsense, but he complied nevertheless, if for no other reason than to bridge the physical distance between them.

"I trust you will share whatever dire fate you find there," he said.

"Certainly."

She took his large hand in her smaller one and turned it

this way and that, gently poking and prodding, tracing with her forefinger the lines that traversed his palm. A frown of intense concentration marked her features.

"You shall live a long life and never want for any material goods," she began slowly, in what he thought was disappointingly standard fortune-teller rote.

"You were close to your mother," she said, "but you lost her at an early age. Your father was quite domineering, almost brutal at times. Your relationship with him was formal and rather standoffish. Even so, he had a tremendous impact on your life."

Better, but not significant. She had probably learned that from the Comtesse or one of the household servants.

"You have an innate appreciation for objects of beauty," she continued. "You are not easily touched emotionally, but once your feelings are affected they run deep. You are profoundly loyal and set high standards for both yourself and others."

She turned his hand toward him and pointed toward a deep groove that ran diagonally across his palm. "Do you see this line?" she asked, a note of excitement in her voice. "That's the line of fate. As you can see, it crosses all areas of your life."

"Is that supposed to mean something?"

"Of course. That's extremely significant," she informed him gravely. "That means that destiny is intervening in your life—events are unfolding around you that have been fated to occur from the moment of your birth."

"I see," he replied, striving to match her somber tone.

He watched her as she searched his palm, feeling almost disappointed. For some reason he had expected to hear something unique from her, but obviously he had given her far more credit than was reasonable. Fortune-tellers were known for telling a person whatever he or she wanted to hear. Women who were unmarried were told they would soon discover true love. Men who were poor were assured they would find riches. The sick and crippled were given false promises of a speedy recovery. Clearly Katya was no different from anyone else who practiced the absurd art of palmistry.

But no sooner had that thought crossed his mind when her intent expression abruptly changed. A look of dark understanding and genuine dismay crossed her features. She let his palm drop and moved slightly away from him. Forcing a strained smile, she said, "That's all I see. As I told you, I'm not very good at this sort of thing."

Nicholas studied her curiously. Although he didn't possess any faith in palmistry, Katya obviously did. And whatever she had seen in his hand had upset her. He lightly placed his finger under her chin and drew her gaze up to meet his. "As I recall, we had a bargain," he reminded her. "You promised to tell me everything you read in my palm, no matter how appalling my fate may be."

"Very well," she sighed, her voice ringing with the tragic tone of a physician delivering a fatal diagnosis.

He bit back a smile. "Perhaps I had better sit down for this."

"A legacy of death has been passed on to you," she said bluntly, reflecting none of his teasing laughter. "You have tried to shield and protect others in the past, but no longer will you be able to do so. You have learned this lesson already. Those who surround you are shadowed by death."

Nicholas sobered. Her words were vague enough to be applicable to almost anyone, yet he couldn't deny the ominous ring of truth contained within her message.

"There is more," she said. "Do you want to hear it?"

"It seems I should."

She nodded and continued, "A man and a woman whom you believed to be close to you have returned your trust with treachery. The woman is no longer present in your life, but the man is. He has betrayed you in the past and will betray you again."

He studied her for a long moment, torn between disregarding her dire prophecy completely and foolishly allowing himself to be drawn in. Finally he succumbed to morbid curiosity and asked, "Can you tell me who the man is?"

"Your brother."

A shock of icy dread filled his belly. Although her words weren't entirely unexpected, it took him a minute to find his voice. In a tone of cool certainty, he replied, "My brother is dead."

"Is he?"

With that simple question Katya plunged directly to the heart of what had been troubling him for months. Tyler's death. Never had he been able to believe that Tyler would take his own life—if only for no other reason than that his younger brother had been far too selfish. Even when confronted with the evidence of Tyler's enormous gambling debts, he still couldn't quite convince himself that Tyler would have been in such despair as to have taken his own life. It just didn't fit.

But if that were the case, where was Tyler now? The question loomed before him, large and unanswerable.

He reined in his errant thoughts, surprised at how deeply Katya's words had affected him. Short of confessing all and giving her a full history of recent events, there was little left for him to say. He decided therefore that his best solution was to return their conversation to its previous light tone.

"Fascinating," he remarked. "But I was hoping you could tell me whether I should wager on black or red at the casino this evening."

Taking her cue from him, the somber expression that had darkened her features slowly vanished. "I'm afraid that wasn't clear," she replied with a soft shrug.

"And what about you?" he asked. "Now that we know

that my own future is so decidedly grim, dare we check to see what the fates have in store for you?"

She shook her head. "It's impossible for me to read my own palm."

"Then let me try."

He reached for her hand and captured it before she could protest. He turned it this way and that, tracing the lines that etched her palm with one finger, just as she had done. "This is most interesting," he finally remarked.

"What do you see?"

"You did a great deal of traveling when you were younger."

Her lips curved in a small, knowing smile. "How incredibly intuitive."

"You have a remarkable talent in sleight of hand and perform well before an audience."

"Amazing. Tell me more."

"I see a man in your future. A tall man with dark hair and an obscene amount of wealth. He has a scandalous reputation, which he no doubt deserves. He gambles, he drinks, and he has been known to engage in empty, licentious affairs. He is harsh, cynical, quick to judge, and at times unbearably arrogant and opinionated. But despite his many faults, there may still be some redeeming quality lurking within the blackness of his soul. You haven't decided yet whether or not you should trust him. You should."

"Why does it seem that my fortune panders to your own base interests?"

He feigned a look of innocent surprise. "Does it?"

"I amuse you."

"You fascinate me," he corrected, astonished at having said it, yet meaning it sincerely.

She gave a sharp, startled laugh and pulled her hand free from his grasp. "You must fascinate rather easily."

"Not at all, little gypsy."

He reached out and gently stroked his fingers along the velvety skin of her jaw. The gesture was entirely unplanned, yet almost unavoidable, as though his hand were moving of its own volition. Katya softly gasped in surprise but she did not pull out of his reach. Her lips parted slightly and her eyes widened as she watched him with a look of open anticipation. She stared at him without moving, as though caught in the same spell of profound sexual awareness that had fallen over him.

"Kiss me," he said.

Her startled gaze flew to his. "What?"

"Kiss me, Katya." When she didn't move, he continued smoothly, "We can't have you appearing too innocent, now, can we?"

"I thought you said that my appearance of innocence was my greatest strength."

"True. But there is such a thing as carrying it too far. A chaste and virtuous mistress—how very appalling. Think of my poor reputation. People will wonder what I'm not doing. Or worse, if I *am* doing something, why I'm doing it so badly."

A shaky smile curved her lips. "You have a remarkable way of rationalizing, don't you?"

"Is it always this difficult to coax a kiss from you?" he countered, then a thought occurred to him. "Do I frighten you?" he asked, searching her eyes.

In the wake of Allyson's death and the scandal that surrounded him, he had developed a reputation as a possessive, passionate lover. A man of dark moods and intermittent fits of rage and jealousy. As a result, anxious mothers kept their daughters protectively removed from his presence, despite the potent lure of his wealth and title. Other women found the very air of death and danger that surrounded him sexually exciting. It sickened him, but he understood it.

Katya's expression told him she hadn't considered that at

all. "I don't think you're as dangerous as you pretend to be," she said softly. "Everyone else may believe it, but I don't. You're really not so terribly frightening."

"Maybe you just don't know me well enough."

"Maybe." Her voice came out slightly breathless, tinged with a husky timbre of desire.

"Touch me," he commanded softly.

She blinked up at him as though confused by his words. Finally a look of skittish understanding showed in her expression. She swallowed hard and tentatively raised one small, delicate hand, studying him as though he were a rabid wolf who might at any moment decide to turn on her. Moving with cautious deliberation, she placed her palm on his chest. The steady beat of his heart instantly quickened. He could feel the heat of her skin through the light linen of his shirt, feel his muscles tense in response to her touch.

Nicholas felt a slight shudder run through him as she brushed her hand lightly over his rib cage, as though her touch were giving life and breath to his body. She traced her hand experimentally over his chest, down the rippled muscles of his stomach and back up to the broad lines of his shoulders. She moved with deliberate care, completely absorbed in her task. Although he doubted it was deliberate on her part, she was teasing him and enticing him in a way that was far more arousing than the most blatant sexual performance of a more sophisticated lover.

Unable to hold back any longer, he wrapped his arm around her and pulled her tightly to him. He lowered his head, crushing her lips beneath his own. Using the pressure of his jaw, he coaxed her lips apart and thrust his tongue inside her mouth, tasting and exploring the sweet depths. There was no finesse in his motions, no loverlike gentleness. His need was too urgent.

After a shocked moment, Katya returned his embrace with a fervor that shook him to his very soul. She wrapped her arms around his neck and pressed herself against him. Her breasts were crushed against his chest, her hips locked against his. She mimicked the rhythm of his kiss, matching the play of his tongue with a fiery ardor that spread a slow heat burning through his veins.

The seducer was quickly becoming the seduced. Nicholas pulled his mouth from hers and let out a soft groan, burying his face in her neck. Katya softly sighed and let her head fall back, giving him greater access to her soft, creamy flesh. He nuzzled the tender skin beneath her ear, then pressed a fervent line of kisses along her collarbone. As he did, a slight tremor ran through her limbs. She clung to his shoulders as though she would otherwise topple over backward.

His prim little gypsy was a wealth of contradictions. Her responses were entirely genuine; no smooth veneer of worldly sophistication masked her need. That realization made him want her even more. He moved his hand along her thigh, against the rustling softness of her skirts. He captured her tiny waist, then lightly traced her rib cage. When his fingers brushed against her breast, however, Katya stiffened abruptly and drew back.

She studied him with a look of startled awareness, as though suddenly conscious of where they were and what was happening between them. A deep rose blush stained her cheeks as she lifted one hand and nervously brushed back her hair. Then she meticulously smoothed her skirt and blouse as if regaining her dignity could only be accomplished by removing any trace of Nicholas's hands.

She took a deep breath and confidently announced, "That won't happen again."

He crossed his arms over his chest and leaned back against the parapet wall. "Won't it?"

"Certainly not. And I would appreciate it if you—" She stopped short as her arm brushed against her reticule and knocked it over.

Nicholas shot forward, capturing the tapestry pouch an instant before it tumbled off the wall and into the sea below.

Katya paled and lunged toward him. "Give that back!" she demanded breathlessly.

He had been about to do exactly that. But her panicked demeanor made him hesitate. He held her reticule just out of her grasp, studying her curiously. "Of course," he said slowly. "What did you think I was going to do?"

She searched his face, then lifted her shoulders in a bored shrug, as though forcing herself to assume a posture of cool indifference. "Nothing," she said carelessly. It would have been an adequate performance, had her eyes not given her away. Her gaze moved from him to her reticule with a look that bordered on nervous terror.

"It's heavy," he commented, watching her face as he weighed the reticule in his palm.

She licked her lips and swallowed hard.

He smiled. "Have you been pilfering through the pockets of Corrina's guests?"

"Have I—? Yes. I have."

"Indeed? How very enterprising of you. Perhaps I should check inside and make certain that nothing has been damaged."

"Go right ahead," she invited tremulously.

"Very well," he rejoined, calling her bluff. He pulled apart the strings that sealed the opening and lifted his hand.

She drew in a deep breath, as though bracing herself for the worst.

Although she had definitely provoked his curiosity, looking inside seemed an undeniable breach of the meager trust they had established. If she was hiding something from him, he would eventually discover it. To force the issue now was wholly unnecessary. Moreover, it occurred to him that if she was lying, he would infinitely prefer that she divulge the truth willingly. With these thoughts in mind, he abruptly dropped his hand and returned her reticule.

"On second thought," he said, "I'll let you keep your little secrets to yourself." He paused for a moment, then finished significantly, "For now."

Eleven

They say the DuValentis are capable of great evil.

I do not believe it. Mother tells me I am a fool to give my trust so freely. She says the signs foretell much grief should the union between our families occur. She harps upon Father to disavow his pledge giving my hand in marriage to a DuValenti. Father will not break his word, of course, and they argue more fiercely every day.

No one seeks my opinion, but I am glad Father will not listen to her. Dare I admit it? Twice I have stolen away to meet Marco DuValenti in private. He seems as anxious to know his future bride as I am to know my future groom. At first his size and strength frightened me: his reputation as a warrior is quite fierce. But now that I know him better, I see a gentleness in him that no one else can see. Today he told me a story of magic faeries that live in the forest and dance atop toadstools when the moon is full. He smiled when I laughed at his childish tales. Then he kissed me.

Mother is wrong. Only good will come of this union.

*K*atya set aside the journal of Sacha Rosskaya with a sigh. So much hope and innocence wasted, she thought. Her ancient ancestor had clearly harbored nothing but faith and affection toward her future husband. In return, she had been rewarded with treachery and death.

Yet even as that bitter conclusion formed in her mind, another thought occurred to her. What kind of man would entertain his future bride with tales of dancing faeries, especially if his true intention was to betray her family and rob them of their lands and wealth? If their union was already a fait accompli, why would he bother to woo her with stolen kisses? That sounded more like a man intent on winning his betrothed's heart than on doing evil.

Katya wrapped the brittle parchment in a soft cotton cloth and returned it to its hiding place in the bottom of her trunk, which had been transferred from the theater to Nicholas's home after her performance that evening. Once the ancient documents were secreted away she turned toward the window and stared out over the moonlit gardens. A soft breeze stirred her filmy white dressing gown and gently caressed her skin. It was past midnight and a heavy stillness echoed through the villa. The servants were long since abed. The only sound was the faint chiming of the clocks downstairs.

Despite the lateness of the hour, she was too restless to consider sleep. A nervous energy gripped her and would give her no peace. The afternoon she had spent with Nicholas still seemed to hold her in its spell. Like a wave crashing again and again against the shore, her every thought turned incessantly back to him.

She had heard all her life that the DuValentis were evil. That they had stolen the Stone of Destiny from the Rosskayas, thereby setting in motion a bloody feud that had lasted for centuries. That the Stone rightfully belonged to her family and that it was her duty to retrieve it. Initially she had used these rationalizations to justify her deception, and for a time it had worked. But no longer.

It would be so easy to lose herself completely in Nicholas Duvall, just as she had nearly done that afternoon. Was she truly so weak that it took nothing more than a few stolen kisses to break her resolve? Or was there something greater between her and Nicholas, some fated destiny toward which she was being inexorably pulled?

The high-pitched screeching of a bat fluttering in the trees outside her window interrupted her thoughts. Glancing outside, she saw that the light scattering of clouds she had noted earlier had been swept away by the soft spring breeze. The sky was inky black and filled with thousands of twinkling stars that seemed to beckon her outside. Her room suddenly seemed suffocating, too small to contain the enormity of her thoughts.

Eager to escape, she drew on a dressing robe and fastened the sash tightly around her waist. She slipped out the bedroom door and into the quiet of the hallway. No candles or gas lamps were lit, but the soft glow of moonlight trailing in through the windows gave her ample light by which to see. She padded softly down the grand circular stair that led from the bedchambers to the formal receiving rooms below.

Once she reached the lower level she turned to her right, intent on retreating to the rear gardens. She moved in that direction, but found herself stopping outside Nicholas's study. Periodically she had heard Nicholas working within, presumably taking care of correspondence or other personal affairs. At other times the door was shut but the room sounded empty. Now the door was opened wide. She hesitated, reluctant to invade his privacy, but curiosity loomed too large for her to resist. After glancing twice over her shoulder to assure herself that no one else was about, she stepped cautiously inside.

The room was thoroughly masculine with thick tables made of dark woods and chairs upholstered in rich burgundy leather. Bookcases filled with leather-bound volumes. An enormous desk cluttered with papers. She tiptoed toward the desk and glanced at the papers. The documents covered a wide range of concerns ranging from shipping and insurance, freight and bills of lading, to other mundane business affairs. The ledgers looked as though they had been carefully scrutinized, for a series of small check marks were penned beside the columns. It occurred to her for the first time that

Nicholas actually worked to maintain his wealth. Until that moment, she thought it had all just been handed to him. Like most men of his stature, she assumed he would leave the running of his business affairs to others. Apparently not.

Other than that surprising discovery, there was not much for her to see. She turned to leave and was stopped by two enormous oil portraits staring down at her.

Her eyes moved first to an enormous portrait of a man sitting astride a huge black stallion. He wore a dramatic black cape lined with deep crimson satin, and it billowed about him as though stirred by a savage wind. She knew at once that the man was Nicholas's father, for the resemblance between the two was striking. Like Nicholas, he was large and powerfully built. He had the same dark hair and aristocratic features, the same piercing, coal-black gaze. But unlike the cool, sardonic expression Nicholas usually wore, his father's mouth was turned down in a disapproving frown, as though the world didn't quite live up to his standards. There was a subtle harshness and lofty arrogance about him that the artist had managed to capture. Katya guessed it was no idle coincidence that his portrait had been painted from a perspective that forced the viewer to look up. The elder Lord of Barrington was clearly a man of wealth and stature, but—if the painting was any guide—a man devoid of kindness. She gave a slight shudder and turned to the second portrait.

Again the dominant figure was Nicholas's father. He stood behind two immaculately dressed boys, his hands resting firmly on their shoulders. Once more the family resemblance made it obvious that they were his sons. Her gaze moved first to the elder of the two brothers. Nicholas looked about twelve. His expression, if it could be described at all, was almost forlorn. His eyes were curiously empty, his features set in a look of grave responsibility. Katya's heart panged at the look of such stark maturity on the face of so young a child.

Her gaze moved next to his brother. Unlike Nicholas, the younger boy's lips were curved in a small, slightly superior smile. His expression was almost haughty, as though he were accustomed to being given whatever he wanted. Their father was standing slightly closer to him, perhaps unconsciously signaling his favorite. Despite that prejudice, the hand resting on Nicholas's shoulder wore the thick band of gold and onyx that bore the sign of the Maltese, sending an unmistakable message as to which of his sons would inherit the DuValenti legacy.

Katya turned away from the portraits and stepped quietly from the room. She moved through the tall glass doors that led from the informal parlor to a stone-and-masonry patio outside. Continuing away from the house, she moved down a wide set of stairs until she reached the formal lawn. Once there, she felt a tremendous sense of freedom and relief, as though a burden she had been wrestling had somehow been lifted.

The lush grass felt cool and spongy beneath her bare feet, luxuriously decadent. A gentle breeze caressed her face and arms and caused her robe and dressing gown to flutter about her. The gardens were bathed in the soft silver glow of the moon, offering an enticing invitation to enter and stroll about. Katya did just that. She wandered along the flagstone path in a seemingly endless maze, moving deeper and deeper into the overgrown gardens. An exotic array of plants and shrubs surrounded her, filling the air with their rich floral perfume.

She took a step toward the gazebo when a movement near one of the benches made her catch her breath. She heard the soft brush of fabric against the stone and realized at once that someone was sitting inside. Katya hesitated where she stood, halfway up the low wooden steps that led within. Her first thought was that it was Nicholas, that he had somehow followed her through the gardens without her realizing it. But the voice that spoke quickly dispelled that irrational notion.

"Are you entering, Miss Alexander, or do you prefer to stand there all night?"

Katya instantly recognized the imperious voice as that belonging to the Comtesse de Fiorini. "No, I . . ." she began, somewhat taken aback. She lifted her hand from the railing and took a step away from the gazebo. "Forgive me. I didn't mean to disturb your solitude," she murmured.

"Nonsense. Obviously you were intending to sit down. I should hate to think that the mere knowledge of my presence would render you incapable of enjoying the night air."

A small smile touched Katya's lips at the undeniable ring of challenge contained in the Comtesse's words. Boldly deciding to accept her offer, she moved up the steps and settled herself on the bench opposite the older woman. "Thank you," she said. "It is lovely tonight, is it not?"

The Comtesse ignored her greeting and raised her lorgnette, her dark gaze indicating clear disapproval of Katya's clothing. Or lack thereof, as Katya was attired in nothing but her nightgown and dressing robe. She self-consciously crossed her ankles and tucked her bare feet under her gown, wondering why she constantly found herself at such a disadvantage with the woman. Despite the lateness of the hour the Comtesse was dressed in a regal walking gown of deep forest green complete with hat and gloves, as though she were expecting company for tea at any moment.

"It appears as though something disturbed your sleep," the Comtesse de Fiorini observed dryly.

Refusing to be baited, Katya replied, "Actually, I found I couldn't sleep at all. I thought a walk through the gardens might relax me."

"Ah."

Silence fell between them. After a moment, Katya ventured, "And what about you? Were you unable to sleep as well?"

"One has less need for sleep as one grows older. I suppose it's God's way of allowing us more time to look back and reflect upon life."

"Perhaps that's why they say our elders are so wise."

"Hogwash. I hear nothing from my peers but the same tired opinions, the same foolish gossip, the same dull lamenting over idiotic schemes and wasted opportunities. There is no wisdom at all, nothing to show for the years they have been on this earth but profoundly wrinkled skin, bad teeth, and creaking joints."

Katya bit back a smile. "I see."

The Comtesse stomped her cane on the ground in a militaristic gesture that uniquely suited her. "So what do you think of the gardens, Miss Alexander?" she demanded briskly.

"They're lovely, truly."

"I quite agree. They were the work of Nicholas's mother. My brother oversaw the construction of the house and the setting up of its furnishings, but it was Marianne who planned the gardens." She paused for a moment, as though lost in silent reminiscence. "She was constantly out here puttering. My brother thought it was beneath her. He directed her to leave the work to the gardeners and staff, but Marianne couldn't resist. She tried to stand idly by but eventually she succumbed to the lure of the soil, snatching up a weed here, planting a shrub there. Nicholas and Tyler used to love puttering along beside her, pulling up worms and digging holes."

"Tyler?"

"Nicholas's younger brother."

Katya's thoughts immediately turned to the portrait of the young, impish boy she had seen in the study. "Were he and Nicholas very close?" she asked.

"Close?" the Comtesse repeated thoughtfully. "Perhaps as young boys, yes. Unfortunately they became quite estranged as they grew older. Tyler had tremendous potential, but I suppose in the end he was too much like their father. Selfish, profligate, reckless, far too arrogant for his own good. His reputation as a notorious rogue preceded him wherever he went."

Katya arched one dark brow. "It appears that that reputation runs rampant among the men in this family."

The Comtesse sent her a disapproving frown. "I take it you are referring to the ridiculous title that is whispered behind Nicholas's back."

"The Lord of Scandal?"

"Yes, that bit of irresponsible nonsense."

"It was Nicholas himself who warned me of his reputation. But from what I've heard, it's well deserved."

"You may also encounter fools who will try to convince you that the world is flat. I suggest you not believe everything you are told, Miss Alexander."

"You are saying that your nephew is a perfect gentleman?"

"Hardly. How dreadfully boring." She thought for a moment, then continued in a tone of somber reflection, "It is almost impossible to say anything completely correct about Nicholas; it is equally difficult to say anything entirely erroneous. He is not an easy man to know, but well worth the effort should you care to try."

"I'm afraid you mistake my place in this household," Katya replied. "I'm here to see if I can assist in recovering the scroll, that's all."

The Comtesse dismissed that with an impatient wave of her hand. "The scroll itself is of little importance. Surely that is clear even to you by now. What Nicholas seeks are answers."

"And you believe I can provide them?"

The older woman studied her in silence for a long moment. "Perhaps. I'm glad you're here in any case, Miss Alexander. For Nicholas's sake. In my opinion he has suffered unnecessarily—both at the hands of society at large, and because of his own feelings of guilt regarding recent events."

"Nicholas has been unhappy?" she asked, unable to reconcile any weakness with the strong, opinionated man she had come to know.

"Burdened," his aunt corrected with a stern frown. "Only the truly self-pitying allow themselves to be unhappy." She paused, then continued curtly, "You are attracted to him, are you not?"

Katya's brows shot skyward. "I hardly—"

"You should be," the imperious older woman informed her. "In my day a man like Nicholas would have been considered quite a catch, regardless of the lurid rumors that surround him."

"I suppose great wealth is a rather potent lure."

"I am not speaking of his wealth and you know it," the Comtesse countered sharply. She paused a moment, then continued with an imperious thump of her cane, "I am an old woman, but I have learned a thing or two about men in my time. Allow me the indulgence of imparting a bit of unrequested advice—advice that will doubtless go unheeded, but I give it to you anyway. Character is what matters most. I would say that this is the ultimate test of any man who walks this earth. Character. Nicholas has that in abundance."

"Does he?" Katya remarked. "How very reassuring. Now I can sleep through the night."

The Comtesse sent her a look of cool reproach. "There are far better things to do with the night than sleep through it. If you haven't learned that by now, Miss Alexander, perhaps it is time you do."

Katya blushed and looked away, uncertain as to how to react to that astonishing statement. She had ventured outside to clear her thoughts, but now her head was swimming with even more questions. She released a soft sigh and stood, moving to the battered wooden railing that encircled the gazebo. As she stared out at the gardens, she realized for the first time that the roses covering the latticework were white. Scores of tiny white rosebuds clung to the thorny vines.

"These roses remind me of Nicholas," she said. "Each time he's given me a flower, it's been a white rose. Yet I can't look at a white rose without remembering a bit of the gypsy lore I heard as a child. My mother told me that a white rose symbolized secrets kept between two people. She said the rose was never given—or received—without a cost."

"Indeed?" The Comtesse mulled over her words. "It may surprise you to know that we English are not without a bit of whimsy of our own when it comes to botany. I seem to recall that Marianne shared a word or two with me regarding the flower as well. Not about the rose itself, but about the tight little buds you see before you. She said a white rosebud symbolized innocence and awakening, the opening of a heart untouched. There are two courses the flower might take: it may stretch toward the sun and become a rich, full blossom, or it may draw inward and wither away."

Katya reached out and brushed her finger over a tight, velvety bud. "And which course do these flowers take?"

"If you look closely, you'll see that the buds are shriveling, the petals turning brown. I don't think they've bloomed once since Marianne died."

"How very sad."

"You are not a thief, are you, Miss Alexander?"

Katya's head snapped up in startled surprise. Unwilling to lie to the Comtesse directly, she temporized instead. "I'm doing exactly what your nephew asked me to do. If he has expressed any dissatisfaction with my abilities, I would prefer he bring his concerns directly to me."

A glint of victory showed in the elderly woman's dark eyes. "I thought not."

Her cane in hand, she rose regally to her feet and moved down the wide wooden steps that flanked the gazebo. Once she reached the flagstone path she turned back to Katya and pronounced, "That's the most interesting thing about secrets. Rarely are they one-sided. Usually both parties are withholding from the other." She gave Katya a piercing stare, as though she could see right through her, then finished evenly, "Good night, Miss Alexander."

With those final words, the Comtesse strode proudly away. Walking with slow, measured steps, she moved across the rocky flagstone path and disappeared into the moonlit gardens.

Nicholas waited until half past noon for Katya to make an appearance for breakfast. When the servants began setting out the luncheon dishes and she still had not surfaced from her room, he set aside the journals he had been browsing and strode upstairs. He moved down the long hallway and rapped purposefully on her bedchamber door.

He heard the sound of swishing skirts and the soft padding of feet across the carpet. Katya opened the door and peered out. Any concern he may have harbored that she had kept to her room because she was unwell was instantly dispelled once he saw her. She wore a simple gown of pale pink muslin that brought out the gentle glow of her skin and the rosy hue in her cheeks. Her eyes were bright and alert—if partially hidden behind the spectacles that sat perched on the end of her nose.

"Oh, it's you," she said, looking more than a little surprised to find him standing there. "I thought you were the maid."

He crossed his arms over his chest and relaxed against the

doorjamb. "I suppose that's my greatest failing," he said. "People are constantly confusing me with the servants."

A small, embarrassed smile curved her lips. "I meant, I was expecting the maid," she corrected. "I've kept to my room all morning and I fear I'm preventing her from seeing to her duties."

"Anything wrong?"

"Not at all. I had some correspondence I'd been putting off and I decided to shut myself in until it was finished." She paused for a moment, then asked abruptly, "Did the Comtesse send you?"

"The Comtesse? No, why?"

She shook her head. "Nothing, I . . . I thought she might have, that's all."

"Well, she didn't." His gaze moved slowly over her form. "So you do wear it down," he observed.

She raised her hand in a self-conscious motion and smoothed it over her hair, as though attempting to bring some sort of order to the mass of silky ebony curls. "I was going to wash it later so I haven't bothered with it." She hesitated, then continued in what sounded suspiciously like a subtle reprimand, "I wasn't expecting company."

"I didn't mean to disturb your privacy. I waited for you in the dining room, but you never came downstairs for breakfast."

"No, I wasn't hungry. I had a pot of hot chocolate and some toast sent up."

His gaze moved past her and to the tray that sat on her bedside table. A few slices of toasted bread, a dish of marmalade, fresh creamy butter, and a small plate of sliced melon and strawberries remained untouched. The rich scent of chocolate wafted through the air. Her bed was tousled and unmade, the sheets were thrown back and the pillows scattered about in seductive disarray. For a moment Nicholas allowed himself the unprecedented luxury of letting his imagination run wild. He imagined coaxing Katya into bed, then slowly disrobing her and making love upon those warm, messy sheets. He imagined running his hands over her body as he learned what pleased her and what did not, slowly exploring every delicate, erotic inch of her form.

Reluctantly returning his thoughts to what had brought him here, he said, "I wonder if I could speak with you privately for a moment."

"Certainly."

"Down the hall, if you don't mind."

A look of surprise flashed through her eyes, then she nodded briskly. "Very well."

She stepped out of her room and allowed him to guide her down the hall. Once they reached the end of the passageway, he paused and pushed open a set of broad oak double doors, gesturing for her to precede him. She glanced inside then looked back at him in wary hesitation.

"Your bedchamber?"

"Yes."

"Exactly what is it you would like to discuss?"

A broad grin curved his lips. "Are you always this distrustful?"

She tilted her chin. "Whenever a man tells me he would like to speak to me, then leads me to his bedchamber for that discussion, yes, I am."

"How very prudent. Does that happen to you often?"

Aware she was being mocked, she replied primly, "It's the principle of the matter that's at issue here."

"Of course." He nodded somberly. "If it's any comfort to you, bear in mind that I have a staff full of servants within earshot. Should I make any gross, untoward advances, you need only raise your voice and they will all come running."

Katya considered that. "True," she agreed, reluctantly stepping inside.

Nicholas followed her and closed the door behind them.

Leaning against the heavy oak panels, he added with a mischievous grin, "They all are in my employ, of course, so should anyone try to intervene on your behalf, I would threaten him with immediate dismissal and banish him from the room."

She sent him a dry smile. "Thank you. That's very comforting."

She turned her attention from him to his room, studying it with open curiosity. Nicholas followed her gaze, wondering if she liked what she saw. His bedchamber was rather large, its masculine furnishings dominated by a huge four-poster bed made of dark mahogany. A stone fireplace occupied one corner; a set of oversized chairs and ottomans were grouped around it. A set of tall windows flanked one wall, offering a sweeping view of the cliffs and sea. On the opposite wall was a huge mosaic made from thousands of pieces of tiny, shimmering tile.

The mosaic showed three mermaids sitting on a cluster of jagged rocks. Towering waves crashed on the rough shore around them, sending flecks of white foam over the ghost-like hulls of ships that had been driven ashore. A full moon hung in the sky, sending silvery beams dancing over the eerie landscape. The mermaids leaned forward, their eyes wide and imploring as they beckoned to a tall, three-masted ship that sailed in the distance. The captain of the ship stood at the helm, his gaze riveted on the mermaids. The ship's wheel was clutched tightly in his hands. His expression was one of pure anguish, torn by the conflicting emotions of terror and desire. In response to the changing light in the room, the scene seemed to shimmer and pulsate with emotion, as though the mosaic were a living, breathing work of art.

Katya moved toward the mural, entirely captivated. After a long moment she drew back, giving an embarrassed laugh as she realized she had allowed herself to become totally absorbed in the artwork. "It's lovely," she said.

"Isn't it?" he agreed. "I commissioned the work from a local artist."

"Did you design it yourself?"

He shook his head. "I had a vague idea what I wanted, but I have to admit that the result was far superior to anything I had originally envisioned." He moved closer and hooked one booted foot over the bedrail. "Since I'm rarely in Monaco, I thought about having it dismantled and transferred to my home in London. But it always struck me as belonging here."

Katya nodded and returned her gaze to the mosaic. "Night is the time when the soul surrenders," she said softly.

"What?"

She started, as though unaware she had spoken aloud. With a small, embarrassed shrug, she repeated, "Night is the time when the soul surrenders. My mother used to tell me that. As a child, I thought she was referring to dreams. Now that I'm older I understand that she meant much more."

Nicholas studied her for a long moment as a feeling of deep understanding swept through him. That was exactly what he had felt the first time he looked at the mosaic. More than any woman he had known, Katya Alexander seemed to have the singular ability to plunge directly to the heart of what he was thinking and feeling. After a lifetime spent engaged in a series of sexually satisfying relationships that were intellectually shallow, he found himself constantly surprised at her remarkable insight.

"I suppose that's why I liked the mosaic so much," he said. "The piece captures the state of longing better than anything I've ever seen."

"Yes, it does."

"Are you familiar with the legend of the Sirens?" he asked. "They were notorious for singing to passing ships and luring them in to wreck on the rocky shores. Apparently their song was so beautiful that the mere sound of it would drive men mad with lust."

She frowned. "That has always struck me as a rather one-sided, male interpretation of the story. Perhaps the Sirens weren't trying to lure men to their deaths at all, but simply attempting to warn passing ships of the danger of the rocky shore. Perhaps they were entirely unaware of their own powers—or their effect on men."

Nicholas arched one brow. "Given that they were women, I find that highly implausible. In either case," he continued dryly, "their beauty was the men's downfall, was it not?"

"The men's own weakness was their downfall," she countered. "They should have had the strength to resist the Sirens' call."

He took a step closer to her and ran his finger lightly along the length of her collarbone. "Have you never succumbed to the urge to surrender?"

She nervously licked her lips. "From what I've seen, total surrender of one's soul—whatever the reason—brings nothing but disastrous results. I much prefer the quiet dignity of resisting temptation."

"Sometimes there's far more to be gained in surrender than there is in shallow resistance."

She tilted her chin to meet his gaze, her beautiful lavender eyes filled with a look of heady sensual awareness. But the moment passed all too quickly. Before he could close the gap between them, she took a step backward and moved just out of his reach.

He studied her for a long moment in silence, then asked, "Do you see the fish along the bottom of the mosaic? At first I didn't notice them at all, then one day they seemed to jump out at me. The seaman is heading toward certain death, the mermaids are sheer fantasy, but the fish are real.

There they are, darting in and out of the shadows and skimming below the surface. Like you, Katya. So elusive. Always skirting away just when I think I have you in my grasp."

She sent him a nervous, awkward smile. "I'm sure you didn't call me in here just to tell me that I remind you of a fish."

"No, I didn't," he agreed. Reluctantly turning his attention away from the mosaic, he moved to his desk and opened a drawer. He retrieved a rectangular case covered in rich black velvet and passed it to Katya. "We'll be attending a gala at the casino tonight. I thought you might like to wear these."

She quietly searched his gaze, then turned her attention to the case. She opened the lid and peered inside. Although her expression didn't change, Nicholas knew well what she had found. Within the velvet case was a stunningly intricate necklace of glistening, square-cut diamonds encircled by shimmering rubies. A pair of matching diamond and ruby earrings completed the set.

"Very impressive," she said. "I take it these are not one of the 'lesser pieces.' "

"No, they're not. As a matter of fact, that little box you're holding in your hands happens to be worth more than the entire contents of my London estate."

"I see." She closed the case and drummed her fingers pensively against the lid. "Is this really necessary?" she asked after a minute.

"What do you mean?"

"The jewelry. Why take the risk that something might happen to it? What if the clasp breaks, or a stone comes loose, or—"

"For a thief, you have a rather peculiar aversion to jewels."

A small, wistful smile touched her lips. "Doesn't that

worry you?" she asked. "What if I were to run away tonight and flee the country with your priceless jewels?"

"I trust you." He waited a beat, then continued smoothly, "And they're insured."

"How very flattering."

He lifted his shoulders in a light shrug. "What would you have me say? Society demands it. The more ostentatious the jewelry, the more readily one is accepted into the inner circles. A man's wealth is displayed not only by his coaches, horseflesh, and estates, but by the quality of the glittering trinkets worn by his wife and mistress. I suppose it's a primitive way of marking one's conquests."

"Primitive, indeed."

Noting her displeased frown, he asked, "Why do you assume I mean to imply that I have conquered you? The jewelry could also be interpreted as a sign that you have conquered me."

"I suppose that's true," she murmured. She thought for a moment, then announced in the regal tone of a queen bestowing a favor upon a lesser mortal, "Very well. I shall wear your jewelry."

"You do me great honor," he replied, biting back a smile. Most women he knew would have given their right arms for such an opportunity.

"So what is the occasion for this grand event we are to attend?" she asked.

"It's a private affair hosted by Monsieur LeBlanc. The casino is donating all of tonight's gambling proceeds to various local charities."

"I see."

"Are you adept at gambling?"

She shrugged. "I have a passing knowledge of how games of chance are played."

"Indeed?" He leaned one broad shoulder against the mahogany bedpost, regarding her curiously. "Can you tell me how to win?"

"Not how to win, precisely, but I can tell you how not to lose."

"Oh?"

She arched one delicate brow in an expression of mocking superiority. "Don't play."

He smiled. "Unfortunately, little gypsy, that's exactly the kind of advice I never take."

Twelve

❦

Marco DuValenti has wrapped me in his spell. I have forgotten what my life was like before I met him. He has tangled my reason and my dreams, choking away all thoughts but those of him. He is like a wild vine spiraling around the trunk of a tree, twisting tighter and tighter until nothing else survives. I am beginning to understand the danger that others warned me of, but it is too late to change my course now. Something in him lures me closer and closer. I feel alive, more alive than I have ever felt in my life. When he touches me it is as though

*T*here Sacha Rosskaya's diary ended abruptly.

Katya shuffled through the pile of ancient papers in her lap looking for more, but they were too jumbled for her to find any semblance of order. As the documents had been passed down through the generations, the thick stack had become hopelessly mixed and mismatched. Records of births and deaths, crop figures, household inventories, religious passages, political agendas, and medicinal folklore were all bundled together under the heading of Sacha's diary.

Katya let out a sigh. It would take hours more of scouring through the brittle parchment pieces to find another clue from the diary. Another time, she might have been content to spend days poring through the documents. But now she felt pressed by an overwhelming sense of urgency to find the answers she sought in the ancient text.

She couldn't help but feel that she and Sacha were following a parallel course. Both she and her ancestor had been warned away, yet they were pulled toward the DuValenti men as though a magnetic force were tugging them toward their fate. Even with the knowledge Katya possessed, she seemed determined to repeat the mistakes made by Sacha. Were the DuValentis really as evil as legend made them out to be? Was there some sort of fatal weakness in the Rosskaya women? Or had something else gone awry between their families, something that had led to the centuries-old feud?

The questions reverberated through her head as she gathered the ancient parchment pieces and put them away. She crossed the room and paused before a tall looking glass, studying her reflection. The eyes that stared back at her were glowing, her skin was flushed. She had been drawn to a gown she had never worn before, one she had never even particularly liked. But for some reason it seemed to call out to her and so she had followed her instinct.

The gown was made of deep crimson satin, and so brazen it was almost theatrical, unlike the demure gowns she normally preferred. It was sleeveless, and designed with a deep, square neckline that served to frame a generous expanse of the soft, creamy skin of her breasts. The fabric was drawn in tightly at her waist, then gathered in tiny pleats that caused the satin to drape around her hips. A garland of rich, handstitched black embroidery framed the neckline and hem of her skirt. She had completed the ensemble with high-heeled black kid slippers and matching black elbow-length gloves. Her hair was piled high on her head in a dramatic pompadour and adorned with one crimson ostrich feather. A few ebony curls spiraled around the nape of her neck, softening the overall effect.

Katya took this in, then her eyes moved to the jewels Nicholas had lent her. They felt heavy around her neck, outlandishly conspicuous. The diamonds shimmered in the soft evening light; the rubies seemed to glow as though lit from within. What had he said? "A primitive way of marking one's conquests." Strangely enough, she did feel marked as Nicholas Duvall's woman. A sense of reckless anticipation flowed through her veins; her skin felt quivery and alive where his jewels touched her throat, as though he were touching her himself.

A small, embarrassed smile curved her lips at that fanciful thought. So much for the rational, analytical Katya.

A clock chimed nine. She took a deep breath to steady her nerves, then picked up the small black-and-crimson reticule that matched her gown. She left her room and followed the sound of murmuring voices to the informal parlor. There she found Nicholas deep in conversation with the Comtesse. Although she hadn't said a word, the soft rustle of her gown gave away her presence, for they both turned immediately toward her.

Her gaze went directly to Nicholas. He studied her in speechless silence, a look of shocked, almost frozen surprise carved on his features. Katya stood unmoving as embarrassment coursed through her. Judging from his look, her attire was entirely inappropriate. But before she could react, Nicholas rose to his feet and moved toward her.

"You look beautiful, Katya," he said, in a tone of such smooth sincerity that she wondered if she had completely misinterpreted his expression.

He was dressed in black, save for the crisp white linen shirt. The severe lines of his tailored clothing suited him well, she thought. He looked elegant and incredibly handsome. The only ornamentation he wore was a tiny ruby that twinkled from deep within the precise folds of his cravat. His dark hair was slightly damp and the fresh scent of soap clung to his skin, adding to his air of rugged sensuality. As her gaze moved briefly over his form she remembered the lean, hard feel of his body. Unlike most men, Nicholas Duvall needed no padding in his jacket, no lift in his boots. The Lord of Barrington was a mass of solid muscle and pure masculine power.

The air seemed to shimmer between them. It was one thing to think about Nicholas Duvall in the abstract, Katya realized, to tell herself that she wasn't the least bit attracted to him and that she could easily betray his trust. But it was quite another thing to stand so close and deny that attraction.

Once, she had witnessed a fellow performer hypnotize a member of his audience. At the time, Katya had thought it was merely a trick. But now she wondered. For as she gazed into Nicholas's coal-black eyes, she felt as though she had fallen completely under his spell.

He raised his hand and brushed his fingers softly along the base of her throat, lightly touching the glittering diamond-and-ruby necklace she wore. "I was curious to see what heat would do to your skin," he said, his voice low and husky. "Now I know. Fire becomes you, little gypsy."

Before she could reply, the Comtesse lifted her lorgnette and studied her critically. "Very suitable, indeed, Miss Alexander," she intoned.

Katya forced her attention away from Nicholas. It occurred to her to wonder if the Comtesse had ever spoken to Nicholas about their conversation, but somehow she doubted it. A subtle air of quiet female conspiracy seemed to hover about the older woman.

"Do you have a wrap?" Nicholas asked.

She nodded and passed him a black lace shawl. As he settled it around her shoulders his fingers brushed lightly against her skin, causing a quivering tremor to race down her spine. Determined not to show the effect his touch had on her, she schooled her features into what she hoped would pass for an expression of cool poise. "Thank you," she murmured.

"If you're ready, the coach is waiting."

"Certainly."

They said their good-byes to the Comtesse, then Nicholas took her elbow and ushered her through the villa to their coach. Once they had assumed their seats the groomsmen urged the team out. They began the descent down the steep road of the Moneghetti, moving toward the soft glow of glittering gaslights that beckoned from the principality beneath them. Katya leaned back against the plush leather seat, listening to the steady clip-clop of the horses' hooves, the rhythmic crunch of gravel beneath the coach's wheels, and the occasional creak of the springs.

In the silence that surrounded them, she turned her attention to Nicholas. As they passed the thick outcropping of jagged, white-capped rocks that she had noted before, she saw his gaze linger there. "Burdened," the Comtesse had said. Perhaps that was the best way to describe the look of private pain and inner turmoil that marked his rugged features. As they moved past the rocks he refocused his attention on her, as though suddenly realizing he had abdicated his responsibilities as host.

"The gown is an interesting choice," he said.

"You don't like it."

"Actually, it's quite perfect for this evening." His gaze moved slowly over her form. "But it seems rather unlike you. What made you select it?"

"The rubies, I suppose," she replied with a light shrug, uncertain how to interpret his mood or his comments. She studied his face within the shadowy confines of the moonlight that spilled in through the windows. "Both you and the Comtesse had such an odd reaction to my appearance. Why?"

He waited a moment, as though resolving an internal debate before answering. Finally he replied, "For an instant when you entered the parlor, your resemblance to Allyson Whitney was striking. I'd never noticed the similarity before. Perhaps it was the way you stood, the way you had done your hair, or simply the gown you're wearing. The last time

I was with Allyson she wore something nearly identical to it."

His unexpected reply released insecurities Katya had never known she possessed. The fact that Nicholas might be attracted to her because of her resemblance to his former mistress was profoundly distasteful, yet it carried an undeniable ring of truth.

"Is that what drew you to me, my resemblance to Allyson?" she asked, amazed at how cool and steady her voice sounded.

"At the time, if you recall, I was far more impressed by your amazing deftness with Lady Stanton's handbag than by your peerless beauty. Much to my embarrassment, it was only later that I came to appreciate your more delicate charms."

Her dissatisfaction with his answer must have shown on her face. "I hope you don't think me so shallow or needy that I would try to relive a failed love affair by recasting the players," he said. "Even if I were to attempt it, you are not the woman I would cast as Allyson Whitney—however superficial the resemblance. You have far too much substance for so negligible a role."

"I see."

As though sensing her lingering doubt, Nicholas continued smoothly, "Whatever occurs between you and me, little gypsy, is solely of our own making. There is nothing else— past or present—that need concern us."

Unfortunately that wasn't true, and therein lay the heart of the problem. They had centuries of history between them, beginning with Sacha Rosskaya and Marco DuValenti. In light of that, her worries seemed hopelessly trivial. Even if he was attracted to her because of her resemblance to his former mistress, was she not guilty of a greater deceit? She had agreed to act the part of his mistress in order to steal the scroll out from under him. If complications ensued because of her lies and deception, were they not entirely of her own making?

Rather than attempt to sort out her tangled thoughts and emotions, she turned her mind to the one element that had initially brought them together. "I presume we are making an appearance tonight in order to continue our search for the scroll," she said. "Whom in particular would you like for me to target?"

If he was at all surprised by her abrupt change of topic, it didn't show. "Very well," he agreed, and commenced to list a number of dukes, viscounts, and earls to whom she might attach herself should the opportunity arise. "Even if you don't find the scroll," he concluded, "I believe that should amount to a profitable evening for you."

"Indeed," she replied flatly. Although she had done nothing but encourage his belief that she was little more than a common thief, she still didn't like it. The label felt base and dirty, a mockery of her parents' good name.

"By the way, how are things proceeding for you in that respect?" he asked. "I trust you've found our little partnership adequately lucrative?"

"Quite, thank you."

"Tell me what will happen next. Have you found a source willing to pay you for your trouble—one who won't ask embarrassing questions when you present yourself to redeem your vast assortment of feloniously acquired baubles?"

"I've made certain inquiries," she lied. "There is a jeweler in the Condamnie who is rumored to be discreet."

"How very fortunate."

"You're amused."

"Intrigued," he corrected. "I've never met a professional thief before. Certainly not one as forthright about it as you." He thought for a moment, then lifted his shoulders in a light shrug. "Or perhaps I'm simply enjoying the fact that the only honest person in attendance tonight happens to be a thief. I find that wonderfully ironic, don't you?"

"I suppose I hadn't thought about it."

Why was it so hard for her to remember that he viewed her as nothing more than a thief he had hired as a means to an end? Unable to meet his eyes, she averted her gaze, her focus intent on adjusting the lace on the hem of her gloves. Fortunately the coach rolled to a smooth and timely stop in front of the casino, sparing her the need for further conversation.

Nicholas stepped out of the vehicle and politely offered his hand, helping her disembark. Glancing around, Katya saw that the Grand Casino was rife with visitors. She wasn't surprised. The exclusivity of the event served to draw far greater numbers than would normally be on hand.

As they moved inside, she was intensely aware of the light pressure of Nicholas's fingers on her arm. Watching the reaction of the crowd as they moved through the bustling salons, she detected the same response to him now as she had on the occasion of the first gala they had attended: coolly deferential greetings, followed by shocked whispers, nervous excitement, and a murmur of giddy speculation trailed in their wake. Throughout it all Nicholas remained stoic and impassive, as though completely insensitive to the clamor his presence created.

"You seem to be causing quite a commotion," she remarked softly as they strode arm in arm through the garishly lit gaming rooms.

Nicholas nodded politely to an elderly couple then tilted his head toward hers, a sardonic smile on his lips. "Really? I hadn't noticed."

"Are you truly so modest? Or merely blind in one eye?"

His smile widened. "How do you know you're not the one causing the sensation?"

"I'm hardly the type to cause a commotion of any sort."

"On the contrary, your weekly performances here at the casino are causing quite a stir," he countered. "Whether you're aware of it or not, you've become the object of much speculation." He led her toward an isolated corner of the room, a small oasis amid the dense crowd. There he stopped and turned toward her, his ebony gaze locking on hers. "Then there's the matter of your appearance tonight. You look beautiful, Katya."

She felt her breath catch in her throat and managed a small, fluttery smile. The moment seemed to stretch between them. She could think of no reply to his words; none seemed necessary. Everything needing to be said was conveyed within the burning heat of Nicholas's dark eyes.

But where the moment might have led would forever remain a mystery. The spell that had fallen between them was abruptly broken as a casino employee approached Nicholas with an offer to exchange his francs for gaming tokens.

Nicholas handed the man a thick stack of notes and received the gold tokens with a word of thanks. He then returned his attention to Katya.

"What do you like?" he inquired politely. "Roulette, baccarat, chemin de fer?"

"I'm not much for gambling."

"I hope you'll make an exception tonight. As my mistress, it's your sacred obligation to toss my money about as freely as a fountain spouts water."

She lifted her shoulders in a soft shrug. "Perhaps I'm a frugal mistress."

"What a ghastly idea."

The appalled look on his face aroused a note of genuine curiosity within her. "Is spending money truly that important?"

"Absolutely," Nicholas averred. "In this society, the more extravagantly and obscenely one flaunts one's wealth, the more renown and stature one gains." He studied her face for a moment, then continued with a slight smile, "I'd forgotten you haven't been in Monaco long enough to see how truly preposterous it can get."

"What do you mean?"

He nodded toward a stunning redhead attired in a deep emerald gown that hugged her every curve. "Do you see that woman there?" he asked. "Her name is Gabriella." He scanned the crowd, then nodded discreetly toward another woman, a breathtaking brunette who wore a gown of shimmering gold. "That's her rival, Lianne."

"Her rival?"

"They're both courtesans," he explained simply. "Each woman claims to be the most coveted courtesan in all of Monaco. As you can imagine, it's a claim that is fiercely debated."

It was a rather dubious distinction in Katya's mind, but she nodded for him to continue.

"One evening Gabriella decided to outdazzle her challenger by entering the casino in an evening gown as low cut as decency allowed and wearing what appeared to be her entire collection of jewelry—tokens she had received as gifts from her various admirers. The lot included four pearl necklaces, an emerald brooch, a diamond tiara, ruby hair clips, and sapphire ear fobs. A few minutes later, Lianne, who had been forewarned of Gabriella's decision, made her own appearance wearing a white dress of classic simplicity and a single diamond drop at her throat"—he paused and illustrated his point by lightly placing his finger on her breastbone—"followed by her poodle bedecked in the remainder of her jewelry."

Katya couldn't help but smile at the women's outrageous antics. Although she hadn't been in Monaco long, she could well envision the scene.

"I must appear rather dull in comparison," she said.

"Hardly." His eyes swept slowly over her body in undisguised appreciation. "Katya, the Goddess of Mystery. The title suits you." He reached for her hand and pressed his fingers against her wrist, causing her pulse to leap erratically. Then he lightly traced the length of her arm, gently caressing her bare skin. "There's fire in your veins, little gypsy. Running just beneath the surface. Don't you feel it?"

Yes, she answered silently, whenever you touch me.

Aloud she said simply, "I think you like to play games. I think you're interested in me because you imagine I pose some sort of challenge."

Her breathless protest was nothing but a feeble attempt to push him away—one she was glad didn't work. The heat that smoldered deep within his gaze did not dim.

"Perhaps," he said. "Or perhaps I see something in you that draws me ever closer. Like darkness chasing light, each inseparably linked to the other." He smiled, then placed his hand against the small of her back, urging her forward into the bustling crowd. "Now go and mingle—before I do something neither of us regrets."

Her mouth dropped open in automatic protest.

His smile widened. "I know, I know. How dare I." He pressed a heavy stack of gold gaming tokens in her hand. "If it makes you feel any better, bear in mind that the proceeds all go to charity. You may be as reckless as you like in good conscience."

Katya moved away from him, her thoughts hopelessly jumbled and her emotions whirling in nervous turmoil. She strolled randomly from table to table, nodding to various acquaintances as she placed her wagers. Occasionally she won, more often she lost. But her mind was scarcely focused on the gaming. Instead she returned again and again to her incredible situation.

Skirting the edge of danger had never particularly enthralled her, but everything was different in the presence of Nicholas Duvall. In fact, just the opposite was true. She had always been overly cautious, prim, and prudent. But at that moment she felt more alive, more essential, than she had ever felt. Nicholas seduced her with his words, his touch, his gaze, his very being.

Awareness of him ran through her veins like fire. No matter where she moved in the room, she knew instantly where to find him. And she was intensely aware that he was watching her. She felt as though she were performing onstage for a private audience of one. The only thing that mattered was Nicholas's approval. Somehow she had lost herself—or maybe this was whom she was meant to be all along.

She had no pangs of guilt about feeling out her prey, casually brushing up against an earl or a viscount and searching him for the scroll. Mindful of her need to maintain her charade as a thief, she occasionally claimed a small keepsake, filling her reticule with pens and snuff boxes and various other gold- and silver-plated trinkets. She moved through the crowd with a deftness she would not have suspected she possessed. The crush of bodies, the noise, and the large amount of liquor most of the guests were imbibing made her task easier. Whereas before she had been nervous about her undertaking, now she felt nothing more than a vague sense of ease, as though her actions were completely natural.

She was beginning to believe that the role she was playing was real—a turnabout as preposterous as believing that the magic she performed onstage was real. Both were equally illusory, but she was falling into it nonetheless. It seemed a night made for magic, and she was no more immune to the spell that Nicholas had cast over her than she was able to resist his touch.

As the evening progressed and the crowd reached its peak, Nicholas drew her to the secluded corner where they had spoken earlier. "Any luck?" he asked.

"Nothing yet."

"Right." His voice conveyed nothing but cool acceptance

as he scanned the crowd. "Do you see that man over there? Lord Jeffrey Chalmers—the portly fellow who's in the process of losing a fortune at roulette?"

"Yes." She thought for a moment and frowned. "But I believe I've already checked his person. He wasn't carrying the scroll."

"Perhaps not on him, but something's making him nervous. I happen to know that he and his wife rented a villa here in Monaco, yet he's left the casino three times tonight and made his way across the street to the Hotel de Paris."

"Is that so unusual?"

Nicholas shrugged. "He's drinking heavily, and it's clear by the way he scans the room before he leaves that he's meeting someone over there. It may have nothing to do with the scroll, but . . ."

"But?" she prompted.

"He and my father were involved in a business deal that went awry—they both lost substantial sums. There was a great deal of animosity between them when my father died."

"And you think he might be striking back by stealing your family's scroll," she surmised.

"I think it's possible. Outstanding moral character is not one of Lord Chalmers's more obvious traits."

"I see." Katya considered the problem for a moment. "If he has a room at the hotel, I imagine he's carrying the key with him."

A small, conspiratorial smile curved Nicholas's lips. "That had occurred to me as well."

Instantly understanding what he was asking her to do, she nodded discreetly and moved away, gliding across the room toward the roulette table. She sent Lord Chalmers her most beguiling smile as she positioned herself beside him. An expression of startled pleasure flashed across his pudgy features; then he sent her a flustered smile in return.

"What color have you been finding lucky this evening," she asked, "red or black?"

His gaze moved over her crimson gown with a look of bleary-eyed admiration. "Undoubtedly red, Miss Alexander."

She nodded and placed her token on red, then formed her lips into a pretty pout as the wheel came up black.

"It's far more complicated than merely choosing red or black," he rushed to assure her, his chest puffed out with pompous dignity. "Do allow me to assist you."

He leaned solicitously toward her and explained the rules of the game. Under his tutelage, she commenced to lose one hundred francs within the space of five minutes. "It appears we are not a lucky combination," she concluded with a soft sigh. "Perhaps I shall try again later."

She smiled and stepped away from him. As she moved to leave the crowded gaming room, Nicholas materialized at her side. She withdrew Lord Chalmers's gold hotel key from within her glove and flashed it discreetly toward him. "I shouldn't be more than twenty minutes," she said.

He nodded. "I'll keep him occupied until you return." As she turned to leave, he caught her arm. "Be careful, Katya."

She considered his grave features and sent him a soft smile of reassurance. "What could possibly go wrong?" she asked lightly.

Their eyes met and held for one long, breathless moment. Nicholas's dark gaze seemed to burn into hers, marking her with deep, possessive hunger. Finally he released her arm and she moved wordlessly away. She exited the casino and stepped onto the paved path that led to the Hotel de Paris.

Amazing what Nicholas could do to her with just one searing look. His mere presence left her intoxicated. She felt light-headed and giddy, completely unstable—as though a thousand fluttering butterflies had been turned loose in her belly. Although she knew her feet were touching the pavement, she moved as though she were swept up in a tumultuous cloud of emotion and desire.

The sound of a soft footfall behind her interrupted her thoughts. Katya glanced behind her only to find the street curiously empty. She gave a mental shrug and proceeded a few more yards when she heard the sound again—the distinct sound of a man's boots striking pavement. She turned abruptly and scanned the street. Nothing. The only movement she saw was the swaying of the palm branches in the night breeze.

Despite the visual assurance that she was alone, her instincts told her otherwise.

Increasing her pace, she moved rapidly toward the hotel and stepped into the grand, cavernous lobby. Once inside, she was somewhat comforted by the presence of the hotel's guests and staff. Even if someone had been following her, she was relatively safe in the hotel. Seizing that reassuring thought, she gave the night clerk a polite nod and examined the window displays of the exclusive shops that filled the lobby. She glanced from time to time at the reflections in the glass, but saw no one who looked even mildly suspicious, let alone watching her.

Her courage restored, she proceeded up the red-carpeted steps to the room indicated on Lord Chalmers's key. She found his room and inserted the key; the door swung smoothly open. Katya took a last glance down the hall. Satisfied that no one was about, she took a deep breath, stepped inside, and closed the door behind her.

The chamber was pitch dark, filled with an empty, hollow silence. She gave her eyes a moment to adjust to the darkness, then cautiously scanned the space. Lord Chalmers had leased a suite, she noted. The room in which she stood served as a sort of formal sitting parlor. To her left was a separate chamber that had been partitioned off as sleeping quarters.

Rather than light a gas lamp and risk detection, she moved toward the window and parted the draperies. The space was immediately flooded with the soft, silvery glow of moonlight. Deciding that this was adequate, she began her search in the bedchamber. She had barely completed her preliminary search of Lord Chalmers's bed, pillows, and dresser drawers, when she heard a faint click in the outer chamber.

Katya froze, her pulse hammering in her ears.

She stood unmoving, straining to hear more.

Nothing.

Nothing but the faint sound of her own shallow breathing.

Then she heard it. A soft, almost imperceptible creak coming from the outer chamber. The sound made by a foot striking a squeaky floorboard. Her heart slammed against her ribs as a wave of terror washed over her. Was there someone in the suite with her? She stood absolutely still, paralyzed by fear.

Finally she summoned the courage to move. Her eyes wide and her heart drumming madly, she padded softly into Lord Chalmers's parlor and scanned the space. To her overwhelming relief, the room was completely empty and still save for the draperies fluttering in the breeze.

The draperies fluttering in the breeze? . . .

Her brows drew together in a puzzled frown. She knew she had opened the draperies, but hadn't the window been—

An arm shot out of the darkness and caught her about the waist, pulling her off her feet. Before she could react, a rough male hand slammed over her mouth, choking off her scream.

Thirteen

❦~❦

"Quiet!"

The word was whispered in her ear with rough urgency. Katya didn't hesitate to ignore the command. She opened her mouth and emitted a muffled scream as she raised her foot and slammed her heel down hard on her captor's instep.

She heard a softly sworn oath, followed by the words, "Dammit, Katya, it's me!"

It took her a moment to recognize Nicholas's voice through the fog of terror that held her in its grip. Once it did, relief poured through her—followed immediately by anger.

"I'm going to release my hand," he whispered, speaking slowly and distinctly. "When I do, don't speak. Don't even move. Do you understand?"

She nodded obediently.

As soon as he removed his hand she spun around and demanded, "What in blazes are you—"

He immediately covered her mouth again.

Katya sent him an indignant glare and moved to jerk his hand away when she heard the sound of voices approaching from down the hall. One voice in particular caught her attention. *Lord Chalmers.* Her eyes widened in horrified understanding as her startled gaze flew to Nicholas. His features grim, he sent her a curt nod and released his hand.

This time Katya made no sound. Instead her gaze moved about the room, searching frantically for a way out. Nicholas must have gained access through the second-story window. While that offered the best escape route for him, it was not an option for her—not while she was dressed in a floor-length ball gown and high-heeled satin slippers. He must have come to the same conclusion, for after a brief glance at the window he turned away and quickly scanned the room, searching for a place to hide.

The obvious solution would have been to crawl beneath the bed. Unfortunately, the mattress was dressed with only a short coverlet; there was no bedskirt to conceal them.

The footsteps echoed closer, then Lord Chalmers's voice carried into the room. ". . . I know I had the blasted thing in my pocket."

"You're certain the door is locked?" responded a female voice.

"Of course it's locked. Why wouldn't it be locked?" Chalmers replied shortly. "Now if I can just find the bloody key . . ."

The doorknob rattled.

Katya's gaze flew to the small table beside the door. With a jolt of dismay, she realized she had forgotten to lock the door behind her. The key rested on top of the table, exactly where she had set it after admitting herself.

The knob rattled again—and then turned. The door began to swing open.

"How very odd," began Chalmers.

The rest of his words were lost as Nicholas grabbed her by the arm and gave her a sharp tug, breaking her free from her frozen stupor. He pulled her to a tall wardrobe that stood between the bedroom and parlor. Throwing open the thick door panels, he thrust her inside then immediately followed, quietly shutting the panels behind him.

The fit was tight—their bodies were pressed together—but the wardrobe was tall enough so that they could comfortably stand. Katya held her breath, afraid to emit even the slightest sound. The heavy tread of a man's boots moving over the wooden floorboards told her that Lord Chalmers had entered the room. The sound was followed by the click of a delicate heel and the soft rustle of a woman's gown.

Her curiosity stirred, Katya peaked through a knothole in the wooden door. She instantly recognized the woman as Gabriella, the stunning redheaded courtesan Nicholas had pointed out earlier.

As Katya watched, Gabriella sent Lord Chalmers a smile of calculated seduction. "The emeralds are beautiful, darling," she cooed. She lifted her wrist and gave the glittering bracelet she wore a soft shake. "If it weren't for your little gift, I'd have nothing to wear with my gown."

"I'm glad you like them."

"They're perfect," she said. "I don't know how to thank you."

Chalmers smiled and drew the ravishing redhead closer. "On the contrary, my dear," he said, "I think you know exactly how to thank me."

Katya lowered her gaze as heat stained her cheeks. Apparently Lord Chalmers's frequent trips to his hotel room had nothing to do with the scroll—and everything to do with an illicit rendezvous with one of Monaco's most celebrated courtesans. With that clear, she would have liked nothing more than to beat a hasty retreat. Unfortunately she and Nicholas were trapped where they stood, reluctant witnesses to the torrid affair.

The ridiculousness of their position was suddenly vividly clear. In a moment of comic horror, she tried to imagine what she would say if Lord Chalmers were to open the wardrobe and she and Nicholas came tumbling out. She bit her lips as a wave of nervous, almost hysterical laughter welled up inside her.

Although she didn't make a sound, Nicholas must have felt her shoulders shake, for his hand came up to steady her. Katya took a deep, sobering breath and forced herself to remain calm. Putting their situation in perspective, she reasoned that they needed to remain hidden for likely no more than an hour—any longer than that and Lord Chalmers's wife would undoubtedly begin to wonder where her husband was.

It might have helped if she had been facing Nicholas so that they could at least communicate. But they had hastily stepped into the wardrobe one right after the other. As a result, they were both facing in the same direction, with her back snuggled up tightly against Nicholas's chest. All they could do was stand silently and wait.

A moment later, she was glad that Nicholas couldn't see her face. She heard the distinctive sound of clothing falling on the floor, followed by Lord Chalmers's low, passionate groan. It occurred to her with unforeseen clarity that people do not make love in total silence. She and Nicholas were about to be made privy to every noise and utterance made by the unsuspecting couple. But short of revealing their presence in the room, there was no way to avoid it.

She heard Gabriella's throaty giggle, followed by a whispered endearment. The sound of high-heeled slippers hitting the floor echoed through the room. Then a whoosh of skirts, a soft thud, and another giggle. Had Gabriella just fallen onto the bed or onto a chair? Before Katya could resolve that question, she heard a wet, rhythmic noise that could only be described as sucking. Was Lord Chalmers sucking his mistress's fingers, or some other portion of her anatomy?

Horrified that she had posed such a question—even if only to herself—Katya tried desperately to divert her thoughts. But she couldn't ignore the sensual noises surrounding her. The soft groan, the tittering laugh, the feathery sigh, the brush of clothing hitting the floor. The sounds were inescapable.

Cognizant that Nicholas was also hearing everything, Katya's embarrassment rose to new heights. What was he thinking as they stood in guilty silence listening to another couple making love? Nervous suspense churned in her belly as she considered his response. Was he caught in the grip of the same sexual tension she was experiencing? Did he relate every sound he heard back to the two of them?

With every second that passed, the space in which they hid seemed to grow even darker and more confined. Hotter. Tighter. Her nerves felt stripped raw and her senses were almost painfully heightened, so alert was she to every sound and motion. She was far too aware of the feeling of Nicholas's body squeezed against hers; too aware of the way his breath softly fanned the back of her neck; too aware of the way his strong, muscular thighs brushed against hers.

Just when she thought she could stand it no longer, Nicholas lifted his hand and traced his fingers lightly from her elbow to her shoulder. The relief that that small physical contact brought was almost dizzying. There was a question in his touch, and Katya replied without thinking. She nearly collapsed against him as he wrapped his arm around her waist, so strong was the desire that had been swelling within her.

He lowered his head and pressed a series of sweet, searing kisses along her shoulder blade, then he shifted slightly and traced his lips over the nape of her neck. As his mouth and tongue made contact with the sensitive flesh beneath her ear, a rush of tingling heat shot through her body. She shivered and threw back her head, giving him greater access to her tender skin.

She felt as though she were melting with yearning, so intense was her need for him. It seemed that the more Nicholas touched her, the more he awakened the fire within her, stoking and building the flames until they threatened to rage out of control. She couldn't get close enough to him. She moved with wanton abandon, pressing her back against his chest, crushing her bottom against his groin, locking her foot around his calf, running her hands down his lean hips—striving unthinkingly to make their bodies one.

Nicholas seemed to be caught in the same torrent of desire that held her in its thrall. His hands wandered fervently over her body with no apparent purpose but to explore and entice. He stroked her thighs, caressed her hips, captured her waist, and tickled her ribs. His touch was magic. Boundless. Reaching beneath the satin bodice of her gown, he cupped her breasts in his palms and moved his thumbs over the taut, hard buds of her nipples, teasing the tender flesh into firm peaks.

Katya drew in a sharp breath, then released a soft, fluttering sigh. She was overwhelmed with carnal curiosity and unhindered by propriety. Her body felt marked, burned by Nicholas's touch. Nothing else mattered. She was vaguely aware of Gabriella's soft panting in the room beyond, of Lord Chalmers's low moans of pleasure. The sounds were were no longer embarrassing, for now they seemed merely a reflection of her own burgeoning fervor.

As he caressed her breasts, she rubbed her bottom against his hips. His manhood leaped to life against her skirts. She experienced a momentary surge of pride at the effect she had on him, but her thoughts quickly turned to baser matters as his hand went from her breast to the juncture of her thighs. He moved his palm rhythmically, cupping her most intimate of places through the crimson satin of her skirts. Katya gasped as shock, apprehension, and desire spiraled through her in equal measure. She arched her back and lifted her arms, reaching behind her to touch Nicholas's face.

As she moved, her hand accidentally brushed against the thick oak panel of the wardrobe door. The door parted slightly, then banged softly to a close.

"Did you hear that?" Lord Chalmers's voice echoed across the chamber like a ricocheting bullet.

Katya froze, as did Nicholas.

"Hear what?" asked Gabriella.

"That noise."

Thick silence filled the room. Katya was afraid to move, afraid to even breathe.

After what seemed an interminable pause, Gabriella spoke. "I don't hear anything."

"Odd," said Chalmers. "I could have sworn . . ." His voice trailed off as he left the sentence unfinished.

Katya heard the distinctive creak of mattress springs, followed by the sound of Lord Chalmers's feet striking the floorboards. Then the general rustle of clothing and the low murmur of conversation reached her ears. As she listened to them dress, it occurred to her that Chalmers and his mistress must have finished their lovemaking before she and Nicholas had. But how long before? Katya had lost all sense of time. Had two minutes passed since she heard Gabriella's soft panting, or twenty?

The lovers' tone turned distinctly businesslike as they agreed upon a time and a place for their next rendezvous. Shortly thereafter, Katya heard the sound of footsteps echoing away from her followed by the opening and closing of the chamber door. Hollow silence filled the room.

She let out her breath in a rush. Nicholas waited a minute, then opened the wardrobe door and stepped out. She quickly followed and stood in the center of the room, lost in uncertainty. After the pitch blackness of the wardrobe, the soft moonlight that filled the room made her feel glaringly exposed. She searched her mind for something intelligent to say, but her thoughts and emotions were too jumbled for her to construct a single coherent statement. Unable to meet Nicholas's eyes, she turned her attention to her gown, devoting her entire focus to restoring order to the soft folds of satin.

"Katya."

There was a note of command in his voice, as though he

knew she was doing her best to dodge his gaze—and he wasn't about to let her. Aware that she couldn't avoid him forever, she reluctantly resigned herself to the inevitable and lifted her eyes to meet his. His expression was curiously flat, stripped of any sign of the fire and passion they had shared only moments earlier.

"Do you regret what happened between us?" he asked.

She studied him in mortified silence. "How would you have me answer that?"

"Honestly."

Honestly. As if it were that simple. Then again, perhaps it was. Although her emotions seemed far too complex to analyze in such a brief space of time, she supposed it ultimately came down to just one question: if she had to do it over again, would she? Yes. Without question. Perhaps she should be stronger, firmer in her resistance to the man. But she wasn't. She could no more resist Nicholas than the tides could resist the pull of the moon. If nothing else, at least that much was clear.

"No," she admitted softly, "I don't regret it."

"Nor do I."

In that brief instant, she saw something astonishing in his expression, something she never dreamed she would see. Relief. As though her answer—and perhaps Katya herself— were important to him. Incredible as it seemed, the aloof, decidedly arrogant Lord of Barrington was not as invulnerable as he appeared.

Before she had time to ponder the ramifications of that extraordinary discovery, he took her arm and guided her toward the chamber door. Once there, he stopped. His dark gaze locked on hers.

"We were interrupted," he said firmly, "not ended. I would have you bear that difference in mind."

★　★　★

Nicholas and Katya left Lord Chalmers's room and made their way back to the casino. Fortunately it appeared that their absence had not been noticed. Resuming the roles they had taken earlier, they mingled freely among the other guests, placing wagers, exchanging gossip, and sipping champagne. But despite her attempts to put forth a facade of graceful tranquillity, Katya's emotions remained too heightened from her encounter with Nicholas to properly focus on finding the scroll.

It seemed incredible to her that the gala had continued in their absence as though nothing significant had occurred, for the shift Katya felt within her was one of momentous awe. A life-changing occurrence as impossible and earthshaking as would be the stars veering off course. Unbelievable, yet it had happened. She and Nicholas Duvall. Brought together by fate and destiny, but why? And to what end? The questions lingered, running unanswered through her mind.

Deciding to momentarily abandon the task of searching for the scroll, she left the crowded gaming rooms and stepped out onto the balcony for a breath of fresh air. She moved down a shallow flight of steps and followed a sandy path that led away from the casino and toward the rocky cliffs overlooking the sea. She walked without direction or purpose, needing nothing but a few minutes' respite from her whirling thoughts.

As she rounded a corner, lost in her solitary musing, she was startled by the figure of a man stepping out from the shadows before her. As he moved toward her, she took an automatic step in retreat.

"Miss Alexander?" he asked.

She let out a sigh of relief as she recognized Jeremy Cooke. "Oh, it's you, Mr. Cooke."

"Forgive me, I didn't mean to startle you."

"You didn't. It's just . . . I thought I was alone."

He gave a polite bow. "Of course. I won't intrude on your solitude."

Realizing he had interpreted her words as a request for him to leave, she hastily asked, "Are you having much luck at the tables tonight?"

"I'm afraid I haven't made a single wager."

"No?"

He shrugged. "My family resides among the class politely referred to as impoverished nobility . . . a fancy way of saying that my ancestors have already squandered whatever wealth we once possessed. Not that I'm complaining, mind you," he averred. "If I had an inheritance at my disposal, I fear I would be every bit as much of a wastrel as my ancestors were. But I would throw the funds away on books, rather than tossing it after spinning roulette wheels."

She smiled. "That makes infinitely more sense," she agreed. She studied him quizzically for a moment. His evening attire was a bit threadworn, but proper nonetheless. With his thick glasses, preoccupied air, and mild manner, he looked like a scholar who would be entirely at home poring through dusty tomes in a library—not someone she might encounter outside a casino in the south of France. "If that's the way you feel," she said, "what is it that keeps you in Monaco?"

"Money," he answered bluntly. "Now that the Season is over in London, this is where the wealth is. If I am to continue my father's research, I must find another patron willing to take Lord Barrington's place. I've already spoken to several potential investors who have demonstrated a lively interest in the project."

"What wonderful news."

"Yes," he said proudly, "I'm quite pleased with the way things are progressing."

They walked together in companionable silence. Of all the people Katya had encountered in Monaco, it was probably with Jeremy Cooke that she felt the most at ease. Despite his age—which she guessed to be a year or two older than Nicholas—Jeremy emanated an awkward, slightly boyish charm that made him seem much younger. Katya made a mental note to ask Nicholas to reconsider funding his research.

"The gardens are lovely here, are they not?" she said after a minute.

"Indeed."

She stopped for a moment beside a rosebush covered with rich yellow blossoms. "Lord Barrington has a score of roses on his estate," she said, "but unlike these, they seem to die before they bloom. I don't suppose you might be able to suggest an antidote?"

"I fear I'm not much of a horticulturist."

"Nor am I."

He suddenly brightened. "There is something I recall, however, that might be of use to him. When I was a child there was an old man who lived in our village, one of the few remaining physicians who still adhered to the ancient custom of bleeding his patients back to health. It never occurred to me to wonder what he did with the blood he drained from his patients until I chanced to pass his garden one day and saw him feeding the stuff to his rosebushes."

"The blood?"

"Indeed. He swore there was a property in it that enriches the soil."

She gave a light shudder. "How ghastly."

"But apparently scientific. He had the most magnificent rose garden I've ever seen."

A shout of boisterous male laughter from the balcony drew their attention to the casino. "I suppose we ought to be getting back," she said.

"Of course." He immediately offered his arm. "Allow me

to escort you. The path is rather uneven and can prove somewhat of a maze at times."

She accepted his arm with a murmur of thanks.

As they moved along the path, Jeremy nervously cleared his throat and remarked, "It's quite fortunate that we met this evening."

"Oh?"

"There is something I should like to say to you, Miss Alexander, only I regret very much that I lack the skill to say it without upsetting you. In truth, I don't know where to begin."

Katya gave his arm a light squeeze. "That sounds rather dire."

"I'm afraid it is," he replied somberly. "At the risk of being indelicate, I am not unaware that you and Lord Barrington have a certain . . . intimate relationship."

Surprised and somewhat taken aback, she replied coolly, "I see."

"I would not presume to mention it," he rushed to assure her, "were it not for the conversation we had on our first meeting."

"I don't believe I follow you."

He let out a sigh. "I realize this is terribly awkward for us both. What I mean to say, Miss Alexander, is that I recognize that you are somewhat new to society here in Monaco. Therefore, should you ever find yourself in danger, I would be honored if you would come to me for help."

"Danger?" she repeated with a light laugh. "Surely you exaggerate."

"Lord Barrington's past does not frighten you?"

"Of course not. I can assure you that any rumors surrounding him are completely baseless. He is a perfect gentleman."

"How very charming," put in a shrill feminine voice from

their left. "I've never heard such a testament of undying loyalty."

She looked up to see Philip Montrove and Corrina Jeffreys standing only a foot or so away, at the point where their paths converged. Katya's instinctive reaction was one of unpleasant surprise; of all the people she had met in Monaco, this pair numbered among her least favorite.

"Miss Alexander, Mr. Cooke," Philip Montrove greeted them in a tone of false cheer. "How remarkable to find you here."

The man was attired in an immaculately tailored black suit accented with a cream-colored silk cravat. Beside him Corrina looked supremely fragile and feminine in a frothy gown of pale blue, a diamond tiara nestled atop her golden curls.

"We were just returning to the casino," Jeremy Cooke said stiffly. A note of annoyance touched his voice, as though he was also unhappy to see the pair.

"Were you?" Montrove said. "Odd, you were walking toward the cliffs. The casino is behind you."

Jeremy's head snapped up as he glanced around with a frown. Then he lowered his head in defeated acknowledgment. "It appears you're correct, Lord Montrove." He turned to Katya and sent her an apologetic smile. "I warned you that the paths form a bit of a maze."

"So you did," she said lightly.

They reversed themselves and fell in step beside Corrina and Montrove.

"I don't think I've ever heard the Lord of Barrington described as a perfect gentleman," Corrina remarked, displaying not the slightest bit of embarrassment at having eavesdropped on their previous conversation. Her lips curved in a smile of amused superiority. "I wonder if Nicholas would be pleased or insulted to hear himself thus depicted?"

"Insulted," replied Montrove dryly. "From what I gather, the Lord of Scandal seems to enjoy his villainous title."

"Nearly as much as everyone in Monaco seems to enjoy talking about him behind his back," Katya put in, her tone one of acid sweetness.

Montrove arched a pale blond brow in cool reproof. "Can you blame us, Miss Alexander?"

She shrugged. "I had no idea there was such a scarcity of suitable topics for conversation."

"Perhaps it's the very unsuitability of the topic that makes it so fascinating. As you must be aware, Lord Barrington and Allyson Whitney left quite a mark on society."

Discussing Allyson Whitney, Nicholas's former mistress, was well outside the bounds of propriety, and each of them knew it. Given that, there was no need for Katya to temper her remarks. "Is that a fact?" she said, affecting a tone of icy disdain. "I wouldn't know. Lord Barrington has shown greater discretion than to discuss his former mistresses with me."

"You're right, of course," Montrove conceded. "I mention their relationship simply because I would be devastated to see history repeat itself. If so tragic an ending must occur, surely it should happen only once."

"Tragic?" she repeated. "That's a bit of an overstatement, is it not? Clearly they were ill suited to each other or their relationship would not have ended."

"Indeed," said Montrove. He toyed for a moment with the cuff of his jacket, his gray eyes cool and aloof. If Nicholas was smoldering fire, Katya thought, this man was ice. "Exactly what did Lord Barrington tell you regarding his break with Allyson?" he inquired.

"To his credit, very little. I can hardly see why that should be a matter of my concern."

"That's either a very brave stance or a very foolish one, my dear. Particularly when you consider the facts surrounding Miss Whitney's shocking death."

Katya had thought herself prepared for any assault they

might make against Nicholas's character. But this caught her completely off guard.

"Her death?" she echoed in a shocked, trembling voice she instantly hated.

"It's not surprising that you would be unacquainted with the horrid circumstances surrounding Allyson Whitney," said Corrina. "The scandal has been quite thoroughly hushed up—at least, in so far as no one would ever dare speak of it directly to Nicholas. Still, the taint of it lingers around him, does it not?"

Too occupied with her own thoughts to be annoyed by the patronizing sympathy in Corrina's tone, Katya nodded numbly as she considered the reception Nicholas routinely received from his peers. It was cold to the point of icy. She had attributed the reaction to Nicholas's character in general, even to his family history, rather than to a specific event. Clearly this was not the case.

Only moments earlier she had experienced a sensation of almost giddy joy as she considered Nicholas. Now, however, a chill ran through her bones and a feeling of ominous dread spread through her limbs. Like her ancestor Sacha, she had deliberately blinded herself to that which she did not wish to see. But this was a foolish luxury she could no longer afford.

Steeling herself, Katya returned her attention to her companions. Jeremy Cooke studied the path as he walked, looking extremely uncomfortable. Corrina and Montrove watched her reaction intently, their eyes glowing with barely subdued excitement. Despite their physical beauty, they resembled nothing more than a pair of vultures eagerly waiting to descend.

With an expression of what she hoped would pass for serene detachment, she inquired, "Now that we've come this far, perhaps I should hear the rest of the story. Exactly how did Miss Whitney die?"

Philip Montrove sent her a slightly superior smile. "Undoubtedly that was what Mr. Cooke was so gallantly trying to warn you about before we interrupted," he said. He paused, then finished with the cool aplomb of a fencing master drawing the blood of a novice who had dared to challenge him, "Lord Barrington murdered her."

Fourteen

*N*icholas studied Katya as they sat together in his coach. It was late, and the only sound breaking the stillness of the night was that of the horses' hooves as they moved ploddingly up the steep path that led to his villa. Since leaving the casino she had been curiously silent, almost reserved. Quite a remarkable change from the passion-flamed gypsy who had fallen into his arms in Lord Chalmers's wardrobe.

"Tired?" he asked.

"Not at all."

"You're awfully quiet."

"Am I?"

A sardonic smile curved his lips. "Do I detect a note of sarcasm in your pretty little voice?"

She turned toward him, her beautiful lavender eyes filled with simmering resentment. "When were you planning to tell me about Allyson Whitney?"

He let out a long sigh and leaned back against the plush leather seat. "Ah."

"Ah? Is that all you have to say to me? Ah?"

He lifted his shoulders in a shrug. "A thief and a murderer. A pretty pair, are we not?"

"I'm not a th—"

"Really? Then how would you explain that collection of trinkets you have in your reticule?"

She stiffened her back as her lips turned down in an expression of prim disapproval. After a minute she said tightly, "It's you we're discussing here, not me."

"I see," he replied solemnly. He regarded her in silence

for a long moment, then said evenly, "Suppose you tell me what you heard—and from whom you heard it."

"Very well. I was walking with Jeremy Cooke when we happened to meet Philip Montrove and Corrina Jeffreys. The subject of Allyson Whitney was raised—as was the matter of her death." She paused and took a deep breath, as though gathering her courage; then she finished in a rush, "They told me that you murdered her."

"And?"

Her brows shot skyward. "Isn't that enough?"

"Apparently I owe them a word of thanks," he replied. "They did not malign my character to the extent that they might have."

"What more could they have said?" she asked, aghast.

"They could have told you that I murdered my brother," he replied flatly. His gaze locked on hers across the shadowy dimness of the coach interior. "You don't think one earns the title of Lord of Scandal simply by disposing of an inconvenient mistress, do you?"

An expression of horrified awakening dawned on her face. "I see."

"Do you?"

Heavy silence reverberated between them. Before he could guess her intention, she lifted her arm and rapped her gloved fist against the roof of the coach, calling for the driver to stop. The groomsman ignored her command, urging the team along at the same even, measured pace. After several subsequent—and considerably louder—attempts to gain the groomsman's attention failed, she folded her arms across her chest and sent Nicholas a frigid glare.

"Do you mind?" she asked tightly.

"Not at all." He tapped his knuckles against the roof. "John, stop the coach."

The groomsman drew the team to an immediate stop. Katya threw open the coach door and stumbled out, moving away from him with what appeared to be blind urgency. She strode silently down the path, finally stopping before the jagged, white-capped rocks that drew him so often to the very same spot. She stared out over the moonlit sea, her brows pulled together in a troubled frown.

Nicholas stopped a few feet away, maintaining a quiet distance. A mist had risen from the sea; it wrapped her in a shroud of shimmering gray fog. The gentle night breeze lifted a few strands of her elaborately styled hair. The ebony spirals danced about her face in soft disarray. As he studied her, he was struck by the slimness of her shoulders, the smoothness of her bare arms, the lissome curve of her spine. Despite her posture of sophisticated independence, an air of fragile vulnerability surrounded her.

"I shouldn't have involved you in this," he said. "You've done your part, you're under no further obligation to me."

She turned slowly to face him, an incredulous smile on her lips. "Are you releasing me from my post with top references, as though I were a housekeeper or a cook? Shall I expect a letter of commendation? Mistress for hire: well-spoken, tolerably attractive, possesses superior aptitude for petty thievery?"

Ignoring her sarcasm, he lifted his shoulders in a faint shrug. "If you like, I can provide you with a train ticket out of Monaco and enough money to comfortably settle your parents' debt."

She placed her hands on her hips, studying him with an expression of irritated disbelief. "How very generous. But what I would like," she said, "is an explanation. Why would anyone believe you murdered either your brother or Allyson Whitney?"

"A minute ago you sounded as though you believed it."

"Don't be absurd," she answered shortly. "Of course I don't."

An exasperated nonchalance filled her voice, as though

the mere idea of his being a murderer were too ridiculous to be entertained even for a minute. Her unhesitating display of loyalty was profoundly unexpected—and profoundly touching.

Nicholas had not planned to fill her in on any of the background that had necessitated having her pose as his mistress. But they had clearly reached a point where keeping her uninformed was no longer practical. He let out a dark sigh and raked his fingers through his hair, wondering where to begin.

Finally he said, "Approximately six months ago I received a wire from the authorities in Monaco informing me that my brother had died, that he had leaped to his death from these very rocks."

An expression of quiet horror showed on her face as her gaze moved from him to the jagged rocks lining the cliff. "How dreadful," she said softly. She ran her hands over her arms as though banishing a sudden chill. "Were the two of you very close?"

He shook his head. "Unfortunately not. With every year that passed, we grew more and more distant. The last time I saw Tyler we had a bitter argument. He had long since depleted the funds my father had left him, yet his gaming debts were higher than they had ever been. I had paid off his debts on several previous occasions, but this time I refused to do so. I'll spare you the details of the row that followed—suffice it to say that the argument was heard not only by all the servants in the house, but by a few neighbors as well. Tyler was livid. He swore he would get the money from me one way or another, and that I would be sorry I had ever refused him."

"What did he mean by that?"

"I'm not sure. We never spoke again. The next communication I had informed me of his death." Nicholas hesitated, sorting through the bleak memories that followed. "I discovered that Tyler was even more deeply in debt than he had admitted when I saw him in London. He was about to lose everything he owned, and I had refused to help him."

"You didn't know," Katya pointed out softly.

"That hardly signifies now, does it?" He lifted his shoulders in a resigned shrug. "Rumors immediately spread through London of the row Tyler and I had had before his death. Evidently society determined that I was directly responsible for his death—by refusing my own brother the money he needed, I left him no choice but to take the honorable course of action and end his own life."

"That's ridiculous," she scoffed.

"Perhaps. Or perhaps there's more truth in that than I want to recognize." He stepped on the jagged rocks, moving across their slick, sea-sprayed surface until he stood nearly at the cliff's edge. He stared down at the tumultuous, swirling mass of sea and rock beneath him. "I never saw his body," he said quietly. "By the time I reached Monaco he had already been buried. Apparently I wouldn't have recognized him anyway; he had been so badly battered by the rocks and waves that he could only be identified by his clothing and possessions."

Uneasy silence filled the space between them.

Abruptly recalling himself, he returned his gaze to Katya. "Forgive me. That's a rather grim bit of news to share."

"Are you certain that it was him?" she inquired, meeting his gaze unflinchingly.

Her question went directly to the heart of what had been eating away at Nicholas for months. Putting aside the swirling emotions of shock, anger, and guilt, what bothered him more than anything else was the sense of doubt and disbelief that lingered over his brother's death.

"No, I'm not," he said. "I knew Tyler, better than I've known anyone in my life. He was charming, impetuous, and shrewdly intelligent. He was also reckless, selfish, and occasionally amoral. But above all, he was a fighter. He would not have been so careless with his own life that he would have thrown it away because he could not face the shame of debt."

Katya nodded. "Your brother is alive. I saw it in your palm. He lives."

A hollow smile curved his lips. "How confident you sound."

"I am."

"Unfortunately, little gypsy, I need more proof than that." He hesitated a moment, then continued, "That's why I hired a private investigator to look into the circumstances surrounding my brother's death. At first I suspected murder—perhaps someone to whom he was indebted had decided to take matters into his own hands. Now, however, I think it may run deeper than that."

"What did you learn?"

"That the abbey where the third portion of the scroll has been kept for centuries had been broken into."

"Yes, you mentioned that. What else?"

Nicholas released a weary sigh. He moved away from the edge of the cliff and came to stand beside her. "I don't know who is currently in possession of the scroll. But I'm convinced I know who stole it from my home initially."

Katya searched his gaze. "Your brother?"

"Allyson Whitney."

Startled surprise showed on her features, then her brows drew together in a troubled frown. "I don't understand."

He thought for a moment, searching for the best way to order the events. Finally he began, "On the night of Allyson's death, she and I attended a ball at Lady Sarah Rathbourne's. The gala was the event of the season, and as such it was naturally mobbed. We had been there a little over an hour when Allyson created a horrid scene, announcing loudly that she had had enough of my insane jealousy and possessiveness. She burst into tears and demanded that I take her home immediately. Her accusations were completely baseless, but that mattered little. As you can imagine, the spectacle did not go unnoticed by the crowd."

"I would think not."

"We left the party and my coachman took her home." He paused, then admitted candidly, "At the time I was vain enough to believe that she had created that little spectacle in order to gain my attention. After my brother's death our relationship—such as it was—had floundered dramatically. I was not the attentive suitor she desired."

"I think your inattentiveness would have been understandable."

He lifted his shoulders in a faint shrug. "To you, perhaps, but not to Allyson."

"What happened next?"

"I wasn't yet ready to return home, so I adjourned to a private club on King's Street. The following morning I was visited by two men from the magistrate's office who informed me that Allyson had been murdered. Her body had been found in an alley in London's east end, strangled to death."

Katya gave a slight shudder. "How awful."

He nodded. "In light of the public quarrel we had had the night before, naturally I was their first suspect. Fortunately I had a score of witnesses who could attest to the fact that I had passed nearly the entire night at the club. That was enough to satisfy the magistrates of my innocence, but not society at large. The rumors immediately began to circulate that I had killed Allyson with my bare hands in a fit of jealous rage."

"I see." She studied him for a long moment. Her expression conveyed neither disbelief nor pity, but merely somber contemplation. "What caused you to believe Allyson was responsible for the scroll's theft?" she asked directly.

"A month prior, she had asked me several questions about the scroll. She even asked me to show it to her. At the time I attributed her sudden interest to the legend of the Stone of Destiny—she was fascinated by jewels of any size, shape, or form."

"So she knew where the scroll was kept."

"She did. And I highly doubt it was a coincidence that it disappeared from my home on the night she died."

"I agree." She studied the horizon, searching the glistening midnight stars as though the answers she sought could be found there. The wind whipped around her as she stood motionless at the cliff's edge, sending her crimson skirts flaring out in the night breeze. After a minute she turned back to him and said, "Is it possible that Miss Whitney might have been offered money to retrieve the scroll from your home—and was murdered before the transaction was completed?"

"I considered that as well." Eager to finish the discussion and put it behind them, he continued matter-of-factly, "I believe that the person who planned the theft used Allyson as a pawn—he intended to kill her all along. He probably suggested she create a scene at Lady Rathbourne's ball as an excuse to leave early and rendezvous with him, when his true intention was to create a motive that would make the authorities suspect me in her death."

"But why would Allyson agree to take part in his scheme?"

"I suspect she thought she would profit handsomely from her role—and that she could get away with it. Had she not been murdered, I never would have suspected her involvement. Her quarrel with me had been entirely fabricated. She would have laughed it off to minor dramatics and expected us to resume our relationship just as it had been before."

"I see." Her expression assumed an air of reserved contemplation—not judgmental, merely thoughtful.

"There's more, but it's mere conjecture on my part," he said.

"I'd like to hear it."

"Very well." He placed one booted foot on the jagged rocks and leaned forward, peering out over the smooth indigo sea. "The person I'm after could have hired a thief to break into my home and steal the scroll. That would have been far simpler, far less risky. He chose instead to hire my mistress, murder her, and then lay the blame for her death at my door. He wants more than the scroll and the Stone to which it leads. I suspect he wants to see me dragged before the House of Lords and branded a murderer before all of London. He wants to see me stripped of my homes and my title and my wealth, to see me hurt and humiliated."

A look of appalled understanding crossed Katya's features. "Would your brother hate you enough to do something like that?"

"I don't know," Nicholas admitted quietly. The thought that it might be Tyler plotting against him burned in his belly like a lump of blistering lead. But no matter how he tried to convince himself that the very suggestion was absurd, he couldn't dispel the notion that it might be true.

"Sometimes I don't know which would be worse," he said to Katya. "The thought that Tyler would hate me enough to fake his own death and conspire against me, or that he came to me desperate for help and I refused him."

"In either case, it wouldn't be your fault."

"Wouldn't it?" he countered sharply. Refusing to allow himself to vent his anger and frustration on her, he drew in a deep breath, then slowly released it. "There is a third possibility," he said. "One I hope you'll help me prove. I may yet discover that I have an enemy I am unaware of. Someone who moves in the same circles as I, someone who knew both Allyson and Tyler. Someone who is here in Monaco right now, watching every move we make. Someone who will strike against me again—only this time I am prepared."

"That's why you involved me," Katya surmised. "To find that person."

"Yes." He hesitated, then said firmly, "But whatever answer we find, I won't run from it—even if it is Tyler who is been behind the plot. Sometimes I think that the worst part of this is not knowing, not having the answers to what truly happened."

"I would imagine so."

"Now that you know the whole story, I won't blame you if you want out. If I could offer you assurances that you'll be safe no matter what happens, I would. But I can't do that."

Taking her silence for an assent that she wanted out, he nodded firmly and continued in a businesslike tone, "Very well. My earlier offer still stands. As of noon tomorrow I'll see to it that you are provided with a train ticket out of Monaco and enough money to comfortably settle your parents' debt. Will that be satisfactory?"

"No, Lord Barrington, it will not be."

He searched her face, studying her in surprise.

She brought up her chin, her lavender eyes glistening with steely resolve. "I didn't run earlier, and I'm certainly not going to run now."

"You're not frightened?"

With an impatient wave of her hand, she brushed that away as though it were a matter of little import. "Nothing's changed," she said briskly. "You've simply made the picture a little clearer. And might I add that you should have done so days ago."

Relieved beyond measure that she wasn't leaving, Nicholas nodded, silently accepting her reproach. "Very well then. Henceforth, there shall exist nothing but complete honesty between us. Are we in agreement?"

For just an instant, an emotion that looked remarkably like

stark dismay flitted across Katya's face. Or perhaps it was simply a trick of the moonlight, for the emotion vanished as quickly as it had appeared, leaving nothing in its place but solemn composure. "Agreed."

Nicholas studied her for a long moment, feeling as though yet another shift had taken place in their relationship. In the silence that followed, he asked, "Why are you staying?"

"You need me," she replied, astonishing him with her honesty. She hesitated a moment, then added softly, "Perhaps we need each other."

Unable to stop himself, he reached out, brushing one hand softly across her cheek. "Perhaps we do, little gypsy."

Fifteen

$\mathcal{N}$icholas sat alone in his study, nursing a brandy and listening to the late-night sounds that echoed through the villa. Katya had retired to her room hours ago, but he was too restless to even attempt sleep. Instead he retreated to his study to try to bring some semblance of order to his chaotic thoughts. Thus far he was having little success.

The portrait of his father seemed to glare down at him, watching his every move with haughty arrogance and stern disapproval. Nicholas returned the stare, lifting his glass to the portrait in a mocking toast. He had always thought that Tyler had inherited the worst of his father's traits. His selfishness, his recklessness, his childlike excesses. But perhaps he was more like his father than he wanted to admit.

For wasn't it unmitigated selfishness—and nothing less—that caused him to experience such immense relief that Katya had chosen to stay? If Nicholas had any conscience he would send her away and out of danger. But something profoundly unique in her kept drawing him back. From the day they had met she had remained on the edge of his mind, filling his thoughts and teasing his senses. If he closed his eyes he could smell her hair, hear her voice, see her eyes. He could taste her lips and feel her skin. She seemed *necessary* to him. As necessary as the air he breathed or the water he drank. It was a sensation unlike anything he had experienced with any other woman. Ever.

He took another sip of brandy. While the fiery liquid rolled across his tongue he imagined what might have happened had he and Katya met elsewhere, under entirely different circumstances. But he could imagine her in no other place. Nicholas was not one to put much store in either luck or destiny, but neither was he immune to the pull of fate. And it felt as though fate had brought them together in Monaco for a reason—whatever that might be.

At the sound of a clock chiming the early hour of two in the morning, he set down his glass and stretched, taking it as his cue to retire. But then another sound caught his attention.

That of a soft footfall creeping past his study door.

He frowned, listening intently. It was too late for the servants to be about, Katya had gone to bed hours ago, and the Comtesse would never have come to pay a call at this hour. Nicholas felt his muscles tense as a furious certainty gripped him that the person who had stolen the scroll had returned for something else. The intruder's steps hesitated in front of his door, then continued stealthily on. Nicholas slowly rose from his chair, left his study, and quietly followed.

He recognized Katya immediately. Her hair was unbound, streaming down her back in a wild profusion of rich ebony curls. She wore a white dressing gown that was tightly cinched at the waist. The long sleeves had been rolled up and the hem trailed past her ankles. She was entirely engulfed in the thick folds of smooth white cotton, giving her the seductive appearance of a woman who had hastily donned her bedsheets rather than her clothing.

She moved silently through the villa, exiting through the glass doors that led to the terrace and the gardens beyond. Nicholas followed at a discreet distance, reluctant to make his presence known. The fabric of her dressing gown took on a nearly translucent glow in the moonlight, making it clear that she wore nothing underneath. As she moved he saw the shadowy outline of her slim, lithe form. The gown billowed about her as though dancing in the breeze, causing the tantalizing scent of her skin to drift back to him. She was an elfin enchantress, a barefooted sprite who lured him out of his home and into a moonlit garden.

Katya was clearly familiar with the grounds, for she moved with a stride that was unhesitating and purposeful, as though she had a specific destination in mind. Finally she stopped at the deteriorating gazebo that had once been his mother's sanctuary. It jealously occurred to him that she might have scheduled a rendezvous with another man. As that dark thought took root, he watched her step into the elevated gazebo. She rested one hand on the wooden rail that flanked her and looked out over the gardens. But her eyes were unseeing, as though she were lost in inner thought. Moreover, there was a stillness about her that indicated she was content in her solitude; that she was looking for no one.

"Katya," he said. He called her name unthinkingly, with no purpose but to make her aware of his presence.

She gave a sharp gasp and spun around. He knew the instant she recognized him, for a look of relief entered her eyes and she gave a light, shaky laugh. "Oh, it's you, Nicholas."

He left his place in the garden and entered the gazebo, coming to stand beside her. Softly he said, "That is the first time you called me by my given name without my demanding it."

"Is it?" she asked. "I am surprised you would notice."

"I notice everything about you."

She quietly searched his gaze; then she turned away, self-consciously tightening the belt on her dressing gown. "What are you doing out here?"

"I was in my study and heard you walk past the door. I thought it might be an intruder and followed."

She nodded; then they stood together in silence, absorbing the sights and smells of the gardens. "Do you come out here often?" she finally inquired.

"Never."

A look of mild surprise showed on her face. "Why?"

"I suppose because my attention is not needed. I have a staff that tends the grounds."

"You never come out here just to enjoy the beauty?"

"No." He had always associated this part of the villa with his mother. When she died, the joy of the gardens had died with her.

"Hmmm," Katya murmured, studying him thoughtfully. She turned back to the gardens. "Your staff does a remarkable job. Except for this one spot."

He followed her gaze and nodded. "So I see. The roses are dying."

"Not dying," she corrected softly, "just failing to bloom."

"Is there a difference?"

"Yes. According to the Comtesse, an important one." Before he could puzzle out the meaning of her words, she continued, "I mentioned to Jeremy Cooke that your roses wouldn't bloom. He suggested that we feed them blood."

"I beg your pardon?"

"I know it sounds rather ghastly, but he said that there's an element in blood that enriches the soil. Apparently he has seen it work."

"Really? How fascinating." Nicholas leaned his shoulder against one of the tall beams that supported the gazebo's roof. "Did he suggest whose blood we use? I would offer mine, but I happen to be using it at the moment."

A small smile touched her lips. "That does leave us in a bit of a quandary, doesn't it?"

They stood together in silence, listening to the sounds of insects buzzing and chirping in the garden. Finally Nicholas said, "What are you doing out here?"

She gave a light shrug. "I couldn't sleep. I thought a walk and some fresh air might help."

"Something wrong?"

Katya said nothing for a long moment, then she turned

and faced him. Her lavender eyes glistened with a luminous inner glow as she replied, "I thought you might come to me tonight."

Nicholas felt his pulse skip a beat as desire leaped to life within him. "And if I had?" he asked. "Would that have been good or bad?"

"I couldn't decide. I suppose that's what kept me awake."

"I see."

She turned away, running her hand along the smooth wooden railing that encircled the gazebo. "I thought at first that what was happening between us was so new, so different from anything I had ever experienced. But then I realized that that wasn't the case at all. That that's why it seemed so familiar. It's happened before."

He frowned, distinctly displeased with the notion that she might be comparing him to some former lover. Yet he couldn't stop himself from asking, "What do you mean?"

Her lips curved in a smile of dreamy reminiscence. "Once when I was a child I was playing in the ocean. The water was totally calm and smooth as glass, but slightly chilly. I was alone in the water and therefore cautious, keeping sight of the beach as I swam, careful not to go too far out to sea. Suddenly I felt this odd, strange current of warm water wrap around me. It started at my toes and worked its way up to my chin, engulfing me completely in its warmth. Before I knew what was happening the warm current had dragged me out to sea.

"It didn't happen immediately," she said. "But slowly, bit by bit, as though the current were taking me in its embrace. Although I knew it was dangerous, it was also strangely comforting and exciting. I didn't want to leave the warmth to return to the chilly water that would send me back to the shore and safety. I was floating, free, exhilarated. After a few minutes, I couldn't fight it even if I had wanted to. The current had become too strong."

"What happened?"

"A local fisherman recognized my plight and reached me in time to pull me aboard his boat."

"Is that who I remind you of? The fisherman?"

"The fisherman?"

"Am I to be your savior?"

Her gaze locked on his. "You're the current," she replied. "Warm, smooth, and dangerous. I'm afraid you'll draw me so far out to sea that I'll never again be able to reach the shore."

He studied her for a long moment, then said in quiet understanding, "Surrender. Would that be so bad?"

She shook her head in an expression of helpless uncertainty. "I don't know. I'm a different person when I'm with you and it frightens me. I feel this strange sense of letting go, of drifting away."

"Have you always been so tightly in control?"

"Yes."

He moved toward her, closing the distance between them. With one hand he reached out, his fingers softly stroking her temple. "Until now."

Her eyes searched his. Her small pink tongue darted out as she nervously licked her bottom lip. Then she nodded. In a low, raspy voice, she whispered, "Until now."

Nicholas wrapped his arm around her and pulled her tightly to him. The soft curves of her body yielded instantly to the lean, muscular firmness of his. He searched her face for any sign of hesitation, half expecting her to pull away. But he read nothing but wary eagerness and open trust.

He lowered his head, moving his lips over hers. His touch was gentle at first, lightly tasting and teasing. But this kiss of sweet exploration quickly sparked and burned with dark, possessive fire. He couldn't get enough of her lips, the taste of her mouth, the scent of her skin. He increased the pressure of his jaw against hers and slipped his tongue inside her mouth.

Katya matched the ardor of his kiss with passion. She lifted her arms and locked them around his neck in an irresistible combination of innocence and sensuality. Her body, soft and yielding, leaned into his as she mimicked the rhythm of his kiss. As his excitement grew, Nicholas drew her closer, tracing the delicate line of her spine from her neck to the small of her back. He cupped her buttocks, caressing the firm, round globes; then he brushed his fingers along the tops of her thighs. She responded with a soft, purring moan issued from deep within her.

As her hips pressed against his, the smooth flesh of her belly rubbed against his manhood, causing his erection, to grow hard and thick. The burning hunger within him ignited and became a dull ache. Suddenly impatient to feel her skin against his own, he lifted his hand and fumbled awkwardly with the ribbons that fastened the front of her gown. As he worked the silky ties free he kissed her jaw, her ear, her neck, then trailed a line of fiery kisses along the delicate length of her collarbone.

Once her gown was partially opened, he nuzzled the shadowy cleft between her breasts with an eager, awkward ferocity, as though starving for the taste of her skin. He was overcome by a sense of almost painful urgency, so intense was his desire for Katya. Nicholas had always considered himself a courteous, even proficient lover. But at the moment he was aware of nothing but his own overwhelming need.

He glanced around the wooden gazebo, his eyes moving from the rough wooden floor to the cold stone benches— both entirely unsuitable for his purposes. But he was too hungry for her, too nakedly needy to wait until they reached the sanctuary of his bedroom. He took her hand and ushered her down the wide flight of stairs that led from the gazebo to the gardens below. He stopped in a patch of lush, dewy grass that was encircled by the white rosebushes. Removing his thick burgundy dressing robe, he spread it out over the grass as a makeshift blanket.

Katya willingly followed Nicholas's lead, completely captured by the magical, sensual spell he had woven around her. She hesitated only when he knelt down and attempted to pull her down beside him. A spark of prim practicality intruded on the sensual fog that had overtaken her.

"We'll ruin your dressing robe," she protested.

"I'll buy another one."

Responding to the undisguised hunger she heard in his voice, she allowed Nicholas to guide her down beside him onto the soft burgundy velvet. His large hands gently stroked her body as she lay beside him, touching her with a captivating combination of passion and reverence. She searched his eyes and saw the smoky fires of desire blazing within their ebony depths. But there was something else there as well. Something that looked astonishingly like raw, overwhelming need. For her.

Awed by the realization he wanted her as badly as she wanted him, she put aside her hesitation and reached out for him, lightly moving her hands over the firm, hard muscles of his chest. Nicholas let out a sound that was half growl, half moan and pressed his mouth against hers once again. The subtle taste of brandy clung to his lips, warming her blood and making her head swim with dizzy desire. She returned his kiss with the same ardent urgency she felt building within him.

Nicholas's large, powerful hands moved over her body with a sure, deft touch, heating her skin beneath the gown. Then he shifted slightly so that she lay flat on the ground beneath him. He propped himself up on his elbows, bracing his weight above her as he reached down and caught the front of her dressing gown between his fingers. Carefully parting the smooth cotton fabric, he traced his fingers lightly along her skin. He moved with slow deliberation, totally absorbed in his task.

As his hand moved from her collarbone to her navel, Katya's attention was caught by the feel of his ring against her skin. The cold, thick band of gold sent an icy shiver down her spine. Although she had tried to avoid thinking about it, the ring provided a jolt of unwelcome reality. There was no escaping the fact that she was about to give herself to her family's mortal enemy.

She drew back abruptly. "Nicholas."

He lifted his head, studying her with eyes that smoldered with desire. "Yes?"

"Will you take that off?"

"What? Oh—of course." His hands reached automatically toward the buttons of his shirt.

"No, not that. Your ring."

His brows drew together in a puzzled frown. "My ring?"

"The metal feels so cold against my skin. Do you mind?"

By way of answer, he pulled off the ancient gold band and stuffed it into his shirt pocket. Then he reached beneath her gown and ran his hand up the silky skin of her thigh. "Better?" he murmured. His breath fanned her ear, all hot, seductive, and spicy.

Katya managed a tight nod. She closed her eyes and took a deep breath, willing her tension away. She knew her request had been nothing but childish superstition on her part. Making him take off his ring would do no more good than knocking wood or hunting for four-leaf clovers. But in some small, foolish corner of her mind, she couldn't help but feel that if his ring were gone, all the bad connected with it would disappear as well.

Nicholas boldly ran his hands over her skin, warming her flesh with his own. His hands seemed to be everywhere at once, and where his hands went, his mouth immediately followed. He kissed her hair, her face, and her breasts. He kissed her ankles, her knees, and the tops of her thighs. He kissed her fingers, her wrists, and the nape of her neck, setting her flesh on fire with his fiery touch. Soon Katya was aware of nothing else. She succumbed completely to the mastery of his touch as his hands worked free the last ties to her dressing gown. He parted the garments and pulled them from her body, carelessly tossing them aside.

A sudden stillness came over him. Katya lay beneath him, naked and vulnerable; she was suddenly awash with trepidation. She fought the urge to cover herself as she searched his gaze for signs of disappointment. Insecurities she had never known she possessed suddenly rose up, threatening to extinguish the heady passion that had engulfed her so completely only moments ago. Were her breasts too large? Too small? Was her waist too narrow, her hips too full, her legs too long?

Much to her relief, however, she read stark approval in his eyes, combined with profound, unmistakable desire. She had thought him a lone, predatory animal when they first met. That same sense struck her now. Something in the way his ebony gaze moved slowly over her body told her that he was branding her as his own. She had always considered herself a thoroughly modern and rational woman. But the notion of belonging to Nicholas Duvall sent through her a primitive thrill that was undeniable.

"Look at you," he murmured huskily. "You're so beautiful, Katya. So beautiful." Kneeling, he lifted his hands and traced them lightly over her body, as though fixing her every curve to memory.

The thrill of feminine conquest coursed through her as she experienced a pride in her body she had never before known. But his words jarred something deep within her. She was not content simply to have him see her. She wanted—needed—to feel and explore his body in the way that he was touching hers. She reached up and tugged at his shirt, popping the buttons off the smooth, crisp linen. Immediately reading her intent, he shrugged off the garment. They fumbled together with the rest of his clothing, lost in their urgency and clumsy with desire.

Once Nicholas was naked he knelt before her in the moonlit garden, his skin glowing like ancient bronze. His body was a mass of hard, sinewy muscle and lean, powerfully sculpted flesh, so perfect that it was almost intimidating. She lifted her hand and placed it tentatively on his chest, as though she wasn't quite certain of her right to touch him. His skin felt hot and curiously smooth; his muscles quivered and leapt to life beneath her hand. Emboldened by his reaction to her touch, filled with both wonder and awe, she lightly skimmed her hands over his body. His dark hair was silkier than she had imagined, his shoulders broader, his muscles firmer. She indulged her wanton curiosity, touching him everywhere—until she reached his manhood.

Then she pulled back her hand as though it had been bitten by a snake.

Katya was not so naive that she lacked a rudimentary knowledge of lovemaking. Once she had even dared to read an anatomy book. But the dry, clinical explanation she had read bore no resemblance to what she was currently experiencing. What about the anxious trembling that seized her limbs, the sensual fog that muddled her thoughts, or the tight knot that filled her belly and radiated warmth through her veins? Why hadn't these been mentioned? If they had been, she could have been prepared.

Or could she have?

Her gaze returned skittishly to Nicholas's throbbing manhood. His firm erection jutted proudly to life against the flatness of his stomach. She swallowed hard as wary skepticism gripped her. He would bury that intimate part of him deep within her? Impossible.

As though sensing her fear, he gathered her in his arms once again, refusing to allow her time to focus on her worries. His lips over hers, he cupped her breasts in his hands. He brushed his fingers lightly over her nipples, teasing them until they rose to firm, stiff peaks. Just when Katya thought she could stand the pleasure of his touch no longer, he brought his mouth to her nipple, gently licking and sucking. She gave a cry of shock and stiffened in surprise, then melted with pleasure. His lips traveled over her body in erotic exploration, kissing her ribs, the hollow curve of her belly, the soft swell of her hip. He lavished her with kisses and caresses, stroking her body until it felt inflamed.

Then he moved his hand, bringing it to rest between her thighs. She instinctively clamped her legs shut in wild panic.

"Easy, Katya," he murmured against her ear. "Open your legs for me, little gypsy."

Gathering her courage, she cautiously inched her thighs apart. As she did, she experienced a momentary, fleeting sense of shame at her response to him. She felt a damp heat between her legs and a pulsating warmth that seemed to radiate from her thighs and spread outward. No doubt someone like Corrina Jeffreys would be cool, dry, and slightly remote. Katya sensed that her own response was entirely unseemly, but she had no idea how to control it.

Fortunately Nicholas gave no indication of displeasure. In fact, just the opposite was true. As his fingers explored the soft folds of her innermost places, he gave a low growl that sounded distinctly approving. He rhythmically stroked the tight pearl of flesh fronting the delicate opening between her legs, causing a shiver of heated excitement to course up her spine.

Katya's restraint vanished as she surrendered completely to her base instincts. Her need for him was overpowering, almost a living, breathing thing, so great was the hunger that engulfed her. Her nails clawed at his back as she writhed beneath him. She heard a strange, faraway noise, something between a moan and a purr, and she was startled to realize that it was she who was making it.

She felt a tremor run through Nicholas as he gave a soft moan of his own. "Katya," he said, her name a breathless sigh that had been torn from deep within him.

He shifted slightly, bracing himself on his elbows above her. His eyes locked onto hers as the tip of his silky shaft touched the folds of her innermost lips. Moving with deliberate, infinite care, he thrust his hips forward and slowly entered her.

Katya's eyes widened with wonder. She felt her body stretch to allow him entrance, then hold his manhood in a tight, firm grip deep inside. Awe and tenderness flooded through her. Their union was so simple and at the same time so intimate and earthshaking. Unable to put her emotions into words, she placed her hands on Nicholas's shoulders, drawing him closer into her embrace.

He slid his hips forward, inching further inside her, then abruptly he stopped. He was clearly holding back, his muscles trembling with the effort of holding himself still. She realized in that instant that he was waiting for something from her, for some sort of acknowledgment or acquiescence. She lifted her hand and ran it lightly over his jaw, instinctively attempting to soothe the tension she saw there.

"Yes," she said. "Yes." She had nothing but a hazy idea of what she was agreeing to, but that didn't matter. She knew only that stopping now would be more painful than anything yet to come.

A look of naked relief crossed his features, followed almost immediately by an expression of harsh regret. He drew back, then plunged himself deep within her. Sharp, stabbing pain intruded into the warm, melting sensation she had experienced only moments earlier.

Katya stiffened in shock and opened her lips to cry out.

Nicholas captured her mouth with his, swallowing her cry as though attempting to transfer her pain to himself. And the sharp ache slowly eased. She let out a sigh of relief as the tension drained out of her.

Feeling her relax beneath him, Nicholas began to move once again. He pulled his hips back, then thrust slowly forward. He moved cautiously at first, as though she were supremely fragile. As the sensual pressure built within her once again, she lifted her hips to meet his. Her hands gently caressed his back, silently urging him on. Taking his cue from her, he began to move faster, stroking her deep inside, moving in an endless, teasing dance of withdrawal and advance that left her yearning, aching for more.

Katya grasped his shoulders and arched her back to meet his steady, rhythmic thrusts. Her breath came in short, hot gasps and a fine sheen of perspiration coated her skin. She was wet and hot, yet her body trembled as though it were the dead of winter. She couldn't stop touching Nicholas; she needed him too badly. Her hands skimmed the bunched muscles of his back, his firm buttocks, his rocklike thighs, moving over his body with almost frantic determination.

She felt as though she were melting and flying at the same time, building toward some unknown goal. A tight knot of liquid fire coiled within her belly, threatening to explode at any moment. She was soaring, climbing ever higher, striving to reach some faraway plateau. Her fingers clenched reflexively as a sudden rush of heat surged through her body. Passion swelled within her. Her limbs tensed, then abruptly relaxed as a thousand stars shattered deep within her, sending waves of shimmering pleasure coursing through her veins.

As she arched her back and cried out her pleasure Nicholas drove into her harder and harder, faster and deeper. He threw back his head, his body shuddering as he gave a hoarse cry of his own. The wet warmth of his seed poured into her, filling her with its rich male essence. Then he collapsed weakly on top of her, as drained of strength as she was.

They lay together atop the burgundy velvet, their slick bodies still intimately joined, locked together in breathless triumph. Katya felt Nicholas's chest rise and fall against her own, heard his heart pound against her ear. Her senses working overtime, she concentrated intently, fixing the moment forever in her mind. She wanted to remember it all: the stars twinkling in the sky above them, the sound of their mingled breathing, the salty taste of his skin, the thick fragrance of the roses mingled with the heady odor of their union, the sticky warmth between her thighs. She suspected she would be sore tomorrow—perhaps she would even experience regret—but at that moment it didn't matter.

After a minute he rolled to the side, taking his weight off her. As he pulled away she tensed, suddenly feeling very vulnerable. She was gripped by an irrational certainty that he would stand and move away, leaving her alone. Instead he drew her to him, her back snuggled up against his chest. He brushed the damp hair from her forehead with a gentle, ministering touch, and he softly kissed her temple. Then he drew his hand lightly over her belly, her ribs and breasts in a meandering, indolent caress. Katya closed her eyes and let out a low purr, a sound that was almost a whimper, of luxuriant relief and satisfied pleasure.

"Did I hurt you very badly?" he asked. Although she couldn't see his face, a gruff note of regret and apology was clear in his voice.

She caught his hand and lifted it to her mouth, brushing his knuckles with a light kiss. "No."

Heavy silence hung between them.

"What are you thinking?" he asked.

Her senses too befuddled to reply with anything but the truth, she asked, "Did I please you?"

He rolled his fingers lightly over her shoulder blades.

"You pleased me, Katya," he answered quietly. "Everything about you pleases me. It sometimes frightens me how much."

There was something vaguely dark about his answer, as though his words contained a foreshadowing of some future unpleasantness. Katya deliberately pushed her fear aside, refusing to allow her grim premonitions to intrude on their intimacy.

"I've heard that some people actually make love in beds," she said, trying to lighten the moment.

"Really?" He made a *tsking* sound with his tongue. "They are obviously lovers of limited imagination."

"Or perhaps the nobility is simply more creative."

"Very astute." He gave her bottom a light, approving pat. "Clearly there's more to you than a ravishingly beautiful body."

"How kind of you to notice."

The warm breeze they had enjoyed earlier grew progressively chilly, until at last they resigned themselves to abandoning the garden and returning to the villa. They gathered their clothing from where it had been strewn and quietly dressed. Katya took one last, lingering look at the place where their bodies had joined, then turned toward Nicholas. Seeing that her gaze had turned toward him, he sent her a soft smile and silently reached for her.

His ancient gold-and-onyx ring glistened in the moonlight as she placed her hand in his.

Sixteen

*K*atya sat alone in her bedchamber with the curtains pulled wide, flooding the room with glorious Mediterranean sunshine. The early morning song of a warbler nesting in the olive tree outside her window drifted in to greet her. Her spirits buoyed by the beauty of the day, she hummed a light tune as she fastened the last of the tiny pearl buttons lining the front of her blouse. Then she moved to stand before the looking glass, checking her appearance one last time before going downstairs to join Nicholas.

Her attire was modest: an indigo riding skirt and matching cropped jacket with a crisp white blouse beneath. Wearing her hair in a thick ponytail, she wore a classic straw boater that was softened by the addition of navy and lavender ribbons around the hat's wide brim. The ensemble was completed by sensible brown riding boots and wrist-length leather gloves. All in all, she decided, her clothing was eminently suited for a leisurely afternoon spent riding.

But as she gazed into the looking glass, she knew that she was searching for more than the mere suitability of her attire. Two weeks had passed since she and Nicholas had become lovers. Although she had embarked on the affair burdened by a nearly overwhelming sense of trepidation, her worries had all but vanished.

As she searched her reflection, she wondered if the heady thrill of her burgeoning romance was visible to everyone who saw her. Did her eyes glow with inner excitement? Were her cheeks rosier? Was her smile more mysterious? She half expected to see physical evidence of their relationship on her skin; surely Nicholas had left his mark somewhere. How was it possible that he could affect her so profoundly heart and soul, yet leave no trace of his touch for others to see?

Even though she was alone in her bedchamber, it felt as though he were beside her. She could still smell the spicy, masculine scent of his skin on her bedsheets. She could almost hear the low murmur of his voice as he whispered in her ear, or the steady sound of his boots echoing down the hall as he came to her room late at night. She saw herself, eager and breathless, trembling with desire, waiting for him in her bed. If she closed her eyes and imagined it, she could almost feel him standing behind her, reaching around to hold her breasts in his hands as he kissed the nape of her neck. She could almost feel the gentle brush of his lips over her skin, the tight knot of warmth radiating from the juncture of her thighs as he slowly entered her, and the way her nipples tingled in glorious anticipation of his touch.

Their lovemaking embraced her like an invisible ghost, holding her tightly in its thrall. It was an odd sort of possession, but one to which she willingly submitted. His presence surrounded her; the very air seemed to pulsate with his being. His touch captured her completely, setting her flesh on fire and making her shudder with so much pleasure that she nearly felt weak. In the two weeks that they had been lovers, they had settled into an exquisite, sensual routine. Or perhaps, Katya reflected, routine wasn't the right word for it, as each night was spectacularly different from the others.

The news of their liaison was likely of interest to no one else—particularly since she had been posing as his mistress since her arrival in Monaco—but to her it was a source of unending astonishment. She felt as though she were a different person. Surely it was apparent to anyone who looked at her that the rational, prudent Miss Katya Alexander no longer existed. Every move she had ever made was always meticulously planned—until now. For the first time in her life she had willingly thrown caution to the wind, allowing the giddy bliss of passion to replace the more tempered path of reason. She gave herself freely, without worrying about the consequences. Most remarkable of all, she enjoyed a stunning lack of shame.

Her only troubling moments came when she thought of the fleeting nature of her arrangement with Nicholas. Where would it lead? Their relationship had been temporary at best, unscrupulous at worst. Her original plan, so brash and daring, now seemed unimaginable. Could she possibly steal the scroll out from under him and leave without a word?

Putting that weighty issue aside for the moment, she turned away from the looking glass and moved across the room to her bedside table. She had taken to poring over Sacha's diary every chance she had; the ancient documents covered the small mahogany nightstand. Katya had become fascinated with the diary, finding parallels to her own life on every page. It seemed as though the destiny she and Nicholas shared was mysteriously entwined with that of her ill-fated ancestor centuries ago.

Katya was driven by the irrational notion that if she could find an explanation for what had gone wrong between Sacha and Marco, she might be able to foresee how her relationship with Nicholas would end. But the excerpts she had read thus far suggested nothing but rapidly escalating affection and intimacy between the medieval lovers—exactly what she was experiencing with Nicholas. Frowning as she pondered that fact, she opened the diary and removed the ancient parchment page she had discovered that morning. Although she had read it so many times it was nearly committed to memory, she scanned the document once again, looking for something in Sacha's words or tone that she may have missed.

Marco came to me again last night. I thought at first it was only a dream, for none but a sorcerer can move through the castle so unguarded, or slip into my room with the silent grace of a shimmering moonbeam. Then his lips touched mine. He is no phantom, but a man of flesh and blood. Only Marco can awaken the fire within me, only he can spark the quivering heat that spreads through my body. Even the rough linen of my bedsheets turns to woven silk with his touch. I know it is a sin to be with him without the sacrament of marriage, but how can I turn him away? Soon we will be together for eternity. Is it so wicked that I should let him claim my body, when he has already laid claim to my soul?

Katya folded the page and tapped it against her lips, vaguely uneasy. Was Sacha's loyalty to Marco commendable or foolish? If the worst-case scenario were true and Marco had set out to destroy her from the very beginning, at least Sacha had been an unknowing innocent, her faith rewarded with cruelty and treachery. But Katya could plead no such defense. She had entered into her liaison with Nicholas knowing exactly what she was doing. Like a willful child playing with matches, she had completely disregarded the danger contained in the lure of the dancing flames.

The kiss of fate. Her mother had told her that it had been bestowed upon her at birth, but she had neglected to mention whether it was a blessing or a curse. Katya let out a sigh. Perhaps only time would tell. She swept up the ancient documents and tucked them neatly away in the hidden compartment at the base of her trunk. Then she picked up her reticule, looped it through the waistband of her skirt, and left the room, heading downstairs to join Nicholas.

She found him in the parlor that overlooked the terrace, enjoying tea with the Comtesse. He rose to his feet the instant she entered the room. The Lord of Scandal, she thought, watching him move toward her with passion in his ebony eyes. How apt the title. Once he had been intimidating. Now he was intoxicating.

Katya fleetingly wondered if her eyes mirrored his. If he saw within her gaze the same longing, the same approval, the same eager rush of desire that flooded through her every time they were reunited, no matter how short the absence. Even if her emotions were as blatantly visible as she feared, she doubted she could hide them.

Fortunately the Comtesse displayed the utmost discretion, acting as though she were blind to the fact that the relationship Katya and Nicholas enjoyed had been profoundly altered. Although Katya knew the regal older woman would never comment on their newfound intimacy, her expression indicated approval.

"Do come in and see the costumes I sent for, Miss Alexander," she said. "It has taken an inordinate amount of time for them to arrive, but at last they are here."

Katya stepped into the room. "Costumes?" she asked. She stopped as her gaze fell on a pair of richly detailed medieval robes that were laid out over a chintz-covered settee. The first was clearly a woman's gown: a long-sleeved smock of soft, misty green, made from a linen so sheer that it was nearly transparent. Over it was a surcoat of rich silver brocade. For Nicholas there was a cream-colored chemise woven from soft flax, a sleeveless tunic, a pair of coarsely knit braies in a deep copper color, and a rich indigo cape heavily studded with jewels. A wide leather belt with a loop that held a glistening dirk completed the ensemble. As her fingers brushed the gleaming blade, a shiver of ominous forewarning raced down her spine.

"If you don't like them—" the Comtesse began.

"Not at all," Katya said, sending her a wan smile. "It's just that they're so . . . authentic."

"They should be. My first husband was an amateur scholar with a particular fondness for medieval lore. He ordered the costumes years ago for a ball we attended in London. He designed them himself and was meticulous in every detail, right down to the very thread with which they were sewn together."

"I see."

"If they meet with your approval, I thought they might be suitable for you and Nicholas to wear to the Fete du Tarasque."

Katya turned to Nicholas with a soft frown. "The Fete du . . . ?"

"Tarasque," he supplied. "It's an annual festival here in Monaco. The Tarasque is a man-eating creature of mythic appearance, part dragon and part lion. You'll find it on many of the heraldic flags in the area. Legend has it that the beast roamed the countryside, laying waste to the towns and villages in its path. Although many powerful knights attempted to slay it, it was a beautiful maiden who finally soothed the ferocious beast with her awesome beauty. Once under her spell, the Tarasque fought alongside the knights against the Saracen invaders who stormed the region."

He paused and folded his arms over his chest, resting against a sturdy mahogany desk. "The taming of the Tarasque is now celebrated with a day of bullfights, outdoor concerts, wine festivals, and a parade in which the beast is carried through the streets in effigy and ultimately tamed by a town maiden. The celebration culminates at night with a huge gathering in the ancient quarter of town." He nodded toward the clothing the Comtesse had sent for. "It's traditional for those attending the gala to dress in medieval garb, hence the costumes."

Now that the reason for the attire had been explained, Katya felt somewhat better. Somewhat. But a lingering sense of apprehension remained as her gaze moved over the clothing. Putting aside her reservations for the moment, she turned to the Comtesse and said, "The costumes are exquisite, but there are only the two. Won't you be joining us?"

An expression of haughty astonishment flashed across the older woman's face. "Heavens, no. That's far too parochial a spectacle for me." She released a mock shudder. "As far as I can tell, the festival is nothing but a blatant excuse for everyone involved to behave with abysmal taste and make complete fools of themselves—not that they need an excuse on any other day of the year, mind you."

"Yet you encourage Katya and me to attend," Nicholas pointed out with a sardonic smile.

She waved a dismissive hand in his direction. "It is entirely proper that youth be wasted in foolishness. I, however, am too old to make a mockery of myself parading around town in the guise of a virtuous medieval maiden. I much prefer to remain here in the company of my servants and my books." She turned to Katya and fixed her with a stern stare. "Provided that you supply me with a full and detailed report as to who attended, what they wore, and what they said—all the latest *on dits*. The more persnickety the gossip, the happier I shall be."

Katya smiled. "Very well."

"Then we are agreed." She gave her cane a decisive thump on the parlor's thickly padded carpet. "Now help me up, Nicholas. I have far too much to accomplish today to waste any more time here."

Nicholas crossed the room and extended his arm, helping his aunt to her feet. The Comtesse gave a cool nod of parting as she strode regally from the room, her ice-blue skirts trailing in her wake.

"She is quite something, isn't she?" Katya remarked once they were alone.

"Indeed." He moved to where she stood and wrapped his arm around her waist, pulling her tightly into his embrace. His lips on hers, he kissed her with a hungry ferocity that warmed her to her toes. After a long, breathless moment he pulled back and softly stroked her cheek. "I consider myself extremely fortunate to have two such remarkable women in my life," he said.

Katya smiled softly. A tight knot of emotion filled her throat as, warmed by the stark sincerity that blazed from their ebony depths, she studied his eyes. There was an underlying current between them, a wealth of emotion that she could feel, even though the words were not expressly spoken.

"If you're ready," he said, "the groomsmen should have the horses saddled by now. I believe Cook has prepared a basket lunch for us as well."

"I'm ready."

They moved through the villa and out to the elaborate stone courtyard fronting his home. Ignoring the groomsmen who were waiting to help Katya onto her mount, Nicholas locked his hands around her waist and lifted her effortlessly into the saddle of a chestnut mare. "Be careful," he admonished solemnly, "her temperament matches her name."

Katya nervously gathered the reins in her hands. "What is her name?"

"Daisy."

She arched her brows as an impish grin curved her lips. "Daisy, is it?" she said, stroking the mare's thick mane. "In that case, I believe I'll manage."

He gave her calf a light squeeze and turned to his own mount, swinging easily into the saddle. A groomsman handed him two picnic baskets. He strapped them on either side of his saddle, then tapped his heels against the powerful black's flanks and sent him into an easy canter; Katya quickly followed. They rode side by side as they moved out onto the quiet road that led away from his villa. But rather than heading east, as they normally did when going into the principality, Nicholas directed them west.

They rode away from the steep banks and rugged cliffs that plummeted to the sea and moved inland instead. Soon they were surrounded by gentle rolling slopes and smooth grassy hills. They moved through fields of wildflowers and moss-covered boulders, past small gurgling streams and dense patches of scrub oak. There was a quiet, subtle beauty to the land that was immediately soothing. While the dramatic cliffs and sparkling sea shouted for attention, the inland areas claimed their praise with a mere whisper.

As they crested a hill they were rewarded with a view of a shallow dale filled with lush, verdant grass interspersed with the brilliant blooms of bright red clary. Caught up in the beauty of the scene, she shot Nicholas a mischievous look of silent challenge and leaned down low over Daisy's neck. She spurred on the gentle mare with two sharp kicks that set her galloping across the meadow. Katya bounced merrily in the saddle, giving a shout of laughter and delight as the wind whipped across her face.

Nicholas caught up with them easily, but gallantly held his horse in check so that the race was neck and neck as they sped down the gentle slope. When they neared the tall chestnut that stood as an obvious marker ending the race, he let her pull ahead. She let out a victorious whoop as she reached the tree and pulled on the reins. Daisy abruptly slowed her pace, causing Katya to waver in the saddle. For one heart-stopping moment she thought she might tumble to the ground, but she caught herself in time and regained her seat.

With a smile of glowing exuberance on her face, she turned to Nicholas and gloatingly announced, "I won."

For a moment it looked as though he would chastise her for her recklessness. Instead he bowed his head in gracious defeat. "So you did."

She let out a deep, contented sigh. "That was wonderful," she exclaimed breathlessly. "I haven't ridden in years."

"Really? I couldn't tell."

"Liar," she said, but she beamed up at him as though he had just paid her the ultimate compliment. Closing the distance between them, she leaned over her saddle and wrapped one hand around Nicholas's neck, pressing a warm, laughing kiss against his lips. She pulled back abruptly, startled and a little embarrassed by her impetuous gesture. The intimacy she and Nicholas shared had always been a prelude to making love; they hadn't yet established a place for spontaneous gestures of affection. Forcing herself to meet his gaze, she searched his eyes for a sign that her kiss had displeased him. But his expression was unfathomable, offering her no clue as to what he was feeling.

Slightly disappointed, she looked away and lifted her hand self-consciously to her hair. "It appears as though I've lost my hat."

"I'll get it for you."

He tapped his heels against the black's flanks and sent the animal racing across the meadow, its powerful hooves tearing up the turf as it ran. Once he spotted her straw boater, he leaned out of the saddle and swept it up in a breathtakingly fluid movement of grace and daring. He wheeled around without a break in stride and urged his mount back toward her, presenting her hat with a flourish.

"You ride beautifully."

"That surprises you?" he asked, picking up on the mild astonishment that filled her tone.

She gave a light laugh. "Frankly, yes. The last time you were out riding, you came into the casino looking as though you had been dragged behind your mount, rather than sitting astride him."

"Not one of my finer moments," he admitted. "Generally I do better than that—although occasionally I have lapses."

"Oh?" she said, sensing a story behind his words. She relaxed back into her saddle as they guided their mounts in a smooth, easy walk.

"When I was sixteen," he began, "there was a certain sophisticated, older woman of twenty-three I was determined to impress. After much careful thought and consideration, I decided that the best way to prove my manhood and win her affection was to demonstrate my prowess on the field of honor—in this case, a local horse race."

Katya smiled. "Did you succeed?"

"That depends on how you define success. I certainly managed to make myself noticed."

"What happened?"

"It was a crowded race, perhaps twenty riders, but I held the lead from the outset. By all accounts, I should have won . . . had I not fallen off my horse as I rounded the last bend."

Her brows shot skyward in alarm. "You did what?"

"Fell off," he repeated. "Actually, my entire saddle slipped from my mount's back, sending me tumbling to the ground with it. The cinch had worn thin enough to break apart. Surprising, really, as it was a relatively new saddle. Apparently the leather was not the quality I had assumed it to be."

"Were you hurt?"

"A broken arm and several bumps and bruises," he replied with a shrug. "My pride was wounded more than anything."

"Because you fell?"

A wry grin curved his lips. "Because I displayed the bad form of knocking down several other riders—and their mounts—when I fell. It had rained rather heavily the night before, so we all sloshed about in puddles of mud like a group of drunken quarrymen. As you can imagine, I turned the entire event into a rather outlandish spectacle."

"I see," she replied solemnly, attempting to hold back her smile at the image his words conveyed.

"Go ahead and laugh," he entreated. "Tyler and I certainly did—months later, of course."

"What about the woman you were so desperate to impress?" she asked. "Did she coddle your wounds and nurse you back to health?"

"Not exactly."

"No?"

"As I recall, she rewarded my noble effort to win her heart with a furious glare for having splashed mud on her silk skirts. Then she left arm in arm with a wealthy duke who was old enough to be her grandfather."

"That's hardly a romantic tale, now, is it?"

"Perhaps not. But the event did teach me two important lessons. The first was not to be overly impressed by a pretty face."

"And the second?"

"Even more important. To check the condition of my saddle before racing headlong across a field."

Katya smiled softly as they rode on in companionable silence. From time to time Nicholas pointed out an interesting land formation, an unusual tree, or a scampering animal. Generally, however, they remained silent, content to enjoy the simple beauty of the day. At last they crested a sharply sloping hill where they had a view of a cluster of ancient stone buildings. A vineyard flanked the buildings to the east; rolling fields of lavender, orange blossom, jasmine, thyme, mignonette, and violet surrounded it to the west and south. The deep toll of a chapel bell echoed out to them from across the valley.

"The Abbey St. Chamas," Nicholas confirmed, following her gaze.

"It's lovely," she breathed.

A quiver of nervous apprehension surged through her as they moved toward the abbey that held the third and last portion of the scroll. So this is where it all ended, she thought. Where the final clue could be found as to the location of the Stone her ancestors had fought and died for. "It's not what I expected," she said after a minute.

"No?"

She shook her head. "I expected to see something far more warlike, with turrets, and towers, perhaps even a moat. After the king went to the trouble of sending his knights to lay siege to the two families, I would think he'd see to it that the scroll remained more tightly guarded."

Nicholas shrugged. "Perhaps the king only intervened because he had no choice—and because it had all grown rather tedious."

"Tedious?"

"The plague that had swept across the region had been checked, a benevolent ruler sat on the throne, and the harvests had been plentiful for decades. With the exception of the constant raids and warring between the two families, it was a time of remarkable peace and harmony. When the clans failed to come to terms over the Stone, I suspect the king had reached the end of his patience. Therefore he simply removed the object of their rage—much as a parent might remove a toy from two bickering children."

Katya might not agree with his description of a glittering blue diamond the size of a man's fist as a mere toy, but the rest of what he said made sense.

"In any event," he continued, "the third part of the scroll was useless without the portions the families held in their possession. And neither clan would have dared to raise arms against the monks who resided in the abbey. To do so would have been the ultimate sacrilege."

"I suppose that's true," she murmured in agreement. As they passed through the gates and entered the abbey's wide courtyard, her attention was diverted by the boisterous shouts of children laughing and playing. She turned to Nicholas with a puzzled frown.

"The monks abandoned the abbey decades ago," he explained. "It's now run by an order of nuns. The Sisters of

Holy Charity, I believe. St. Chamas is the site of one of the region's largest orphanages."

As he finished speaking a group of children ran into the courtyard, swarming around them with gleeful, excited shouts. Nicholas smiled and greeted them in French as he swung down off his mount. He untied the larger of the two baskets that had been strapped to his saddle and set it on the ground; then he moved to Katya and lifted her from Daisy. The children pressed closer, flooding them with a series of animated questions, each shouting to be heard over the other. As Katya's gaze moved over the group of children, she noted that their ages ranged from those so small they still tottered when they walked, to young adults who shepherded the group.

"I hope you'll forgive the children's excitement," called a soft female voice from behind her. "We don't receive many visitors."

She turned to see a woman attired in the long brown robes and stiff white wimple of a nun; a thick wooden crucifix hung from her neck. Once the woman reached them, Nicholas performed the introductions. "Katya, I'd like you to meet Sister Helena, the abbess here at St. Chamas. Sister Helena, Miss Katya Alexander."

Sister Helena offered her a warm smile. "Welcome to St. Chamas, Miss Alexander," she said. Katya returned her smile, immediately at ease in the other woman's presence.

Nicholas lifted the large basket he had untied from his saddle and handed it to the abbess. The sweet smell of almond and cinnamon wafted from within it, causing the children to clamor even louder for attention. The abbess smiled at their enthusiasm and turned to a pretty young girl of perhaps sixteen. "Trina, will you take the children into the kitchens, please?" she said as she passed her the basket. "Perhaps they would enjoy a little milk with their sweets."

Once the children had departed, Sister Helena turned to

Nicholas and said, "I received your message, Lord Barrington, and the generous gift that accompanied it. If you like, I can take you directly in to see the scroll."

"Thank you."

They trailed behind her, exiting the courtyard and moving into the largest of the ancient stone buildings. It took a moment for Katya's vision to adjust to the dimness of the Gothic interior. Once she could see, she noted that they had entered some sort of communal room. Huge rectangular wooden tables flanked by long benches filled the cavernous space. On the perimeters of the room were large bubbling vats and shelves filled with hundreds of tiny vials.

"We are a working abbey," Sister Helena explained. "In the spring we cut the flowers from the surrounding fields and distill the essence into perfume. In the fall we harvest the grapes from the vineyard and make wine. Our profit is small, but it is enough to pay for most of the costs associated with running the foundling home here at St. Chamas."

"Have you been having any more trouble with thieves breaking into the abbey?" Nicholas asked.

Sister Helena shook her head. "Mercifully no, not since those first two incidents."

They moved from the large communal room through a barrel-vaulted cloister that led to a large chapel with spectacular stained-glass windows. Sister Helena proceeded to lead them up a steep stone staircase located at the rear of the chapel. "All of the abbey's ancient manuscripts are held in a chamber just beyond the belfry," she said. "This particular area has always served as a place of solitude and study; I believe the documents you seek may have been created in this very room," she said with a soft smile, "but this is only a guess."

As they moved up the staircase, Katya turned and whispered to Nicholas, "Isn't this cheating?"

"Cheating?" he repeated with a smile. "I don't think so.

The scroll must remain at the abbey until it is properly claimed, but there was never a decree forbidding either family from looking at the portion held in its trust. I would imagine both families came to view the scroll, but gained no more insight from it than we will."

She frowned. "What do you mean?"

"You'll see."

Sister Helena removed a key from deep within the pocket of her robes and unlocked a heavy wooden door. Katya's heart suddenly doubled its pace as fear gripped her. What if there was something on the scroll—an inscription or a drawing—that would reveal her identity? Why hadn't she told Nicholas who she was? She swallowed hard as the questions reverberated through her mind.

The abbess swung open the door and beckoned them to enter. "I'll be in the refectory if you need me," she said.

Not trusting her voice to speak, Katya nodded her thanks and stepped inside. The musty smell of the leather-bound tomes that lined the floor-to-ceiling bookcases assaulted her nose; dancing dust motes were reflected in the beams of bright sunlight that filtered in through the chamber's narrow windows. She scanned the room, noting the crudely constructed table and chairs, the heavy candle sconces on the walls, the ornate plasterwork that covered the ceiling.

As her gaze moved around the room, her eye was suddenly caught by an ornate parchment piece that lay spread over a tall wooden stand. *The scroll,* she thought, her breath catching in her throat. There it was: the third part of the ancient triptych her family had warred over for years.

She moved instinctively toward it, as though drawn by a magnetic force. A shiver ran down her spine as she studied the intricate drawing that filled the top half of the parchment. It depicted a man and woman dressed in medieval bridal garb holding hands as they stood before an altar. Above them was a deadly dagger, poised as though ready to fall and tear them apart. Beneath them was a glittering blue diamond. Katya quickly skimmed the ancient Latin text that filled the remainder of the sheet.

"You read Latin?"

She nearly jumped, so engrossed had she been in her study. "I do," she replied.

He nodded. "As you can see, the scroll gives a brief summary of the events that occurred on their wedding day."

"Yes."

"Perhaps your grasp of Latin is better than mine. Unless there is something I'm missing, the only clues contained within this document are the few lines found at the very bottom."

Katya turned her attention to the portion he indicated. " 'Rosskaya and DuValenti,' " she read aloud. " 'The two are as one. Learn this and out of darkness will come light.' " She drew back, vaguely disappointed. "Is that all?"

He leaned against one of the heavy desks that filled the room and folded his arms casually across his chest. "According to legend, it will all make sense once the three scrolls are joined," he said. "The scroll that was taken from my home describes a series of landmarks: rocks, trees, caves, that sort of thing. An ancient treasure map, if you will."

Just like the scroll her family possessed. "And where one scroll ends the other begins," she said. "This should be the final clue necessary to find the Stone."

"So they say."

"The two are as one," she repeated musingly. "Perhaps a tree that is split in two?" she suggested. "Or a cave with two entrances? The Stone might be buried there."

"Perhaps."

"You don't sound convinced."

He hesitated for a moment, then said, "I've always felt that that was more a riddle than a clue. As though the answer were right in front of me but I couldn't see it."

"There is another possibility," she said slowly. "Do you see the ornate illustrations that border the edges of the document? When the three scrolls are laid side by side, they may form a word or a final clue."

He looked impressed. "I hadn't considered that. The clue may not be in the text at all." He moved to stand next to her, a frown of intent concentration on his face. His gold-and-onyx ring glinted in the sunlight as he slowly ran his hand over the scroll.

Beware the Maltese. The words echoed through her mind, but the warning rang hollow. She was no longer afraid of Nicholas. Now her only fear was of losing him.

"Why did you bring me here?" she asked.

He turned toward her, searching her eyes for a long moment before answering. Finally he replied, "I'm not certain. It seemed appropriate somehow. I wanted you to see the scroll, I don't know why."

Tell him! her mind screamed. *Six simple little words: I am Katya Zofia Rosskaya Alexander.*

She stood frozen in mute uncertainty as the words clogged her throat and a tight knot of nervous apprehension filled her belly. Some nameless instinct held her back. Perhaps he had already gained physical proof of who she was and was waiting for her to confess her deceit. But she couldn't do it. Not yet. Just a few more days, she thought. Once they had discovered who had stolen his scroll, she would tell him who she was.

"Is something wrong?" he asked.

She forced a tight smile. "No, why?"

"Nothing. I thought you looked upset, that's all." He lifted his shoulders in a light shrug. "If you're ready, we can leave at any time."

"Fine."

The sound of their footsteps reverberated around them as they moved down the steep stone staircase that led to the chapel. When Nicholas took her elbow to guide her back to the courtyard Katya hesitated, glancing at a small alcove beside the altar. "Do you mind . . ." she began.

"Not at all. I'll wait for you outside," he replied, allowing her a moment of privacy.

She knelt and said a brief prayer, then lifted a long taper and lit a candle for each of her parents. As she made her way out of the chapel, she paused at the donation box located against the back wall. Then she untied the strings of her reticule. Into the depository went Lord Teecham's watch fob. Sir Garvey's sterling silver fountain pen. The Duke of Pallister's diamond stickpin. Lord Rutherford-Green's gold-plated snuff box, as well as sundry other trinkets she had acquired during her stay in Monaco. Once her reticule was empty she breathed a sigh of relief, feeling immeasurably unburdened.

As she stepped out of the dimness of the chapel and into the brilliant spring sunlight, her gaze moved immediately toward Nicholas. Unaware of her presence, he stood in the midst of a group of laughing children. As they tugged at his pants and shouted for his attention, he carried on in a calm, orderly manner—lifting each child one at a time for a brief ride on his gelding's back.

Katya felt her heart swell within her chest as she watched him. She let out a sigh and faced the stark reality she had been desperately trying to avoid.

She had fallen in love with her family's ancient enemy.

Seventeen

$\mathcal{N}$icholas held Avignon tightly in check as he rode. Although his high-spirited mount was accustomed to racing across the verdant meadows, clearly Katya was not an experienced rider. She had handled Daisy fairly well on their way to the abbey—with the exception of that idiotic race—but he was not about to tempt fate again. He kept their pace slow and leisurely, biting back a smile as he watched her ride. She bounced up and down in her saddle, her feet flailing about in her stirrups, her hair tumbling down her back in adorable disarray, and her cheeks blooming with color.

Once they were halfway to the villa he gestured to a quiet spot off the familiar path on which they traveled. He led her down a small valley to a grove of shady cork oak. A small stream carved its way through the valley, gurgling past them as it flowed over moss-strewn rocks. Swallowtail butterflies floated through the air, pausing from time to time to suck the nectar from the heavy blossoms that filled the clearing.

He drew Avignon to a halt and said, "I thought we might stop here for lunch."

"Perfect," she agreed with a smile.

She placed her hands on his shoulders as he lifted her from her mount, the heady scent of her skin drifting all around him. Desire surged through him but she moved out of his grasp to stand near the edge of the mossy bank before he could act on it.

He turned to the basket that hung from his saddle and untied it. The first item he removed was a bottle of wine, which he placed between two jutting rocks in the stream to chill. Then he spread a blanket over the soft grass, took a seat, and set the basket down next to him. Katya immediately moved to join him, smoothing her skirts around her as she sat down and leaned against a fallen log.

"Do you like curry?" he asked.

She hesitated a moment, then wrinkled her nose and shook her head.

He set aside a ceramic tureen. "So much for the fish stew." Lifting the next item from the basket, he inquired, "What about garlic?"

"Yes."

"Oregano?"

"Absolutely."

"Basil?"

"Of course."

As he emptied the contents of the basket, she cheerfully spread the bounty across their blanket, sorting the oven-roasted chicken, delicate cheese pastries, fresh fruits, crusty baguettes, and candied tarts and figs. Once she had accomplished her task, she lifted a leg of chicken and took an enthusiastic bite.

A small smile curved his mouth as he watched her. "Please don't feel you have to feign a delicate appetite on my account."

She swallowed, then a bubble of laughter escaped her lips. "I'm starving," she announced with an unapologetic grin. "I'll have to count my fingers when I've finished just to make sure I haven't bitten one off."

They ate their meal at a leisurely pace, content to enjoy the food and the quiet beauty of the day. Once they had finished, she let out a satisfied sigh. "I don't think I'll ever eat again."

He smiled. "I hope you saved room for a little wine."

"That sounds lovely."

He stood and went to retrieve the bottle he had placed in the stream. To his surprise, she followed him. She glanced around at the open meadows, then down at the stream, then up at him. Clearly she had something on her mind, but he couldn't begin to guess what it was.

"I wouldn't imagine this spot is visited too often," she finally ventured.

"I wouldn't imagine so," he agreed.

"In that case . . . how terribly uncouth would you think me if I were to take off my boots and soak my feet in the stream for a few minutes?"

"Actually, I was considering doing the same thing," he lied.

An expression of guilty pleasure lit up her face. "Were you?"

"Indeed."

In truth, Nicholas's mind had been on seduction, for he could think of no better way to pass an idle spring afternoon than making love to Katya beneath the shade of an ancient oak. Furthermore, he had not splashed around in a gurgling stream since he was a child. So the suggestion held a definite appeal—if only because it persuaded her to remove a bit of her clothing. Granted, her boots were not the ideal place to start, but it was a step in the right direction.

She seated herself on a flat rock beside the bank. While Nicholas turned and lifted the wineglasses from their picnic basket she bent down and removed her boots. The rustling of the lace and petticoats beneath her riding skirts, he decided, was the most alluring sound he had ever heard. Next she removed her stockings, allowing him a glimpse of the satiny skin of her thighs. She folded the stockings neatly and placed them on the mossy bank beside her boots. Then she stood and moved toward the stream. Her feet were small and delicate, her ankles perfectly proportioned.

She sat on the edge of the bank and plunged her feet into the water. A huge smile broke across her features as she released a sigh of pure contentment. The naked response was typical of Katya, Nicholas thought. The woman had an enormous capacity for pleasure and wasn't embarrassed to show it, regardless of whether the occasion was enjoying a picnic or responding to his lovemaking.

He passed her a glass of wine and sat down on the mossy bank beside her. He removed his own boots and socks, rolled up the legs of his pants, and submerged his feet in the stream. The water felt amazingly good as it caressed the soles of his feet and whirled between his toes. He lifted the glass to his mouth and took a deep swallow of the cool white wine. It was light and tangy, with a slightly sweet bouquet.

Following his lead, Katya took a small sip of wine and sighed, twirling her toes in the water. "This is heaven," she said. She tilted back her head and smiled as a soft wind rustled her skirts. "What's that breeze?" she asked dreamily.

"It's called a *mistral.*"

"It feels wonderful."

"Just wait a few days. It can blow out of the north for weeks at a time, so hot and dry it's been known to drive some of the locals nearly mad."

"Truly?" She thought for a moment, then lifted her slim shoulders in a shrug. "Well, right now it feels wonderful."

She glanced about her and absently plucked a smooth stone from the grass. She closed her fist, then opened it with an impish smile, revealing a handful of tiny yellow daises. She opened her palm and scattered the flowers in the breeze, watching as they fluttered away.

"Magic," she said.

"Very nice."

She was, Nicholas thought, an improbable thief. An improbable mistress, for that matter. She smiled and leaned back on her elbows, a posture that thrust out her breasts and served to emphasize the smooth curve of her hips. But he suspected the sensuality conveyed within her movement was entirely accidental on her part—he doubted that she was even aware of just how arousing her position was.

Nicholas had been fortunate to have known a variety of women in his life. But in retrospect they all blurred together to form one forgettable mass. Granted there were some who pleased him more than others, but none who truly touched him. Their relationships had been part of an obligatory social ritual, as perfunctory as finding a partner for a business venture, or finding the right cook or wine steward. Quite simply, the women had fulfilled his sexual needs and social requirements. When the affair ended, they parted amiably.

But what he shared with Katya was profoundly deeper than that—and growing deeper every day.

She turned toward him with a soft smile, interrupting his thoughts. "I'm glad you invited me to accompany you here," she said. "Now I know that it truly exists."

"The abbey?"

"No. This place. I used to dream about it."

He frowned. "You mean like some sort of prophesy?"

She gave a startled laugh. "Nothing that extraordinary. I mean the silly kind of dreams that children dream, the make-believe kind."

"Tell me about them."

She shook her head. "I'll sound foolish."

"Not to me."

She regarded him with uncertainty, then slowly began, "When I was young my family traveled constantly, touring our show from city to city. In some ways it was very exciting, but in other ways, well . . ." She looked up at him and gave a light shrug. "I suppose that's human nature, isn't it? Always wishing for something other than what we have."

"What did you wish for?"

"A house. Someplace I could truly call home."

He smiled and nodded in understanding. "You mean a great big beautiful palace?"

"No, nothing that grand," she said immediately. "I'm too practical for that—I prefer dreams that are attainable. What I wanted was a simple brick house with rose gardens in back and a white picket fence in front." She gestured to the surrounding countryside. "In my dreams, the house sat in a meadow just like this one. There was a small church not too far from here, and a school just over that ridge," she finished, pointing to an imaginary spot beyond the horizon.

Nicholas arched a dark brow. "You had a school in your dream?"

"Absolutely. Since we constantly traveled, I spent most of my time with either my parents or with other adults. But in my dream there was a school full of children my own age just beyond the next hill."

"Imaginary playmates?"

"Dozens," she averred. "In my mind I spent hours entertaining them, impressing them with incredible feats of magic and regaling them with stories of my travels." A small, wistful smile crossed her face as she turned toward him. "I warned you I would sound foolish."

"You don't sound foolish at all."

She splashed her feet in the stream, sending ripples across the surface. "What about you?" she asked after a moment. "What did you wish for when you were a child?"

Somewhat taken aback by the question, he thought for a minute, then shrugged. "Nothing," he replied. "I suppose there wasn't anything I needed."

"Not need. Want."

He shook his head. "Nothing comes to mind."

"Hmmm. When you're rich, I suppose you don't need to dream at all. You simply ask for something and you receive it." She studied him for a moment in somber contemplation. "I wonder if that's good."

He arched one brow. "Are you telling me that I can

attribute all the gross deficiencies of my character to the fact that I was raised with too much money?"

She laughed. "Most of them, anyway."

"That's encouraging."

Her expression slowly sobered as she studied him. "I can't picture you as a child. Even in the family portrait hanging in your study you couldn't have been more than eleven or twelve, yet you looked the same as you do now."

He smiled. "Perhaps a little shorter."

"True." She matched his smile with one of her own. Then she cocked her head to one side, a look of rapt curiosity on her face. "Tell me, what were you like as a little boy?"

Nicholas took a sip of wine and announced flatly, "Boring."

She gave a short, sharp burst of laughter. "In what way?"

"Too stoic, too staid, too conscientious. I rarely played as a child. I *organized*."

"What does that mean?"

"That means I never played games, instead I organized teams. I never ran through the woods just for the fun of it; instead I collected leaves and organized them into books alphabetically by species. I organized my clothing, my schedule, my schoolwork. I made it a point to handle everything in my life with the utmost care and efficiency."

"Was your brother the same way?"

Nicholas nearly choked on his wine. "Tyler?"

Katya smiled and arched one brow. "I take it that's a no."

"God, no." He let out a low laugh and shook his head. "Tyler was the opposite of me in nearly every way you could imagine. Wild, defiant, completely unpredictable." He paused for a moment, then continued, "Sometimes I think we deliberately opposed each other."

"What do you mean?"

He raked his fingers through his hair, at a loss as to how to put his feelings into words. "I was groomed from birth to inherit my father's titles and estates," he finally began. "For as long as I can remember it has been drummed into my head that nothing is more important than preserving our family legacy. Nothing. As the firstborn male heir, it fell upon me to assume the role of Lord of Barrington. I took that duty very seriously when I was young—probably too seriously," he admitted with a rueful smile.

"In what way?"

"Everything I did was an effort to please my father—I suppose I wanted to prove that I was worthy of carrying on his name. I was determined to mold myself into the proper little lord. It used to drive Tyler mad."

"Because he was jealous of your relationship with your father?"

"Because he thought I was a complete fool," Nicholas corrected with a smile. He brought up one knee, resting his elbow on it. "Trying to please our father was as futile a pursuit as trying to drown a fish. It simply couldn't be done. Tyler was intelligent enough to recognize that from a young age. The more demands were put on him, the more he rebelled. In some ways I think our father respected that far more than he respected my eager attempts at approval."

"I see."

He shrugged. "In truth, in some ways I envied Tyler his freedom, his total fearlessness. He may have respected my judgment, my sense of sacrifice and commitment. But we had each chosen a course and we refused to budge. I was the responsible, somber brother. He was the uninhibited, reckless one. It became a point of honor between us to prove how different we were."

Katya nodded. "What about your mother?" she asked. "What was she like?"

He thought for a moment, lost in bittersweet reminiscence. "Gentle, kind, beautiful," he finally replied. "Tyler and I both adored her—that was probably the only thing we had in common. When she died, the thin thread that held us together as a family began to unravel. The older I grew, the more rigid I became—and the wilder Tyler became. After a while the gulf that separated us was too large to bridge. But I never thought it would lead to—"

He stopped abruptly and shook his head, refusing to give voice to the thought. Had Tyler hated him enough to fatally plot against him? Was his brother capable of murder . . . or suicide? It was inconceivable, yet the possibilities loomed too large to be ignored. And if this was the case, to what extent was he, Nicholas, responsible for the gulf that had divided them?

"Tyler was as stubborn and prideful as I am," Nicholas continued. "I know what it cost him to come to me for the funds to pay off his debt. I should have given him the money."

"You must have had your reasons for refusing him."

"I thought so at the time, but now I wonder."

"What do you mean?"

"Everything that had been brewing between us for years finally came to a head that night in London. I accused him of being a reckless, profligate rake, a childish embarrassment to the family name. He accused me of being as cold and arrogant as our father had been, harsh and unyielding like an old man. I refused to see it at the time, but now I can't help but feel that he may have been right. Perhaps I was using my power and money to force him to bend to my will. If so, he was right to tell me in no uncertain terms to go to hell." He paused, then shook his head and let out a low sigh. "I doubt he meant to, but Tyler did me a bigger favor than he could possibly have known."

"In what way?"

"By forcing me to come here to Monaco to search for him," he replied. "I have never enjoyed staying at my father's villa. Too many memories, I suppose, most of them unpleasant. But on the occasion of this visit I've been even more uncomfortable here than usual. It has taken me a while, but I have finally realized why."

"Why?"

"Because it reminds me too much of my own home."

An expression of soft understanding showed in Katya's eyes. "Is it too late to change that?"

"I hope not."

Until his recent arrival in Monaco, Nicholas had thought his home in London a paradigm of the virtues of orderliness and routine. His servants moved about in hushed, measured steps, his meals were served with prompt efficiency, and his rooms held such a quiet stillness one could hear the clocks tick. At the time, he thought he was running a well-ordered household. Now, however, he saw an emptiness in his life that he had never noticed before, a rigidity that bordered on fanaticism. Time passing and life going nowhere. Tyler had been right. He was becoming just like their father.

What he needed, he realized with startling clarity, was a touch of mayhem. Profound disorder to shake the routine that filled his days. For a brief moment he imagined a home filled with noise and clutter. Children laughing and playing, toys scattered about, and pets scampering underfoot. Servants who smiled rather than whispered. Clocks that couldn't possibly be heard, even when they chimed the hour. A wife lying next to him in bed at night.

"You have such an odd look on your face," Katya said. "What are you thinking about?"

"You."

She gave a light laugh and tossed a pebble into the stream. "That explains the look—it must have been a frown I detected."

He sent her a small smile in reply, but he wasn't at all focused on her light banter. Instead his thoughts were turned inward. Nicholas had never considered himself superstitious, yet now he felt haunted by a vague fear that was as senseless as the dark omens about black cats or walking beneath ladders. He couldn't shake the suspicion that he and Katya had crossed some invisible line. That as long as she had feigned being his mistress, she was safe. But now that things had changed between them, he feared, she had been put in a position of jeopardy.

Rationally he knew that his feelings were foolish. Surely their newfound intimacy and affection were visible to no one else. Surely she was in no more danger now than she had been on the first day of their little ruse. Yet he couldn't help but worry, uncertain whether his intuition was a result of events occurring around them or whether it was caused by the heated emotions escalating between them.

He studied Katya in silence as the golden sunlight streamed all around her. With her skirts tucked up to her knees and her feet splashing in the stream beneath her, she made a fetching picture of unparalleled beauty and innocence. In that instant he was overcome by a sense of purpose and resolve that had been missing since his arrival in Monaco.

Until that moment, Nicholas had been wracked by conflicting emotions and uncertainty. Depending on the hour or the day, his feelings had run the gamut: pain and shock at Tyler's betrayal, guilt at how he, himself, may have contributed to the suicide, rage that someone may have killed Tyler, and remorse at what had passed between them. These various emotions, powerful as they had been, were now eclipsed by a single feeling that was stronger than anything he had ever experienced. A dead certainty that he would kill anyone who tried to harm Katya. Anyone.

Apparently feeling his gaze on her, she turned to him and asked, "What is it?"

"Nothing."

"Hmmm." She studied him for a moment, then arched

one brow and said in a playful tone, "You're acting very mysterious this afternoon, Lord Barrington. All these cryptic looks you're giving me."

Before he could reply, she gave a sharp squeal and leaped up from her spot on the stream bank. She stomped her feet, then turned to him with an embarrassed laugh. "A fish," she said. "It just wiggled over my foot."

He smiled and reached for her. "Have I told you yet today how beautiful you are?"

Her expression sobered as she moved her hand self-consciously to her windblown hair. "I'm a mess."

He shook his head and made a soft *tsking* sound. "How remiss of me. I must have neglected my duty." He pulled her closer and guided her down onto the lush grass beside him. Then he brushed his hand softly across her cheek. "You're beautiful, Katya."

She searched his eyes as a hushed silence fell between them. After a long moment she said softly, "I never know quite what to do with you."

"Anything you want."

A mischievous smile curved her lips. "Anything?"

"Anything."

Her gaze locked in his, she raised one small, delicate hand and placed it against his chest. He felt the heat of her palm through the light fabric of his shirt. She moved her hand slowly, watching his face as she traced a path lightly over his chest, down the rippled muscles of his stomach, then back up along the broad lines of his shoulders. His muscles tensed beneath her hand and a slight shudder ran through his frame, as if she were giving life and breath to his body.

He tilted back his head and closed his eyes, awed by the emotions she could stir in him with just one touch. It was as though Katya alone could awaken an innermost desire that had been lost within him. Finally he could hold back no longer. He wrapped his arm around her and pulled her tightly against him. He kissed her with a hunger he could not restrain. Her lips carried the crisp, tangy flavor of the wine; her tongue tasted as sweet as the berries they had eaten with lunch.

Katya returned his fervor with a passion that shook him. Maintaining their kiss, she locked her arms around his neck and pulled herself onto his lap. Her breasts pressed against the hardness of his chest. Her thighs crushed against his. As their embrace deepened, she wriggled her bottom on his lap, sending a fire through his loins. He felt his manhood leap to life beneath her, straining at his pants and thrusting against the softness of her skirts.

The seducer was quickly becoming the seduced. Nicholas pulled his mouth from hers and let out a soft groan, burying his face in her neck. Bunches of soft, springy curls brushed against his cheek. Her hair smelled fresher than spring rain. Her skin felt softer than silk. As he traced a line of fiery kisses from her ear to her collarbone she let out a soft, kittenlike whisper of a moan and let her head fall back. A tremor ran through her limbs and she clung to his shoulders.

He drew his hand over the velvety flesh of her inner thigh as she ran her fingers down his back. Katya's unconcealed responses to his lovemaking, her tremors and moans and soft purrs, made him want her even more, heating his desire until it nearly burned out of control. His prim little gypsy was a wealth of contradictions. She was both capture and surrender. She was the spark that lit his veins and the water that would extinguish his need.

With one hand he clumsily worked free the buttons that held closed the front of her blouse. He tugged it off her shoulders, then pulled down the straps to her white cotton camisole until the garment sagged about her waist. His gaze moved to her breasts; he was awed by her fragile, womanly beauty. She was almost too beautiful, he thought, as his fingers lightly caressed her flesh. Like uncovering a perfectly shaped porcelain sculpture—but one that pulsated life and radiated warmth.

Her breasts were soft and round and pretty. Her nipples were deep rose and tilted upward toward the sky, beckoning him to take them into his mouth. His fingers moved over her ribs, then along the fragile line of her collarbone.

"Katya."

Her name was torn from his lips, a low murmur that was part groan, part wish, and part primal recognition, as though it had been like this between them for centuries. He cupped her breasts in his hands, amazed at how soft her skin felt against his calloused hands. He lowered his head and nuzzled his face between her breasts, drinking in the warm, womanly scent of her skin. Shifting slightly, he drew a nipple into his mouth, teasing it with his tongue into a firm, hard peak.

He heard her sharp intake of breath as she writhed beneath him, digging her fingers into his shoulders. Suddenly she tensed and stiffened her spine.

"Nicholas."

Something in her tone made him draw back. She looked beautiful, her lips soft and rosy, her hair cascading down her shoulders in wanton disarray.

"Did you hear that?" she asked.

"Hear what?"

"I thought I heard—"

Her words were cut off by a shower of pebbles raining down the grassy bank opposite them. Nicholas jerked up his head in the direction of the sound. Silhouetted against the brilliant sunshine was the tall figure of a man—a man who had been watching their every move. Before Nicholas could utter a single oath, the stranger turned and raced toward his mount.

Eighteen
❧❧

$\mathcal{K}$atya quickly tugged her blouse and camisole back into place as Nicholas plunged across the shallow stream and scrambled up the steep slope. She tensed, listening for the sound of angry shouts or fisticuffs. Instead all she heard was the distinct rhythm of hoofbeats echoing furiously into the distance. The person who had been watching them was getting away.

That fact was confirmed moments later as Nicholas climbed down the sheer bank and made his way across the stream.

"Did you see who it was?" she asked.

"No. The only view I had was of the back end of his horse, and even that was moving too quickly for me to get a good look."

"Oh."

She searched her mind for something intelligent to say, but her thoughts and emotions were too jumbled for her to construct a single coherent statement. The state of Nicholas's attire didn't help. He wore no shirt, revealing the vast expanse of his bronzed chest and stomach. His pants were soaked to the middle of his thighs, showing every muscle and sinew in his long legs. His dark hair was disheveled, doubtless from her having combed her fingers through it only minutes earlier. His ebony eyes—eyes that had been filled with heat and passion—were now guarded and alert.

"Do you think it had something to do with the scroll?" she finally managed, forcing her thoughts back to the issue at hand.

He lifted his shoulders in a casual shrug. "Perhaps. Perhaps it was nothing but a bored farmboy looking for something more interesting to watch than a herd of sheep grazing in a pasture."

She nodded and attempted a sophisticated smile, amazed that he could be so indifferent. He might be so accustomed to midday dalliances that he could make light of what had passed between them, but she enjoyed no such irreverence. She searched for a suitable jest that would match his tone, but once again her mind came up blank. What was expected of a man and a woman who had just shared the kind of passion and intimacy they had shared? A light, teasing remark and the whole liaison was laughed off? Was it nothing but a way to pass an otherwise dull afternoon, or merely her own insecurities that made her read more into his tone than she should?

Unable to resolve the question, she turned away and sat down on a low stump to pull on her stockings and boots. She stood and moved toward Daisy, giving Nicholas a murmur of thanks as he lifted her into his saddle. For the first time that day, his hands did not linger about her waist. Instead he moved with brisk efficiency, dropping his arms and turning away the moment she was seated on her mount. Then he swung into the saddle of his black and tapped his heel against the gelding's flanks, sending the animal into a smooth, rolling gait. They moved side by side, making light conversation as they rode. But it was evident from his expression that he was as disturbed by the incident as she had been. An air of somber preoccupation hung over them both.

Once they reached the villa, Nicholas adjourned to his study while Katya retired to her bedchamber to rest before her performance that evening. But the rest she sought eluded her completely. Finally succumbing to the impatient energy that seized her, she threw open her window and paced a bit before it, allowing the warm wind to gently brush her skin. Within a matter of minutes her attention had turned to the false-bottomed trunk at the foot of her bed. She removed the clothing she had stored within and released the hidden spring, opening the compartment that contained Sacha's diary. She had become addicted to the journal, searching the words contained therein the way a sailor might search the sky looking for guidance among the stars. Katya carried the ancient documents to her bed and spread them around her as she sifted through the fragile stack. After two hours of translating badly smeared Latin and faded bits of ancient French, her head was pounding and her spirits were sinking. All she had uncovered for her trouble were a few transcripts of religious sermons, household inventories, bills of lading, and two letters written by a knight—a rather boorish and conceited knight, she thought—attempting to woo his lady love by cataloging his awesome battle skills and deeds of daring.

She stacked the bundle of parchment papers back together in irritation, wishing someone before her had assumed the task of sorting and separating out the relevant pages. It would take her days more to get through the scrambled mass of papers. As she lifted them, one withered piece of parchment escaped the bundle and drifted down to fall into her lap. She gave it a cursory glance as she moved to stuff it back inside.

There is evil afoot.

Immediately recognizing the writing as Sacha's, Katya froze, her attention riveted on the page.

There is evil afoot. I am frightened in my own home. Perhaps I should not admit this, even in these pages, but who other than me will read these foolish scribblings? Where else can I turn to reveal my despair?

Sometimes I think he must be mad. He professes to love me, yet his intensity frightens me so. How foolish I was, how wholly vain to let myself be flattered by his attentions. Now it is too late. Last eve I felt his gaze upon me and turned to see him watching me. His eyes were cold, yet they burned with a deep, possessive fire. He doesn't think I understand but I do. He no longer sees me. I have taken the form of his vengeance.

I have spoken with Father but my fear only angers him. He will not listen. Even if I were to waver in my conviction to marry—which I certainly do not—it is too late to plot a new course. The king's emissary and his men have already arrived.

In a matter of days—nay, hours—I will become Marco DuValenti's wife. I tremble to think what might happen once the ceremony has taken place. But I must trust in the fates that have brought us together. Perhaps Father is right. Perhaps I am only behaving like a nervous, foolish bride and there is nothing to fear. I pray that it is so.

Katya set down the page as a wave of grim comprehension and defeat washed over her. So Sacha had learned to fear Marco. The realization was a bitter blow. She had been so certain that if she kept digging she would find some explanation for what had gone wrong between the ancient lovers. Instead she had found verification of the DuValentis' quest for vengeance, the essence of the feud that had torn their families apart for centuries.

She let out a sigh and stood. She had foolishly been tracking her relationship with Nicholas to that of Sacha and Marco, reading parallels in every line of her ancestor's diary. The first meeting, the giddy blush of awakening desire, the heady bliss of sexual satisfaction, the thrill of falling in love. Each deepening emotion had been repeated between her and Nicholas. She had been certain that finding a happy ending for them—or at least an explanation for what had gone wrong—would mean a happy ending for her.

But no longer.

The ancient legends had brought her this far, but now it

was up to her to set her own course. It was time to move forward. Katya gathered up the parchment pieces and resolutely put them away in the bottom of her trunk. She felt a sudden urge to see Nicholas, to feel his strong arms around her. She wanted some physical assurance that the tragedy that had befallen Sacha and Marco would not touch them.

She left her room and proceeded downstairs, searching for Nicholas in his study. The room was empty; a hollow stillness rang through the chamber. Katya moved to his desk and ran her hand over the leather chair where he customarily sat.

"Are you looking for Nicholas, Miss Alexander?"

She glanced up to find the Comtesse elegantly poised in the doorway, one slim hand resting on the ivory-carved handle of her walking cane. She sent her a soft smile and moved away from Nicholas's desk. "I am."

"Unfortunately he's already left. He thought you were resting and didn't want to disturb you. He asked me to convey to you that he had some business to attend to in town and would see you after your performance this evening."

"I see." She hid her disappointment with a polite nod. "Thank you."

"If you have a moment, may I ask how you are progressing in your search for the scroll?"

"Not very well, I'm afraid. We're rapidly running out of suspects. Either my touch isn't as deft as Nicholas assumed, or the person who has the scroll has hidden it someplace where we can't possibly find it, perhaps locked away in a hotel safe, buried in a garden, or . . ." She paused, shrugging her shoulders. "Who knows where it could be?"

The Comtesse let out a sigh. "I suppose it was unrealistic of us to expect that the person who had stolen it might be carrying it on his person." She moved into the room and seated herself on a small burgundy settee. "I suspect Nicholas is aware of that as well," she said. "Perhaps he hoped that if the two of you made a flamboyant appearance here in Monaco, your presence might help to draw out the thief and force him into making a move."

Katya nodded. "I thought of that as well."

"But it hasn't worked."

"No, it hasn't."

"I see." An expression of quiet pain filled the Comtesse's gaze as she turned toward the portrait of Nicholas and Tyler seated before their father. "Perhaps the person we're seeking can't risk making his presence known. With each day that passes, I can't help feeling that the truth has been before us all along and we have simply refused to see it."

"You mean Tyler?"

The older woman hesitated for a long moment, then finally replied, "Yes."

"Then you don't believe he's dead?"

"No, I do not."

"You'll think I'm foolish, but I read Nicholas's palm," Katya blurted out. "His brother lives, I saw it."

A small, sad smile curved the Comtesse's lips. "You're no more foolish than I have been, for my opinion is based on nothing more than an old woman's sentiment. In my heart of hearts, I can't help but believe that I would feel it if Tyler were gone." She thought for a moment, then shook her head. "But if Tyler is alive, why would he continue to let us believe that he is dead?"

"Nicholas mentioned that his brother had accrued a vast sum of gaming debts—debts that Nicholas refused to settle. Could Tyler have fabricated his own death in order to escape his debts?"

"Certainly not," the Comtesse objected immediately. "He would not have done anything so cowardly."

Katya paced for a moment before Nicholas's desk. "If we are correct, where does that leave us?" she asked. "If Tyler was not murdered and did not commit suicide, and if he is not hiding from his debts—"

"Then why has he not shown himself?" the Comtesse finished for her with a dark sigh. "We could talk all day, yet we keep circling around the same answer, do we not? It would appear that Tyler has been behind the scheme to steal the scroll all along, and was likely behind Miss Whitney's death as well." An expression of profound sorrow filled her eyes as her gaze returned to the portrait she had been studying earlier. "I know he had his faults, but I would not have thought him capable of something this . . . ugly."

"Indeed," Katya replied, glancing away as she brushed a piece of lint from her skirt.

Although she had tried to keep her tone neutral, it was evident from the Comtesse's expression that she had not succeeded. The older woman's mouth tightened into a grim line as her gaze narrowed. "Obviously you do not share my shock at this appalling turn of events, Miss Alexander. I can only assume that this is because your opinion of Tyler differs profoundly from my own. Am I correct in my assumption?"

Katya hesitated. "I never knew Tyler. I have only heard others speak of him."

"I take it you are referring to the baseless, demeaning gossip that pervades society here in Monaco."

"Yes," she admitted.

"I should like to hear those rumors."

"I'm afraid I'll only offend you by repeating them."

"I expect you will," the Comtesse replied, drawing herself up into a posture of regal assurance. "But I would appreciate an honest answer nonetheless."

"Very well." Although Katya had never sought out gossip regarding either Tyler or Nicholas, neither had she attempted to avoid it. Given the scandal that had surrounded them, it would have been impossible. "From what I've heard," she said, "behavior of this sort would not be entirely uncharacteristic of Tyler Duvall. Rumor has it that he was an arrogant ne'er-do-well, a profligate rake, completely self-absorbed, appallingly impertinent, and lacking in any sort of discipline. Apparently he was the image of his father in both temperament and appearance."

"I see," the Comtesse replied slowly. "How very enlightening. So that is what is said."

She rose from the settee and moved to the window, leaning heavily on her cane as she stared out over the magnificent gardens. The early evening light cast a soft shadow over her slim frame and immaculately coiffed silver hair, giving her the appearance of uncharacteristic frailty.

Katya felt a sudden pang of remorse at having spoken so brashly and immediately tried to soften her words. "I suspect those rumors are as absurd as the ones that surround Nicholas," she said.

The Comtesse turned to her and waved an imperious hand. "Do not attempt to mollify me, Miss Alexander. It has been my experience that rumors generally have some basis in fact—however distorted they may grow once they are spread." She lifted her shoulders in a faint shrug. "The objection I have is not in the content of what is being said, but in its narrowness."

"I'm afraid I don't understand."

"Tyler was a selfish rogue," the older woman conceded, "of that I have no doubt. But he could also be charming, as charming as the devil himself. Just as my brother William was charming in his day—and kind, and loyal, and gallant, and a host of other traits you find so compelling in Nicholas." The Comtesse gazed for a long moment at the family portrait that hung on the wall before them, lost in silent reminiscence. Finally she turned to Katya and smiled softly. "That surprises you, doesn't it? I can see it in your face."

"I— Yes, it does."

Katya's impression of Nicholas's father—one that was reinforced by both Nicholas himself and by the dark, menacing portrait that hung in his study—was that of a harsh, cold, arrogant man who had little time or patience for either his wife or his sons.

"Has Nicholas spoken to you of the DuValenti curse?" the Comtesse asked.

She frowned, not quite sure how that was related to the subject at hand. "He mentioned that he believed the Stone of Destiny was cursed. Is that what you're referring to?"

"Indirectly, yes. From the day that wretched stone was bequeathed to us, the men in this family have lost the women they loved. It is rumored that once we retrieve the stone, that tragedy will be forever lifted. Perhaps it is nothing but a bit of ancient foolishness. Or perhaps it is true, and that is the burden we must bear. I only know that my brother was deeply affected—forever changed, if you will—by that curse."

Katya nodded somberly. "Nicholas told me his mother died when he and Tyler were young."

"She did," the Comtesse agreed. "But I am not speaking of Marianne. I am speaking of the woman William loved."

A heavy silence fell between them. "I see," Katya managed at last.

"I've shocked you again, haven't I?" the elderly woman said, her ebony eyes glowing. "You have a very expressive face, Miss Alexander. Far too revealing for your own good, I suspect."

The Comtesse returned to the settee and settled herself on the firm cushions. She took a moment to arrange her gray silk skirts, then continued evenly, "Her name was Louisa. Her father was a bricklayer . . . or perhaps a stone mason, I don't recall. Nor do I know how she and my brother met. Perhaps he saw her walking in the village, or crossed her path while out riding. In any event, I did not learn of her existence until William sent me an impassioned letter telling me that he had fallen madly in love. He sent page after page, extolling Louisa's virtues and praising her extraordinary beauty. He intended to marry the woman. I knew from the moment I received his letter that he had written to me in order to gain my blessing and approval."

"Did you give it to him?"

The Comtesse's fingers tightened around the head of her cane. "No, I did not."

"Why?"

"The woman's father was a common laborer. Her mother took in laundry and mending from the local townspeople. Yet their daughter should marry the Earl of Barrington? Impossible." She paused for a moment, studying Katya intently. "How sour and disapproving you look, Miss Alexander."

"If your brother loved her the way you say he did—"

"Do you truly believe it's that simple?"

"Yes, I do."

A look of profound sadness was etched upon the older woman's face. "If only that were true. Rarely are one's passions so completely pure—and one's life so free of duty and obligation to others that one can do whatever one pleases."

"I don't understand."

"From the moment William was born, it was ingrained in him that his foremost obligation was to his title and his lands. To that end, he was destined to marry another member of the nobility. Years earlier our parents had made arrangements with Marianne's family to arrange my brother's suit. Although they were not yet formally pledged, in the eyes of society at large their courtship and marriage was a fait accompli. The course my brother's life would take had long ago been chartered by others. To throw it all away for the sake of some bricklayer's daughter was an affront not only to our family, but to our status and position in society as well."

"Is that how you replied to his letter?"

"Yes. That is exactly how I replied. Perhaps I was even harsher."

The Comtesse fell silent for a long moment, gazing inward· as though reviewing painful, timeworn memories. At last she continued, "In my defense, I assumed my brother's fixation with the woman was nothing but a temporary infatuation. Or perhaps a way of putting off the burden of marriage. In short, I thought it would pass."

"Did it?" Katya asked.

"No. It did not." She paused again, then let out a heavy sigh. "I was William's last vestige of hope. Without my support, he knew he stood no chance in going against our parents' wishes. Had he done so, he likely would have lost his title, his lands, his financial support, everything he had. Then what could he have offered his bricklayer's daughter?"

"Himself."

"Indeed. In my brother's case, I believe that would have been enough."

"What do you mean?"

"I saw them walking together once—William and Louisa—shortly before he married Marianne. They were arguing fiercely, presumably about my brother's upcoming nuptials. What struck me most at the time was my brother's expression as he looked at her. I had always heard that love could transform a man. I knew in that instant that it was true. His face was an image of both agony and adoration, as though he were hanging onto her every word even in their bitterest moment, memorizing the way she moved, the way she spoke, the color of her hair, and the shape of her eyes." The Comtesse's gaze locked meaningfully on Katya's. "The men in this family love very deeply, or not at all."

Ignoring what appeared to be a blatant reference to her relationship with Nicholas, Katya asked, "What happened between the two?"

"My brother married Marianne, as was his duty. Louisa married almost immediately as well; a nobleman, I believe, but a man with no wealth of which to speak. I thought it would end there, but I was wrong."

Katya frowned. "What do you mean?"

The Comtesse lifted her shoulders in a small, defeated shrug. "Marianne was the right woman for William only in regard to class and breeding. Although their marriage was civil, that indefinable spark that is so essential between two people was missing from the start. Marianne was kind and gentle, a doting mother to Nicholas and Tyler, and a gracious hostess to their guests. But she was far too docile to suit my brother. Although we never spoke of it, I suspect she was unhappy in the marriage as well. Shortly after Tyler was born she moved out of the bedchamber she had shared with my brother and into her own suite of rooms."

Katya nodded thoughtfully. "And what of Louisa? Did your brother ever see her again?"

"Yes. On many occasions. But do not misinterpret my words, Miss Alexander. My brother never broke the sanctity of his marriage vows. Louisa lived only a few days' ride away. Months would pass, then his longing to see her would grow so great that he could not resist the temptation of riding to her home just for a glimpse of her walking the grounds, running some small errand, or riding through the woods."

"But he never spoke to her?"

A look of deep sorrow crossed the Comtesse's normally reserved features. "After their break, she returned all his letters unopened and refused to see him when he called." She paused, then finished softly, "I understand she died suddenly one winter of pneumonia. William didn't learn of her death until weeks later. I believe a large part of him died with her."

Katya turned her gaze to the portrait of Nicholas's father, studying him in an altogether new light. "How very sad," she remarked, then she returned her gaze to the Comtesse. "Do Nicholas or Tyler know any of this?"

"No. My brother swore me to secrecy and I have honored his request—until now."

"Why now? Why did you tell me?"

The Comtesse planted her cane firmly on the rug and rose to her feet, moving to stand before the portrait of her brother. She studied the painting for a moment in contemplative silence then turned and replied, "Because I do not want William remembered like this. Harsh, cold, arrogant." She paused, then shook her head. "I am not trying to excuse my brother's behavior. I am only attempting to offer an explanation for what made him the man he became. I believe the loss of Louisa cost him more dearly than any of us could have suspected. William grew more and more bitter as the days went by, more and more withdrawn. When Nicholas and Tyler were young, I watched them struggle so hard to gain their father's approval, desperate for some small sign of affection. But there was nothing there. Eventually they simply stopped trying. I can't help but wonder what might have happened had they been aware that their father's anger and withdrawal had nothing to do with them. Would it have hurt or helped had they known the truth?"

"I've found that withholding the truth rarely leads to a good end."

From across the room, the Comtesse's dark eyes glowed with satisfied victory. "Exactly," she said. "Our lives are the sum of the choices we make. It has been my experience that the longer a secret is kept, the more damage it does once it is revealed."

She knows. She knows who I am. The thought jolted through Katya's mind with a startling awareness that left her temporarily speechless. But surely that was impossible. Surely it was nothing but her own feelings of guilt that were making her read into the Comtesse's words something that was not there.

Carefully considering her response, she asked, "When do you plan to tell Nicholas about Louisa?"

"As with any other matter in life, proper timing is essential. Although the explanation of his father's behavior may mean little to him at this point, he deserves to hear the truth. He should have heard it long ago."

Before Katya could summon a reply, the Comtesse strode regally across the room, pausing at the door to the study. "I do not know whether the DuValenti curse exists," she said. "Perhaps the only curse that befalls the men in this family is that of loving passionately, but unwisely. I do hope for Nicholas's sake that this is not the case."

This time there was no mistaking the fact that she was speaking directly to her. Katya tilted her chin and met the older woman's gaze. "I hope so, too."

A whisper of a smile crossed the Comtesse's stern features as she glanced around the study. "In the end," she said, "that is all we really have." She lifted her arm and gestured vaguely around the room. "The houses in which we live, the clothes we wear, the titles we flaunt, and the horses we ride are nothing but trinkets, silly little toys we invent to amuse ourselves while we pass our time on this earth. But to love with one's heart and soul—and to be loved in return—surely that is a glimpse into heaven."

On that amazingly unexpected statement, she turned abruptly and left the room, her gray silk skirts trailing in her wake.

As Katya moved through the backstage area of the Grand Casino, traces of the conversation she had shared with the Comtesse echoed through her mind, filling her with a quiet sense of resolve. It was time she revealed to Nicholas exactly who she was. In fact, she would have done so immediately, had he been at home. Instead she had resigned herself to speaking to him later that evening. Rather than feeling overwhelmed with worry about her decision, she felt remarkably unburdened, almost carefree for the first time since she had arrived in Monaco.

She paused at the backstage curtain to observe the act that was onstage. A beautiful French chanteuse and her handsome partner sang a romantic duet written especially for them. Once the song had ended, they would perform two stormy pieces from a Verdi opera, then finish with a heart-wrenching ballad. All in all, Katya estimated that she had roughly twenty minutes before she was due onstage.

She sneaked a peak at the audience. The theater was packed, she noted. Although the audience watched the chanteuse and her partner with expressions of polite interest, an air of subtle impatience seemed to fill the crowded room.

They were waiting for her. The Goddess of Mystery.

Perhaps it was immodest of her to recognize that fact, but the evidence was inescapable. Every one of her performances had been sold out. She had built a reputation of renown throughout Monaco, to the point where she was recognized wherever she went. Despite Monsieur Remy's constant requests that she add more shows to her schedule, Katya had consistently declined, claiming that the scarcity of her performances added more to her appeal than would making herself readily available to her audience.

But that was only part of her reasoning. In truth, she had no desire to spend more time away from Nicholas than she already did. Although she enjoyed performing, it was not in her blood the way it had been in her parents'. She derived a certain amount of satisfaction from knowing she could perform her father's repertoire of illusions with nearly the same level of skill that he had employed, but that was the extent of her pleasure. The rest of it was almost mechanical.

As she waited to move onstage, she mentally reviewed the changes she had made to her act. Nothing significant, really. She had added a routine in which she appeared to float above her assistants and had removed one in which she cupped fire in her palm. The rest of the alterations had been minor: a few changes in costume and stage direction. The Gun Trick would be performed last, as usual, but tonight she would pretend to catch the bullet in a silver bowl, rather than in her hand.

She turned away from the curtain and moved to check her props one last time. As she crossed the bustling backstage area, her eye was caught by a glimmer of glistening gold. Assuming that one of the dancers who had performed earlier had dropped a piece of jewelry, she bent down to scoop it up. But the item she found was distinctly male—and distinctly familiar. Balanced in her hand was a solid gold cuff link embellished with an onyx stone into which had been carved the emblem of the Maltese.

Nicholas's cuff link.

Her heart skipped a beat as a rush of giddy expectation surged through her. Smiling, she glanced around her, but saw no sign of Nicholas. Perhaps their paths had crossed, she thought. The backstage area was small but quite busy—with the various performers, musicians, and stagehands bustling back and forth it was not uncommon to miss someone entirely. He had probably gone to look for her in her dressing room. Anxious to see him—if for no reason than to receive a quick kiss for good luck before her performance—she hurried off to her private dressing room. She lifted her skirts and raced through the crowded halls. Barely managing to stifle a giggle of excitement, she threw open the door and breathlessly called out his name. Silence answered her. The room was empty.

Swallowing her disappointment, she moved back to the stage area. She glanced all around her, but saw no sign of Nicholas. He must have looked for her, then returned to his seat for her performance, she reasoned. As she moved toward the stage, Monsieur Remy, clad in a formal, tightly fitting black suit that gave him the unfortunate appearance of a waddling penguin, drew up beside her.

"Good evening, Miss Alexander," he said brightly. "I understand you've made some changes to your show."

She smiled. "Just a few. One should always keep one's performance fresh."

"Indeed."

He rocked back and forth on his heels as they stood side by side watching the chanteuse and her partner. As Monsieur Remy's beady eyes darted from his performers to the subtle shifting and rustling going on in the audience, a tight frown curved his lips. It would not be long, Katya guessed, before the singers were looking for another engagement.

"You didn't happen to see Lord Barrington this evening, did you?" she inquired.

"Who?"

"Lord Barrington."

"Ah. So that's his name." He nodded. "You did know him after all."

Katya frowned. "What do you mean?"

"The man I met before. I mentioned him to you in my office on the day you applied for this engagement. Do you not recall?"

She stared at him blankly.

"Your parents' agent," he said. "He was here again tonight."

A tight knot of vague, ominous dread coiled in her belly. "Are you certain it was the same man you saw before?" she asked.

"Quite certain. He was here perhaps thirty minutes ago, near the table where you store the props for your performance. I called out to him, but he turned and left before I could speak to him."

"What did he look like?"

Remy gave her an odd look, then pursed his lips in thought. "He was quite handsomely dressed," he began. "Formal jacket and trousers, starched white shirt. He was a tall man with dark hair . . . and I seem to recall that his eyes were dark as well. He looked to be in his early thirties."

"Can you tell me anything else about him?"

"It was weeks ago that I spoke with the man," he said with a shrug, "but I remember that I didn't like his temperament. He was quite curt, quite impatient. As though he were accustomed to ordering people about all day. He was most displeased when I refused to allow him immediate access to your parents' belongings. But as I informed him, I had already received your letter informing me that you were en route—"

"Thank you, Monsieur Remy," she said, abruptly turning away as the singers took their final bow and the heavy red velvet curtain fell. The moment the audience's applause died down, the stagehands began to scurry about setting up her act. Katya placed a restraining hand on the arm of the man who was wheeling her prop table toward her assistants. "Just a minute, please," she said.

Her gaze moved painstakingly over the table. A prop placed even a fraction of an inch off could make a difference between a smooth illusion and one that appeared fumbling and inept. She ran her fingers lightly over the objects before her, scrutinizing each item. The cups, the balls, the wand, the mirror. Her every instinct told her that something was amiss, but nothing looked as though it had been disturbed.

She silently lifted the gun. It felt cold and heavy in her hand. Carefully cracking open the chamber, she emptied out the bullets into her palm. Three blank cartridges, each of them carefully marked.

Remy came up to stand beside her. "Is there something wrong, Miss Alexander?"

The mellow strains of the sitar reached her as the orchestra began the opening notes of her performance. She was due onstage in a matter of seconds.

She replaced the blanks in the chamber and gave him a

small smile, slightly embarrassed at her show of nervousness. "No," she said. "Everything looks fine."

"Very good." He nodded at the stagehand to finish his setup, then gestured for her to precede him. "I believe your audience is waiting."

She took her place onstage, readying herself for the Birth of the Butterfly, her opening act. Her concern over the man who had been posing as her parents' agent faded to the back of her mind as she focused her attention on the performance. She moved from illusion to illusion with the graceful fluidity her father had taught her, never hesitating and never faltering, luring her audience into the magical land of the enchantress.

As her show reached its finale, her assistant, Hubert, withdrew the gun from the prop table and held it before the captivated crowd. He selected two volunteers from the audience to join them onstage to inspect the piece and fire the weapon, thus proving its deadliness. That accomplished, the volunteers took their seats.

Hubert took his position upstage while Katya moved downstage. She calmly met his gaze as she lifted the shallow silver bowl with which she intended to catch the bullet he fired. She was ready; she knew exactly what to do. The split-second timing had long ago been perfected: the gun would fire, a backstage hand would ring a bell to give the illusion of a bullet striking metal, she would wave the bullet she currently palmed in her hand at the audience, making it appear as though she had captured the deadly shot in the silver bowl she held. All neat, tidy, and dramatically effective.

Hubert raised the gun.

He pointed it directly at her.

The drumroll intensified as the audience collectively caught its breath.

As she stared down the barrel of the gun, she experienced a sudden tingling sensation in the back of her scalp, a feeling that was part alarm and part intuition. Something was wrong.

He pulled the trigger.

In the millisecond that followed, Katya was dimly aware that the repercussion of the blank cartridge sounded much louder than it normally did.

She felt a strong shove against her chest, as though a mule had kicked her between the ribs. Then stabbing pain, followed immediately by heat. Burning, scorching heat.

The stage abruptly tilted and began to spin.

Afraid she was going to faint, she reached out for something to hold on to, but her hands came up with nothing but air. Fortunately, however, she did not have far to fall.

The floor obligingly rushed up to meet her.

Nineteen

His heart in his throat, Nicholas fought his way through the swarming crowds that filled the theater. Nearly all the audience had risen to their feet; their distressed cries and agitated milling about added to the pandemonium that filled the room—and made it that much more difficult for him to reach the stage. At last he made it to the front row and leaped onto the stage.

His gaze went immediately to Katya. She lay motionless where she had fallen, surrounded by panicked assistants, distraught stagehands, and other performers who had rushed to the stage. Her lifeless pose instantly seared itself into his mind; for one heart-stopping moment he stood unmoving, paralyzed by the agonizing certainty that she was dead.

Then he heard a stagehand's frantic cry for a physician, followed by another's call for smelling salts. The import of the words slowly sank in. She wasn't dead. *She wasn't dead.* The realization was like air to a drowning man, shaking him free from the stupor that had gripped him.

Nicholas shot forward and dropped to his knees at Katya's side. He reached for her hand and grasped it firmly in his. Once again he was struck by how small and fragile, how very delicate it felt within his larger one. He pressed his fingers against her wrist. Her pulse was strong and regular, its steady beat more reassuring than words could be.

His gaze moved searchingly over her form. A bruise was forming near her left temple. Her skin was pale and her breathing was shallow, but mercifully there was no sign of blood. He was vaguely aware of someone kneeling beside him, then of a stranger's hand reaching to brush Katya's hair from her face.

"Don't touch her!" Nicholas snarled instinctively.

The stranger drew back, an expression of appalled shock on his face. "I'm a physician," he stammered. "Dr. Ellwood."

Nicholas slowly absorbed the information, then gave the man a curt nod, gesturing for him to proceed.

"There's a cot in the back," a nearby voice suggested.

At Dr. Ellwood's nod of assent, Nicholas gathered Katya in his arms and carried her to the backstage dressing room indicated by the stagehand. He set her down gently on the narrow cot and took a step backward, allowing the physician room to perform his examination. As Dr. Ellwood's long, slender fingers gently poked and prodded, Katya suddenly awakened, struggling against the physician as though terrified for her life. Nicholas instantly stepped forward to soothe her, but his ministrations seemed to only intensify her agitation.

A heavy dose of laudanum finally quieted her enough for Dr. Ellwood to complete his examination and—to Nicholas's overwhelming relief—report that Katya would recover unharmed from her mishap. Apparently a real bullet had filled the chamber of the gun she used for her finale, but rather than striking her directly, the shot had ricocheted off the silver bowl. The impact of the bullet striking the bowl had deeply bruised her sternum and knocked her flat. After gaining the physician's assurances that he would pay a visit tomorrow to check on her condition, Nicholas called for his coach to be brought around to the backstage entrance.

He sat with Katya bundled limply in his lap, staring out over the moonlit landscape as they left the principality and made their way up the steep slope of the Moneghetti. Her breath fell softly against his chest, low and steady. Amazing how simple the act of breathing was, and yet how profoundly comforting.

As he traced his palm absently over her arm he felt suddenly unburdened. Since his arrival in Monaco he had been cursed with an inability to see the situation clearly, to separate the important facts from the unimportant. His mind had been filled with too many questions. What if it was Tyler who was out to destroy him? Had Allyson been involved? Who else would want to see him ruined? But now the questions all faded away. The meaningless chatter that had clouded his thoughts, all the contingencies and what ifs, suddenly cleared, leaving him with a sense of astonishing clarity and resolution.

Someone had tried to kill Katya.

The details of who and why no longer mattered.

It was time for the macabre little game to come to an end.

Katya felt as though she were floating, surrounded by a deep, misty haze. A familiar, masculine scent drifted around her; a cool expanse of starched linen brushed her cheek. She felt wonderfully secure, if somewhat groggy. As her senses wakened, she realized that, in a sense, she truly was floating. Nicholas was carrying her in his arms.

Dull curiosity spread slowly through her. Where was she, and why was he carrying her? She knew the answer was right before her, but reaching it was like fighting her way to the surface of an icy lake. The closer she came to it, the more conscious she was of the terrible ache in the center of her chest—worse every time she drew breath—and the steady pounding that filled her skull. No, thank you, she decided. Definitely not worth the effort. She closed her eyes and let out a contented sigh as she burrowed in against Nicholas's chest, letting herself slip back into the foggy haze.

When she woke next, she was dimly aware of her surroundings for the first time in what felt like days. She was in bed in her chamber in Nicholas's villa. Pale peach light filtered in through the windows. Dawn? she wondered. Or was that the soft glow of twilight? Her gaze skirted the room, then came to a stop as she saw Nicholas.

He was slumped over in a small chair that had been pulled up next to her bed. His eyes were closed and his breath was low and even, as though he had just dozed off. As she studied the chair—a fragile, undeniably feminine chair that had been upholstered in an apple-green silk damask—it occurred to her that he must be uncomfortable. If he wanted to sleep, surely he would be more comfortable in bed with her. She lightly tapped his knee to wake him and tell him so.

His ebony eyes instantly snapped open. He straightened in his seat, his gaze searching her face with somber intensity. "Welcome back," he said; then he gently asked, "How do you feel?"

"As though I've been run over by a team of wild horses," she replied honestly.

A hint of a smile touched his lips. "I would imagine so."

"What time is it?"

He pulled a watch from his pocket and gave it a cursory glance. "Nearly five."

That hardly helped. "Morning or evening?"

"Morning."

She nodded. Her speech, she noted, was slightly slurred; her tongue felt thick and heavy.

He reached for her hand and held it in his. "Do you remember what happened?" he asked.

Katya found she had to concentrate intently in order to reply. Her thoughts seemed to tumble through her mind in a completely random manner, tossing about from one point to the next with no coherence whatsoever. But despite her mental disarray, a feeling of vague alarm and foreboding hung over her. There was something very important she needed to remember, something fundamental, but it hung just out of her reach. The more she tried to focus on that elusive memory, the more it skirted out of her grasp.

Letting the thought go for the moment, she struggled to summon a reply to his question. "I was onstage," she said slowly. "Something went wrong."

"You were performing the Gun Trick, do you remember?"

The Gun Trick. Yes. She remembered standing onstage: the audience, the curtains, the music. She remembered hearing the drumroll that always accompanied her finale as Hubert pointed the gun at her. She remembered feeling a sharp, searing pain in her chest. Then nothing. Blackness. "Yes," she said slowly. "I remember." She searched his gaze. "What happened?"

"I was hoping you could tell me."

She thought for a long moment and reached the only logical conclusion she could. "The gun must have misfired."

He frowned. "Has that ever happened before?"

"No, never." She shook her head and let out a soft, embarrassed sigh. "What a finale."

"You certainly had your audience on its feet."

"I can imagine." She gave a rueful smile and struggled to sit up, but found to her irritation that her arms were too weak to support her.

"Easy," Nicholas soothed, reaching forward to assist her into a sitting position. He propped a pillow up behind her. "Better?" he asked.

She nodded. Her limbs felt like rubber, her chest ached, her head was pounding, and her thoughts were totally muddled. But given her circumstances, she felt remarkably well.

"Dr. Ellwood examined you last night," he said. "All things considered, you were damned lucky. Evidently there was a live bullet in the chamber. Fortunately it ricocheted off the bowl you were holding. Although it didn't penetrate the bowl—or you—the force of it was hard enough to knock you off your feet. You have an awful-looking bruise right here," he paused and lightly touched his fingertips to a spot just over her heart, "but there doesn't appear to be any swelling and your ribs aren't fractured. You hit your head when you fell and gave yourself a pretty nasty bump, but that appears to be the extent of your injuries."

"My head—is that why I feel so groggy?"

"Possibly. It might also be the lingering effects of the laudanum Dr. Ellwood administered to help you sleep." He hesitated, then continued, "You put up quite a fight when he tried to examine you, do you remember?"

She hadn't thought of it until that moment, but suddenly she remembered the stark, cold terror that had gripped her, the overwhelming desperation she had felt to flee. She also remembered the anxiety that had seized her just before Hubert had fired the gun. *Why?* There had been a reason for her fear, but now that reason escaped her entirely.

Her memories were nothing but vague, fragmented shadows; she found herself entirely unable to put them into any semblance of logical order. It seemed as though all she could understand at the moment were simple concepts, questions that required nothing but a yes or a no answer.

To that end, she glanced down at the simple cotton nightshirt she wore and asked, "Did you remove my clothing?"

"Yes. Do you mind?"

She shook her head. It was a thoughtful gesture, particularly since he had made no attempt to make himself more comfortable. With the exception of removing his jacket and loosening his cravat, he still wore his formal evening attire.

He shifted slightly in his chair, leaning forward. A note of solemn gravity came over his features, but his voice was low and gentle. "Did you see anyone suspicious backstage?"

Her pulse skipped a beat and her breath caught in her throat. There had been someone backstage before her performance, someone who had frightened her. But who?

Think! she commanded herself. But the harder she focused on the question, the more her fear rose, choking off her thoughts. Her memories skirted away and out of her grasp as though deliberately eluding her. In the end she was chasing nothing but dark, ominous shadows. There was definitely something there, something she needed to see, but she couldn't quite grasp it.

Worse still, the laudanum was once again taking its toll on her. Her eyelids were growing heavy, her limbs felt even weaker than they had earlier, and the mere effort of putting her thoughts into words seemed to drain her of every ounce of energy she possessed.

"Katya, try to remember," he urged. "Who did you see backstage?"

She gave a soft yawn and lifted her shoulders in a light shrug. "Only you."

He frowned, clearly taken aback. "Me?"

"You didn't come to see me before my show?"

"No."

"That's odd, I could have sworn . . ." She let her voice trail off as she searched her mind. Hadn't Nicholas been there? She distinctly remembered running down the crowded backstage hall toward her dressing room, her heart beating with excitement and expectation, confident that she would find him inside. In that regard her memory was crystal clear. But had he truly been there? For some reason, she couldn't remember actually seeing him.

"I had some business to attend to in town," he said, interrupting her thoughts. "I didn't make it to the casino until your performance was well under way."

"You weren't there?"

"No," he repeated, "I wasn't."

"Oh." She leaned back against her pillows and sent him a wan smile. "I suppose that was nothing but a bit of wishful thinking on my part."

"I suppose so," he agreed. He began to ask her another question, then his gaze moved slowly over her face. "You're tired," he said.

"So are you." She reached out and lightly traced her fingers over the rough, dark stubble that shadowed his cheek. Judging by the look of him, he had passed the entire night sitting in that cramped chair beside her bed. She drew back her bedcovers and patted the space next to her.

He hesitated. "I don't want to hurt you."

She yawned again. "If this incident has taught us nothing else, at least it proves that I am not fragile, does it not?"

A small smile curved his lips. "I suppose that's true."

That said, he kicked off his shoes and carefully climbed in beside her, not bothering to remove his shirt and pants. As the mattress sank beneath his weight Katya rolled against him, curling up with her back against his chest. He wrapped his arms around her and pressed a light kiss against the nape of her neck. "Am I hurting you?" he asked.

"No."

She felt wonderful. A little sore, perhaps, but warm, sleepy, and content. The scent of Nicholas's skin drifted around her; his warm breath lightly fanned her cheek. She reached for his hands and graced his knuckles with a light kiss, then burrowed into the cool linen sleeve of his shirt. As she did, she felt something press against her cheek. She drew back, frowning slightly as she stared at his sleeve.

In that instant the dark memories that had haunted her came back in full force, skittering through her mind at a pace too rapid for her to grasp, leaving nothing but horrified alarm in their wake. Something was wrong, but she still couldn't identify what it was. She only knew that the feeling of stark dread that had lodged in her belly earlier had returned tenfold.

Think! she commanded herself once again. She reached for the memory, mentally stretching for it, battling the drugged fatigue that threatened to overwhelm her and take it away. Her gaze narrowed on Nicholas's arm. She studied the long sleeve of his shirt, the crisp white linen, the starched cuff, the ornate gold-and-onyx cuff link.

The *single* ornate gold-and-onyx cuff link.

He had lost one cuff link.

And she had found it. The memory came flooding back in a sickening rush. She had found Nicholas's cuff link near her prop table just minutes before she had been due onstage. Obviously he had been backstage before her performance.

As she considered that fact she suddenly remembered something Monsieur Remy had told her. The man who had posed as her parents' agent weeks earlier had been backstage as well—a man Remy had described as in his early thirties, tall, with dark hair and eyes, and an inborn air of arrogance. Were he and Nicholas one and the same? The possibility seemed too ludicrous to consider, yet she could not banish it completely.

Would Nicholas have tried to gain access to her parents' belongings?

Why had he lied to her about having been backstage?

As the questions reverberated through her mind a feeling of sinking dread spread through her limbs and a quiet panic filled her heart. The answers had to be faced, but at the moment they were overwhelming. The warmth of Nicholas's body, the softness of the sheets, and the lingering effects of the sedative were all too strong to resist. The fatigue she had been battling finally took hold, dragging her down into a deep, fitful slumber.

When Katya woke next, the room was awash with brilliant midday sunshine. She was alone. Apparently Nicholas had left at some point that morning, although she didn't recall him slipping out of bed. Glancing at the small brass clock atop her dresser, she saw that it was nearly noon. Seven hours had passed since she last awoke.

To her relief, the grogginess she had experienced earlier was gone. In its place was a keen sense of clarity and purpose. She sat up, swung her legs over the side of the bed and stood, testing her body's reaction. A dull throbbing echoed through her head, and there was a deep ache in her chest, but aside from these she felt remarkably sound.

A feeling of quiet resolve filled her as she attended her toilette and drew on a simple cotton blouse, a riding skirt, and a pair of sturdy boots. She could no longer brush aside the worries that had engulfed her earlier that morning. It was time she faced the truth, whatever it might be.

She had naively assumed that she had kept her true identity a secret from Nicholas, but now she wondered. Had he known all along that she was a Rosskaya and used her to gain access to her family's scroll? Had he been determined to seduce her into giving the scroll to him, or to use her until he found the ancient parchment himself? Highly unlikely— *extremely* unlikely, she amended—but possible.

And then what? she thought, following that train of thought to its natural conclusion. He had found her scroll, therefore her usefulness was at an end? He had sneaked backstage and deliberately sabotaged her act, intending to make it appear as though she had accidentally died while performing? The very idea was so preposterous it was laughable.

Not only that, it was easily proven false. She counted the reasons why on her fingers. First, she had seen her scroll yesterday, safely hidden away in the false compartment of her trunk. Second, her parents' deaths had been accidental. Third, there were any number of reasons why Nicholas might have kept the truth from her regarding his presence backstage . . . she just couldn't think of them at the moment. Fourth, just because Monsieur Remy's description of the man who had posed as her parents' agent matched Nicholas perfectly, it didn't mean it actually was him. She could simply bring Nicholas to Monsieur Remy and ask if he was the man who had been posing as her parents' agent. Fifth— She stopped counting and let out a sigh. She could stand there counting for days but it wouldn't prove a thing. Or *dis*-prove a thing, she mentally corrected herself. The only way to do that was to physically verify the evidence.

To that end, she crossed the room to where her trunk was stored. She lifted the lid and emptied it of the assorted clothing. Then she touched the spring that released the hidden compartment and removed the false bottom. Relief immediately poured through her as her eyes moved over the assortment of books and papers. She immediately saw Sacha's diary, as well as the bundle of ancient parchment. From the looks of it, nothing had been disturbed. She shifted the books and moved the papers aside, searching for the scroll.

Odd.

It wasn't there.

A tremor of icy apprehension raced down her spine. It *had* to be there. She had seen it only yesterday, just before she and Nicholas had left for the abbey. Fighting back a surge of wild panic, she thrust her hands along the bottom of the trunk, frantically searching for the scroll. When that failed, she dumped the trunk upside down, scrupulously examining each piece. Twice. Then again.

Nothing.

Her scroll was missing.

Katya swallowed hard and rocked back on her heals, fighting her escalating emotions of stunned disbelief and budding hysteria. Someone had stolen her scroll. His brother, Tyler? Perhaps, but surely one of the servants would have seen him in the villa. *Nicholas?* Could it be? Could she truly have misjudged his character so completely? But if he hadn't taken it, who else could have? She searched her mind, but returned again and again to the same conclusion.

Nicholas.

The Lord of Scandal.

His reputation had been well deserved after all. An image of his face loomed before her as a sickening mixture of dread and distress lodged deep within her belly. How could he have touched her the way he had? Not just the way his hands had caressed her body, but the way his eyes had peered so deeply into her soul. Had that been nothing but a sham? Impossible. Or was it? While he kissed her mouth and stroked her flesh, had he been entirely devoid of emotion? Was he capable of that level of betrayal? Her hands began to shake and for a moment she thought she might be physically ill.

Beware the Maltese.

The firstborn son of the DuValentis. Her family's ancient enemy. She had been warned all along, yet had refused to listen. She had tumbled headlong into his arms, not even putting up a token resistance. For the first time in her life, she had shed the thick shield of prudence and caution that had habitually preceded her every act. She had loved Nicholas Duvall with her heart and soul. Passionately. Completely. Foolishly.

She repacked her trunk, handling each item as if placing it just so was of the utmost importance. The mindless, repetitive task gave her time to find the strength she needed. She was not beaten, she decided. She may have lost the scroll, but she would not give up. Not yet. Not so long as the blood of her gypsy ancestors flowed through her veins.

She had only a part of the answer she required. The rest could be found only at the casino. With that in mind she stood and gathered her reticule and gloves, then turned to the door of her bedchamber. She marched resolutely downstairs, stopping at the foot of the curved staircase as Edward Litell, Nicholas's personal secretary, stepped from his master's study and closed the door behind him.

"Mr. Litell," she called.

He turned toward her, an expression that could almost be defined as a smile softening his normally austere expression. "Miss Alexander," he returned, striding toward her. His cool blue eyes moved briefly over her form. "I heard of your accident last night. How wonderful to see you looking so well."

"Would you please send word to the groomsmen to have Lord Barrington's coach readied for me immediately? I have some business to attend to in town."

He hesitated. "Immediately?"

"Is that a problem, Mr. Litell?"

"Regrettably, yes. Lord Barrington has requested that Dr. Ellwood return this afternoon to check your condition. He should be arriving within the hour."

"In that case, you may inform both Dr. Ellwood and Lord Barrington that I am not in need of a physician's services. As you can see, I am quite fully recovered."

"So you are."

Katya spun around at the sound of Nicholas's voice behind her. Her heart skipped a beat and her breath caught in her throat at the sight of him. He was so incredibly handsome, she thought, as she regarded him with a raw, aching awareness. He stood with one broad shoulder against the wall, studying her with a look of quiet intensity. She had assumed he was out of earshot, behind the closed doors of his study. But judging from the shiny red apple he held in his hand, he was coming from the kitchens.

As Litell moved away, Nicholas said, "I didn't expect to see you up and about so soon. How are you feeling?"

Katya had to battle the urge to confront him with the fact that her scroll was missing and to demand an explanation. He couldn't possibly have done—she began, then stopped herself. Clearly her emotions could not be trusted. What she needed now were facts. Cold, hard facts.

"I'm fine," she replied, keeping her voice cool and formal.

"Are you certain you're ready to be up and about?"

"Quite certain."

"Very well." He paused, then continued lightly, "Now what's this I hear about you going into town?"

"If you don't mind, I should like to borrow your coach this afternoon. I have some business to attend at the casino."

"Can't it wait? Dr. Ellwood should be here shortly and—"

"I'm afraid it can't. I'd like to leave now, if you don't mind."

He frowned, searching her face for a long moment in silence. Was there something different in his gaze? Something dark she had never seen before? Or was she merely imagining it?

"Is anything wrong?" he asked.

"Not at all."

"You seem upset."

She stretched her lips into what she hoped would pass for a confident smile. "Merely hurried," she corrected. "I didn't intend to sleep so late. I have an appointment to meet with Monsieur Remy to review my schedule of performances for next month."

"Given last night's mishap, surely he would understand if you can't make it."

"Perhaps. But I would like to go nonetheless." She hesitated, then continued in a rush, "Why don't you join me? I don't believe you've ever met Monsieur Remy. He may have a little insight to shed on last night's—"

"I'm afraid I can't," he replied, cutting her off. He lifted his shoulders in a light shrug. "Some other time."

Katya nodded. "Yes, some other time." Idiot! she screamed at herself. Why had she mentioned Remy's name? Surely Nicholas knew the man could identify him.

Before she could guess his intention, he reached out and gently brushed a stray curl from her forehead. A shiver ran down her spine as his fingers brushed her skin, but it wasn't the tremor of sensual anticipation she normally felt when Nicholas touched her. Instead, it was a shiver of ominous foreboding. His eyes locked on hers as he drew his fingers up her arm in a light caress. In a low, dangerous voice, he asked, "Is there something you're not telling me, little gypsy?"

She swallowed hard and moved out of his reach. "I don't know what you mean."

"We had a pact, don't you remember? Complete honesty."

"Yes. I remember." So naive, so foolish.

He studied her face for a long moment in silence, then said simply, "The groomsmen should have the coach ready shortly. Is there anything else you need?"

Yes! her mind screamed. You! But all she could manage was a feeble shake of her head. "No."

"Then I won't keep you any longer." He nodded politely and stepped aside.

"Thank you."

She swept past him and moved toward the door. As she exited the room, she noted a wisp of charcoal-gray silk skirts and glanced to her left to see the Comtesse comfortably seated in the front parlor, a book in her lap. Undoubtedly she had overheard their entire exchange. Katya sent her a polite nod—and received in return a silent stare that was completely unfathomable. Before she could utter a word, the Comtesse turned her head and went back to her reading.

Just as well, Katya thought, making her way toward the courtyard where Nicholas's coach awaited her. She was not capable at the moment of idle chatter. Her jaw hurt from clenching her teeth and her throat felt as though it had been filled with sand. She couldn't swallow, couldn't speak, could barely see past the tears that blurred her vision.

Katya turned away from the window as the coach began its descent into town. She had expected she would feel *something* when she saw Nicholas. Rage, anger, pain, grief, fear—perhaps a combination of all these emotions. But what she felt instead was entirely unanticipated, and even worse to endure.

Longing. Longing to touch him. Longing to laugh with him. Longing to confront him with the fact that her scroll was missing and to demand to know where it was. Longing to turn back the clock just twenty-four hours, back to a time when she trusted him entirely.

So shattered were her thoughts and so grim her emotions that she felt as though she had just sat down in the carriage when the groomsman pulled the team to a stop in front of the Grand Casino. She exited the coach and strode wood-enly through the bustling gaming rooms toward the theater. She pulled open the broad doors and stepped inside, her footsteps echoing through the vacant hall.

As she reached the backstage area she nodded politely in greeting to the performers rehearsing their acts. She smiled and murmured empty words of thanks at their expressions of shock and concern over her accident, but it was evident that she was in no mood to talk. The small crowd that had surrounded her upon her arrival quickly dissipated, leaving her alone.

Someone had gathered her props and returned them neatly to her table, she noted. As she ran her fingers over the various pieces, all essential items for a conjurer, a chill shot down her spine. She had stood just like this last night before she stepped onstage.

She lifted the gun and cracked open the barrel chamber. It was empty now, but last night it had held three blanks. Or had it? Her gaze moved to the thick silver bowl that had figured so prominently in last night's illusion. A heavy line disfigured the center of the bowl—the path the bullet had taken as it had ricocheted off the silver. She fingered the bowl thoughtfully as she considered the ugly bruise that marred her chest. If not for the bowl, the bullet would have traveled right through her.

Was it fate or merely blind luck that she had decided to change her act? She had introduced the silver bowl on a whim, because of the variation and dramatic appeal it added to the routine. Until then, she had caught the bullet in her hand. Had she done that last night, she would have been killed.

Clearly she was supposed to have died onstage . . . just as her parents had.

The realization sent the quiet horror that filled her soaring to a new level. She set down the gun and scanned the backstage area until she found the large wood-and-glass tank her parents had employed for their finale. Katya moved slowly toward it, a feeling of imminent dread balled tightly within her belly. She had not examined the tank since her arrival in Monaco; until that moment, she had had no reason to.

She traced her hands over the tank, a frown of deep concentration on her brow, as though listening for the piece itself to tell her what had happened. There were two locking mechanisms by which the tank was operated. The first was to the door the audience saw—the door through which her father had stepped when he entered the tank. The second was to the hidden compartment at the floor of the tank, through which her father exited and her mother entered. Katya pulled open both doors and examined the locks, finding nothing amiss. The locks clicked shut and released as smoothly as they had when the tank was new.

Not yet satisfied, she stepped inside the tank, pulling the door closed behind her. She examined the seams of the glass and wood, looking for any clue as to what might have happened. Finding no sign of tampering, she grasped the tiny lever that would release the door latch from the inside and gave it a quick tug.

Nothing. The lever didn't work. Katya tugged again, harder this time. Still nothing. She bent down to try the lever that controlled the secret door on the floor of the chamber. Again, nothing. She was trapped inside. Sickening understanding spread through her. The release levers worked from the *outside*. But once her parents had been inside the tank together they had had no way of escaping.

Nor did she, she belatedly realized. But while she could cry out and bang on the wood to gain the attention of those around her, during her parents' performance the tank had been filled with water, thus making it virtually soundproof. As that stark realization took hold, claustrophobia overwhelmed her, choking off her thoughts. Before she could call out for help, however, the tank door swung open. Her heart beating wildly, Katya spun around, expecting to see Nicholas standing before her.

To her relief, it was Monsieur Remy who held the door open.

"I hadn't expected to see you so soon, Miss Alexander," he said as she stepped from the tank. "How are you feeling?"

She ignored the question, bending down to reexamine the tank's locks. She immediately found what she had missed before. The inside release levers had been filed down—not enough so that it would be immediately apparent. But enough to prevent them from working.

Her parents had been murdered. The conclusion was inescapable.

"Is something wrong?" Remy asked, wringing his hands as he studied her with an expression of nervous anxiety and wary confusion.

Katya nodded slowly. "Yes, I'm afraid so."

A look of horrified understanding immediately showed on Remy's face as his gaze traveled from Katya to her parents' underwater tank. "You don't mean——" he began, then broke off abruptly, making the sign of the cross.

"Who handles the security for the casino?" she asked.

"Monsieur Chatelain."

"Is he discreet?"

Remy's head bobbed up and down as tiny beads of sweat appeared on his forehead. "Very discreet."

"Good." She quietly closed the door to the tank. "I should like to speak with him," she said. "Immediately."

Twenty

Marco waits for me in the great hall. It is nearly noon: in minutes I will be his bride. At dawn I climbed the Saint's Tower and said a prayer of safekeeping for us both. As I finished, the clouds parted and a ray of golden light shone down. I do believe my prayer was heard.

Sacha's final entry. Katya had nearly missed it entirely, so small and tattered was the scrap of parchment on which it had been written, as though it had been jotted down in a rush before she had left for her wedding ceremony. Katya had found it three days ago, just after she had returned from speaking with Monsieur Chatelain, the chief of security for the Grand Casino.

Sacha's words were neither comforting nor informative, but they did seem eerily prescient. Particularly now, as Katya stood alone in her bedchamber in Nicholas's villa dressed as a medieval bride.

As she finished her toilette for the Fete du Tarasque she studied herself critically in a floor-length looking glass. Perhaps her costume was historically accurate in detail, but it was sorely lacking in believability. She might be dressed in the guise of a medieval bride, but her eyes did not glisten with the eager joy one might expect to see in a young bride's gaze. Instead the eyes that stared back at her were flat and hollow, shadowed by pale circles.

With the exception of the simple crown of flowers she wore, her hair was completely unadorned, cascading freely down her back in a rich mass of ebony spirals. She wore a long-sleeved, finely woven smock of misty green coupled with a surcoat sewn from rich silver brocade. The bodices of each garment had been cut in deep squares, revealing an enticing glimpse of the soft curve of her breasts. An ivory-and-green-striped kirtle emphasized the narrowness of her waist and the gentle sway of her hips.

Clearly the costume had been designed to evoke an image of both innocence and sensuality. But whether or not it succeeded she could not judge. Nor did she particularly care, she decided, turning away from the mirror with a dull sigh. Her appearance was of little concern. She felt shaky and exhausted to the point of numbness, but her nerves had been too tightly wound for her to sleep. Nor could she eat. In fact, she had been able to do nothing from the moment she had discovered her parents had been murdered.

Her encounters with Nicholas had been deliberately brief and empty. Although he had come to her room in the evenings, she had claimed fatigue and turned him away. Inside herself, however, she had clung to his every word, his every nuance of tone, his every small gesture, analyzing everything over and over again in her mind. Surely she was wrong about him. The phrase echoed through her entire being, both a wish and a prayer. But one that she suspected was entirely futile. If the ancient legends were correct, their fates had been determined long ago.

In an attempt to avoid further contact she had kept mainly to her bedchamber, but the precaution had been unnecessary. Both yesterday and today she had watched him mount Avignon and ride out shortly after dawn, not to return until dusk. She had no idea where he went, nor did she ask. In truth, she strongly suspected she already knew. Now that he had found her scroll he was hunting for the Stone. But at the moment this was nothing but dark suspicion. Soon—possibly tonight—she would know for certain.

As that grim thought filled her mind, the sound of a hall clock striking eight drifted into her room. She could delay no further. Nicholas was waiting for her. Summoning her resolve, she left her bedchamber and made her way downstairs.

She found him standing alone in the back parlor, one knee propped up on the windowsill, his hands clasped behind him as he stared out over the sparkling Mediterranean. He was dressed in the costume she had seen days earlier. He wore a doublet woven from pale flax and a sleeveless tunic upon which was embroidered the emblem of the Maltese. The copper-colored braies that covered his long legs were tucked into a pair of rich leather boots. Completing the costume was a jewel-studded cape of indigo velvet.

The attire suited him. She watched as a warm breeze blew in through the open window and tossed the cape about his powerful shoulders. He looked like a beautiful medieval prince, she thought, her heart aching anew as she studied him. He seemed lost in thought, completely unaware of her presence. She read firm resolve in his expression, as well as profound sadness. Katya paused, frowning. Was she projecting her emotions onto him, or did he truly seem deeply troubled?

"Nicholas."

She called his name without thinking, shattering the stillness that had enveloped him. As he straightened and turned toward her, she noted that he wore a wide belt slung low across his hips, from which was suspended a glistening dirk and a thick leather pouch.

He studied her for a long moment, his ebony eyes glowing with an inner fire. Then he crossed the room and took her hands in his. "You look beautiful, Katya," he said, bending down to kiss her softly.

It was nothing compared to what they had experienced before. Just a mere whisper of a kiss—a light brushing of his lips against hers that left her aching for more and remembering everything they had shared in the past. Longing. Surrender. Rapture. How was it possible, she thought? Given everything she suspected him of, how could she still feel anything? Yet she did. With every fiber of her being.

The DuValentis are a merciless clan, not to be trusted at any cost. They are fierce in battle and swift to revenge. They will do anything to get their hands on the Stone.

The words echoed through her mind but the warning rang empty. It was too late. Is this what Sacha had felt? she wondered dimly. Had Marco had the same effect on Sacha that Nicholas had on her? Did the mere scent of his skin, the sound of his voice, the feel of his touch stir something within her that she had never felt before? Perhaps this explained why she had yielded so willingly to her fate.

"I have a favor to ask of you," he said.

Apprehension coursed through her. "Yes?"

Nicholas lifted his hand and displayed a delicate gold necklace adorned with a small, glistening white rose carved from mother-of-pearl. "Of all the jewels my family possesses," he said, "this simple piece has always been my favorite. It belonged to my mother. It would do me great honor if you would wear it tonight."

Katya nodded wordlessly, fighting back a rush of bittersweet sentiment as he bent forward and fastened the clasp about her neck.

Once the necklace was secure he studied her for a moment in silence, his eyes glowing with a deep, satisfied emotion she couldn't begin to define. Was it possession she read in his gaze, or something darker? Before she could speak, he reached forward and brushed his fingers over the chain. A ghost of a smile curved his lips as he traced the shallow path of the delicate gold. "A primitive way of marking one's conquests," he murmured, almost as though to himself. Then he straightened and intoned politely, "If you're ready, the coach is waiting."

She searched his eyes, searching for some deeper meaning

behind the necklace, but his gaze was unfathomable. "I'm ready," she replied.

As they stepped out into the courtyard and made their way to the coach, a strong, hot wind buffeted her skirts. The Mistral was at its height, she noted. It seemed appropriate somehow that the weather should be at its most savage. She wanted the climate to reflect her emotions. Thunder and lightning, vicious rains and howling winds. Landslides.

Once she and Nicholas were seated inside, the grooms- men pulled the coach smoothly out of the drive, moving down the steep slope that led to the principality. She had always found the gentle rocking and swaying of his coach deeply soothing. But now it seemed as though every motion, every jarring bump and rolling turn, was designed to put her body in contact with his—to force their knees to brush or their hands to touch. His presence seemed all-engulfing. No matter how she tried to divert her thoughts, he was all she was aware of.

"You're awfully quiet," he said, breaking the silence that had been between them. "What are you thinking of?"

Katya forced a small smile. "The weather," she replied automatically, lifting her shoulders in a light shrug.

"The Mistral." He nodded in understanding. "I believe it's at its peak. It should be subsiding in a day or two."

"I see." She turned and stared out the window, watching as the strong winds buffeted the cypress and pine that spread across the landscape. She returned her gaze to Nicholas, studying him through the dimness of the moonlit interior. Once again she noted the faint expression of pensive, almost pained resolve that was reflected on his chiseled features. "You're quiet as well," she remarked softly. "What are you thinking?"

He was silent for a long moment. Finally he replied, "I'm thinking how little I knew my father." He arched one brow and finished dryly, "Not that that's a complaint, mind you. Merely an observation."

Uncertain where the conversation was leading, Katya merely nodded.

"The Comtesse spoke to you about the woman my father had been in love with, didn't she?" he asked.

"She did."

"I can't help but wonder if it would have made any difference had Tyler known."

"You don't think he might have suspected?"

"No, never," he replied with certainty. "Neither did I. Yet in hindsight it makes perfect sense. Duty and sacrifice. For as long as I can remember it has been drummed into my head that nothing was more important than preserving our family legacy. But I never suspected what lengths my father would go to to do so." He paused and shook his head as his fingers ran absently over the blade of his dirk. "I suppose none of us truly know what we're capable of until we're put to the test."

His words caused a shiver to run down her spine. Aware that her emotion would show on her face, Katya turned away, staring blindly out the window as they descended from the Tête du Chien and entered the bustling traffic of the principality. Fortunately Nicholas seemed as disinclined to further conversation as she was, and heavy silence once again filled the coach.

She watched as revelers dressed in medieval garb spilled out into the streets, gaily drinking and dancing and calling out merry insults to one another. Vendors pushed carts selling roasted meats on a spit, coarse breads, and candied fruits. Jugglers, musicians, and troubadours wandered about, performing on street corners and inside cafés. From the appearance of the crowds, it looked as though all of Monaco had turned out to celebrate the taming of the Tarasque. Although Katya had no interest in the festival, it gave her a

point of focus, something other than Nicholas on which to
direct her attention.

"It's amazing, isn't it?" he remarked after a few minutes.

"Quite," she managed.

As she stared into the bustling crowds, her thoughts
turned to the conversation she had had days ago with Monsieur Chatelain. A tall man with a hound-dog face, stooped
shoulders, and an air of infinite sadness, he looked as though
he expected nothing but the worst from mankind and was
rarely disappointed. He had listened patiently as Katya had
related her involvement with Nicholas and the events that
had occurred since her arrival in Monaco, occasionally interrupting her to ask pointed questions, or steering her politely
back on course when she strayed off the facts.

She had almost expected—almost hoped—he would tell
her that her suspicions were ludicrous and that she was behaving like an excitable child. Instead, after examining her
parents' water tank and the silver bowl she had used the
night she had been injured onstage, he had calmly informed
her that her instincts were probably correct and that she truly
was in danger. Until he and his men were able to unveil the
person behind her mishap at the theater, he advised her to
carry on as she normally did, acting as though nothing were
amiss.

It had been his opinion that if another "accident" were to
happen, it would likely happen tonight, while they were
surrounded by throngs of people. As rich and powerful as
Nicholas was, even he could not risk the suspicions that
would arise if Katya were to fall victim to a fatal accident
while at his villa. Too many questions would be raised—
particularly after Allyson Whitney's disturbing death in London.

Suppressing a shudder, Katya returned her attention to
Nicholas as the coach rolled to a smooth stop in the
Fontvieille, one of the principality's oldest sections. As she

exited the coach, she noted that the entrance to what was normally an open market square had been somewhat blocked by the placement of two huge towers and an elaborate drawbridge—obviously constructed to resemble the entrance to a medieval castle. A group of men dressed as knights of the Crusade stood guard, allowing entrance only to those who held invitations. Rows of seashells filled with olive oil and single burning candlewicks lined both sides of the walk, gently illuminating the entrance.

Katya gazed about her in wonder. The square had been transformed into a bustling medieval keep. In one corner, knights paired off, displaying their prowess with swords. In another corner a cluster of peasant women spun wool into yarn. She saw hunters and horsemen, milkmaids, shepherds and plowmen, farcical court jesters and obsequious courtiers, queens and fishwives, lowly serfs and haughty nobles. A beautiful maiden paraded serenely through the grounds atop a gentle white mare whose forelock bore the single horn of a unicorn. Children scampered and played underfoot, pigs and goats rooted through piles of straw for scraps of food. If not for the grim circumstances that had brought her here, the setting would have captivated her entirely.

As she scanned the crowds, her attention was caught by a rather stoic-looking friar who stood alone. Monsieur Chatelain was not by nature a jolly man. He looked even more pained and conspicuous than usual standing in a crowd of boisterous celebrants. Although her gaze momentarily fixed on him, he was professional enough to look right past her, displaying the same level of interest in her that one might show toward a fence post. But his presence and that of his men was reassuring nonetheless.

Remembering Chatelain's advice that she act as though nothing at all were amiss, she turned to Nicholas and placed her hand on his forearm, asking in a tone of false brightness,

"Is there anyone in particular you would like me to target this evening?"

He frowned. "What do you mean?"

"Is there anyone you would like me to check for the scroll?"

"Ah. The scroll." His tone sounded slightly distant, as though he were speaking more to himself than to her. Then he met her gaze and smiled softly. It wasn't the lazy, sexy sort of smile she was used to receiving from him, however. It was more the blank sort of smile one might give while exchanging empty pleasantries with a stranger.

"Come," he said. "The tournament is about to begin."

He placed his hand on the small of her back and guided her toward a large field overlooking the harbor. As they neared, Katya heard the blare of trumpets, followed by the low murmur of an excited crowd. Banners fluttered in the strong breeze. Large tents had been set up to encircle the field, beneath which were gathered Monaco's most distinguished citizenry, all dressed in an exquisite variety of medieval finery.

Nicholas paused at a table to retrieve two chalices brimming with spiced wine and passed one to her. They made their way into the crowd and watched as the jousting commenced. In a magnificent display of thirteenth-century pomp and pageantry, two men outfitted as warrior knights mounted their powerful steeds, lowered their lances and shields, then charged each other at full speed. The audience collectively held its breath as the charge ended in the center of the field in a brutal clash of armament.

Although the spectacle was impressive, it did not hold Katya's attention. Nor, she sensed, was Nicholas entirely captivated. A restless energy seemed to consume him, just as it did her. From time to time his fingers moved to the dirk and leather pouch that hung suspended from his belt, as though reassuring himself that the items were still there.

Once the jousting had ended they moved across the grounds to watch a display of crossbow and archery. Then on to exhibits of medieval candlemaking, dyeing of wool, and falconry. They watched jugglers and acrobats perform feats of great daring and skill, listened to a medieval choir, sampled grilled meats that had been dusted with cinnamon and curry, and witnessed a spectacular demonstration of swordsmanship. But despite the remarkable quality of the exhibits, Katya could see that Nicholas was no more interested than she. Like her, he seemed to be moving mechanically from display to display as though it were nothing but a chore that must be accomplished.

At length they reached a wooden stage that had been constructed near the grounds that overlooked the harbor. A group of minstrels, dressed in multihued jackets with peacock feathers bobbing from their caps and bells strung about their ankles, stood on an elevated platform above the stage. They called out to the passing crowds, beckoning their audience to draw closer. As soon as a sufficient number had gathered they lifted their instruments and commenced playing a merry tune, filling the air with the sounds of their lutes and viols, lyres and tambors. A group of dancers stepped onstage and swung about in a festive, whirling dance as the audience clapped along.

Once the music ended the dancers stepped back and the minstrels struck up a new tune. A sweet, haunting melody floated out over the crowd. A troubadour moved to the center of the stage and began to sing, telling the story of a wandering knight who had lost his lady love. The final lilting notes of the song drifted away, but the musicians continued to play as dancers once again took the stage. But this time there was no merriment in their movements. Their bodies swayed in time to the melody in a graceful, almost hypnotic series of twists and turns. After a moment the dancers ges-

tured for a few members of the audience to join them onstage.

To Katya's astonishment, Nicholas immediately placed his
hand on her elbow and propelled her toward the stage.
"Come," he said. "Let us show all of Monaco that the Lord
of Barrington and his lady are in attendance."

As Nicholas generally preferred to remain in the background, the move was very unlike him. Then again, Katya
remembered the first ball they had attended together. He
had been determined to make them both as conspicuous as
possible. For whatever reason, this seemed his intention once
again.

As they reached the platform he swept the indigo cape
over his shoulder and wrapped one arm around the small of
her waist, then grasped her hand in his. Katya's body pressed
against his as they swayed in time to the minstrel's melancholy tune. The troubadour softly resumed his song, telling
the wistful story of love and loss. Following the lead of the
performers who remained onstage, Nicholas guided her
through the dance, executing a series of sweeping motions
that drew them near then pulled them apart.

Until then, Katya had managed to keep her feelings tightly
in check, maintaining a polite, cordial distance between her
and Nicholas. But now she discovered just how fragile were
the walls she had put up. She couldn't say whether it was the
words of the song that were her emotional undoing, or the
fact that she was once again in Nicholas's arms. All she knew
was that her resolve to remain aloof was shattered.

They moved as only lovers could, swaying to an inner
rhythm that had long ago been established between them.
With each brush of his body against hers, a sense of aching
tenderness and desire blossomed within her. She was over-
whelmingly aware of every motion, every slight touch, every
breath that fell against her cheek. Her senses were almost too
heightened; a rush of warmth swept through her body and a

knot of sexual expectation coiled tightly within her belly. She remembered how safe and secure she had felt within his embrace, how profoundly correct their bodies felt together. As the troubadour sang of false pride and loss, she longed to throw caution to the wind, to tumble heedlessly back into the sanctuary of Nicholas's arms.

But sanctuary was no longer to be found there, she realized with a jolt of pained awareness.

They had come full circle. There was nothing between them any longer but the ancient legends. The greed and mistrust that had kept their families apart for centuries had risen once again.

As they swayed together she felt the brush of his hip against hers. The small dirk and the leather pouch that hung suspended from his belt pressed between them. In that instant curiosity combined with icy determination. He had checked and rechecked that pouch several times already that night. Whatever it contained must be of some importance.

Her scroll, perhaps?

There was only one way to find out. Emboldened by the success she had enjoyed to date with her sleight of hand, she removed her hand from his shoulder and let it slide ever so gently down his back. As they swayed in time to the medieval melody, she brushed her body against his.

"You seem quite familiar with the steps to the dance," she said, hoping to distract his attention.

"Do I?"

She moved her palm lightly over the thick leather of his belt. "Indeed. One would almost think that—"

His hand immediately came up to clamp on top of hers as her fingers made contact with the small pouch.

"Your touch is smooth, little gypsy," he whispered against her ear, "but not undetectable." He gave her hand a light squeeze, then released it. As he brushed a kiss over her forehead he murmured softly, "Leave it alone for the moment, will you?"

Shock, disbelief, and anger coursed through her. Her cheeks flamed and she stiffened her spine, withdrawing slightly from his embrace. "I was merely curious," she said.

His indigo eyes reflected only cool amusement. "You couldn't have asked me?"

"I thought—" Katya began, then stopped and looked away, her thoughts and emotions in turmoil. Short of accusing him of stealing her scroll, murdering her parents, and attempting to murder her, what could she possibly say?

Fortunately the moment quickly ended. The minstrels finished their tune and set down their instruments. Anxious to retreat, she turned away and moved off the stage, Nicholas following behind her. As they merged back into the crowd, she scanned the area for Monsieur Chatelain. She found him only a few yards away, standing near a pen of livestock. Because her focus had been on Chatelain, she did not notice Corrina Jeffreys and Philip Montrove until they materialized at their sides.

"Well done, Duvall," said Montrove, a thin smile on his face as he brought his hands together in slow, sardonic applause. "And you as well, Miss Alexander," he added, giving her a graceful bow. "What a stunning medieval pair the two of you make."

Corrina appeared as exquisitely feminine as usual, Katya noted, her gaze moving over the other woman's gown of ice-blue brocade. In the past, Katya had based her dislike of the pair on their constant disparaging remarks toward Nicholas. Despite the fact that those remarks had proved to be accurate reflections of his character, she found she felt no more warmth toward them than before. Their presence amounted to nothing more than a vague annoyance that must be temporarily tolerated—like a summer cold, unruly children, or ants at a picnic.

Therefore she paid little attention to the conversation, turning instead to watch the troubadour as he once again resumed center stage. Rather than singing, he knelt down on one knee before a young maiden. In a fervent demonstration of courtly love, he began to extol her many virtues, praise her beauty, and promise to devote the remainder of his life to demonstrating his unending adoration.

Katya was only half listening until she heard Montrove turn to Nicholas and dryly remark, "Rather bland, don't you think? Surely even you could do better than that, Duvall."

Nicholas shrugged. "I fear I have no poetic abilities"—he paused and lifted Katya's hand, pressing the back of it to his lips—"even when gifted with so beautiful a subject upon which to lavish my words."

"In the spirit of the occasion, name one virtue," insisted Montrove. His gray eyes moved over Katya in wintry appraisal. "Tresses of spun moonlight, lips as soft as rose petal, skin smoother than freshly churned cream . . . What is the virtue you would praise above all others?"

"Therein lies my problem. How does one narrow it down to one single virtue when there are so many from which to choose?"

"Try."

Nicholas turned to Katya and regarded her steadily for a long moment, a flicker of undisguised deviltry glistening in his ebony eyes. "I suppose if I had to name one virtue that I hold dear above all others, it would have to be her honesty."

The distinct glimmer of challenge contained within his words was unmistakable; a private thrust and parry of sorts. "Indeed," Katya murmured, refusing to allow him the upper hand, "clearly Lord Barrington admires in me that quality which I find so compelling in him."

"How very refreshing," said Montrove in a tone of infinite boredom. "Lovers who are drawn to beauty of the soul, rather than the baser lure of the flesh."

A dull roar coming from the grounds south of them drew their attention away from the conversation. Katya saw a rapidly swelling mass of people moving toward them, laughing and jeering as they ran alongside a huge green-and-gold monster that writhed slowly through the crowd, swishing its tail and spewing flames of red tissue paper from its mouth.

"It appears the evening is drawing to a head," remarked Montrove as he gestured toward the frenzied crowd. "It must be time for the taming of the Tarasque."

The mythical beast was preceded by a group of murmurs dressed in black robes, their faces covered by grotesquely distorted animal masks. They raced in the forefront of the crowd, performing feats of random foolishness and acrobatic skill, then dashing off from time to time to pull in a woman from the onlookers and spin her around in a frenzied dance while their audience roared its approval.

As they approached, Corrina grasped Katya's hand and pulled her along beside her into the path of the celebrants. "Do hurry, Miss Alexander," she urged. "The murmurs select the maiden who will have the honor of taming the Tarasque."

Although Katya had no interest in taking part in the festivities—particularly not in so principal a role—it seemed easier to play along for the moment than to attempt to break the grip Corrina had on her hand. In any case, Nicholas and Philip Montrove waited for them only a few feet away.

In what seemed like mere seconds the crowd reached them and they were swept up in the jubilant melee. Two murmurs broke free from the group. One took Corrina by the hand, the other reached for Katya. His face was completely covered by the ferocious and rather gruesome mask of a wild boar. He held her wrists in an iron grip as he whirled her around, spinning her until she was nearly dizzy.

The mob swelled around them, shouting and laughing, making her feel as though she were being carried away on the crest of a giant wave. She searched for Nicholas in the crowd, but the faces that surrounded her were all a blur.

At length the roar of the crowd faded and the murmur released her. Katya stumbled to a disoriented stop. As the murmur raced on without her she surveyed her surroundings in some confusion. Rather than keeping pace with the Tarasque, the murmur had released her in a rather solitary spot away from the masses. She had joined the crowd near the livestock bin and the platform stage. Now she stood alone on the cliffs that overlooked the harbor. She gazed about her in an attempt to place her whereabouts, but it was rather difficult to see. The only light was that of the crescent moon hanging low in the sky.

As the warm wind buffeted her skirts she turned in the direction from which it blew. Her heart leaped to her throat as she suddenly caught sight of a man standing only a few feet from her. He stood alone gazing out over the sea, one booted foot propped up on a rock, his indigo cape billowing about his shoulders. He was so still she had missed him entirely at first glance.

She had missed him, but obviously he knew she was there, she realized, as a shiver ran down her spine. He must have heard her stumbling, awkward halt as the murmur abruptly released her hands.

Noting his dark hair and indigo cape, as well as his height and posture, Katya softly called out, "Nicholas?"

The man straightened and slowly turned. "I'm afraid I disappoint you."

His face was at once familiar and yet at the same time unknown. She took an instinctive step backward in fear, then recognition sunk in. Jeremy Cooke, she thought, breathing a sigh of relief.

"Jeremy—hello," she said with a soft laugh. "I seem to be forever mistaking you for Nicholas, don't I?"

"Do you?"

She studied him with a small frown as she moved toward him. "You're not wearing your glasses, are you?" she said. "That's why you look so different. I don't think I've ever seen you without them."

"Somehow they didn't seem appropriate to medieval attire."

"I suppose not." Her gaze moved briefly over his clothing. "Very noble. I take it you are a knight."

"Alas, no," he replied, shaking his head. "It seems times have not changed since the olden days. Armor has always been a prerogative of the upper classes, worn by only the wealthiest of lords. I might aspire to knighthood, but I'm cursed with an inability to afford the chivalric glory of full armor. Thus you see before you a mere knight's apprentice." A self-deprecating smile curved his lips as he gestured to his costume. "A lowly squire, if you will." He paused for a moment, then continued, "Fortunately those heavy suits of armor you see in museums were not long in fashion. In time, the preoccupation of fighting men shifted to weapons of offense, rather than defense."

"Indeed?" Katya murmured politely.

As though abruptly recalling himself, Jeremy said, "You must be seeking Lord Barrington."

"How did you know?"

He lifted his shoulders in a small shrug. "From what I've seen, the two of you are not long parted."

"Actually," she said, "we were separated when the Tarasque swept through. I believe he's waiting for me at the site of the symbolic taming."

Jeremy Cooke frowned. "Are you certain?"

"I— Yes, I think so."

"Odd. I saw him just a moment ago, speaking with Lord

Montrove and Miss Jeffreys. I believe they stepped into the caves to see the remarkable display of medieval alchemy."

"Into the caves?"

"Yes. Shall I take you to him?"

Katya hesitated. She followed his gesture to the face of the cliff, noting for the first time the flickering light emitted from the caves below. Uncertainty gripped her as she glanced around, looking for some sign of Monsieur Chatelain, but he was nowhere to be seen. He had probably lost her when she was swept up in the wild mob surrounding the Tarasque.

"Or if you prefer," Jeremy continued, "I would be happy to escort you to the jousting field where the taming of the Tarasque is to take place. I may be a poor substitute for the Earl of Barrington, but it would be my honor to stand in for him until he finds you."

She considered his offer. Although she would feel more comfortable back among the bustling crowds, her wisest course was probably to seek out Nicholas. Even if Monsieur Chatelain had lost sight of her, undoubtedly he had kept Nicholas in view. Besides, she reasoned, what harm could come to her if the group contained not only her and Nicholas, but Jeremy Cooke, Philip Montrove, and Corrina Jeffreys as well?

That decided, she gathered her courage and sent Jeremy a small smile. "Actually, I haven't seen the caves yet myself. Why don't we start there, then we can all return to the jousting fields together?"

He nodded politely. "As you wish." He led her toward the edge of the cliff then stopped, frowning as he glanced back at her. "I hope you won't think me too forward if I ask for your hand. It's difficult to see, and the path is rather narrow and rocky."

"Of course." She extended her arm and placed her hand in his. As they made their way along the ledge she was glad for the security of his hand. Strong gusts of wind threw her off balance. On two occasions she lost her footing and would surely have slipped were it not for his firm grip. Although it was too dark to see exactly where they were, she could hear the faint thunder of the waves crashing against the rocks below.

"Why would they have placed this exhibit in the caves?" she asked. "Everything else I've seen has been so easy to reach."

"In the spirit of authenticity, I suppose," Jeremy answered. "The church reigned supreme in medieval times, you'll recall. Alchemists were considered heretics. Anyone who pursued science was thought to be in league with the devil. Hence they were often tortured for their beliefs, imprisoned, or burned at the stake. They routinely hid their experiments, working in underground laboratories or caves such as this one, anywhere they wouldn't be discovered."

"I see."

At last they reached the entrance to the cave. "I think you'll enjoy this," he said, stepping aside to let her enter.

Katya stepped inside. Flaming torches propped in the crevices of the rock walls filled the interior with flickering golden light. She glanced around, seeing makeshift wooden tables upon which were propped an odd assortment of bellows, crucibles, odd-shaped bottles, glass vials, and bowls filled with powders and liquids. The air was heavy with the smell of burning charcoal and brimstone. On one table a thick book sat open next to a quill and an ink pot. Scientific scribbling filled the pages, as though the person working had been momentarily called away. Aside from the echo of the howling wind, the interior of the cave was silent.

She turned to Jeremy and said, "They're not here."

He gave a light shrug. "What a shame. We must have missed them."

"I suppose we ought to return to the jousting fields."

"Yes, I suppose we ought," he agreed. But rather than turn back to the entrance, he moved toward a display of bottles and vials. He dipped his hand in a bowl and thoughtfully rubbed the powder contained therein between his fingertips. "Did you know that the science of alchemy dates back to the times of the ancient Egyptians?" he asked. "For centuries mankind has been attempting to discover the secret formula to what is known as the Philosopher's Stone. This magic substance, it was thought, could be dissolved and the liquid derived from it would turn any common metal into gold. A tiny drop of the substance, when taken internally, would convert old age into eternal youth and beauty. Fantastic, isn't it?"

Katya hid her impatience with a polite smile. "Yes, it is."

"The middle ages were a fascinating time. Your ancestors should have been quite at home then. Magicians flourished, as did gypsies. They professed an ability to predict the future, were capable of striking the unlucky with curses, made charms and talismans of good fortune, and sold powders that were thought to inspire love or hatred in those who consumed them. They helped to spread the belief that a man's destiny was written in the stars, or revealed within the palm of his hand." He paused, shaking his head. "And all the while those who practiced pure science were hunted and condemned."

She frowned. "You're not exactly putting my ancestors in the most flattering of light, are you?"

"Perhaps not." He sighed. "So much ignorance and superstition. But I suppose you're right—it can't all be blamed on gypsies and magicians. Do you know what truly causes ignorance? People being too ready to believe anything they're told. One must consistently question the so-called facts, don't you agree?"

"Yes, I do. Now if you don't mind—"

"You look beautiful tonight, Katya."

Not only was his remark totally unexpected, something about his tone chilled her. "We should leave," she repeated, more firmly this time.

"How that costume becomes you. A bride, is it? Lovely."

Katya moved toward the cave entrance, but Jeremy Cooke was there first, blocking her exit.

"Are you frightened?"

Her heart slammed against her ribs as her every instinct shouted for her to run. But she had nothing to gain by showing her fear. Tilting her chin, she replied curtly, "Don't be preposterous. Of course I'm not."

A small smile curved his lips as he took a step closer. "Perhaps you should be."

Twenty-One

*N*icholas frantically scanned the thinning crowd looking for Katya. She was gone, had disappeared entirely in the wake of the Tarasque. His gut tightened in horrified disbelief. She had to be here. He had been watching her intently, his gaze never straying as she had been whirled and twirled by the murmur who had claimed her hand. Although he hadn't taken his eyes off her, she seemed to have vanished as completely and inexplicably as she did when she was onstage.

Dammit!

Where? A tight coil of panic and dread knotted in his belly. He had been attempting all night to draw out the person who had been out to destroy him—now he was terrified that he had succeeded. Was he too late? He banished the thought, refusing to let it take hold.

Move! his mind screamed. Find her! With that simple, elemental thought taking precedence over any other, his legs obeyed, carrying him off toward the spot where he had last seen her.

Katya took a deep breath as her eyes darted past Jeremy's shoulder, looking for a way out. But there was nothing beyond the mouth of the cave, nothing but a narrow path that ran along the face of the cliff and a sheer drop to the sea below.

Even as she was seeking a way out, disbelief was registering in her mind. Jeremy Cooke? Was he the one who had been behind the murders and the theft of her scroll? It seemed impossible to believe, yet why else would he have brought her there? As she considered this, a tiny bud of relief blossomed inside her, swelling within her chest until it temporarily replaced her fear.

It wasn't Nicholas. *It wasn't Nicholas.*

That realization gave her the strength she needed. Hiding her emotions for the moment, she studied Jeremy coolly, assuming an expression of haughty disdain. "If this is meant to be a joke, Jeremy, I find it in rather poor taste, don't you?"

"I think we both know that it's no joke, now, don't we?"

She brought up her chin. "I don't know that at all."

"Come now, Katya, you're not stupid. Except perhaps for your taste in men." He thought for a moment then smiled, lifting his shoulders in a languid shrug. "But then every woman has at least one fatal flaw, doesn't she?"

Katya studied him in silence, forcing herself to remain calm and to logically consider her options, eliminating every possibility one by one. Her first choice was to simply call his bluff and walk away. Unlikely, but certainly worth a try. Her second choice? To stall him until help arrived. Again unlikely as the caves were so remote from the rest of the festivities and no one had seen her enter. Her third and final option was one of last resort: to use physical violence to escape.

Deciding to attempt to exercise her first option, she said shortly, "I've had enough of this." It came as no surprise, however, when Jeremy blocked her exit as she tried to sweep past him and gain the narrow ledge outside.

"I'm afraid I can't let you leave yet, Katya."

"Just how do you intend to keep me here?"

"With this if I have to," he said, flourishing a gun from the inside of his cape. "But I sincerely hope you won't be so foolish as to force me to use it." He gestured to a rickety chair that stood beside a table. "Do make yourself comfortable."

Acting meekly obedient, she sat down in the chair.

"Now where were we?" Jeremy said, as a satisfied smile crossed his lips. "Ah yes, women's fatal flaws. Would you like to hear Allyson Whitney's fatal flaw?"

Katya studied him silently as a feeling of sinking dread filled her belly.

"The lovely Miss Whitney was truly a creature of greed. Do you know how much I had to promise her in return for the simple task of removing Nicholas's scroll from his home? Fifty thousand pounds—as if I had that kind of money."

"So you killed her instead," Katya said, her voice a mere whisper.

"Not personally, of course. It's amazing how simple it is to find people willing to carry out that sort of nasty work, particularly in London. And for sums considerably less than fifty thousand pounds, mind you."

"And what about Tyler? Did you have him killed as well?"

"Yes." A troubled frown creased his brow. "Unfortunately the French are much more difficult to deal with when it comes to crimes of that nature. Stubborn and entirely unreasonable. I wanted a body. Physical proof that Tyler Duvall was dead. Instead they chose to countermand my instructions and shove him off a cliff. I had to take their word—the word of two thieving murderers—that he was in fact dead. In truth, I'm still not entirely satisfied."

"It's so difficult to find good help these days."

"Sarcasm doesn't become you, Katya."

"Tell me about my parents."

"Ah. Your parents. Now that was regrettable. They seemed like such pleasant people." He shrugged. "Do you know how long it took me to trace the scroll to your mother? Years, Katya, years. Your ancestors were not easily found. But I persevered and my hard work was rewarded. In fact, I almost had the scroll in my hands until Monsieur Remy received your letter. After all I went through you snatched the scroll out from under me. Not very kind of you, was it?" He studied her with a quizzical frown. "Does Nicholas know who you are, by the way? Rosskaya and all that?"

"You're sick, Jeremy," she replied quietly. "You need help—a doctor."

"On the contrary, I'm not sick at all. I'm angry. Very, very angry."

"At whom?"

"Nicholas, of course," he replied, in a tone that was almost cheerful. "The Lord of Barrington. I've hated him for decades—I've made it my life's work, if you will."

"Why? Because he canceled the funds for your father's research?"

A flash of dark rage showed on his face. "There, you see, Katya, you're ignorant. You're choosing to be ignorant. All you have to do is ask yourself a few simple questions."

"What questions should I ask?"

He moved toward her. Using the barrel of his gun, he lifted the delicate gold chain she wore. She barely suppressed a shudder of revulsion as the cold steel pressed against her throat. "Let's begin with this pretty little necklace you're wearing, shall we?" he said. "It's been passed down through my family for generations, did you know that?"

"*Your* family?"

"Yes, my family. All the DuValenti men give it to the women they love."

In the midst of the shock and horror that enveloped her, Katya felt a momentary surge of joy as his words echoed through her head. *All the DuValenti men give it to the women they love.*

Nicholas had given it to her.

"Did you ask where the necklace came from?" Jeremy railed, drawing her attention back to him. "Or did you just blindly accept it—the way you blindly accepted the fact that

Nicholas was William Duvall's firstborn son? *My* mother should have worn it, not Nicholas's."

Katya's eyes widened as comprehension slowly dawned. "Louisa," she breathed.

Jeremy pulled back his gun as a flicker of interest showed in his eyes. His *dark* eyes, she thought. Eyes that were so similar to Nicholas's. How many times had she seen him from behind and thought he was Nicholas? His height, his build, his dark hair. And without his glasses, the facial resemblance was even more apparent.

"You know of my mother?" he asked.

Uncertain of his reaction, she replied cautiously, "Yes, I do. The Comtesse told me about her just a few days ago. She said that Louisa was the only woman her brother truly loved."

She had hoped the words might offer some consolation. Instead, they only seemed to make him more furious. "Loved?" he spit out. "He never loved her. He abandoned her—and me. She was never good enough for him, or should I say, not good enough for him to marry. Bedding her was something altogether different, wasn't it?" He paused for a moment, pacing angrily before her. "When Lord Barrington discovered that my mother was carrying his child he arranged her hand in marriage to Rodney Cooke, a man desperate enough for money to agree to take part in the deception."

"What do you mean, desperate for money?"

"*He paid him.* He paid him to marry my mother and keep his mouth shut. It was all done very discreetly, of course. One lump sum after the wedding vows were exchanged, one tidy check each month thereafter. All done under the guise of funding Rodney Cooke's scholarly research. There never was any research, of course. For that matter, I don't know if the man could even read—I certainly never saw him do so. Rodney Cooke spent his days knocking my mother and me about and his nights locked away in his study getting completely soused." Vile disgust showed on his face for a long moment, then he slowly composed himself. "But none of that mattered to William Harrison Duvall, did it? The only thing he wanted to ensure was that the world never know that his firstborn son was an unwanted, lowborn bastard."

A wave of profound sadness washed over Katya. "I don't think he ever knew—"

"He never wanted to know," Jeremy interrupted sharply. "He chose to be ignorant."

She studied him silently, lost for words.

"Now do you understand?" he demanded. "None of this is random. It's not as though I'm a madman roaming the streets. Do you see how meticulous I've been, down to the very last detail? Everything I've done has been done in order to teach Nicholas Duvall a lesson."

"What lesson could any of this possibly be teaching him?"

"Loss," he answered curtly. "Nicholas Duvall's presence not only humiliates me, but deprives me of my birthright as well. From the day he was born he has taken everything that should have been mine. Therefore it is my duty to teach him about loss."

"You're holding Nicholas responsible for the mistakes of his father?"

"I was held responsible, wasn't I?" he demanded. "Now it's his turn to suffer. I want to see him lose everything. His mistress. His brother. His lands, his title, his reputation. Everything that should have been mine." He lifted his gun and waved it carelessly in her direction. "The woman he loves."

"That was you the other night in the theater," she said flatly. "I found Nicholas's cuff link shortly before my gun misfired."

"Clever girl. But I had hoped the authorities would find that incriminating bit of evidence—after your unfortunate demise, of course." He began to pace before the mouth of the cave once again, moving with almost frantic, jerky gestures. "Actually, the fact that you lived worked out in my favor. Divine intervention, if you will. This is much better. Neater. Nicholas should be here at any moment. When he arrives I'll confront him with the fact that I'm his older brother. He'll fly into a rage and try to kill me. Unfortunately, he'll shoot you instead. Then I'll be forced to kill him in self-defense." He tapped his gun nervously against his thigh as a victorious smile flashed across his face. "An altogether fitting end to the Lord of Scandal, don't you think?"

Katya studied him across the flickering lights of the cave. So the legends had been right after all, she realized. *Beware the Maltese.* The DuValentis' firstborn son. But *Jeremy* was William Duvall's firstborn son, not Nicholas.

The emotions she had felt earlier, the shock, the rage, the pity, the horror, all slowly evaporated, leaving nothing in their place but a grim will to stop him. Her gaze darted to the table by which she sat, examining the surface for some kind of weapon. But she found nothing but bowls of various sizes. As she surveyed the contents—charcoal, brimstone, and saltpeter—a rush of hope surged through her. While Jeremy ranted, she pulled a soft linen handkerchief from the kirtle of her costume and filled it with a generous pinch from each bowl, moving with the same care and discretion she might have displayed onstage.

Jeremy stopped pacing just as she finished tying her handkerchief into a firm knot, securing the volatile powders within.

"That's why I must have the Stone," he concluded. "It will help to solidify my position as the DuValenti heir apparent. In any case, I already have Nicholas's scroll, and I'll find yours eventually. You may as well tell me now where you've hidden it."

"But I thought—" she started, then broke off, studying

him in blank confusion. If Jeremy hadn't stolen it from her room, who had?

"Why don't you put the gun down, Cooke?" called a low, steady voice from the entrance to the cave.

Nicholas.

Katya surged to her feet, her linen handkerchief balled tightly in her fist, biting back an urge to shout for him to run. As his gaze moved over her, she watched the relief in his eyes turn to steely determination. He stood unmoving, his powerful form silhouetted in the moonlight, his cape billowing behind him in the wind. In that instant she knew she didn't have to warn him away. If Jeremy Cooke thought he could go up against Nicholas Duvall and win, he was sadly mistaken.

"Are you all right, Katya?" he asked tersely.

She nodded. "I'm fine."

Jeremy waved his gun. "Do come in, Nicholas, we've been expecting you. Slowly . . . there. That's far enough. Back against the wall, please. Now keep your hands where I can see them."

Katya glanced past Nicholas, looking to the entrance of the cave for Monsieur Chatelain and his men, but she saw no sign of them.

"I was just attempting to convince Katya to reveal the location of her family's scroll," said Jeremy. "It means nothing to her now, merely the difference between a quick death and a painful one."

"Yes, I heard. But you're a little late, Cooke. The scroll won't do you any good."

"Why is that?" he sneered. "You don't think I'll be able to find the Stone?"

A small smile curved Nicholas's mouth. "I already have."

Tense silence filled the cave, then Jeremy's face slowly darkened with rage. "You're lying."

"May I?" Nicholas asked coolly, his hands moving to his belt.

Katya noted immediately that the dirk he had worn earlier was missing. The only item suspended from his belt was the leather pouch she had tried to lift earlier. She watched as he removed it, slowly pulled apart the thin rawhide strings that secured the top, and upended the contents into his hand.

A magnificent pale-blue diamond filled his palm. The Stone glowed with a shimmering brilliance, as though pulsating with an inner life. Incandescent rays of warmth emanated from it and filled the cave with light.

Katya felt her breath catch in her throat. The Stone of Destiny. It really did exist.

"A simple trade," said Nicholas evenly. "The Stone for Katya."

Jeremy slowly tore his gaze away from the diamond. "A trade?" He hesitated, as though carefully considering it. Then he said, "I have a better idea. I'll simply kill you both and take the Stone."

As Jeremy raised his gun, Katya's gaze shot to Nicholas. Their eyes met for a fraction of a second—a second that seemed to stretch into infinity. Then everything seemed to happen at once.

Jeremy leveled his gun on Nicholas and drew back the trigger.

Nicholas reached inside his cape, presumably for a weapon of his own.

Katya hurled the balled linen handkerchief at Jeremy's feet.

The subsequent explosion rocked the interior of the cave, pitching them all to the ground. Flames shot up as Jeremy Cooke's screams echoed through the thick black smoke that filled the air. She heard the sound of men's frantic shouts, followed by the sound of boots as they rushed by her. Monsieur Chatelain and his men? But she couldn't see anything.

As she struggled to rise to her knees she felt Nicholas beside her, pulling her to her feet and out of the cave.

His arm wrapped securely around her waist, he tugged her with him across the narrow ledge that led away from the cave. Once they reached the safety of the rocky overlook he released her. They both fell immediately to their knees, coughing and gasping for breath. Katya's eyes burned and her lungs and throat felt as though they had been stripped raw.

After a long moment he choked out, "Are you all right?"

She swallowed hard and answered in a hoarse voice that she barely recognized as her own, "I'm fine."

"What the hell was that?"

"A little something I mixed from the bowls I found on the table. Charcoal, brimstone, and saltpeter."

Nicholas's eyes widened in surprise, then in glowing approval. "Gunpowder," he said. "I'd forgotten your flair for drama."

She lifted her shoulders in a small shrug. "My father used it once in his show." She coughed again, then shook her head. "I'm afraid I was a little too generous with it though, wasn't I?"

Nicholas smiled. His teeth appeared pearly white against the black mask of smoke and ash that coated his skin. "That depends. Were you attempting to knock Cooke to his feet, or flatten a mountain?"

She started laughing, laughing until she couldn't stop. Laughing until tears were streaming down her face, and then she was crying, and she couldn't stop that either.

Nicholas gently gathered her into his arms, stroking his hand along her back in slow, soothing motions. "I know," he murmured against her hair. "I know. I feel exactly the same way."

* * *

Katya studied her face in the looking glass of her bedchamber. The costume the Comtesse had loaned her was ruined, but at least she had managed to remove most of the smoke and ash that had coated her hair and skin. With this accomplished, she could delay no further. Nicholas was waiting for her downstairs. Time to face the music.

Nervous tension filled her as she made her way to the back parlor. She stepped inside, noting that the Comtesse was there as well. As usual, the older woman appeared regal and composed, giving no sign of what she might be feeling inside. Did she know that Katya had been lying to them, intending to steal their scroll since the day she had first arrived in their home?

With that ugly thought reverberating through her mind, she lifted her gaze to Nicholas. Like her, he had removed his smoke-ravaged costume; he wore simple black trousers and a crisp white lawn shirt. Her gaze moved to his face. He looked so handsome, she thought. So . . . honorable. Regret poured through her and her heart felt as though it were sinking within her chest. How could she ever have suspected him of murder?

He lifted a flask of amber liquid. "Can I pour you a drink?"

For the first time in her life, she felt that she could truly use one. But as comforting as it might be, she preferred a level head. "No, thank you." He gestured for her to be seated, but she shook her head. Her nerves were too raw for her to sit. "I'd rather stand, if you don't mind."

He nodded politely. "As you wish."

An awkward silence filled the room. Finally Katya said, "Have you heard anything about Jeremy Cooke?"

"His legs were burned pretty badly, but he'll live."

"Good." She shook her head helplessly as she looked from Nicholas to the Comtesse. "Perhaps this is wrong of me to say, given all the horrible things he did, but I almost feel sorry for him."

"I can't help but share your sentiment, Miss Alexander," replied the Comtesse. "My brother told me about Louisa, but I never knew there was a child involved. Had I known . . ." Her words trailed off as she shuddered. "What a ghastly mistake William made by attempting to bury the scandal. No wonder it haunted him for the rest of his life."

Katya's curious gaze turned to Nicholas. "What would you have done," she asked softly, "had you known about Jeremy years ago?"

Nicholas splashed a generous amount of the amber liquid he had offered her into a glass and took a deep swallow. "I don't know. Something." He let out a sigh. "Simply knowing the truth would have explained so much. It needn't have come to this."

"It's such a waste," murmured the Comtesse. "Such a dreadful waste."

"I—" Katya began, then stopped abruptly, swallowing hard. "I don't know where to begin."

Nicholas set down his drink. "Why don't we start with the basics?"

She cringed at the subtle hint of irony and anger that clung to his words. "Very well," she managed.

"If it's not too much to ask, I'd like to know your name." He paused, eyeing her sternly. "Your *full* name, if you don't mind."

"Katya Zofia Rosskaya Alexander."

"Rosskaya," he repeated slowly. "Rosskaya. Now that's interesting. I don't remember you mentioning that before."

Not knowing what to say, she remained silent.

"And you never were a thief, were you?" he asked.

"I never claimed to be. I simply never corrected you when you presumed that I was."

"What about the jewelry I saw you take from Lady Stanton's bag?"

"If you recall, you warned me that she and her husband may have stolen from me. As it happened, you were right—but I was too embarrassed to admit it at the time. Nor did I want a grand confrontation with the Stantons. It seemed far simpler to retrieve the jewelry on my own."

"And that's what I witnessed," he said, shaking his head in disgust. He studied her for a long moment, his expression unfathomable. "Were you ever planning on telling me who you were?" he asked quietly.

Katya glanced from Nicholas to the Comtesse. Deciding to adhere to a policy of strict honesty, she admitted, "Not originally, no. When you came to me with your proposal that I pose as your mistress, it seemed the perfect opportunity to retrieve the scroll, find the Stone, and settle my parents' debts. In retrospect the plan seems rather crass, but in my defense I didn't know you at all—except for what I heard about the DuValentis through my family's ancient legends." She gave a wavering smile. "As you might imagine, none of that was very flattering."

He crossed his arms over his chest, regarding her steadily. "No, I would think not."

She swallowed hard and rushed on before her courage deserted her completely, "But then I came to know you—and the Comtesse," she added, sending the older woman a fleeting smile, "and I realized I couldn't possibly steal the scroll from you."

"How very comforting."

"In fact, I nearly told you who I was the day we returned from the Abbey St. Chamas. But you had already left for town and there wasn't an opportunity before my show. That night, when the accident occurred onstage—"

"You thought I was deliberately trying to kill you?" he interrupted, his brows lifting skyward in astonishment.

"Monsieur Remy told me he saw a man who matched your description earlier that evening by my prop table. I found your cuff link there so I presumed it had been you. But you told me that you hadn't been to the theater at all. When I discovered my scroll had been taken from my room . . ." She lifted her shoulders in a helpless shrug. "What else was I to think?"

"I see."

She sent him a troubled frown. "But if you didn't take the scroll from my room, and Jeremy didn't take it, who did?"

"I did, Miss Alexander," replied the Comtesse regally.

Katya turned to her in startled surprise. "You did?"

"Yes. Day after day I waited for you to reveal yourself to Nicholas. But you never did. When your foolishness nearly cost you your life, I took the liberty of interceding. But do not think for a moment that I enjoyed playing the part of an interfering old crone. I'll have you know that that is the last time I shall attempt to save you from yourself."

"But how did you know?"

"I mentioned earlier that my first husband was an amateur aficionado of medieval lore. He was fascinated by my family's legacy, and by the Stone of Destiny. To that end, he studied not only our ancient heritage, but that of the other family involved—the Rosskayas. He related to me that the women of that line were gypsies who were renowned for their beauty and their striking coloring: ebony hair and unusual lavender eyes." She paused, giving Katya a significant glance. "According to his studies, legends foretold that the two families would come together again one day in yet another battle over the Stone. And perhaps, to right the wrong that had taken place centuries earlier."

"Amazing," Katya murmured. Then she turned to Nicholas and said, "But you only had one scroll from which to work—mine. How did you find the Stone?"

Nicholas smiled. "One scroll was all I needed. All anyone

ever needed." He turned to the table next to him and took out an ancient piece of parchment. "Come look."

Katya moved to stand beside him. "That's my scroll," she said.

"Correct. And this is the scroll Jeremy Cooke convinced Allyson to steal from my home. As it turns out, he *was* carrying it on his person. Monsieur Chatelain returned it to me shortly after Cooke was arrested."

As her gaze moved from one scroll to the other, astonishment rose within her. "They're exactly the same," she breathed.

"Down to the smallest detail," he confirmed dryly. "For centuries the puzzle had been where does one scroll begin and the other end? But as it turns out, that was the wrong question. The answer has been right before us the entire time."

" 'Rosskaya and DuValenti. The two are as one. Learn this and out of darkness will come light,' " Katya said, quoting the scroll that they had seen at the Abbey.

Nicholas smiled. "Both families have held the key to finding the Stone all along. We just didn't know it."

"Amazing, isn't it?" the Comtesse said, rising to her feet. "It's a shame my first husband is no longer alive. He would have enjoyed that tremendously—a bit of medieval trickery, if you will." She moved to the door, then turned back and announced imperiously, "Difficult as it may be for you to believe, Miss Alexander, I have been cursed with a romantic heart. I have always believed that our families should put this matter behind us once and for all. To that end, I shall now absent myself and leave the two of you alone to work out the remainder of this tangled mess. But I expect a full and satisfactory resolution by morning."

Nicholas watched his aunt sweep out of the room, leaving them alone. In the silence that followed, Katya stepped self-consciously away from the scroll, moving across the room to stare blindly at the rows of books that filled the shelves. Beautiful, he thought. But in so many ways still a mystery to him. He watched her wander aimlessly before the bookcase, trying to interpret her expression. Was she nervous? Relieved? Angry? Or did some other emotion capture her mood? Cognizant that she needed a minute to collect her thoughts, he waited patiently for her to return her attention to him.

At last she did. "Why did you bring the Stone to the festival tonight?" she asked.

"I expected to find Tyler there," he replied. He lifted his shoulders in a small shrug. "Like you, I had my own theories as to who was behind the theft. I intended to offer him the Stone in return for his promise to leave and never return."

"And if he hadn't accepted that offer?"

Nicholas's mouth tightened to a grim line. "I don't know. If he had tried to hurt you, I believe I would have killed him."

"I see."

She stood unmoving, as though uncertain what to do or say next. After everything that had passed between them, it should have been possible for them to bridge their differences. But an awkward gulf of unsaid words hung between them, keeping them apart.

At last Nicholas said, "I've been thinking about my father quite a bit during the last couple of days. It seems that he and I had even more in common than I thought true when I spoke to you of this a few days ago."

"Oh?"

"He tried desperately to control every element in his life—so much so that he was willing to give up the woman he loved and his child. They didn't quite fit in with the way he wanted his life to be." He shrugged and smiled sadly. "In a sense, he won. He had neatly organized his life so that it was just the way he wanted it to be. Eminently proper, orderly, and controlled. But he was completely miserable."

"And you were the same?"

"Yes." His ebony eyes locked on hers. "Until I met you."

As he watched, her expression seemed to suddenly lighten; her eyes glistened as though lit from within. Breathlessly she asked, "What do you mean?"

"I mean that the only thing that frightened me more than loving you was losing you."

Her eyes grew wider, then a quivering smile curved her lips.

Throwing caution to the wind, Nicholas continued, "I couldn't control the way I felt about you. I always expected that I would love someone quietly, coolly, and rationally. But you exploded into my heart. I tried to check my emotions from the very beginning—I thought at first I would only love your body. But I couldn't limit it, I couldn't confine it to one small part of your being, any more than I could love your smile but not love your eyes. Or love your scent but not love your skin. I found I loved your spirit and your strength. Then I loved your mind. Then I loved your soul. I was no longer setting the terms, and it took me a while to accept that."

"I see," she managed hoarsely.

In the thick silence that ensued, Nicholas leaned against the heavy mahogany desk and studied her expectantly. "Well?"

"Well?" she echoed tremulously.

"Now that I've just shared that ridiculously maudlin sentiment, you might return the gesture and tell me how you feel about me."

"I might? . . ."

To Nicholas, standing there with his heart on his sleeve, it seemed to take an inordinate amount of time for his words to get through to her. But at last Katya broke free from the astonishment that seemed to have been holding her in its grip. She raced across the room and hurled herself into his arms, nearly knocking him over in the process. "Yes," she cried fervently.

He gave a low chuckle as he tightened his arms around her. "Yes, what?"

"Yes, anything," she exclaimed in giddy exultation. "Everything."

He pulled back, searching her eyes. "Katya, do you love me?"

"Yes," she breathed. "Oh, yes. Yes. I love you, Nicholas."

He smiled. "Now that, little gypsy, is exactly what I've been waiting to hear."

Twenty-Two

Katya woke slowly, naked and sleepy. She sat up and looked around the room, not quite certain what had disturbed her. The gentle, golden light of early morning filtered into Nicholas's bedroom. The sunlight reflected off the tile mural that filled the wall behind her, sending shimmering rainbows bouncing off the soft cotton of the bedsheets.

She realized immediately that Nicholas was gone. Glancing at his place beside her, she found a single white rose on his pillow. With a smile she lifted the rose to her cheek, inhaling the sweet, delicate scent. Then she leaped from the bed and quickly dressed. She rushed downstairs and out the back parlor, hurrying through the gardens until she finally reached the gazebo. Once there, she skidded to a breathless stop, staring at the sight before her in amazement.

Nicholas stood alone in the battered gazebo, sending her a smile of tender welcome. Thousands of white roses blossomed all around him. The heavy white blooms clung to vines that covered the wooden rail; they hung gloriously from the lattice roof. Roses bloomed around the base of the stone wall, near the wide steps, and in the bushes nearby. Rose petals covered the ground in a blanket of white velvet. The intoxicating scent of the rich blossoms was palpable in the air.

As Nicholas held out his hand Katya moved dazedly toward him. "When did this happen?"

"A few days ago. I've been saving it as a surprise."

"I love it," she said, gazing around her in wonder. "I love you," she added, snuggling against his chest.

He wrapped his arms around her and gave her a tight squeeze. "I like the sound of that."

"Do you? In that case, I'll have to say it more often." She thought for a moment, then said, "Do you know that I first realized how you felt about me while a madman was holding a gun to my throat?"

He drew back and studied her face with a frown. "Jeremy Cooke told you that I loved you?"

"Indirectly." She lifted the slim gold chain with the mother-of-pearl rose and twisted it between her fingers. "He told me that the DuValenti men give this necklace to the women they love."

"True. But I should have told you sooner."

"When did you first realize you loved me?" she asked, genuinely curious.

Nicholas thought for a moment. "The night we spent hidden together in the armoire," he finally replied.

A blush stained her cheeks. "So it was nothing but naked lust that swayed your affections."

"Your body is exquisite, little gypsy, but that's not what I'm referring to." He frowned slightly, then continued, "At least, not entirely. I'm not quite sure how to put it into words—you felt as though you were a part of me. As essential as water or air. It was at that moment that I couldn't imagine my life without you in it."

She stood on her tiptoes and brushed a gentle kiss against his cheek. "I'm glad."

"And what about you?" he asked with a cocky smile. "When did you come to the intelligent conclusion that you couldn't possibly exist without me?"

"I think it was the day we went to the Abbey. I saw you standing outside, playing with the children in such an orderly fashion, making them all line up for their pony rides, and this beautiful light seemed to fall all around you . . ."

Nicholas arched one dark brow. "I think you're mistaking me for a saint."

"Hardly," she returned, smiling.

He took her hand and led her wordlessly to the soft, dewy grass between the rosebushes. To the spot where they had first made love. At that time, Katya remembered, the gardens had been filled with dark shadows and somber moonlight. Now golden sunlight fell all around them, bathing the spot in its rich, warm light. A soft blanket awaited them, and a bottle of champagne cooled in a sterling-silver icer. The sweet scent of cinnamon sugar and tangy fruit drifted from a wicker basket.

They made slow, lingering love. Once again the garden was filled with the sound of their sighs. They stroked and kissed and petted, exploring each other's bodies as though they were entirely new to one another. In a sense, they were. The love they shared added new depth to their lovemaking, making it richer and fuller than it had ever been. By unspoken agreement, they held back as long as they could, stretching out the moment. At last they reached their climax and fell shuddering into each other's arms.

After a long, breathless moment, Nicholas rolled onto his side and gathered Katya into his arms. "I want to spend the rest of my life surrounded by this perfume."

She took a deep breath and nodded. "The roses are wonderful," she agreed.

He shook his head. "They're nice, but that's not the perfume I'm referring to."

"No?"

"I meant this," he said. He drew his hands lightly down her back, then caressed her hips and buttocks. "The way your skin smells after we make love." He placed his cheek against her breast and inhaled deeply, letting out a contented sigh. "Essence of Katya."

She gave a soft sigh. "Any more remarks like that, Lord Barrington, and we may never leave this garden."

They took turns dressing each other. The occupation was not as enjoyable as stripping the clothing from each other's bodies in a frenzied fit of passion, but it was pleasant nonetheless.

"I think our bodies were made for each other," she announced immodestly as they finished dressing.

"Really?" Nicholas returned dryly. "Was this remarkable conclusion reached before or after you tried to have me arrested?"

"Discreetly arrested," she corrected. "I had no intention of having you paraded through the streets in chains like a common criminal. I made certain Monsieur Chatelain was made aware of your rank and status."

"How considerate. You would spare me any embarrassment, yet you wished me locked away for fifty years."

"Well . . . yes."

"You really would have done it." He studied her face for a long moment, an expression of awe and astonishment on his features. "God. I don't know whether to hate you or respect you for it."

"Monsieur Chatelain promised me that he would be most discreet," she assured him. "As director of security for the casino, he spends his time dealing with dukes who are caught cheating at baccarat, earls who steal linen from restaurants, viscounts who drink to excess and beat their wives—"

"You're throwing me in with that lot?"

"In my defense, you *were* acting strangely that night. All that talk of family duty, preserving your legacy, and not knowing until that moment what you were capable of . . . It was positively frightening."

"If you recall, I was convinced at the time that I would

very shortly be put in a position of having to kill my own brother."

"I didn't know that," she protested. "I was frightened, confused—I thought I was losing my mind; I had to speak to someone."

"I believe I was available."

"True, but at the time I was sure you were a maniacal killer who was only after the Stone—"

"Thank you, that's very flattering."

"And then the next minute I was convinced that I loved you so desperately I wouldn't be able to live without you."

"Better."

"It's not as though I'm the only one who made a mistake," she pointed out. "You thought I was a thief."

"If you remember, I jumped to that insulting conclusion *before* I knew you, not after."

"True." She hesitated for a moment, then asked softly, "How can I make it up to you?"

"You already have."

"Have I?"

"You asked me once what I would wish for if I could have anything in the world. At the time I didn't have an answer. Now I do. Several, in fact."

"What would you wish for?"

"I'd like a wife I adore," he began. "I'd like to spend more mornings in bed and more nights in front of a fire. I'd like to read books instead of ledgers. I'd like servants who smile rather than whisper. I'd like a child or two—or ten."

"Ten?!"

"And I'd like these roses to bloom year after year."

In a voice of aching tenderness, she asked, "Is that all?"

"For the moment, but I'm sure I'll have more demands later. I'm known to be quite unreasonable."

"And if I promise to spend the rest of my life trying to fulfill your every wish?"

He studied her with solemn intensity. "I'll hold you to it."

Her heart swelling within her chest, she brushed her fingers lightly across his cheek. "I take my promises very seriously."

"So do I, little gypsy. So do I."

Epiloque

❦

$\mathcal{S}$pring was in the air. Katya could smell it in the wind and feel its warmth in the base of her spine. As she lifted her face toward the sky a smile of deep satisfaction touched her lips. The Mistral had long since faded, leaving nothing behind but a soft breeze to stir the air. Puffy white clouds floated overhead and larks sang from the trees. The gardens were abloom with flowers.

It was her wedding day.

It was absolutely perfect.

As she stood alone looking out toward the sea, she felt a pair of strong male arms wrap around her as a deep voice murmured in her ear, "Regretting your vows yet, Lady Barrington?"

"No, but then I only took them twenty minutes ago—just before my groom deserted me."

"Foolish man."

"I quite agree. Do you always let your secretary call you away like that?"

"Edward Litell received a letter for me. A rather urgent letter."

Something in his tone made Katya turn around to study Nicholas's face. "What is it?"

"See for yourself."

He handed her a worn, cracked, and badly smeared envelope that carried the faint aroma of sea salt. As she peered at the scribbled writing on the outside of the envelope, astonishment shook her. Then wary joy quickly took its place.

"From Tyler?" she asked.

He nodded. "Apparently it was mailed months ago, but it

﹍e a rather circuitous route from my estate in Devonshire,
﹍o my home in London, then here to Monaco."

She searched his eyes, her heart bursting with pleasure at
the joy and relief she read there. "What does it say?"

"Go ahead and read it—or try. Maybe you'll have better
luck than I did."

She opened the letter to find that it was as badly decayed
as the envelope. From the looks of it, it had been soaked in
either sweat or salt water, or perhaps a combination of both.
Still, a few of the words were legible. She scanned them,
then looked up at Nicholas with a soft frown. "Tyler's been
aboard a ship this entire time?"

"From what I can gather, Jeremy Cooke's men tried to
double their fee. They took Cooke's money for allegedly
killing Tyler, then sold him off to a ship in the harbor. Impressed labor, I gather."

"Isn't that illegal?"

Nicholas smiled. "Very. But the ordeal seems to have
done Tyler some good. Did you read the bottom?"

Katya squinted at the last paragraph. "Something about
swabbing decks?"

"According to this letter, the captain actually dared to
make him *work* for his keep. Tyler goes on and on about it,"
he continued, his smile widening.

Katya matched his smile with one of her own as she returned the letter. "I can't wait to meet him."

As they strolled back toward the villa, Nicholas remarked,
"It seems to me the curse we DuValenti men share is not one
of heartache, but one of incredibly poor timing. I should
have known about my father's affair years earlier and that
Jeremy was my half brother. I should have known Tyler was
alive and that you were a Rosskaya. And lastly, I should have
known we held the key to finding the Stone all these years."
He shook his head. "Think how many problems we could
have avoided."

She sighed. "Speaking of the Stone, what do we intend to do with it?"

"I intend to make you a wedding gift of it," he announced, tracing his finger lightly along her collarbone. "Do you think it would make too heavy a necklace?"

She wrinkled her nose. "A bit flashy for my taste. Besides, *I* had intended to use it to make *you* a wedding gift."

"Oh? What did you have in mind?"

"I thought it might serve as an orb for a royal scepter. That way you'll have something to thump on the carpet while you order your servants about."

"Rather regal . . . but fortunately no longer my style."

"Actually," she said slowly, "I do have one other idea."

She related it to Nicholas, watching as he considered it for a moment.

He slowly smiled. "Perfect."

Having changed out of their wedding attire and into comfortable clothes for riding, Nicholas and Katya stepped from the villa and strode arm in arm toward the stables.

"You cannot be considering deserting your guests," called an imperious voice from behind them, stopping them cold.

They turned slowly around. "Yes," Nicholas replied with a cheerful smile, "we are."

"Good." The Comtesse nodded approvingly. "Perhaps they will take the hint and depart themselves. I've had quite enough of them dirtying our carpets and peering into our china cupboards." She shifted her gaze to Katya. "I will not be so bold as to ask where you and my nephew are going," she said, "but I would appreciate a brief word with you, if you don't mind."

"Of course."

The Comtesse gestured to the ancient parchment pieces she held in her hands, her eyes shining with triumph. "I have been studying these diligently for the past week, and I believe I've solved the puzzle. I simply could not abide believing that Marco had murdered Sacha, and I think I've finally been able to uncover proof of his innocence."

"You have?" Katya said breathlessly.

"Do you recall the love letter written by that awful braggart knight?"

"Vaguely."

"I found more of them. Dozens. Apparently when Sacha spurned his affection by marrying Marco, he vowed he would take his revenge. I believe that's what had Sacha so frightened. She was terrified about what might happen *to* Marco—never was she frightened of him."

As Katya considered that, she remembered an excerpt from Sacha's diary. "It is no longer me he sees. I have become the object of his vengeance." "Yes," she said slowly, "that makes sense."

"I'll show you the letters when you return," the Comtesse said, giving a satisfied nod. "The men in this family love very deeply or not at all. Marco loved Sacha. I am convinced of it."

"Speaking of letters," Nicholas said, "I have one you should see."

The Comtesse frowned as she peered at the envelope he passed her, then radiant joy lit up her face. "That dreadful boy," she scolded. "He should have written months ago. Now I suppose it will take me hours to decipher his writing. He always had such deplorable penmanship . . ." Her voice trailed off as she turned back toward the villa, Tyler's letter clutched tightly in her hand.

Nicholas and Katya exchanged a smile, then strode to the stables. They mounted up and rode at a leisurely pace across the rolling, verdant hills that brought them to the Abbey St. Chamas.

After enjoying a quiet afternoon visiting with the nuns and the children, they gathered their belongings and returned home. But there was one particular item they left behind.

A dazzling blue diamond the size of a man's fist glittered within the abbey's humble wood donation box.